# SOUTHERN WINDS A' CHANGING

Other books by
Elizabeth Carroll Foster

Carroll Frontiersmen: From North Carolina 1805 to Arkansas 1987
Virginia Carrolls and Their Neighbors, 1618-1800s

# Southern Winds A' Changing

*A Novel*

**Elizabeth Carroll Foster**

iUniverse, Inc.
New York   Bloomington

# Southern Winds A' Changing

iUniverse books may be ordered through booksellers or by contacting:

iUniverse
1663 Liberty Drive
Bloomington, IN 47403
www.iuniverse.com
1-800-Authors (1-800-288-4677)

Because of the dynamic nature of the Internet, any Web addresses or links contained in this book may have changed since publication and may no longer be valid.

Certain characters in this work are historical figures, and certain events portrayed did take place. However, this is a work of fiction. All of the other characters, names, and events as well as all places, incidents, organizations, and dialogue in this novel are either the products of the author's imagination or are used fictitiously.

ISBN: 978-0-595-48384-6 (pbk)
ISBN: 978-0-595-71802-3 (cloth)
ISBN: 978-0-595-60475-3 (ebk)

Printed in the United States of America

In memory of my high school English teacher,
Miss Marjorie Walker

To all of those who earned my gratitude thank you.

They are too many to name, including family members who were interested and nudged me along. My husband, John, who allowed time and showed patience. My daughter-in-law, Karen Jones Foster, who read and commented on an early draft.

The Southern Maryland Wordsmiths, especially Jane Deborah Vincent and Audrey Hassanein, who read parts of an early draft.

The Village Writers of Hot Springs Village, Arkansas, who rooted for me to get this book in print. Some had a special hand in the final draft: John Achor, Pug Jones, Dr. Fred Boling, Margaret Morrell, John Tailby, William G. (Bill) White, Madelyn Young, Gene Heath, Linda Hamon and Judy Carroll. They had the courage to point out mistakes and parts that didn't work.

My endearing friend, Jan Stoorza, who read part of an early draft and encouraged me.

My English teacher, Marjorie Walker, who read chapter after chapter and encouraged with such words as, "This is the kind of book I like to read."

Lastly, Nancy Rosenfeld, Nina Catanese and Beth Skony, who did the best they could for me.

It is not, what a lawyer tells me I *may* do; but what humanity, reason, and justice, tell me I ought to do.

Edmund Burke 1729-1797

And the rose like a nymph to the bath addressed,
Whish unveiled the depth of her glowing breast,
Till, fold after fold, to the fainting air
The soul of her beauty and love lay bare.

The Sensitive Plant (1820), pt.I,1.29
Percy Bysshe Shelley 1792-1822

# PROLOGUE

▼

## 1972

A deep sigh lingered in the near-silent room. Upstairs, Allise lay pale and sedated in the four-poster bed. A bedroom window was cracked for freshness, allowing a light breeze to flutter a corner of the sheer curtain. Like a playful Puck, it beckoned to the ledge.

Maizee led the doctor and Miz Allie's husband downstairs to the front door. "Pneumonia," Doctor Chance said. "She will need constant care." Maizee's eyes pooled, and he said, "Now, Mrs. Gains, she's likely to recover."

She wanted to tell him about Miz Allie's long sufferings. Like most everyone in Deer Point, she had doubts about young Doctor Chance, who replaced Deer Point's beloved old Doctor Walls after forty years of service to the town. She glanced up at her middle-aged son, Nate, who waited on the upstairs landing. Closing the door behind the doctor and Mista Dro, she trudged back upstairs. Pausing at the bedroom door, Maizee motioned to Nate. They entered to resume their morning vigil over Miz Allie and wait for Mista Dro to return from King's Drugstore.

Maizee pulled the rocker to the bedside. Sitting straight as a rod, she moved back and forth. Glancing at her son, she wondered what ran through his head.

Nate sat in the overstuffed chair near the window. Long legs stretched forward with one foot crossed over the other. His eyes were set on the movement of the curtain, but as far as his mother could tell, the scene didn't register in his mind.

Maizee rocked to the beat of Allise's shallow breathing. Suddenly she stopped. "Lawd, Miz Allie, you's too good." Whispered words caught in her throat. She wiped her nose and stole another look at Nate. He appeared oblivious to her, and she renewed the metronome-like movement of the chair.

A timorous smile softened her withered blue lips. Pride in her son was beyond measure. *Miz Allie awways bragging on 'im, saying he smarter 'n most and more handsome ever year. It's true,* she thought.

Sunlight splashed across the floor at Nate's feet, casting his skin the color of smooth raw leather. *Cain't deny his white blood.* Maizee grimaced. *He didn't want to even when a black stamp didn't count for much. Things a changing though. Old ways just a blowing in the wind.*

Tall and slender like the man who sired him, Nate's fingers curled over ends of the chair arms. He looked to be carved in stone. Lincolnesque. In ordinary circumstances, his slate gray eyes—"Cajun eyes," they said—commanded attention.

Maizee thought about how unlikely Miz Allie's relationship with her had been. A white and an African-American woman living like sisters. She leaned toward the frail body, looking into its ashen face. Their love and devotion to each other was as comforting as the shaft of light streaming through the window. *Spent hours in here with her and the chil'ren. She be ten years older 'n me, but she treat me equal. Like the sun rising ever' morning, we depend on each other.* She remembered darning socks in that chair. Nate on the floor with Peter and Cleesy. All three bent over the Monopoly board or a jigsaw puzzle. Always a quiet game that let Miz Allie read on the lounge. *Most good in Nate's life begin here wid this brave woman.*

Closing her eyes, Maizee rocked, letting her mind wander until concern grabbed her again. "You done suffered too much. Be too good for y' own good," she scolded, remembering Miz Allie saying she believed in a universal being in a world evolving in time, in place, and in truth. *So do I, but time be slipping away,* she thought.

Then, as though it were whispered in her ear, she knew her friend wouldn't recover. There had been one other such insightful moment when she knew Miz Allie would triumph over polio. The epiphanies amazed and baffled her. *Why ain't I more sad about her going?* she wondered. Pondering their thirty years together, she knew she must release her friend just as she had let her mother, Rebekah, go. *Miz Allie done earned some peace.*

They had aged together. Maizee's skin once held the sheen of a polished chestnut, and was as smooth as chocolate cream poured over God's own fine mold. At some age, cropped gray hair topped a face turned taupe. Allise's beauty had spun many heads. Auburn hair once framed her milk-white skin. Now snow-white hair blended into the pillowcases sent from Pennsylvania. Her eyes, like a chameleon, changed from blue to gray to green, reflecting the color she wore. Now, sunken beneath the brow, they seemed to recede from things seen in her lifetime.

Each spring, Miz Allie waited for the first blooms. Maizee stopped rocking and leaned over to sniff yellow jonquils she placed on the bedside table that morning. Her dark almond-shaped eyes snapped across the room, capturing the window light and settling on Nate. She ran her fingers over the smooth surfaces of the rocker's arms and caught a whiff of lemon oil she had rubbed into the wood. The sturdy oak chair reminded her of the many years she and Miz Allie couldn't speak of Mista Quent. Years after his death, Miz Allie said he had the rocker made for Peter, their first born. She said it didn't match any other piece of dark mahogany in the room then, and still didn't.

Maizee sighed. *When she's gone, me and Nate cain't pay no more on the debt for the best years of our lives.* Shaking her head, she knew she couldn't let Mista Dro know what she was thinking. She studied the black-and-white snapshots on the table. *Peter and Cleesy, me and Nate, and Mista Dro. All framed by Miz Allie's eye and captured in the old Brownie box camera.*

As if compelled, Maizee's eyes swept the wall of family portraits above the bed. She scanned likenesses of the elder DeWitts with their young sons, Mista Quent and Mista Sam; of Miz Allie and Mista Quent's wedding in Philadelphia; and Miz Allie's parents. The hand-tinted image of a World War II soldier in an olive-green uniform brought a crease to her brow. And she rubbed her arms as if the skin crawled over sinew and bone.

Across the room, Nate kept his solitude, but Maizee had stumbled onto a troublesome memory. She struggled with a haunting September evening in a cotton shed. Lost to that which knit their lives together, her images rolled back the years. Years when their lives—hers, Nate's and Miz Allie's—were inextricably entwined and staged in a time and place.

# CHAPTER 1

▼

**1932**

Allise DeWitt could deliver her first child anytime. Standing in the kitchen, her husband's flannel robe hanging loosely over her expanded girth, she felt nervous. She should eat for the baby's sake, but thoughts of food made her nauseous. Her eyes pled with her husband as she kissed him goodbye. "This might be the day, Quent. Please hurry home."

Holding his straw hat, he said, "I know, Allie, but I have to be in the fields to see that the niggers don't waste time when they're suppose to be picking cotton."

After seeing him out the door and listening as Sam, Quent's brother, drove the farm truck down the back alley, she trooped upstairs to the bedroom and sank down on the chaise lounge. Allise lay there several hours before the cramps began. Fearful of the unknown, she trudged back downstairs and phoned Doctor Walls.

Arriving soon, the doctor said cramps were an early phase of delivery. "I'll examine you later, Allie. Get in bed and rest up for your labor. You're probably in for a full day." With her settled, he sat in the overstuffed chair near the window. She felt comfortable in his presence. Glancing at him, she thought he must have sat like this with so many patients over the years.

\*     \*     \*     \*

On the farm on this first day of cotton picking season, by sundown all the sacks were weighed and farm hands were on the path to the tenant houses. All but one. In the weighing shed, a human mass heaved and grunted over Maizee Colson. Each hard thrust between her legs dropped Quent's cold

1

sweat on her dark skin. Searing pain shot through her sunbaked arms pinned against the floor. She lay in paralyzed submission, tears oozing from her eyes transfixed on a dark corner of the ceiling. Maizee wanted to cling there in the cool, darkened place, apart from the scourge being inflicted upon her body.

Giving one last guttural groan, he rolled onto the coarse, dirty cotton sacks, minutes before emptied of the day's pickings. His heavy breathing cut through the thick silence.

Sensing his vulnerability at that moment, Maizee wondered what she should do. Without moving, she saw him stand. Glimpsing white flesh disappear inside his trouser leg, she imagined her fingers reaching out to claw it. Staining his whiteness with his own blood. Staining her fingers with his blood.

He looked down at her nude form and sneered. "Get up, girl! You ain't hurt. Go on home." Without a backward glance, he pushed the sagging door and stepped out into the mid-September evening, heated yet from a blistering Arkansas summer.

Maizee heard voices drift across the evening stillness. "Gawddamnit, I'm starved! Allie may be having a baby and you taking on wenches." Mista Quent had roused his brother, Mista Sam whom she had seen dozing in the truck beside the shed.

"Let's go, Sam. I'm hungry, too." Mista Quent sounded more of tiredness than the usual sharpness of his orders.

Maizee listened to metal slam against metal as the rickety old truck bumped down the rutted lane to the highway. When no longer heard, she knew the men were on the highway headed for Deer Point, seven miles due east of the Chalu River.

Alone in the windowless shed, Maizee felt detached from herself, looking down on a body, not wanting to enter it. Chilled, she pulled an empty sack, reeking of musty cotton, over her nakedness and rolled onto her side. Motionless, knees drawn to her chest, thoughts exploded in her head like charged wires touching each other.

In the flick of a second, she came to her knees, wailing, "Nig-ga!" Whimpering, her fists pounded the dirt-strewn floor. Then, as suddenly as whimper and pounding began, it ceased. Staring wild-eyed, she watched her clenched fists relax into nothing more than callused hands incapable of harming anyone. Breathing hard, anger boiled up again. On her feet and poised like a mad dog ready to attack, she snatched up a long, empty sack, wadded one end and spun it round and round. The shed filled with frenzied motion. Hoes and weights propped against the walls, and tools hanging from nails, all crashed to the floor, settling about her. Letting the sack drop, she breathed in harsh gasps. Then, her legs buckled, and she sagged to the floor, limp and spent. For some time, she sat amidst the rubble, then pushing to her feet, she pulled on white bloomers and a flour sack dress, tied a sweat-stained red bandanna about her head and walked out into the night.

Trudging across the field in the darkness, she wondered how long it had been since everyone left. "Momma! She be mad. Gonna die when she know! What I gonna tell her?" Maizee tried to hurry, but her body was past taking commands.

Nearing the Colson tenant house, her mind dredged up an ugly word she was forbidden to use. Sixteen years old and the eldest child of black sharecroppers on the DeWitt farm, she wasn't dumb about the thing that had happened to her. *Momma and Daddy cain't do nothing. Jest hafta put up with white folks.*

She opened the back door and swept through the kitchen, past her mother and younger sisters. Rebekah glanced up from a dishpan of steamy water on the cookstove. "You late! Where you been, girl? Lookey, ain't no reason to go off sulking in there." Her mother's words trailed her through the curtained doorway between kitchen and bedroom. "Ain't nobody feel sorry for ya. Ever'body here slaving in that cotton patch same's you, and you loafing off so's somebody else hafta do yo share of the work."

Maizee sat on the bed, chin cupped in her hands. She imagined five-year-old Dessie May's face puckering at their mother's harsh tone. Nine-year-old Josephine known as Li'l Joke cleared supper leftovers from the red, oilcloth-covered table. Maizee felt a pang of guilt. Clearing the table and drying dishes were her tasks. Sweat streamed down her momma's face. Fire in the wood-burning cookstove died slowly, like the heat under the tin roof tempered all day by the Arkansas sun.

Rushing through the kitchen, she noticed her mother and Li'l Joke still wore grubby white kerchiefs knotted at their napes. Maizee jerked off her bandanna, wadded it and wiped her scalp. *White folks calling my plaits pigtails.* Holding the head cover as if it were repulsive, she flung the wad against the wall behind the bed frame.

From the kitchen above the clatter of dishes, Rebekah's words reverberated throughout the "shotgun" house. A gun fired through the front door would send a bullet straight through all three rooms to exit out the back door.

Listening to her mother's frustration, Maizee felt the same bone-tiredness all her family endured. Small-framed like her daddy, she didn't tire easily. She had his sharp features, slender build and medium height, but not the look of milk

drops seen in his bloodline. *Daddy don't stumble too much. When he do, he be the first to laugh at hisself.*

On summer nights, Jonas Colson sat on the porch leaning against a post. Cass and Dalt, Maizee's younger brothers, rested against the weathered wall. An evening ritual of cooling off before bedtime. Maizee imagined her daddy's work-hardened hands draping limply between his raised knees. *Does he have enough laughs left in 'im to bear what's happened to me?*

While they would pay no attention to scolding in the kitchen, she knew the whole family depended on her mother's get-up-and-go to prod them through each day. The kitchen would be in order, and kindling piled beneath the stove for cooking a predawn breakfast when Rebekah went to the porch.

"Get on out there." Her mother urged Li'l Joke and Dessie through the middle bedroom, past Maizee and out the front door. From the porch, she heard her say, "Jonas, I don't know what's wrong with our girl, but I sho gonna find out." Rebekah came back into the room and plopped down on the bed beside her. "What be going on, chile? You ain't got some silly boy hanging round that cotton shed, has ya?"

"Nome." Her mother couldn't see her tears in the dark room, and she hoped the quiver in her voice wasn't noticed.

"Listen t' me, Maizee, you knows y' cain't be coming in here late like you done tonight, shirking yo work." Her tone softened. "Stuffs gotta be done, chile. Li'l Joke and Dessie still gotta bathe off fore we can go t' bed."

"I know, Momma."

"I declare I don't know how we ever gonna make it in these old cotton fields." Her mother leaned forward on heavy arms. Chubby hands weighed on her knees, pulling her dress taut as a tent over a high round belly. "All us is tired jes so tired." She sighed, pushed from the bedside and waddled back toward the porch.

Without a thought that Mista Quent might take her again, Maizee decided not to tell her parents what he'd done to her. *If daddy was t' go to 'im about it, they'd take him out in the night and kill 'im.*

She lay in the darkness, thinking Mista Quent probably be laughing right now bout what he done to her. Conjuring pictures of what she should have done to him in the cotton shack, Maizee listened to Cass and Dalt snoring in the front room and her parents' snores in the same room in which she, Li'l Joke, and Dessie shared a bed.

Her mother turned on the coarse muslin sheet. *She be too tired t' sleep.* Mad at me, she thought, hearing Rebekah leave the bed and slip through the front room to the porch. Moments later Maizee sat on the stoop beside her mother, the night stillness stretching between them, and she felt the urge to tell her secret. "Momma something—"

"What? I's tired. You better not tell me some little old boy done got you with chile. I be so mad. Me and yo daddy liable t' kill 'im."

Maizee shuddered. *What I gonna do? Cain't tell 'em.*

They sat there on the porch, slapping at mosquitoes, making sharp popping sounds in the night. Usually, Maizee didn't think much about the weather, but the typhoid-carrying insects made her wish for an early fall, a time when the frogs on Moon Lake stopped croaking. Resting her chin on arms folded across her knees, she said, "Momma, the heat making me sick ever' day." She didn't like to invent a falsehood, but meeting Mista Quent would be worse than telling a lie.

Rebekah spread her legs and flapped her gown between them to create a little air. "Chile, you know you gotta be in that field tomorrah." She stood, and Maizee followed her back to bed. Lying on the lumpy mattress beside her sisters, her mind filled with dread, and her body shook with fear. It was hard to think beyond the reality of that evening. *What's gonna happen t' me?*

∗     ∗     ∗     ∗

Allise's day unfolded in pain. For much of it, she lay on her back, eyes closed, and a dull ache wrapping around her torso. The doctor dozed, small, round specs perched on his nose and an open book across his rotund abdomen, rising and falling with each breath. *He's probably delivered babies all night and is exhausted,* she thought, trying to move without waking him.

Later, she noticed he stood at the window. Pulling a watch from his vest pocket, he said, "Two, going on two. Must examine you, Allie. Lift your knees and spread." She winced. Probes of her body, even if by a kindly old doctor, felt like a violation.

When he returned to the chair, Allise curled into a fetal position and tried to pull Philadelphia's teeming streets, its chugging trolleys, and ringing church bells into a pool of focused thought. Needing her mother, she rubbed her backside and groaned, and the doctor wedged a pillow at her back. Pressing into the support, she rolled tired eyes up at him and said. "I lost my teaching position because I was pregnant. Did you know that, Doctor Walls?" He said he wasn't surprised, and she pushed back tears. "Fresh out of college, I came here to be the best teacher I could be." Suddenly she wailed, "O-oh, where is Quent?"

Hours had passed when the phone rang downstairs, and the doctor hobbled down to answer it. In a few minutes he returned, breathing hard and holding his watch. "It's four o'clock, and I must run to the office to dress a wound." After another examination, he took her hand. "First babies take the longest time, Allie. You're coming along, but it's going to be awhile. You will be fine for I'll be just a few minutes."

She begged for water. "My mouth is dry." Pulling down the sheet, he said she couldn't have water. Allise watched him plop a gray fedora on his head and walk out with a worn-leather medical bag in his hand. Feeling abandoned, she whispered, "Please hurry."

Lying there, she remembered the day Quent abandoned her after she directed an outburst at him. Feeling as big as a hippo and ugly, she had ranted about losing her job and never being invited into Deer Point homes. He said, "Oh, Allie," and she screamed her name was Allise. That everyone called her 'Allie,' and she hated it. At that point, Quent walked out of the house.

Allise had wanted to blame her tirade on being pregnant. She had needed him to listen. I need him now, she thought. Alone and scared, her discomfort became more acute.

After what seemed an eternity, Allise heard the doctor's returning footsteps on the stairs. He deposited hat and bag on the lounge, and she cried in a raspy whisper for water. He asked about a clean washcloth, found one and wet it under the bathroom spigot. She sucked on it and quieted until her moans became a constant plaint.

Doctor Walls dozed when suddenly, her knees came up with a sharp pain, and she cried out, "Dear God, is this day ever going to end?"

He took the watch from his vest fob. "It's near six." He stroked her hair. "It *will* end, Allie. Always does." He lifted the sheet. "You're dilating normally. Won't be long." Pulling the sheet back over her, he said, "The baby's in command now."

"Baby's in command," she mocked. "Do something! Why isn't Quent here?"

"S-sh." He smoothed her hair and patted her lips with the damp cloth. When she quieted, he sat with watch in one hand, book in the other and dozed till another loud cry roused him. He grabbed for the falling watch, and the book thudded on the floor. At the bedside, he held the watch. "Past seven. It's coming now." Shushing her, he waited.

Allise gazed into his gentle face. "Do you know I'm a Quaker? A Friend."

The doctor nodded and patted her hand. "Don't push if you have the urge."

She lay back, thinking the last nine months had been the longest of her life, and now her baby would be born anytime. Allise recalled Deer Point women saying any decent pregnant woman would stay home out of public view. Unheeding of their dictates, she had wandered about to places she had never been. Strange looks came her way.

Now, licking her parched lips, she imagined the judgments behind those looks. Her mind wandered. She and Quent had laughed at the silliest things during their courtship, but he didn't laugh *that day. Just walked out. Walks away from unpleasantness.* She massaged her hard belly. *I need him. He'd be here if he knew the baby was coming.*

Sweat beaded Allise's forehead. A muscle squeezed, pushing the baby toward the birth canal, and with her back to the doctor, she shouted,"Quent." Doctor Walls touched her shoulder. Thinking it was her husband, she clutched his hand and moaned, "Quen-nt." She turned. "Oh-h, Dr. Walls." Gasping on the ebbing pain, she groaned into the next contraction and tried to squirm into another position. "Oh dear God! Why isn't he here?" Muffled words rested on a desperate need, then she heard a rumble in the back alley. Quent's shouts trailed into her languid conscience, and she released a weak sigh.

Heavy footsteps crossed the porch into the kitchen, the foyer and up the stairs. Allise followed them, and her concerns eroded like sand in lapping waves. Quent burst into the room, crept up behind the doctor and whispered, "Is the baby coming, Doc? How's Allie?"

Doctor Walls came off the chair. Raising an eyebrow, he asked, "Where in the name of heaven have you been? Your place was here beside Allie."

Quent's eyes failed to meet hers. She watched his helpless, questioning gaze lock on the doctor. Concentrating on his face, she wondered if it belonged to a man who was about to become a father. He looked disheveled. Light brown hair, normally parted and combed back to each side, fell across a furrowed brow. She lifted a limp hand to his cheek, then another contraction forced a warm gush between her thighs. "Oh, I'm wet!"

"Hold on," Doctor Walls said. "The baby's coming. When I tell you, push hard."

The overhead fan beat the air, but the late summer heat had nowhere to go. Strands of dark, auburn hair pasted Allise's face, and her skin glistened with sweat. Forceful pains brought hoarse gasps. Clamping onto Quent's arm as he mopped her with the cloth, she screamed, "Where were you?"

"Push, Allie. Push again. There's the shoulders!" Pushing with all her might, suddenly the pain was gone. The doctor held the baby by his ankles and gave him a whack on the bottom. The surprised newborn, having emerged from a safe warm place, cried out. "It's a fine boy, Allie." Dr. Walls wiped the infant with a towel.

The baby lay in the curve of her arm. "I love you, Doctor Walls," she whispered.

"I know, dear. Most new mothers do." Beneath the trade-mark mustache, he smiled at Quent, who didn't seem to have a smile to return as he bent to kiss her forehead. The doctor took the baby to the cradle and helped the new father remove the soiled bedding before sitting down to fill out a birth certificate.

Allise watched Quent leaf through the DeWitt Bible. He wrote on the "Births" page: *Peter Weston DeWitt, Friday, September 17, 1932, 7:30 p.m.* Before fading into sleep, she thought, If he loved me, he would have been here.

Sometime around dawn, the baby's cry aroused Allise. Already dressed, Quent lifted Peter from the cradle as though he were a piece of fragile china. Clutching him to his chest, he placed the baby beside his mother and went for a basin of warm water, soap, and a washcloth before going downstairs to make breakfast. The baby slept, and Allise had a fresh-bathed glow when he returned with a breakfast tray. Placing it on her lap, he sat on the bedside. "I'm not a cook. Sam cooked for us after Mama died."

"Um-m." She smacked. "Who said you couldn't cook, love?"

Quent smiled as she bolted down the last bite of scrambled eggs and toast. He set the tray aside and picked up the baby. Sliding against the pillows beside her, he pulled Allise into the circle of his other arm. "You are radiant, honey, as though you didn't go through an ordeal."

She smiled, pushing away the blanket to reveal a crop of fuzzy blond hair. Admiring the tiny pink face, Allise beamed up at her husband. "Isn't he beautiful?" Small fingers curled about hers. "Peter Weston DeWitt, you will be as handsome as your father." She wanted to hold this tender moment forever.

"You think so?" Eyes not meeting hers, he appeared chagrined.

The moment dissolved, and she knew something was wrong. *Is he afraid of being a parent?* Holding her child's hand, she thought of the day she and Quent met on the Pixley Hotel porch. She fell for his devilish ways. Their six-month, fun-filled courtship didn't prepare her for the quiet, withdrawn man he had become. Now, he showered her with attention, but something bothered him. *Don't know how to approach him. If I knew he was pleased about our baby …* Working up courage, she said, "Are you happy with—"

"Course I'm happy." But she heard a lack of enthusiasm. She couldn't see his eyes to tell if happiness filled them. "I guess I oughta do the dishes," he said. Struggling from the bed with the sleeping infant, he placed Peter in the cradle and took the tray downstairs.

Allise heard dishes rattling in the porcelain sink and thought of their lives together. Her husband's up and down moods left her insecure. In recent months, there were more downs than ups. Were their fun times lost in the number three? *Are we crossing a line between past happiness and what might be in the future?* A mother at twenty three, she needed assurance Quent would share their new responsibility. She wanted past, present, and future to fuse into something she could count on. Suddenly, parenthood overwhelmed her. *Strange, a desire to be a mother but fear of what it entails. Does Quent fear it, too?*

Turning, she saw him standing in the doorway. He said he was ready to go to the post office, and she fussed about being confined. He smiled. "Yeah, well Doc Walls says seven days, and I'm here to see that you stay in bed."

She heard the front entrance close, and soon her mind went to a June day when she stepped from the train in Deer Point. *Three years ago.* Old Tate, the first person she spoke with, leaned on a depot dolly beside the tracks. Removing a black derby, he held it over his chest and mopped his brow with a crumpled red bandana. White teeth gleamed in his dark face. "I'm Tate, Ma'am. Calls me Old' Tate round here. If you gwine up there, can I help wid 'em suitcases?" He had pointed up the hill. "It be three blocks."

She followed behind his slow determined gait up the sidewalk, holding her yellow straw hat in place and gazing in storefronts along Hemple Street. Shading her eyes, Allise had squinted through hardware and drugstore windows and stopped to admire bank buildings, one of neo-classical, Greek architecture. Moving along, a sweet, yeasty aroma took possession of her senses. The smell of fresh baked bread wafting from Henmann's Bakery had reminded her she hadn't eaten since the train stopped in St. Louis. She muttered about being hungry, and Old Tate let the dolly rest on the sidewalk, pulled a packet from a canvas bag slung over his shoulder and offered it.

Unfolding the paraffin paper, Allise wolfed down a barbeque sandwich and listened to him tell of cooking over an open pit in his backyard. "Make hot tamales, too. Wrap'em in corn shucks' t' hawk t' hungry passengers." He had chuckled. "My tamales be a bit peppery, too hot for some."

They had started on uphill to the Pixley Hotel. Standing before the two-storied structure, Allise took measure. Like magazine photographs, it fit her notion of stateliness and southern gentility. Ell-shaped, the hotel faced half a block along Hemple and winged down Third Street another half-block. Columned verandas wrapped around both wings, upstairs and down. Black shutters dressed floor-to-ceiling windows, and huge oaks between sidewalk and street provided shade on the building. Rocking chairs lined upstair and downstair porches, and swings hung at each end of the front lower level. Looking amused as she took in surroundings, Old Tate said, "Built thirty years ago. Be a busy place once."

Across the street, grounds of the brick courthouse with two-towers and a detached jail took up an entire city block. Large oaks shaded the government square, reminding Allise that day of the historic part of Philadelphia. She had scanned the hotel's white clapboard and found it in good repair. The mellowness of Old Tate's soft drawl enchanted her. His kindness and the reminder of her native city had made her feel safe.

Old Tate's well-regarded in the community, and most everyone depends on him for one skill or another, she thought now.

That summer, she wasted no time before school opened. Acquainting herself with the small Arkansas town, she walked down Third Street past the courthouse and stopped at a corner to read a sign across Maple Street. Black-on-white lettering noted: *Newtown Church, Founded 1898.* Crossing Third, she passed the post office, vacant lots and law offices on the way back to the Pixley.

On another day, she began exploring at First Street where train rails traced the southern border and divided white town from one section of Colored Town. Walking northward, through business blocks, she had reached the residential area, following it to a point where it edged up against woodlands, a distance of about two miles. Before returning to the Pixley, she ran upon the bell-towered Methodist church and the high school where she would teach English.

On her walks, she discovered that white town fanned out on three sides from the six-block business square. Westward, it abutted a block-wide vacancy separating it from the main part of Colored Town. She had written her family, "I'm pleasantly surprised by Deer Point. Men are extravagantly chivalrous. I think I shall fall in love with the South."

Now there in bed, she recalled a letter sent to her family during Christmas break from school and two years before her dismissal from teaching because she was pregnant.

"People," she had written, "are friendly in public, but I'm not invited into their homes for social events. They draw a line. You're not a Deer Pointer if not born here. Papa, you would call this provincialism."

Sighing now, she thought of having Quent home for a whole week. Looking over at their sleeping baby, she lamented, "Your daddy goes back to the farm soon, but you will be my joy, Peter."

Around noon, he came from the post office and walked into the bedroom. She invited him to sit beside her while he read the mail.

"No letters of interest." He stretched on the bed and ripped open envelopes. As he read, she remembered waiting for him to walk up the street from the post office soon after she arrived in Deer Point. Watching from behind her upstairs window in the Pixley, she had admired the tall, good-looking man. Now, with a coy smile, she touched his arm and said, "Darling, do you remember the day we met? You strolled to the porch where I sat in the swing." Quent paid her a quizzical glance, and disregarding it she continued in the saucy manner. "You deliberately dropped your mail. You did! Trying to distract me."

"Why you little snip!" He feigned surprise. "You saw me coming, didn't you?"

Giggling like a school girl, she hummed, "'By the light of the silvery moon' Do you remember leaning against the banister and whistling? Tipped your hat and said, 'Miss Weston, we should spend some time together.'" Her teasing mock brought him up against the pillows with a look of amusement. "I had already determined to meet Mr. Handsome," she whispered. "That day just cinched it." She leaned back. "Your ways were simply captivating, Mr. DeWitt."

Quent reached for her. Pulling her close, he guided her hand to his swelling need. "So-o, you set a trap for me, did you?" He fell into her playfulness. "And all this time I've thought I caught you. I want you, Allie." He tried to make a move on her.

She felt guilty for arousing him. "Darling, we can't. Anyway, we'll wake the baby."

"I know." He pulled back, laid the mail aside and rose from the bed.

Despite her guilt, happiness shrouded Allise like a warm blanket. "Quent, I wanted that day to never end. We were so awkward." Familiarity made their laughter easier now.

"Ah, Allie." He looked down at her. "You're still pretty even with this bobbed hair," he said, rumpling it.

She squeezed his arm and reminded him of what Sam said about southern women letting their men think they were in control. Quent didn't respond, and she felt uneasy with the near-grin on his face.

✱    ✱    ✱    ✱

Rising with Saturday's sun, Maizee dreaded facing the day. Pulling on a dress, she parted the curtain to the kitchen and began mixing a corn pone. She thought of Mista Quent's wife. *Only seen her from a ways when she sit in the car beside the field.* Pouring the mix into a cast-iron skillet already heated on the stove top, she shoved it in the oven.

Her mother hustled Jonas, Dalt, Cass and Li'l Joke out the door and yelled, "We be coming in a few minutes." The screen door banged as Rebekah turned back to the kitchen. She swished about as though rushing into tomorrow, throwing another slab of wood in the range, and pulling three quarts of home-canned pinto beans from a shelf. She poured them into a speckled enamel pot with fat and waited for a full boil before pushing the pot to the back of the stove to stay warm. "Let's go!" she yelled to Maizee and Dessie.

Maizee opened the oven door and patted the cornbread lightly on top. Testing done, she removed it from the oven to the back of the range. With the day's meal underway, they rushed out to join the rest of the family in the field.

Rebekah went in a full trot, pulling Dessie by the hand. Trailing behind, Maizee scanned the field for Mista Quent. Like the boss man he was, he would be standing there, legs spread apart, hands on hips and wearing a wide-brimmed straw hat that made him easy to spot. She would willingly drop into a pit rather than face him. Her mind raced between seeing him and how to tell her parents he had raped her. He was no where in-sight. She began picking beside her mother, slowly, stopping often to look for him.

"Get t' picking, girl, if you don't want Mista Quent to own yo hide," Rebekah yelled after a while. "Yo sack ain't even bulging yet."

Maizee speeded up and thought of a plan if he appeared. She would say she felt sick and needed to get out of the heat. It was close to eleven o'clock when she glanced up and saw Mista Sam head their way and stop at the row's end. "Allie had a baby Friday night."

"Oh, lawd gawd, Mista Sam. A boy or a girl?" Rebekah asked. Told it was a boy named Peter Weston DeWitt, she said, "I knows Mista Quent be happy about dat boy." She pulled cotton from the last boll on the end stalk and asked, "That why he ain't out here?"

"Yep. He's staying with Allie." Without further explanation, Sam moved down to where Jonas, the boys, and Li'l Joke picked.

Over the week, Maizee was relieved to have Mista Sam weighing the cotton sacks.

Monday, near quitting time, she picked beside Jonas and the boys when she looked up to see Mista Quent staring at her from the end of the row. Turning in a panic, she began down the next row, away from him. Thumbs hooked over back pockets, he grinned and ambled off toward the cotton shed.

At day's end, she waited in the shed for him to weigh her sack. Unhooking it from the scale, he moved toward her, trying to block her way. She stepped in the direction of the door, and his free hand reached out to curve over her buttock. Maizee jumped, and easing around, she backed out of the shed.

At the end of the next two days, when she started walking homeward with the other pickers, Quent called her back into the shed. He grabbed and threw her to the floor. It took only minutes to have his way. While he pulled up his pants, she tore from the building and streaked out across the field, tears bathing her face. "Wanna kill 'im." She repeated the words over and over until she reached the well behind the house. Washing sweat and field dirt away, she threw hands full of water at the semen between her thighs and wiped dry on her dress tail.

Each morning after those two days, he met her with a conquering glint.

Sore hands from boll cuts didn't even register as she picked and schemed ways to evade him. She knew he would try again. That evening, the other pickers emptied their sacks on the wagon and started across the field when Quent called her to the shack. Barely inside, he grabbed her. She flailed and kicked, fighting against him with all she could bring to bear. He slammed an open palm across her nose and jabbed a fist into her cheek, knocking her to the floor. In seconds, Maizee's arms held his weight. When it was over, she fled across the field again, knowing she would have to tell her momma and daddy.

Everyone had gone to the porch, and Rebekah eyed her from across the supper table. "What's going on, honey? What happened t' yo face?"

Haltingly, Maizee said, "Momma, Mista Quent in the cotton shed. He took me! You know? He done it four times now." Light from the kerosene lamp reflected in doleful eyes turned to her mother.

"You saying what I thinks you saying, chile?" Maizee thought her mother's question held more understanding than disbelief. Standing, she drew Maizee into her heaving bosom. "Lawd help us, what's we gonna do? A white man done took you. Miz Allie done had a baby!" Her anger surfaced. "Mista Quent jes like his old daddy, Mista Joe." Maizee sobbed, and Rebekah held her until she seemed emptied of all emotion. "Go to bed, chile. Tomorrah, we gonna decide what to do."

Maizee knew no matter how much her momma ranted, she cared for all of them. And she knew tomorrow's decision would hold her fate.

# CHAPTER 2

▼

While nursing Peter, Alise thought of the day she and Quent sat in the swing on the Pixley Hotel porch. He took off his hat and placed it on his lap. After a time, he asked, "Will you go to church with me?"

"I'm a Friend, Quent." Seeing his puzzlement, she had said, "You know, a Quaker."

"Don't know about 'em, but can't be too different. I'll see you Sunday at ten thirty."

She felt pretty walking into Newtown Church on his arm, wearing her yellow straw hat with daisy trim and white voile dress with puffy sleeves. Quent looked ready to explode from pride. Adult eyebrows raised, followed by whispering behind hands. Choir members exchanged sly looks that seemed to infer their favorite son was about to be snared. All the while, Brother Rigdon stared down from the altar. After the service, Quent introduced her to his friends, and all had laughed about youngsters turning in the pews to gaze at Allise.

Quent's season of wooing took them through the last heat of that long, sweet summer. They breezed about town with the top down on his little Ford roadster. One evening, after seeing *Broadway Melody* at the Rialto and enduring sweaty odors swirled about by high ceiling fans in the movie house, they drove out into the countryside.

Now as Peter drew nourishment from her breast, Allise imagined the car's headlights pitching streams of light into the deep woods that night. Wind flipped a narrow white ribbon holding her bobbed hair. She nestled in Quent's arm, thinking of how handsome he was in a double-breasted pinstripe. Suddenly, the "clank, clank, clank" of a wooden bridge roused her. "Where are we?"

He threw back his head, laughing in that way she found thrilling. "Willow Creek Honky-Tonk is ahead." Pulling onto a grassy area with parked cars and horse-drawn wagons, he pointed to a dim light in a building hard to discern among the trees.

Pushing loose strands of hair under the ribbon, she had sat forward, peering at the dance hall. "Brother Rigdon says this place is a 'den of iniquity.' He said Mason jars of whiskey are brought here from stills. My papa wouldn't like knowing where I am."

Quent laughed again. "Forget Brother Rigdon. Forget your papa's wrath. Let's go dancing, Allie."

He called me 'Allie' that night. I didn't like it, but I didn't object, she thought, going on to a happier memory.

That night at the dance place, she played with folly, casting thoughts of Papa to the wind. Swept off her feet, she wanted nothing more than to share her life with Quent. Their courtship flowered with the town's encouragement before they knew she was a Friend. Soon her "Yankee ways" drew disparaging looks. In my mind, they now think Quent made the wrong choice, she thought.

Five months after their encounter on the Pixley veranda, Allise wrote to her family about their engagement. At Christmas break, Sam had accompanied them East to be Quent's best man in their wedding.

The baby released her nipple. She smiled at his milky lips and wished she could be this contented always.

*     *     *     *

It was Saturday, but the Colsons were not going to town. The evening before, Mista Quent said they were to pick cotton today. After breakfast, Rebekah herded Dalt, Cass and Li'l Joke outside and yelled after them, "Dalt, don't forgit t' tell Mista Quent that Maizee be sick. Me and yo daddy be coming later." The screen door banged behind her. "You stay right there, Jonas," she ordered, turning back to the kitchen.

Maizee saw her daddy's puzzled look. She grabbed the makings for a corn pone and watched Rebekah swish about as if rushing into tomorrow. She threw another wood slab into the firebox and slid an iron skillet daubed with lard across the stove. Any other morning, Maizee would have made the cornbread before breakfast, but today was different.

Measuring ingredients into yellow cornmeal in an earthenware bowl, she waited for her mother to explain to her daddy why they would be late to the field.

Adding an egg and buttermilk, she released her agitation in the blending. The disturbance in her mother's normal rush made her more apprehensive.

Rebekah pushed a playful five-year-old Dessie away. At the water shelf, she poured liquid over dried beans and pork bones in the enameled pot, placed it on the range and shoved in more wood. With the evening meal underway and the tin percolator emptied into Jonas' cup, she shoo-ed Dessie outdoors and plopped down on a chair.

The bread mix sizzled as Maizee poured it into hot grease. Placing the skillet in the oven, she eased onto a chair across from her parents. Her stomach churned as if to turn inside-out. Leaning on the table, she listened to Rebekah tell Jonas about what Mista Quent did to her. Face cupped in her hands, she couldn't look at her daddy.

He leaned back on two chair legs. When her mother finished speaking, the front legs hit the floor with a thud. Elbows digging into knees, Jonas hid woes in his hands.

Moments slipped by. No one spoke. Rebekah drummed stubby fingers on the table. "What we gonna do, y'all? We hafta get Maizee away from here. Take her to Althea's. If she gonna have Mista Quent's baby ..."

Maizee whimpered and dropped her face to the table on folded arms. Jonas raised up. "Bekah, that's fifty miles from here. How we know yo sister gonna keep Maizee? Don't know she gonna have a baby." He pounded the table. "It don't make no sense."

"That the trouble! We *don't* know!" Rebekah said, and Maizee sniffled. "Our chile be scared t' death of that man, Jonas." She reached for Maizee's hand. "Jes don't know, honey. I was awake all night, thinking. Gotta ask Mista Quent if we can borrah the truck."

"He ain't gonna let us use that truck!" Jonas echoed his wife's exasperation.

"Don't matter, we gonna ask anyway. We'll see what Althea says. What else we gonna do? Ain't no doctor close t' here. Hafta go for him with a wagon and mules. Ain't no way t' call Doctor Walls." Rebekah moved around the table and placed a hand on Maizee's shoulder. "This be our chile, Jonas."

"What we gonna tell Mista Quent about needing the truck?"

"Maizee's sick! Taking her closer to a doctor. Althea'll keep her, you'll see."

Bewildered, Maizee dried tears on her dress tail. *I ain't done nothing. Why I gotta leave home?* It only took a thought of Mista Quent to send a shudder through her.

"If she ain't with chile we'll git her home somehow." Rebekah patted her hand. Neither Maizee nor her daddy had another solution. "That settles it, then," her mother said.

Maizee knew those were fated words.

Quent's dark moods became more frequent after he returned to the farm. Questions plagued Allise. Did he worry about their financial means? The loss of her teaching salary wouldn't concern him. *It didn't contribute much. Maybe he feels the pressure of doctor bills.* Depressed times weigh on everyone, she thought, trying to remember when his personality flipped. Was it when she gave in to that moment of frustration? *I didn't apologize.* Now, he returned home late most every night without a word of where he'd been. She had no answers. More often than not, Peter was the only connection between her and Quent.

Later, they sat on the couch with their son sleeping in her arms. She caught his father gazing at him with a look of total adoration. "He's utterly dependent on us," she whispered.

"Uh-huh." Quent drew her head to his shoulder, tucking it beneath his chin.

"Quent …" Knowing raw emotion embarrassed him and unable to see his face, Allise searched for words. "Are you worried about our family responsibilities? I—"

"Oh, Allie!" His disgust was unmistakable, and she thought their moment together was spoiled, but he kissed her forehead and eased from the couch. "Be back in a jiffy."

Upstairs, she put the baby in his cradle, turned back the bedcovers and puzzled over how to reach her husband. Sam had said Southern men didn't burden women with unpleasant things. He had slapped his thigh and laughed when she said she didn't think much of that practice. Quent had rubbed his temple and stared at Sam as if groping for a reason to find their talk funny. We've changed, Allise thought.

Suddenly, she heard heavy bumping up the stairs. Quent entered the room backwards, pulling a rocking chair. He stopped to catch his breath and said, "Mr. Andrews made it. You like it?"

"O-oh, yes," she said, and he positioned the sturdy oak rocker next to the cradle. She threw her arms around his neck and kissed him. He grinned, showing a line of even white teeth, a flash of contentment.

In bed first, she watched Quent undress. Jumping in beside her, he held her to his lean hard body, and she felt his burning need. She never had his hunger. Her need was his affection, but Allise wanted to prove her love by giving her body. She treasured their tender moments and tried to ward off an intangible something wedging between them.

✷     ✷     ✷     ✷

Saturday, Rebekah peered out at the sun bursting over the horizon. She turned back to her daughter. "Not a cloud in the sky, Maizee. Yo daddy's gone t' get the truck. We going to Texas today." Too filled with dread, Maizee didn't respond.

Her daddy returned from the wagon shed. "Mista Sam said he would drive the truck over here. He say we gotta let Dalt and Cass stay behind and pick cotton if we wanna use the truck. I told him 'Okay.'" Jonas went outside and stood at the picket gate, waiting.

In a few minutes, Sam drove up in the truck. He stepped down from the running board and went to lean against the fence. Wedging his hands in the back pockets of work pants, he watched the Colsons load up.

When everyone was aboard, Jonas turned the crank and climbed behind the wheel.

Sam ambled over to the idling truck. "Quent was madder 'n' hell about y'all wanting t' go to Jefferson. He said t' remind you that our cotton has to be ginned before others flood the market. Cain't feel safe about things these days, Jonas." Having set the warning, he added, "Quent said we can't give in to ever' whim you niggers have. Get back over here soon's you can. Else we'll all be in trouble."

Lying on a folded quilt on the truck bed, Maizee imagined her daddy hunched over the wheel, a muscle ticking in his cheek. His eyes wouldn't meet the white man's. She heard him say, "Yassa, Mista Sam. I knows."

Sitting beside Jonas in the cab, Rebekah held Dessie on her lap. "If this old truck holds up, we'll be home tomorrah." Her tone oozed defiance.

Maizee knew her mother had no time to waste on a preachifying white man, not even Mista Sam. The truck rumbled down the lane. Li'l Joke sat against the cab with nothing to soften her ride. At the highway, Maizee noticed her mother peering through the rear window. *She sounded brassy a minute ago, but now she got worry all over her face.* Be wondering if this old truck gonna break down, she thought.

Beyond Mista Sam's sight, Maizee sat up as the truck approached the river bridge. She folded the quilt into a seat behind the cab for herself and Li'l Joke.

Soon, the drone of the engine and gravel striking the fenders set her nerves on edge.

Almost an hour had lapsed when she noticed there was no road noise. Bens-burg's sidewalks teemed with Saturday people. Some stood in groups, stooped and nodding, laughing and gesturing in unwieldily ways while waiting for the stores to open. Yoked horses tethered in vacant lots swished flies with their tails. Some snorted, shook their manes, and pawed hooves at the ground in vain attempts to fight boredom. The girls gaped at their first city sights as Jonas urged the truck along. Her daddy hadn't driven in town often enough to feel at ease, and Maizee cringed each time he stomped on the brake.

Suddenly, Li'l Joke jabbed her and pointed to a man running beside them blowing a whistle and shaking a fist. Maizee tapped the rear window and shouted around the truck, "Stop, Daddy!"

Jonas caught sight of the policeman motioning him to the curb. He stopped and stepped down from the truck.

"What'sa matter with you, boy? Didn't you hear me whistle at that intersection?"

"Nawsah. I didn't even see you. Old truck's pretty noisy. I sho didn't hear—"

"I don't know about you niggers. This yo truck, boy?"

"Nawsah. Belong t' the DeWitt Farm over cross the river. Mista DeWitt let me borrah it t' go down to Jefferson."

"Well, I'm gonna give you a two-dollar ticket or ten days in jail. Take y' choice. You niggers belong on wagons. You gonna mess around and kill a bunch of folks, be in jail a lot longer than ten days."

"Yassir," Jonas said, and Maizee gasped. *What we do if daddy go t' jail?* She peered around to see him pull bills from the bib pocket of his overalls and hold out two to the officer. Pocketing the remaining dollar, he started to explain, "I didn't mean t'—"

"Makes no difference," the officer said, shoving the bills in his pocket.

Outside Bensburg, they jolted on for miles, then her daddy stopped at a stream to add water to the truck's leaky radiator. While he dipped and poured, her mother prompted the girls to look for their Masling cousins when they reached town. "It's Saturday. All of 'em be in town," Rebekah said. Maizee had not seen Aunt Althea and Uncle Moses' family since they loaded on a wagon two years earlier and crossed the Chalu River into East Texas.

With a full radiator, Jonas drove into Jefferson an hour before noontime. Maizee and Li'l Joke, forgetting their mother's request, gawked at people as their daddy inched down the main thoroughfare as though unsure of which direction to take. Soon, Rebekah spotted her sister's son, Ward, on a street corner and called to him.

Ward hopped on the running board, and when all the Maslings were collected, they headed for Colored Town.

Arriving at the Masling's house, Maizee helped her cousins, Henny and Ester, gather late peas and the last tomatoes from Uncle Mo's garden. Then, Aunt Althea sent her girls to a nearby grocery. Her daddy and Uncle Mo sat in cane-bottomed chairs in the shade of a huge mulberry tree, and Ward sat backed against the tree trunk. Speaking in quiet tones, they watched Lil' Joke and Dessie race about the yard.

Maizee sat on the back stoop, listening to her mother and aunt talk in the kitchen. It was hard to concentrate beyond the reality that her family would be leaving the next day without her. She heard Rebekah's aggravation. "Sho, she'll help! Maizee be a good girl. She be little, but strong. Maybe not like Henny and Ester, but strong enough. She be scared t' death of Mista Quent. I don't want her around him." Aunt Althea said she might get work cleaning white folks' houses.

They kept talking about her having a baby. "I want her with somebody knows about birthing. Too many black women done died, Althea. Mista Quent jest like his old daddy. Don't care nothing about us coloreds. Mista Sam, now he's different, but he did rile me about Mista Quent's warning." Her mother mocked him, and both women laughed.

Aunt Althea said she didn't need to be told about the DeWitts. "Remember Mo saying he didn't owe his soul to them and his body t' sharecropping? Him and Ward hire out the wagon and mules t' haul whatever they can lift and the mules can pull. Some days, they wait at the train station. Haul drummers and their sample cases t' stores. Do yard work, too." She and the girls washed for white folks. One laundry took all day and they worked five days a week. "I tell you, Bekah, hanging over wash pots, scrubbing on a rub-board, rinsing and hanging to dry gets to y' back. We press most ever'thing. Old flat irons get mighty heavy when y' tired."

Her mother told her aunt she knew all about washing and ironing. Rebekah's annoyance came though loud and clear to Maizee. The Maslings' life sounded a lot like sharecropping. *They may control their work days and not owe the plantation owner, but all the same, they have the work wearies.* She glanced at the shotgun house and found it not much different from their house on the farm. Tired from the long day, her stomach rumbled from hunger. Her aunt was saying she knew a good midwife who delivered a lot of babies. Fear gripped Maizee. She cupped her chin and set her knees swaying. *What's gonna happen t' me?*

That night after eating a late meal of leftovers, Maizee helped clean the dishes before joining others on the porch. The drone of voices lulled Lil' Joke and Dessie into sleep on a quilt pallet. Sitting on a porch step, Maizee looked resigned and was soon laughing at the shared family lore.

Banter turned serious when Uncle Mo mentioned hard times. "Hardly been any other way. If old Sook and Dolly keep hauling and getting us there, I guess we gonna make it." He chuckled, making light of their plight

"Well, you know what they say about old mules, Mo," her daddy said. "They tote a lotta wear on their faces and don't have much left over for the hind legs." Laughter rippled across the darkness. A lull allowed him to tell of his encounter with the Bensburg lawman.

"Ain't never gonna be no different for us coloreds." Aunt Althea shook her head. "There's a old woman here tells about a gang of white men in Texas and Arkansas and Louisiana killing niggers during Reconstruction. She was a little girl on the plantation when that gang rode in. They tell them niggers they come to organize a colored militia t' catch the white men that doing the killing. Lining 'em militia niggers up in a open field, they say they want 'em t' practice killing them mean white men. Then them white men shot all of 'em niggers dead right there. Turns out that gang was the very ones doing all the killing. That old woman cain't forget. Talks about it all the time."

A hush dropped like a curtain on the final act of a play. Uncle Mo stood and stretched. "We best get to bed if you folks intend t' git a early start home in the morning."

Maizee lay on the quilt beside her sleeping sisters, but dread of morning kept sleep at bay.

\*     \*     \*     \*

Allise rested on the chaise, reading her father's letter while Peter slept. She laid it aside and picked up *The Philadelphia Inquirer* he had sent. It told of factory closings and unemployed workers. In the Fine Cut Barbershop for a hair bob, Allise had overheard men talking about work hours being cut and low pay. A full week's work brought twelve dollars. "Dollars are squeezed," one man had remarked. Another mused, "Franklin Roosevelt will be elected come November, and things will get better." Quent went into the last planting season with grave trepidations, she thought. *Life seems to have gone out of him.*

Returning to the *Inquirer,* Allise read about a black Muslim who preached racial separation to illiterate or semiliterate Negro migrants from the South. Do colored people want to be segregated, she wondered. Earlier her father mentioned that Friends planned a freedom ride South to protest Jim Crow laws and to register voters. Did it take place? she wondered. Disparaging remarks were made about colored people, and she read of despicable acts against them. There seemed to be a deliberate mind set against the race. *I cannot allow my child to be prejudiced.* I won't allow it, she promised herself.

Life in Philadelphia was so different, she thought. Her father and his colleagues sat in the parlor comparing John Dewey and other philosophers. They shared ideas on social ills, politics and religion. Her father's Swarthmore

College students, including herself, had sat on the floor listening with rapt attention.

After graduating from college, Allise read in Quaker literature of a need for teachers in the South. Enthusiastic about educating young people, she arrived in Deer Point with limited knowledge of regional differences. Grounded in northeastern training and experiences, she never guessed her feelings would become so conflicted. There's something to be said for the quietness here and a slower pace, she thought. *I'm an outsider looking at a culture I know little about. Our baby will grow up here.* She remembered having doubts about bringing a baby into the world. *How could I have doubted? I couldn't bear a tragedy like the Lindbergh kidnaping.*

The *Inquirer* kept Allise in touch with the world, as did her father's letters and the books he sent. The Deer Point *Weekly*, a one-room library of donated books, and town gossip were her only other sources of information. The *Bensburg Daily* arrived in the mail a day late. Like most in town, the DeWitts didn't subscribe to it, but Quent had bought a radio. Few others could afford such a luxury.

Peter roused from sleep, and she went to change his diaper. Then, standing in front of the mirror, Allise gazed at her image. Tired eyes from sleepless nights stared back. Feeling tacky in the print dress, she changed and dressed the baby to go to the market. Daddy Joe will cheer me up, she thought.

Her husband's father fondly called Daddy Joe turned the farm over to his sons after opening the meat market on Main Street. His shrewd business sense allowed him to make a profit when others failed. Quent told her that as a young family man, Daddy Joe spent winter days in the courthouse foyer listening to the older farmers. After a few years of heeding their successes, his father had turned his inherited farm of two hundred-fifty acres into twelve hundred. His holdings increased through bids on tax-delinquent properties and mortgage foreclosures. Grooming his older son to become a farmer, he sent Quent to the state university to learn farm management.

Quent was nineteen and in the first year of college when his mother, Berniece, died. His father and seventeen-year-old Sam remained in the Filbert Street home after her death.

Soon after their marriage, Allise thought it was poor judgment on Daddy Joe's part to make her husband the farm manager for it was Sam who had an innate interest in the land. Sam became the farm flunky. Quent often boasted about his knack for working farm hands, implying his brother lacked the backbone to be a boss. Sam seemed to take his older sibling's jabs in stride, misleading Allise to believe the brothers had a close relationship.

It was plain to see now, that they couldn't be more different in disposition and appearance. It was said Sam was predisposed to his mother's benign nature. He was short and swarthy like his dad, exuding earthiness. Book learning didn't interest him after high school, but his love of the farm ran deep.

Quent, on the other hand, had penetrating blue eyes, light hair and his mother's good looks. Allise was drawn to him like a lightening bug to darkness.

Marrying into a family that offered no female companionship, her insights into the DeWitts developed slowly over the last three years. She discovered her husband had a yen to fly airplanes. Already bound to the farm when the first plane landed in a grassy field near Deer Point, he was left with a fantasy. "Stunt flying taking people for rides," he said, "that's exciting and less risky than farming." He said nature ruled farming. When Allise asked about nature controlling flying, he said, "Aviators just don't fly in foul weather." His faraway look had not seemed to include her.

For weeks, Quent had left during the baby's first feeding and returned at night after he slept. Cotton sales were brokered and now he worked part-time at the market. Sam and Jonas tended the farm jobs till spring planting, and Allise thought her husband would have more time for Peter.

A chill ran through her as she viewed herself again in the mirror. *Does he feel obligated to Daddy Joe? Resent being kept from his dream?* I spend too much time trying to figure out my husband, she thought. The baby squirmed in his cradle. She ran a brush through her hair, picked up Peter and headed to the market.

Allise made the market every morning. Now, she returned on a late fall day. The sky azure, like after a good rain, was clear and pleasant. It brought out her nesting qualities. Ready for a change, she stood, hands on her hips and studied the bedroom, looking to rearrange furniture. She went about boring tasks, pondering the track of their everyday lives.

Rubbing Old English Furniture Polish into the dark wood of the highboy while her baby slept in the crib, she thought it was again time to go to church

with Quent. *I haven't been since the women thought I disgraced myself with a pregnant belly.* She smiled, remembering.

Maizee had been with the Maslings five months. She did her best to heed her mother's advise to be good and help with the work. With the patience of her father, she adapted to the routine, helping with the cooking, cleaning, and putting out laundries. Some Saturdays, she went into Jefferson, and always on Sunday, to church.

On this Sunday morning, Aunt Althea handed her a hankie and offered the jar of Vaseline. "Me and my girls use it for gray, scaly legs."

A spring shower sent everyone running to the small whitewashed church with an abbreviated bell tower rising from the roof crest over the door. Settling on a rough-hewn bench, Maizee caught her breath and strained over a protruding belly to wipe droplets clinging to her legs. Dabbing with the handkerchief, she caught a whiff of vanilla coming from the stout woman in front of her. She wore a large, black, straw hat with a wide brim turned back from her forehead. It was the only hat in the room, and she wondered how the woman came by such finery. Maizee always turned to pretty hats in the *Sears, Roebuck* catalogs. Feeling like a "field nigger," she fidgeted and smoothed Aunt Althea's faded print dress over the bulge of her mid-section. Even in her condition, the dress swallowed her like Jonah in the whale's belly. Sighing, she thought, it wouldn't be long now before she could go home.

Thunder rumbled in the distance as the storm pushed northeastward into Arkansas. The choir and congregation swayed to the song, and Aunt Althea's rich *a capella* voice reminded Maizee of her momma. She sang and clapped to "Rock! Rock! Rock of ages! Oh Sweet Jesus, when we called up there."

On the last note, hallelujahs and amens echoed, and Brother Miles paced before the pews with a Bible on his palm. "Oh, Lawd!" He laughed, shaking his head. "We's rejoicing. Bless you, Brothers and Sisters, for that fine singing. The Good Book says, 'Serve the Lawd with gladness, come before His presence with singing.' Amen! Let me hear some more a-amens." Shouts from the congregation died out and he said, "Now, it says in Psalms 126: 'the Lawd saved His people in captivity, and they was like in a dream. Laughing, singing, and saying the Lawd done great things for 'em.'" He paced, speaking of the Lord's greatness, then glancing at the Bible, read, "'Turn agin our captivity.' They crying reaping joy, going forth to bear his seed. Believing he'd come agin."

Maizee whispered "Amen."

The preacher said, "Lawd, we rejoice in Jeremiah's words. He tells of gnawing hunger cause the crops done failed. Prayed to the Lawd about sins they'd done. Back slidings!" Pausing, he mopped his brow, then went on. "How the prophets done told 'um they'd have peace. But God told Jeremiah the prophets lied in his name. Give a false vision. He didn't tell 'um to speak for him. 'Even if Moses and Samuel stood before me, my mind couldn't be to these people.'" Pausing again, he stared at his congregation. "'Cast 'em outta my sight,' he told Jeremiah." Preacher Miles threw the words out to his people. "God ask, 'who have pity on you, Jerusalem? You forsake me.

I stretch out my hand and destroy you! I'm weary of yo repenting.'" Voice softening, Brother Miles said, "and Jeremiah poured out his heart. 'Yo words was found, They was my joy. I'm called by yo name, Lawd God of hosts.'"

Laying the Bible aside, he said, "Oh yeah, Brothers and Sisters. We gonna repent our wicked ways, and the Lawd gonna deliver us outta the hand of the vile. We gonna rejoice in him. Hallelujah! Amen!" With that, he was preached out, and the church rocked with song again.

The sermon struck a chord with Maizee. "That preacher sho knows how t' make y' soul feel good." She walked home beside Henny and Ester. One hand rested across her abdomen when she felt something move. The life sustained within her womb had been no more than an "it," no more than a misery borne by her body. Something to be rid of as soon as possible. She had felt such shame when she wrote her parents of her condition. Now, the thought of life inside her made all the difference in the world. "I gotta write Momma and Daddy again," she said. "Tell 'em somebody gonna write when the baby comes."

She longed with all her rekindled soul to be with her family on the Chalu River.

# CHAPTER 3

▼

Allise and Quent waited in the living room for Daddy Joe and Sam. All were dressed for Sunday service, the baby in a lace-trimmed white gown with shirred yoke and three tiny mother-of-pearl buttons below a Peter Pan collar. "When are you women gonna quit putting boys in dresses?" Quent asked. Laughing, Allise made baby talk with Peter, and Quent smiled at her nonsense as he smoothed the baby's blond fuss with a small hairbrush.

Just then the doorbell rang and Daddy Joe called upstairs from the foyer. "We're here. Where's that boy, Allie?" He stepped into the living room. "Oh, here you are. I came t' see how much he's growed."

Allise stood and met him. "How much can he grow in a day's time, Daddy Joe?"

"You'd be surprised. He'll be grown before we know it." Sam grinned and mussed the fine hair Quent had just arranged.

"We better get going," Quent pulled on his suit coat.

A cloud, moving from the southwest, threatened them as they approached the church door. Two ushers waited for Allise to pull back the baby's white blanket. One said, "We heard it was a boy. Been waiting to see him."

The other rubbed Peter's cheek with his forefinger. "He's fine-looking." Quent beamed over Allise's shoulder.

"Ain't he something?" Daddy Joe boasted, and Sam showed unbridled wonder.

Allise said she should take him in out of the chill. "Oh, yeah. Don't want t' make 'im sick." The men stepped aside, and smiles greeted them from both sides as they walked down the aisle. Taking their places, Allise placed a diaper over her shoulder and settled Peter on it as the choir sang "from whom all blessings flow"

A stocky, bald-pated Brother Rigdon gazed from the altar. Staid solemnity molded his face as though he were impervious to imagination, surprise or any other emotion. On the last note, he asked parishioners to open Bibles to Second Corinthians, and he read: "who comforts us in all our affliction, so that we may be able to comfort those who are in any affliction with the comfort which we ourselves are comforted by God."

Allise glanced at Quent, hoping he could find peace in the pastor's message. His moods were often as dark as moonless nights. He suffered alone, and she suffered as keenly if not more than he during times of his withdrawals. She dropped her thoughts and again gave her attention to the pastor.

"Turn to the psalmist. This godly man cried out to God, knowing to whom he must turn. Knowing the source of all his strength." Brother Rigdon preached all around the premise that God is the rock of ages. "In conclusion," he said, "I implore you, my friends, *never* forget God is our strength." Looking out on his flock, he displayed no joy in declaring the kingdom of heaven. He stepped down from the altar and waited for lost souls to come forward as Ellen Crews pumped the organ for "Bringing in the Sheaves."

Allise bundled up Peter and followed those pausing at the door to shake the pastor's hand. Some told him he preached a fine sermon, but she said, "Pastor Rigdon, from the Second Corinthians verse it's my impression God comforts us so we will know the feeling of being comforted." Gazing into his eyes, she waited before blundering on. "Doesn't God comfort us so we'll want to comfort others? I think God expects us to help each other."

He made a guttural sound, and his face went red. Those standing on the steps drew closer, and Allise felt a churning disquiet. She switched the sleeping child to her other shoulder. "Perhaps I didn't make myself understood. I mean ... well, I was taught an obligation to others. It does no harm to be reminded of that Christian duty. We complain and ask favors of God, but neglect to teach how to be with each other. How can we ignore lessons to comfort when we're told to love our neighbors as ourselves?"

"Tsk, tsk, tsk." Mildred Howard's tongue wagged at her husband.

The Widow Burns shook her head and said loud enough for all to hear, "The idea anyone would question our preacher's interpretation of God's word." She turned to Quent. "Berniece DeWitt was a pillar of this church. Your mother would flip over in her grave if she could hear such talk. DeWitts, like all the rest of us, believe the Bible is God's word."

Onlookers gasped, and Mildred found her voice. "I don't know how you Quakers worship, but here we fill church pews to hear our preachers explain the Bible's words. We don't question the Bible or our pastors. They're called by God Almighty himself!"

Allise wanted to explain she meant only to ask the minister's opinion of her interpretation. Dumbfounded, she thought it wasn't this way in Friends' meetinghouses.

Quent glanced up at the threatening clouds. Squeezing her arm, he herded her down the steps as she grappled with Peter's blanket. Hurrying beside him, Allise felt eyes stabbing into her back. She turned to see Sam and Daddy Joe trailing after them. They chuckled, and reaching the car, Sam convulsed into thigh-slap-ping guffaws. "I'll tell you, Allie, you really set 'em off," he blurted.

"You're amused? I fear Mrs. Burns and Mildred will seal my fate in this town."

"Your fate's probably sealed all right, honey. They'll see to it." Quent held the door open. "Hurry. Clouds are moving fast from the southwest. Let's get home."

Leaving her ill-fated future in the hands of church ladies, they were almost home when Allise exclaimed, "Oh, my!" Holding up Peter, she revealed a large damp spot on her lap. "He soaked his diaper right through to my dress."

"Did you baptize your mother, son?" Quent's eyes gleamed with devilment and Allise giggled like a young girl.

At home, she laid out their dinner, then seated at the table, she mimicked a woman who sat behind them in church. "'He's a pretty baby, Quent. He's got a fine-looking daddy. Looks just like you.'"

Daddy Joe and Sam laughed, and she protested. "They ignore me. I get the message that they want this Yankee girl to just fade away. Well, I'm here to stay! And Peter is my child, too."

Daddy Joe put a hand over hers. "Atta girl, honey. Don't let 'em old biddies gitcha."

Quent changed the subject. "When I picked up the truck from the Colsons', Jonas said they left that sick gal in Texas." He placed his napkin on the table. "Rebekah said she was too sick to work on the farm. I told her it was a good thing there wasn't a work load till spring."

Sam's head drooped like a cowed hound dog's tail.

It was the first Allise had heard of an illness on the farm. Now that the baby was here, she wanted to know the tenants. While they continued to talk about the farm, she mulled over her blunder with Brother Rigdon. Did the men in her family gave a whit about how other people saw them? She needed friends but wanted to feel she could disagree with them and be respected. I'll go to church with Quent but be with God in my own way, she thought.

Allise judged the passing of time by Peter's age. Standing over the cradle, she watched him sleep. His lips moved in a sucking motion. *You don't need to nurse, you little dumpling.* Tiptoeing to the bureau, she took a paisley-covered box from the drawer and removed a book titled, "Memories of Baby." It was a gift from her mother.

Sitting on the chaise, she opened it and read a few passages before turning to the last written page dated April 17,1933. Recording the present date, she wrote: "Peter is now eight months old. It takes little to evoke laughter from him. I'm rewarded with toothy smiles, two on bottom, two on top. He bites and I complain. Holding onto the nipple, he turns mischievous blue eyes up to me. Already, he is developing his father's impish ways. What would I do without our baby to amuse me?"

Just then, Peter sat up, crawled to the end of his crib and stood up. Mr. Andrews had stabilized the cradle with slats when he was able to move about. Allise lay the book aside and consulted the time. She changed his diaper and sat in the rocker to nurse him. Pushing strands of blond hair from his forehead, she marveled at the resemblance to his father's baby pictures. *You can resemble him, but please don't be moody, darling.* Cotton season approached. She could expect anything from outbursts to spells of solitude from Quent. He often went days without sharing a thought with her.

Peter relaxed the nipple. Cutting daring eyes up at her, he grabbed her pendent watch and jerked it. "You little devil!" Laughing, she loosened his grip and lay him on the poster bed to blew "phlub-bs" on his tummy. He cackled and waited for another.

That evening, Allise sat at the kitchen table, waiting to tell Quent about his son's latest accomplishment. He walked in, pitched a letter down and while eating his reheated dinner, thumbed through other mail.

She picked up the letter from her father. Dated May 30th, he wrote:

**Having reached the Great Wall already, Japan pushes deeper into China. Mankind should give up warring against himself. I have great expectations for the "new deal." People are singing, "Brother, Can You Spare A Dime?" Investors are as nervous as cats. His appointment of Frances Perkins to be Secretary of Labor and first woman in a presidential cabinet was a good move. I still root for your gender, Allise.**

**Maybe you read that English was proposed as an international language? Apparently, it didn't gain momentum, but the proposal shows democratic countries have something to be desired.**

**How are you, Quent, and Peter? I would like to see my grandson.**

*Your loving Papa,*

**W. P. Weston**

Slumping over his plate, Quent snarled, "Wonder what your papa thinks about the farm problems. He and Roosevelt remind me of my old professors, sitting behind their desks, hovering over books and reports. Don't know diddlely about down here in the dirt."

"How can you speak of Papa like that!" Her words snapped like green beans, and his laugh was sarcastic. Allise wiped Peter's face and thought of slinging the soiled cloth at Quent. Instead, she whirled and threw it hard against the porcelain sink. Wanting to understand and respect her husband, she was unable to make sense of what was happening to them. She argued with herself, then as usual, she rationalized, *He's stressed. I know he respects my father.* Folding the letter, she laid a hand on his muscle-hardened shoulder. "Everyone is worried, Quent. Papa and the president do what they must. You're doing what you must. We'll be fine."

Propped on an elbow, Quent rested his head in his palm and sighed. "Allie, where is the money gonna come from? May not raise enough hogs t' pay the Nigras with meat. I can't farm cotton for five cents a pound. Seven hundred acres planted, oughta be a thousand. Talk is, if cotton's over-produced again, we'll be ordered to plow it under."

Days passed, and he spoke hardly a word. She wanted to wrap him in a protective cloak, like she would a child, and kiss away his concern. Something held her back.

Next morning, Allise made breakfast when Quent walked into the kitchen wearing a white shirt, and tie. "I'm meeting Daddy at the market. We're gonna try t' find a way to pay the market expenses. He expects me to make the farm pay for itself."

"You will, dear." His concern about losing the crop to a plow-up order had surprised her. The year before, when over-produced cotton met a plunging market, Quent worked through the winter in his father's store. She had no idea how the family would survive if he wasn't hired again. Her husband approached his twenty-seventh birthday. The depression was in its third year. He'll be an old man before his time, she thought, placing toast, eggs and bacon before him.

Quent ate quickly and returned upstairs. She cleared the table and rubbed lemon oil on the dining room sideboard when she heard him on the phone. "Sam, don't stop for me this morning. Daddy and I are going over the ledgers today. Keep after the hands to finish planting," Hanging up, he walked in, pecked her on the cheek and left for Joe's Market.

Poor Sam, Allise thought. Of late, the two brothers crossed swords more often than they agreed.

It was after midnight when Quent crawled into bed. She patted his shoulder and lay awake, listening to him toss and turn.

Next morning, Allise commented about his look of desperation. "We huddled over market and farm books all day, looking for funds to carry the two operations through cotton sales in the fall," he said.

Hardly were his words out before the doorbell sounded. It was Daddy Joe. He didn't look any better than his son. Bluish veins bulged on his temples and his skin had an ashen tone. Quent didn't appear worried about his known heart condition, so she dismissed her concerns. Her father-in-law pulled a chair to the desk where Quent waited. "There's no other way, Daddy. We hafta borrow the money."

"I've never borrowed money in my life, son!"

Quent glanced up from papers on the desk. "Yeah, I know, but unless you know some other way, let's go to the bank." Before Daddy Joe could reply, her husband cursed President Roosevelt for issuing emergency powers over farmers. "Of all the years, he picks this one. Let's go to the bank," Quent said, knowing over-production brought on the regulation.

Daddy Joe heaved himself from the chair, and Allise saw them out the door.

She was yet to realize how the government regulations had sent shock waves through the farming South. Nor did she know that Sam had promised not to mention plow-up rumors to the tenants. She made lunch and sat waiting for them to come from the bank.

Soon, they returned, and after lunch they discussed what should be told to the tenants.

That evening, tools were being stored when Quent, Allise, and Peter drove up to the farm shed. Quent stepped from the car and walked to the door held open by Sam. Watching from the car, she thought, Poor Sam all soiled and sweaty. Straining to hear, she suspected her husband was telling him about the mortgage deed given on the market for a five-hundred-dollar loan.

The farm hands stood off to one side waiting to be dismissed. Quent motioned for the seasonal workers to come closer. "Y'all be back here Monday morning t' finish up." He waited for them to leave, then turning to the Hattens, the Spinners, and Colsons, "I guess y'all oughta know what's ahead."

Some of the tenants stared at their feet. Others shifted from one tired leg to the other. Dusty, sweat-stained faces squinted at a fading sun as though seeking light to shine on some dark unknown fate lying before them. Jonas stood, arms folded across his chest, watching barefoot youngsters run about in a furl of dust. They giggled, pulling at their mothers' skirts and hiding behind them.

"I don't hafta tell y'all things are bad." Quent motioned to Sam. "We'll keep the farm running, but when weeding's done, y'all will probably wanna look for wage jobs."

Rebekah's round face contorted, and black men kept their heads lowered, staring at the ground, the source of their only hope. "You can stay in your houses," Quent said, "but if you're not working on the farm, we'll have to charge rent. Any emergency needing cash, you see Sam. We'll do what we can, but it better be an emergency. When chopping's done, each family will get five dollars extra."

Allise scanned dark faces for signs of fear, anger, any emotion deeper than uncertainty and resignation. As far as she could tell, only Rebekah appeared ready to speak.

Quent started toward the car, paused, kicked up loose soil and stared down at it. Turning, he said, "Y'all can charge at Daddy's store." He turned to Sam. "Tell 'em that's it." Before Sam could say anything, Quent seemed determined to make himself understood. "That's the way it's gonna be till the cotton's sold." His tone softened. "It's not gonna get better soon, and I hope y'all find work." He waited as though expecting someone to speak. No one did, and he blurted, "Hell! If the damn president makes us plow up, it'll get worse."

Allise caught Sam's stunned look. He stuttered out a dismissal, and most of the tenants straggled off in groups of twos and threes, mumbling among themselves. Jonas and Rebekah were left standing. Ah there's a defiant face, she thought as Rebekah gripped Jonas' shirt sleeve and nudged him forward. "Mista Quent, farming's all we know. You gwine need hep come picking time."

Quent ignored her and told Jonas he had been the best help on the place. "If you wanna stay on and take your chances, I'd rather have you than any of the others. But you got to understand it's gonna be risky."

"Yassa, I sho understand." Rebekah loosened the hold on her husband's shirt.

"I've been meaning to ask, Jonas, when's that gal of yours coming back?"

Rebekah came on quickly. "We don't know, Mista Quent, she still be real sick."

Quent whirled around, climbed into the roadster and drove away, leaving a fog of dust for Sam and the Colsons. Speeding along in silence, he appeared disturbed. Allise felt concerned for the tenants. "Tomorrow, I will write to the Philadelphia Friends for clothing, food, and other needs," she said. "I will go to the churches here—"

"You'll what! I don't want people thinking we can't take care of our own, Allie. Why you wanna go messing in Nigra business? They will make-do." One hand left the steering wheel, waving his apparent exasperation. "Market credit is like paying 'em. They're never out of debt. Dried peas and beans will take 'em through winter. Till their gardens produce, they will eat cornbread and pokeweed."

Allise's mouth puckered with determination. Tomorrow, she thought, I will send a letter to the Friends' service committee in Philadelphia.

Monday morning, she pushed Peter's pram to the post office. After depositing the letter, she rolled the baby's carriage up the sidewalk to the parsonage. Must strike just the right chord with Mrs. Rigdon, she thought, ringing the bell. The pastor's wife appeared at the door in a bibbed apron over a loose-fitting, print dress. Her eyes flared at Allise, and her smile seemed forced. Having questioned Brother Rigdon's sermon, Allise cautioned herself to hold her tongue. Ignoring the woman's annoyance, she said, "Hello, Mrs. Rigdon. Isn't it a nice day?" She lifted Peter from the wicker pram. "We came from the post office, and I said, 'Let's say hello to Mrs. Rigdon.'" She gave the woman a winsome smile, and the cheeky face of a hundred wrinkles softened.

With a flourish of hand, she invited them in and led the way to the parlor. "Well, it is nice weather," she contended, walking ahead. Her dress stopped at mid-calf over cotton stockings and black oxfords. Offering no other hospitality, she motioned Allise to sit.

In due time, Allise broached the reason for her unexpected call. "Mrs. Rigdon, everyone suffers now, but I'm concerned for farm tenants. Quent says when the chopping is finished, our hands will have to look for jobs. The likelihood of Negroes finding—"

"Uh-hum." The woman shifted on the ancient, wood-framed couch that might have been pillowed comfort at one time, but heavy bodies had wedged permanent dimples into the cushions.

With a tinge of guilt, Allise played her trump card and watched the woman tug at her apron strings. "I expect our tenants and others to need help. Everyone is having a hard time, but to give when we're not well off, it's like the biblical woman who gave her last mite. Mrs. Rigdon, the plight of farmers could be an opportunity for the church to do good." Now, she had her attention. "If the situation wasn't so sad, it would be laughable," Allise said. She raised her hands in exasperation. "We don't have much, but we're above mere existence. What will they do without warm clothing and food this winter?"

Like dark switched to light, Mrs. Rigdon beamed. "Why it's an ideal project for the Auxiliary. Every year, we take our out-dated Sunday School literature to the coloreds, but the ladies want a new project. You should join our Ladies Auxil—"

Allise wasn't surprised the invitation ended abruptly. She wouldn't be well received in the auxiliary. It didn't matter, she had the pastor's wife hooked. "I'll deliver the goods and help the ladies sort, clean and box collected items."

"Why, they'll love it. They want to do good for God's glory and His blessings."

Allise recalled her father saying, "blessings come through the enhancement of God's creation." Then he had asked, "Do you think God made us merely to receive blessings? No," he added, "God wants us to be good stewards of what He created like Noah with the animals." It would be interesting to have a dialogue with Mrs. Rigdon on these points, but better judgment told her not to challenge while ahead.

Peter turned grumpy. He was wet and in need of a nap. Standing, she said, "Mrs. Rigdon, let's go to the other churches. They should help, and the black church, too."

"Well, I don't know about that, Allie." A long-suffering sigh escaped her thin lips. "Churches don't tend to combine efforts, and down here, we don't engage black chu—"

"Nevertheless ..." Allise bit her tongue and begged. "Please, Mrs. Rigdon, go with me to the other white churches. You will make the difference with those pastors."

"If Mr. Rigdon says it's all right, and if the ladies want the project. I'll call you," the woman said.

Just then, Peter's crying reached a point beyond control, and Allise said goodbye.

During the day, she returned to the talk with Mrs. Rigdon many times before Quent came home. "Sorry I'm late." He stood in the kitchen doorway. "Chop-ping's finished."

"That's good news." Reheating his long-overdue and over-cooked meal at the gas range, Allise gave him a side-ways glance and wondered about his mood.

He slumped onto a chair. "All the help's leaving. Short crew this morning. Can't keep farming with only Nigra women and kids. Farming's going t' hell." Doke Spinner, one of the three tenants, had jumped a freight train headed for St. Louis or on to Chicago to find work. Jake Hatten went to the lumber mill in town to ask for a job, Quent said. "We kept dogging the Colsons and the hired help till chopping was done."

Sensing her husband's depression, Allise decided this wasn't the time to tell about her day. She set a plate before him, and hearing Peter's cry upstairs, went to change his diaper and rock him back to sleep. Her heart ached for Quent's frustrated state; yet, she felt conflicted. *What does he expect from the tenants and me? What must I do?* Her papa's pearls of wisdom popped into her mind. He said there were times to express oneself and times to just listen. Allise whispered, "God, let me find patience."

The next morning, she thought Mrs. Rigdon might call. When she didn't, Allise chose a Kelly green dress from the closet, pulled it over her head and walked before the vanity mirror. Closing in on her image, she saw the color reflected in her eyes. He likes me to wear this, she thought, brushing short, reddish hair back in place.

Peter stood, holding onto the dresser. He was nine months old but still needed something to steady himself. She picked up her child and went downstairs. With a worn blanket underarm, she lifted a basket of fried chicken and potato salad from the table and walked out to the roadster. Pulling open the rumble seat, she stored the food and blanket, seated Peter beside her and closed the car door.

Quent looked pleasantly surprised when they arrived with picnic fare. The brothers were accustomed to egg sandwiches that didn't spoil in the heat. Sam grabbed up Peter and danced like a merry cricket. Allise laid out the blanket, placed the dishes on it and insisted that Jonas eat from their bounty. He sat off to one side, eating and gazing out across the first planted field. Healthy plants were already six to eight inches high.

As far as an eye could see, lobed, gray-green leaves spread across the river flood plain. "Cotton's king down here, Allie." Quent spoke with pride. "No one's old enough to remember any other plant in its place." He took a bite of salad. "Um-m, good."

Sam swigged tea. "No one's apt to remember. Won't plant nothing but cotton."

Peter sat on Allise's lap, waiting for skin to be pulled from a drumstick and handed to him. The child squirmed away from her and crawled across to Sam. "I'm dirty, Peedy." Wiping the child's hands with a paper napkin, he laughed. "I told Quent we oughta plant some fields in corn. If cotton's plowed under—"

"Hell, Sam!" Quent removed his hat and rubbed his forehead. "It costs as much to plant corn as it brings on the market." He gave his brother a look of disgust.

"At least you can eat corn." Sam directed his comment at Allise and laughed.

She glanced back at Jonas, sitting on the grass near the plow and mule. "What will you do, Jonas, if—"

"Don't worry about him. He'll hunt and fish," Quent scoffed. "Jonas is made of strong stuff. Aren't you, boy?"

Allise saw Jonas wince. She turned away, hoping he didn't know she noticed.

Maizee sat at the kitchen table where a morning sun streamed in. She wrote in large printed letters on a postcard: *I miss home. Ester will write when the baby comes.* Laying the pencil aside, she recalled Aunt Althea saying, "When that baby gets here, ain't gonna be no sleep, girl. Better hope it don't have colic." Everything she heard sounded as if the misery would go on. Glancing at the card, she imagined one of her brothers reading it to her momma and daddy.

She, Dalt, and Cass had attended the rag-tag school on the south corner of the eastern edge of the DeWitt farm. Built as a church, the sway-roofed, wooden structure served as a classroom for Negro children living near enough to walk. School was held three months of any year a teacher could be engaged to take students through the sixth grade. No child had ever advanced that far. They grew older year after year, waiting for a teacher.

Maizee signed her name, printed the address and left the card on the table. Pulling herself up, she pressed hands into her back and trudged outside. Two soot-blackened pots coughed up steam. In one, soapy water puffed and fumed over linens. White clothing simmered in the other. Nearby, dark colors filled two baskets, ready to be punched down in the boiling turbulence once white pieces were taken to rinse tubs. Aunt Althea rubbed dark blue trousers over the scrub board as Henny and Ester traipsed up and down beneath clotheslines with damp rags, wiping them clean for hanging the judge's laundry to dry.

That evening on the way home from his office, the judge picked up fresh linens and clothing, every item folded or pressed and on hangers. After he had come and gone, Uncle Mo, sitting at the supper table, said, "If it rained cross the river like here, there'll be a bumper cotton crop this year. Make them DeWitts happy."

Maizee wished rain for her folks' sake. She envisioned her mother throwing a ham bone into a pot of beans and setting it on the stove to simmer, then stirring up a corn pone and prodding her field-bound family out the door. Her daddy and others would be weeding and thinning when she got to the field. *Come evening, all be trudging home one more bone-weary, end-of-May day. They be aching like me bending over them wash pots.*

After supper, she sank into bed and lay awake in the dark. Running a finger around her protruding navel, she thought her momma would be glad to get the card. Although only fifty miles away, Maizee might as well have been a thousand from her family.

She awoke with a keen sense of that distance. Time seemed to move forward one day and two back. The load she carried put a strain on her frame, and Aunt Althea reminded her daily that the baby would come any day now. Rennie Mae had said it was due in June.

"Well, it's June." Hands on her hips, Maizee braced herself and muttered, "Gonna be home soon." Walking out to the boiling pots, she punched sheets beneath roiled water.

Flicking away streams of sweat from her face, suddenly, she dropped the punch stick and grabbed her lower belly. "Aunt Althea." She whimpered and bent into the burst of pain.

Althea looked up from the scrub board. Recognizing Maizee's distress, she sent Ester for the midwife and yelled at Henny, "Git in the house and fix that bed for birthing."

Within minutes, Rennie Mae and Ester came breathless into the bedroom.

Maizee squirmed and moaned, but she heard Aunt Althea shoo her daughters back to the wash pots. "Dat washing gotta go on jes as sure as dis baby gotta come." Between the intermittent birth pains, she listened as her aunt divided attention between the backyard laundering and her suffering.

One after the other, pains came with ever-increasing velocity and intensity. Stripped and drenched in sweat, Maizee shone like polished jasper. She said she wanted to die.

Rennie Mae cajoled, comforted and mopped her face. She crammed a rolled rag in Maizee's mouth when her hands latched onto the cast iron headboard. By mid-afternoon, the soon-to-be mother screamed. Rennie Mae warned, "Don't push, chile. Ain't time, yet."

Maizee heard a basket drop to the floor. She watched Aunt Althea whip out a pillowcase, flip it over the ironing board and whisk the flat iron in a nervous frenzy.

Henny and Ester came to the door. Althea asked if they had eaten. Henny said they had supper and their daddy and Ward sat under the mulberry tree. "They listening to the screams and staring their uselessness," Henny said. They had gone back to the kitchen to wash the dishes when Maizee heard the midwife say, "This baby coming. Push, Maizee! Push! Come on, give another big push. You doing okay. Dis baby's a-coming."

Maizee strained. "Wanna die I wanna die!" She gasped between clenched teeth and groaned through another uncontrollable strain.

Rennie Mae chuckled. "It's a big old boy. Look here, Maizee." She held the newborn for her to see. "You got a fine baby boy. Lawd! Ever'thing gonna be awright."

Moments before, splitting pain left no space for concern. Now, gazing at the baby, emotion swept Maizee's face. Her eyes followed the midwife and Aunt Althea to the table where they wiped and wrapped her son. "He gonna be a beautiful baby when he gits a little color," Rennie Mae said, holding her child beside the bed.

"Uh-huh," Maizee mumbled. Her last thought was of home. Sleep fell over her like a cool sheet warding off the room's stalled heat.

# CHAPTER 4

▼

Cotton plants grew tall as anxiety mounted in the farm community. All indications pointed to the plow-ups. What all the other farmers dreaded.

Allise descended the stairs and walked into the living room with a freshly bathed Peter in her arms. Quent tuned the radio to the evening news. It was H. B. Kaltenborn's voice:

**Cotton farmers have another bumper crop underway. It threatens the market. Today, the Secretary of Agriculture announced that cotton fields, estimated at ten million acres, are to be plowed. This will drive up prices.**

Quent released a long sigh and pushed back on the sofa, resting his head, His eyes were closed and he rubbed his forehead, a sure sign of distress. Allise plopped Peter on the rug, tossed his night clothes and ran behind her husband. She pressed lips into his tousled hair.

The baby crawled out of the towel, pulled himself upright at his father's knee and stood in innocent nudity, looking up at him.

The next day, an August sun beat down on Arkansas earth with the dogged force of something ancient and natural. It drew moisture from the pores of every living thing. Allise pulled the roadster up behind the farm truck and sat, waiting under the full glare of sun, to bring out the picnic fare. A heat rash popped out in the creases of Peter's arms and legs. She fanned him with a folded diaper and hoped that exposing their baby to the awful heat proved to her husband she cared about the labor wasted on a doomed crop.

Allise had witnessed Quent and Sam's relationship grow more and more discordant. They stood at the edge of the field, a safe distance from each other and apparently in self-muzzled silence. Sweat stained their shirts as they stared down the row of thigh-high cotton plants and Jonas, who plodded behind a mule toward them.

She fanned and watched them watch Jonas. Turning her attention to the black man, Allise noted his trance-like gaze to one side of the animal. He tugged on the reins, geeing and hawing straight on the row. *He appears content with his life pattern, as though it were meant to be. Maybe he is merely compliant. What are his feelings about losing healthy plants to upturned earth? Cotton is all he can count on for his family's welfare. What would he say if I could ask my questions?*

Jonas started down another row, and Quent and Sam looked around at a more distant field, also under the plow. Allise turned, too, and saw the bothered soil release a cloud of dust. She removed a towel from the jar of iced tea, patted Peter's face, arms, and legs, then draped it over his head.

Sam took a step toward his brother. He drew shoulders up around his neck and rubbed his palms together in an agitated manner peculiar to him. The first time Allise saw it, she had wondered about such a strange, nervous compulsion. She strained to hear what he said to Quent. Obviously, he was trying to reconcile one of their ongoing spats.

"Ain't nothing we can do about it, Quent. Still have time t' plant something."

Quent told him to forget it, but Sam pleaded. "Something to sell at the store or the Nigras can eat. Why does Daddy think you ..." He spun around and walked to the car. "Gawddamn it! There's gotta be some use for them fields. Sow 'em in turnip and mustard greens" He leaned against the car.

Allise wanted to apologize for Quent, but she didn't. She laid the blanket in the shade of the car, and they ate mostly in silence, only answering Peter's babble.

Leaving Quent and Sam in the field, she drove around the lane to the Colson house. Stopping, she saw swirls of dust blow across the yard where Li'l Joke and Dessie used a brush broom. They ran toward the car, scattering a flock of speckled chickens that scratched in the dirt. Clinging to the picket gate, they peered at the white woman.

Allise didn't want to leave Peter unattended. She smiled. "Hi, girls! I'm Mrs. DeWitt. What are your names?"

"Li'l Joke," the taller one said. "She be Dessie."

"Well, Li'l Joke, would you ask Rebekah to step out here, please?" Allise knew some tenants by first names, but this was her first stop at a tenant house.

Rebekah appeared, and seeing Mista Quent's wife, she grinned. "Where's that baby, Miz Allie? Bet he growed a peck." Allise saw a round vulnerable face as inviting as bread pudding. It was like looking into the woman's soul. "Is he walking?" she asked.

"He tries," Allise said, removing sacks from the rumble seat to the running board. She explained the sacks contained used items. Shown Peter's outgrown baby clothes, Rebekah said she would give them to someone with a baby. Allise told her about the church project. "If approved, may I bring items to you? You won't be offended—"

"Sho nuff, Miz Allie. We ain't too proud. Gonna be scratching t' survive way things is. Ever'body round here's in the same shape we's in."

Allise thanked Rebekah and waved goodbye to Li'l Joke and Dessie.

Back home, she wondered what Quent would say if he knew what she had been up to. She rang the parsonage. The pastor's wife answered the phone. "Why Allie, I've been meaning to call. The ladies like the idea, and my husband says we can ask the other ministers, but Allie, we draw the line on the black church. It doesn't seem proper—"

"I can't imagine the impropri—" Again, she bit her tongue. "Never mind, Mrs. Rigdon. I visited the farm. Rebekah agreed to store the goods and get word to others."

Mrs. Rigdon said an announcement would be made in Sunday School as well as from the pulpit on Sunday. "Is Tuesday suitable for making rounds of ministers?"

Allise agreed and hung up. She was grateful for the woman's help but loathed the insensitivity and indifference to the Negro church. I'll go alone to visit the black pastor, she thought.

Tuesday morning brought relief from the heat, but Peter squirmed and fussed on the seat beside her, and Allise sang, "Who's afraid of the big bad wolf?" He turned a questioning gaze up to her. "Not me! I'm not afraid of the big bad wolf," she said. He delighted her with a toothy smile as they pulled up to the parsonage.

Mrs. Rigdon came out and planted herself firmly on the seat. Giving a sidelong look at Peter, she asked, "May I hold him?"

Surprised at her request, Allise nodded and prayed he wouldn't wet his diaper while settled on the grandmotherly woman's lap. After several church visits and a diaper change, they drove away to see Brother Thomas, the last minister.

He met them at the chapel's lacquered, double doors. His boyish face made Allise question his age. Short and stocky, he wore eyeglasses, and his pale skin made her think he spent too much time behind a desk preparing sermons. He welcomed them into the sanctuary with a soft voice and a smile.

Sun cast a soft yellow hue through arched windows. Stained glass behind the raised altar depicted Christ's pain on the cross. The pulpit painted white was left of the altar, and right was the baptismal font. A far cry from a Quaker meetinghouse, Allise thought. She liked simplicity. No altar, plain wooden benches, no distractions, rituals or formalities. Just a place to be with God.

Brother Thomas appeared pleased to see Mrs. Rigdon. He chucked Peter under the chin, charming him with baby-faced smiles. Then, considering their proposal, he promised to put the idea to his ministerial board. On the church steps, Allise paused. "Brother Thomas, what do you think about inviting the black church to participate?" As she probed his face, out of the corner of her eye, she saw Mrs. Rigdon flee to the sidewalk below.

The church leader jammed hands into his pockets and watched her descend. He avoided Allise's steady gaze and stared down at his toes, raising up and down in his shoes.

She waited with growing exasperation. "I thought ... Never mind." She thanked him and said goodbye to his relieved look.

From the car, Mrs. Rigdon waved Peter's hand at the pastor, and Allise said, "Well, we've had quite a day." The older woman agreed without looking her way. She stopped in front of the parsonage. "Mrs. Rigdon, I guess I shall never understand this strange black and white relationship. Why can't we be more accepting of differences?"

The pastor's wife fixed a gaze squarely on her. "It isn't hard to understand, Allie. Everyone just accepts the way it is down here."

✳   ✳   ✳   ✳

The government-ordered plow-up reached the Maslings by word of mouth, and Maizee overheard her uncle talking about it. "What my folks gonna do, Uncle Mo?"

"I wisht I knowed, girl. It's sho gonna be hard. Sho is."

Worried, she had gathered up her sleeping son from the bed and held him like a security blanket.

Now, Maizee gazed out the bus window at fields skirting the highway. Workers bent over rows, picking cotton in the unplowed fields. Other fields lay barren and baking in the late summer heat. Thinking of October's cooler weather, less than a month away, she pulled the cord for the Greyhound Bus to stop. Balancing two-month-old Nate on one arm, she hooked a cloth bundle over her shoulder and stepped down from the door. With a thin blanket over Nate's head, she stood on the shoulder of the road, waiting for the vehicle to pull away.

Gears wrenching and tires grinding into heat-absorbed gravel, the bus left a signature of dust and smelly fumes in its wake. Once it was well down the road, Maizee let the bag slide to the ground. Removing the blanket from

Nate, she placed him on her shoulder, picked up the bundle and scanned the fields. "We's home, Baby Nate." Up the lane, she spotted her mother, waddling like a fatted duck in her direction. Rebekah's bosom jiggled like a bowl of Jell-O, and hands flailed above her head. Lil' Joke and Dessie ran ahead of her. All the commotion struck an old fear in Maizee.

Mista Quent was out there somewhere. If he saw them running, he would look to see why. Dropping the bag again, she cradled Nate and felt for the switchblade knife bound by cloth above the knee inside her left thigh. Purchased with coins from Aunt Althea, the weapon was her secret, and she wore it constantly. An edgy glance about revealed nothing untoward. She lifted the bundle and welcomed the excitement racing toward her.

Rebekah reached out fleshy arms. "Maizee! Honey, let me see that boy."

Holding out the baby to her, she said, "It's good t' be home, Momma." She stooped to embrace Li'l Joke and Dessie, who clung to her waist.

"It's sho good to have y' back, honey. Ester's card say you named him Nathaniel. That sho is a powerful long name t' hang on a tiny body." She gazed at the infant in her arms. "He's beautiful, Maizee! Sho is."

"Yes'm, he is. I didn't have no name for him till Brother Miles, he be the preacher over in Jefferson. He say Nathaniel means a gift from God. We call him Nate." Her sisters begged to hold the baby, and Maizee smiled. "Li'l Joke, you and Dessie hafta set down cause he's sho a heavy load."

Reaching the house, they collected chairs and took them to the porch. "You wore out, ain'cha, chile?" Rebekah asked. Maizee was tired but her attention never deflected from her baby as the younger girls took turns with him.

Soon, Jonas and her brothers washed off field dirt and ate their supper. Then, Maizee stood over them, guardedly smiling at their shy "cooche-coos" for her son.

She bedded Nate in a large wooden box to which Jonas had attached rockers. Rebekah had made a quilted-padding for the inside. As before, Maizee crawled in bed with her sisters in the room shared with their parents. Except for a long layover in Bensburg, her trip from Jefferson had been like riding a bumping, swaying camel with desert heat whipping her face. Sleep soon beckoned.

During the night, Nate's first movement woke her. She sat on the bedside, letting his mouth work at her breast. Stroking his cheek, she recalled Aunt Althea's prediction of little sleep. I's waked up and tired but he's a good boy, she thought. Sighing contentment, not even an uneasy peace at the edge of her mind could dim the comfort of being home and holding her baby.

At daybreak, Maizee nursed Nate in the kitchen and watched the familiar routine. Rebekah shooed Jonas and the boys out the door with Li'l Joke and

Dessie trailing behind. At the cotton shed, they would get sacks, and pick and empty numerous times into high, side-boarded wagons. Jonas would haul a load to the gin and return with cotton seed.

Breathing hard, Rebekah sat across from Maizee. "You gone so long, chile, we got catching up t' do." They talked for some time before Maizee took the baby to his makeshift bed. She returned and stood at the window, staring out toward the sheds. "Mista Quent ain't out here much no mo'," her momma said. "Not since the cotton been plowed up." Rebekah drummed fingers on the table. "Yo' daddy say he still the boss, telling Mista Sam what t' do. DeWitts don't set foot in here. Talks t' Jonas outside the fence."

"I don't ever wanna see Mista Quent agin, Momma." Hate coiled around the words, and anger-filled eyes turned to her mother. "He cain't ever see me and Nate. Ever'body, Daddy, the boys, and Li'l Joke and Dessie, they gotta know they ain't suppose t' tell Mista Quent and Mista Sam I'm back. I cain't pick cotton, or he'll—"

"Hush, chile." Rebekah said she didn't have to pick cotton. "You can take care of Nate, cook and do some cleaning. I sho don't want 'em t' know you here. I'll tell Leona Spinner and the Hattens t' tell the DeWitts you still in Texas."

✳     ✳     ✳     ✳

After visiting the ministers, Allise helped the food and clothing drive get underway, then one day, she drove into Colored Town. Stopping in front of a rundown building, she saw a sign clinging precariously over the door. It read: "Turner's Store." A colored man sat on a soft drink crate backed against the store front. Before she could leave the car, he stood and disappeared inside.

Carrying Peter on her hip, she entered the screen door and let it bang behind them. A strong caramel aroma greeted her. Sorghum molasses dripped into a bucket from the spigot of a wooden keg. Light entered the long, narrow room through one window and the door, and one bare, fly-specked, light bulb, dangling from the ceiling, shed a hazy glow throughout. The place took on shadowy, jagged shapes of stacked boxes, crates of Coca Cola, and strawberry, orange, and grape soda pops. Cobwebs stretched from the hanging light cord to dusty shelves lined with canned goods, jars of Levi Garrett Snuff, and medicinals.

In the dim light, Allise spotted the storekeeper behind a short counter crowded with opened cartons of chewing gum and tobacco, and a tall jar of pickled pigs' feet. The bulb shone directly down on the counter and the man seated on another upturned crate.

His mouth gaped as she approached him, exposing a few stained teeth in otherwise toothless gums. Time, the sun or hardships had left him wrinkled like a raisin. He spat into a tin can held beneath his chin, and looking up, was careful to avoid her eyes. If I could peer into his eyes, what would they convey? she wondered. "Hello," she said, facing his masked blankness and sensing the wall between herself and his stories. "I'm Allise DeWitt. Can you tell me where I might find the minister of Mt. Zion Church?"

"Yes'm. That be Brother James." Seemingly ill-at-ease, he shifted about. Allise said she didn't catch his name, and still not looking at her, he said, "I be Dodd Turner."

She wanted him to see her smile. "Mr. Turner, I need to speak with the minister. Does he have a phone?" Dodd said he didn't, and she said, "Where does he lives?"

"Lives right back there." He indicated and said the preacher wouldn't be home because he worked in the woods. "His wife oughta be home, though." Dodd followed her outside and pointed to a house. "It be the tall house back of the church."

Allise thanked him and returned to the car.

The two-story, unpainted clapboard set back a few feet from the dirt street. Allise swung Peter on her hip, stepped up to the front porch and rapped on the door.

A stout, middle-aged woman answered with a questioning look. "Yas'm?" She opened the screen door a bit more and shooed a brown chicken from the porch. Allise introduced herself and Peter. "You be Mista Quent's wife, ain'cha? I cooked for Miz Berniece before she died. Yes, Ma'am, I heard about y', Miz Allie. Come in and let me see that baby." White teeth gleamed through her broad grin.

The connection between the woman and Quent's late mother made Allise feel less awkward. She saw another round, black face, and like Rebekah's, it, too, revealed an open soul. Entrusting Peter to her outstretched arms, she caught a fresh-baked scent and said, "Um-m, something smells really good."

"I was icing a cake. Come on in and we'll slice it. Lawd, this is a fine boy." She led them to a kitchen and handed Peter back to Allise. "Sit there," she pointed to a table chair. "It'll be ready in a minute."

"The cake smells delicious. I'm afraid cooking isn't my strong suit, Mrs.— "

"Jes call me Elfreeda." She swiped frosting, then cut a slice. Taking the baby, she watched Allise take a bite. "Peter be a fine name," she said, jiggling him on her knee.

The moist, yellow cake, rich with eggs and butter, smelled of vanilla flavoring. "Um-m." Allise smacked her lips at Peter. She continued to eat and explain what brought her there.

Elfreeda said her husband worked as a timber cutter for the sawmill, and she would tell him about the tenant project when he came home.

Finishing the last bite of cake, she and Peter left with a promise to visit again.

A few days later, Allise delivered the Philadelphia Friends shipment to Rebekah and returned home minutes before Quent came for lunch. He worked in the market after the cotton and seeds were sold. When he returned to the store, she and Peter went to Newtown Church.

Chatter waned as she walked into a beehive of activity around the collection boxes. Greeting the ladies, she began sorting when one woman said, "I don't know why we hafta be so fussy over river niggers. Lazy, no-good-for-nothings clog our sidewalks on Saturday, laughing, talking loud, and spitting ever'where.

The room fell silent, and Allise waited for someone to speak. She knew the women held their disquiet in anticipation of what she would say. Inspecting and placing garments on piles, she began sounding a devised version of the Seven Dwarves marching-off-to-work song. "We wash, we fold, all in one box. Hi ho, hi ho, we label sex and sizes." Dropping the rhythm, she looked at the woman. "Would we do less for needy white people?"

Bent over their tasks, no one uttered a word. The outspoken one wouldn't look at her. Allise was tempted to walk out and leave them to their biases, but, getting things to the river farmers was more important than her pride.

Several days later, boxes were ready to be delivered to Rebekah. Sun beamed on a crisp fall day, and Allise sat beside Sam as he herded the old farm truck from one church to another, collecting them. "I know God is saying 'Amen' to good works." She hummed to Peter, and Sam smiled at her off-key tune. Reaching across, he put a hand on her shoulder.

"You make fun of my singing." She laughed and removed his hand. Seeing his pensive look, she asked, "Do I remind you of someone, Sam? Lost love?" He seemed to struggle with a fake smile. She regretted teasing, but his longing looks disturbed her. At times, her fondness for him was greater than what she felt for Quent. *Does he … No-o, I remind him of someone.* She dismissed the thought as they pulled up to the Colson house.

No one came out to meet them. They unloaded on the porch and went to find Jonas.

As the days passed, mild temperatures relented to a late fall chill. Allise and Elfreeda cleaned and packed the items collected from the black church. Allise printed on each box in large letters: Mt. Zion Church. With the loaded boxes in the rumble seat, they headed for the Colson tenant. Li'l Joke came out to meet them. She said the cartons took all the available house space, and everything was moved to the black church near the back of the farm. "Momma be over there now."

Driving up to the church, they saw Rebekah peering through the window. She rushed out to greet them in a red, wool coat, smelling unmistakably of moth balls, and urged Allise to take Peter indoors. "Cold in there, too, cause the church got cracks big enough t' 'pitch a cat out." She pulled the coat tighter, "Me and Elfreeda will tend t' this."

Inside, Allise watched them unload the car. Then, she walked to an opposite window and looked out on a stand of tall oaks. Someone sat astride the fence stile. *Young man with a rifle?* Must be a hunter, she thought. Clutching Peter, she returned to the unloading. When everything was inside, and sacks and boxes were arranged, all hurried back outside.

Elfreeda took Peter on her lap, and Rebekah looked concerned. "Miz Allie, y'all be real careful about riding out here t'gether. Ain't looked on kindly for white folks t' be riding round with colored lessen whites in the back seat being chauffeured some place."

Allise glanced back at the fence stile. The hunter wasn't there. They waved to Rebekah already scampering down the path toward out-of-sight tenant houses below the hill. Turning onto the highway, she scrutinized all vehicles. Though they were few and far between, she drove slowly, glancing often in the rear view mirror. "Elfreeda, I would not have you ride in the rumble seat when there is an empty seat right here."

Quent was home when she arrived. Handing Peter to him, she started their meal and explained where she had been. He shook his finger. "Mark my word, Allie, you're gonna regret this business."

Letting his remark slide, she didn't tell about a hunter sitting as still as an Irish setter on point. She couldn't risk his demand that she cease the activity for the farmers.

The temperature still had a cutting edge Sunday morning. Walking as fast as she could, Maizee toted Nate along the tenant trail to the black church. Worshipers from the opposite direction rushed up another path leading to the stile. Rebekah had made known that food and clothing awaited them, and a larger number of women than usual walked toward the church.

Leona, wife of former tenant Doke Spinner, rushed past Maizee. At the crest of the hill, she halted and yelled back, "Oh, Lawd! Come look, y'all!"

Pushing ahead, they saw an empty space where the church had been. Speechless, they gaped at the scorched earth. Once-large oaks were dwarfed into black obelisks. Fire-eaten posts burdened by sagging wires, leaned into each other. Recently plowed-up cotton fields proved a blessing in disguise. They kept the blaze contained within the churchyard.

"The church was here Wednesday when we unloaded stuff," Rebekah said. Maizee thought her mother sounded as if trying to reassure herself that she wasn't dreaming the scene.

Women and children milled about, mumbling among themselves. Some picked up sticks and stirred the ashes. Others walked among charred remains of wooden crosses that marked the few graves of those buried before any of them could remember. Their place of worship, their idle school and counted-on cache of winter items, all turned to ashes.

Maizee stood outside the scorched square with Annie Hatten and Leona. Their cheeks were tear-stained. Rebekah stepped up to them. "Tears ain't gonna bring back 'em goods!" she said. "Ain't gonna get no new church, neither."

"Momma, what we gonna do?" Maizee tried to calm her mother's frustration.

"I don't know, honey, jes don't know." Rebekah sounded hopeless.

Jake Hatten, the designated lay preacher, signaled them to gather about. He quoted scripture from memory, then he said, "We don't need that building. *We's* the church! Gonna stand right here under God's sky and give thanks for all he done give us. Bekah, you gonna lead us?"

"Yes, Lawd God!" Rebekah raised closed eyes heavenward, and in a sing-song fashion, lifted her voice to resonant heights. "Sometimes y' give us heavy loads, and we don't know why." Someone shouted "Amen," and she continued. "This be awful hard t' bear, Lawd. We don't know who done this to us. Ain't likely t' know in this world. How's we gonna feed and keep our chil'ren warm, God?"

"How, Lawd?" came the echoes. "How?"

"Lawd God," she held the rhythm of despair. "All we got is Lawd Jesus t' keep us going. Thank ya, God, for the savior, and thank ya, Lawd Jesus, who give his all." Ending, her chin rested on her chest. She wagged her head side to side, as if to rid it of images and fill it with rapture.

Jake said, "Yassa, thank ya, Lawd, and amen. Now, let's sing."

"When it look like the sun ain't gonna shine no mo'," Rebekah began. Notes issued from the depths of her being, and others joined in, before she built to a crescendo.

"A-amen!" Jake said. "Now, let's go on home. Time t' think about what t' do. Remember," he added, "when we ain't got nothing else, we got Jesus."

Worshipers straggled off in twos and threes toward paths leading away from the burned area. Maizee clasped Nate to her body and tried to stay close behind Jake. He walked alongside a sharecropper from the Touvin farm. Turning a somber face to him, Jake said, "I wonder what time the fire was and did anybody see it?"

"I don't know, but I bet nobody did. That old building be dry as a powder house. Burnt fast. I suspect ever'body be keeping warm round the stove that day."

"You remember when the Klan lynched Cobb Akins years ago?" Jake asked. "Said he stole from the Bradmont Plantation Commissary. We gonna hafta watch ever move."

Maizee trusted Jake like a favorite uncle. Her parents had spoken of hooded men lynching Negroes and burning crosses. Fearful, she pulled her coat snugly around Nate.

Monday morning, Jonas met Sam at the cotton shed and gave him the news. He rushed back to Deer Point to tell Quent about the fire."All the donated food and warm clothing in the church went up in smoke," Sam said.

Allise's stomach dropped like an elevator. She set a cut orange before her husband. "Sam, I'll make breakfast for you. How do you like your eggs?"

He said he had eaten, and glancing up from the orange, Quent frowned. "Didn't I tell you? You're fools! When you mess around with Nigras, y' always come out a loser."

"I ain't no fool, Quent, and neither is Allie! You can call *me* one, but how dare you call *her* one! I oughta slap you up side the head." Sam lifted a closed fist.

"Oh, heavens!" Allise jumped up and caught his arm. "Sit down, Sam."

With an amused grin and no apparent sympathy for the tenants, Quent said she would cease her efforts for the farmers. "You don't know what you're messing with, Allie." Turning to Sam, he said, "If it's the damned Ku Klux Klan, those hooded devils could burn all our Nigra houses. Then what would they do?"

Sam chortled. "There ain't been no Klan round here as long as I can remember."

Angry defiance flashed in Allise's eyes. "I won't stop, Quent, as long as things are collected for them." She wanted to blame God and people like her husband, and fume about all the injustices. Taking deep breaths, she said,

"We should watch our behavior, lest the baby starts mimicking us. I really don't want to cause trouble, Quent, but our tenants need help." Calmer words didn't reflect her inner turmoil. "Do you think the sheriff should investigate the burning of the church?"

Ignoring her complaint about behavior, he yelled, "Gawd! That old church wasn't worth a dime. Investigate what?"

"It was worth a great deal to the Negroes. The food and clothing—"

"I tried t' tell you to leave the Nigras alone, didn't I?"

"Yes, you did. Please, have it make sense to me, Quent. Make me understand how doing good and fostering friendships can end in such disaster."

"You've got to *see* the way it is down here. It's always gonna be this way. You don't *want* to understand."

Sam tried to speak, but his brother raised a hand to shush him. Neither she nor Quent had eaten more than a bite from their plates. Allise snatched them up and dropped them with a clatter into the sink. With her back to him, her husband couldn't see her breathing in and out, fighting to suppress the ugly thoughts that pushed to be unleashed.

When she felt she could be rational, she said, "I don't believe it has to be this way."

# CHAPTER 5

▼

Allise loaded boxes from Mt. Zion Church and Philadelphia in the rumble seat. Back in the house, she pulled on her coat and removed the Prince Albert Tobacco can from a pocket. Sitting down on the chaise, she pondered what to do. Two days after the fire, she had sneaked out to the burned church site. Finding the half-empty tin near the door, she wrapped it in a rag from the car and slipped it into her pocket. *Should I show it to Rebekah?* Undecided, she put it back in her pocket and picked up Peter.

They sped along a straight stretch of highway banked on either side by tall loblolly pines. She suspected the hunter on the stile had dropped the can. *But why would he be at the church door? If only I could share my concern with Quent.*

Rebekah heard the car drive up and came out to meet her, buttoning on the red coat.

"I brought things from Philadelphia and Mt. Zion. Very few Deer Point items since the fire, Rebekah." She left Peter on the front seat and stepped down from the running board to help unload the boxes. When finished, Allise asked her black friend to sit in the car with her. "A question simmers in my mind, Rebekah. Who burned the church?"

"Some saying could be the Klan did it but cain't say why. Ain't no reason, Miz Allie. Too, they ain't been no Klan trouble round here in years, not since Cobb Akins. Ever'body scared outta their wits. I'm telling y', it don't make no sense, but, Miz Allie, ain't no way that fire coulda started without mischief."

Neither spoke for a moment. Then, "The last time we were there, I saw a young man sitting on the stile watching you and Elfreeda move boxes inside. He had a rifle. I thought he was a hunter and didn't consider him a threat. Now, I wonder. What do you think?"

"Them McPhersons! That old man done served time in the state pen for making liquor. Left that pore old woman alone t' corral 'em four mean boys." Anxiety clouded Rebekah's face. "The one on the stile was probably Murks. He the oldest. Their daddy owns forty acres next to the church." She paused, then, "'Em boys slithering up through that high grass behind the church and peeking through 'em cracks in the wall. They snicker when we having service. Do it many a Sunday. We try t' ignore 'um, but it's mighty hard."

Allise took the tobacco can from her pocket, unwrapped and held it out. I found this near the entrance to the church. Do you suppose—"

"'Em boys awways got Prince Albert in their shirt pocket. I don't wanna say much.' Em McPhersons mean. No telling what they do next, we go saying they set that fire."

"No, we mustn't. But I ..." Allise lifted the gold watch about her neck. "I must run." She reached for Rebekah's hand. "I'm sorry about the church."

"Jake say *we's* the church, Miz Allie." She stepped down from the car.

"I agree with Jake." Allise watched her friend walk away, then called after her, "Rebekah, ..." She wanted to promise the church would be rebuilt, but her call went unheard. It was just as well, she thought. *Quent would never agree to it.*

She headed back toward Deer Point when driven by impulse, Allise suddenly swerved from the highway and threw her arm across Peter to protect him. She drove up the only road that could lead to the farm house. The road ended where a mailbox announced "McPherson." She stopped before a dilapidated old house flanked by toppling barns and leaning sheds. Rusty plows and a harrow, looking more like an instrument of horror with its spikes, lay haphazardly abandoned. With Peter on her hip, Allise rapped on the sagging wooden door. In a moment it cracked a bit. "Mrs. McPherson?"

"Yes'm." The door opened to a slender, stoop-shouldered woman, pushing wisps of gray hair back from her face.

"Hello. I'm Allise DeWitt, Quent's wife. Are your sons home?" Her heart beat a crazy rhythm, and she wondered why she risked coming to this place.

"Yes'm. Come in by the fire. It's Miz DeWitt, Briley."

Too late to turn back, Allise offered her hand. "So, we're farm neighbors." Shown a chair near the fireplace, she held Peter's mittened hands out to the open heat. "The fire feels good. We're having a cold season." Wanting to get to the bottom of the mystery but unsure of her approach, she reached out to them with caution. "Mr. and Mrs. McPherson, I'm here about the church that burned on our farm. I suppose you're aware of it?"

They nodded, and she went on. "I was at the church on Wednesday before the loss was discovered on Sunday. That day ..." She looked directly at one of the boys. "I'm sure I saw *you* that day. Do you wear an aviator-style cap?"

"Yeah, that's Murks." Briley threw a sly grin at his son. Light from the window fell on the boy's reddish blond hair. He leaned forward in a straight-back chair to stroke the white cat rubbing against his legs and said nothing.

Allise unbuttoned her coat and removed Peter's mittens and outer wrap. Eying Murks, she thought he didn't appear unnerved. Suddenly doubt was no longer a consideration. "Yes, it was *you* sitting on the stile with a rifle. Had you been hunting?" His daddy scowled at him, and the other three boys bent over their knees, trading sly grins. Their mother, standing behind her husband, twisted a loose strand of hair. Allise waited. When he didn't respond, she said, "I'm wondering, Murks, if you saw anyone else around the church that day?"

"Nome, shore didn't," he muttered, slouching back and poking hands in his pockets. He kept his eyes on the cat, now stretched on the floor in front of him.

Allise reached into her pocket for the can, unwrapped and held it up for them to see. "I found this Prince Albert Tobacco tin near the steps of the burned church. It may be nothing, but perhaps you know someone who uses this tobacco."

Briley McPherson jumped to his feet and towered over Murks. "Boy, whatcha doing at that church? Ain't that when you toted canned goods in here as if I don't feed you enough?" Briley clenched his fists and looked ready to throw a punch into his son's jaw.

Murks held arms around his head, shielding it. He rose from the chair, and dodging his father, went to the back of the room, slithered down against the wall and hid his face.

Mrs. McPherson put an arm across her flat chest. Resting an elbow in one hand, she covered thin cracked lips with the other. Her face and body carried the legacy of a cowed woman as she eased back near Murks. The three brothers shifted on their chairs, eyes downcast, as though waiting for something to happen.

Allise flinched at Briley's unexpected move and questioned anew her impulse to be there. Bracing herself, she vied for his attention. "Please, Mr. McPherson." His fists relaxed, and she searched for a way to defuse the situation. From some depth of being, words came. "I'm not really, I'm not here to accuse your son or anyone, Mr. and Mrs. McPherson." She glanced around to reassure mother and son. "If your son knows ... You see, a rumor has the Ku Klux Klan doing it, and people are frightened."

Calmer but with a threat still hanging, the father said, "Boy, if you know anything tell this lady now, or I'll beat it outta you when she leaves." He stood and went to remove a hanging strop from behind a door. Murks grimaced. He glanced up at his mother, cringing nearby.

"The church is gone, Mr. McPherson. We don't wish to bring a case against anyone, only to ease people's minds about the Klan." Allise surveyed the scene and thought she shouldn't have come here. Briley McPherson's threats had her on the edge of the chair and pressing Peter to her body with both arms.

She was close to voicing doubt, when Murks said, "Awright, Daddy! I will."

Mrs. McPherson gasped, and his brothers shifted about. One, appearing to be the youngest, swiped a hand beneath his nose and made a snuffing sound. Everyone seemed to wait. Only a monotonous thwacking of the clock's pendulum, swinging to and fro on the fireplace mantel, was heard.

Murks stood and paced back and forth, rubbing knuckles into his eyes. It took time for him to gain his voice. "I watched you," he indicated Allise, "with 'em two niggers. I'd already been inside, seen all that stuff, and there they was agin, toting more stuff in for 'em. Jes ain't right. You with 'em niggers, and all." He glanced at her with disgust. "When they quit going t' the car, I snuck up through the grass back of the church for a peek. Couldn't hear much, so I jes waited till y'all left. When ever'body was outta sight, I went back inside. Took out two sacks of food. That's all! Two sacks."

Murks threw up his hands as if to stress the minuteness of his crime. He clutched the back of a chair, appearing to be finished. When no one spoke, he seemed goaded by the silence. "I-I was gonna leave. I was, Mama!" Assuring her, he turned back to Allise. "Then I remembered you, a white woman with them niggers, standing in there all friendly wid 'em. Mama, you and Daddy didn't raise us like that." In an agitated state, he went on.

"'Em bitches and a nigger lover!" He turned to Allise. "Nuff food in there t' feed Cox's Army. I dumped ever'thing."

Without moving a thread's width, Allise encouraged. "And then what, Murks?"

Everyone in the room seemed to hold their breath. He swiped beneath a runny nose with the back of his hand. "I put the two sacks down on the steps and rolled a cigarette, then I grabbed a handful of dry grass, went back in there and threw it on a pile of clothes. Lit it off with my cigarette."

Allise could all but hear a collective nervous intake of air. Briley's shoulders drooped, and the strop dangled from his big hand. His wife's crying was silent as the cat curled its tail about her legs, lending its purrs to the ticking clock. Murks struggled to hold back tears until unable to, his snarly, mottled face relented. "I'm scared, Mama, so sc-scared." Sniffing and wiping, he tried to control his emotions.

Though close enough to touch, neither mother nor son reached out to the other.

Thinking they wanted to, Allise's heart ached for them. She eased her hold on Peter and thought they needed each other but seemed unable to give or receive love. It's easier to hate Negroes, but surely they hold goodness inside, she thought. Peter hadn't squirmed or made a peep. *Does he sense the turmoil around us?* Her attention returned to the McPhersons. "Murks. Mr. and Mrs.," Allise indicated the chairs, "all of you, please. May we talk about this for a few moments before I have to leave? There are things I want to say." Obeying, they took seats, avoiding each other's eyes and hers. "Now, I admit I was fearful of coming here today, but I'm glad I did." She turned to the distraught boy. "Murks, I think you are genuinely sorry for burning the church." She didn't ask, "Are you?" but the question was implicit in her tone.

Swiping at his eyes, he nodded. "Yes'm, I am."

"I think you did it out of anger and frustration with me." Allise paused, waiting, but he said nothing. "Whatever your reason, I wish I could help you overcome your apparent feelings for Negroes. Only you can do that. They're different and only our creator knows why, but in the end we're all human beings." Thoughts crowded in. Lowering her voice, she asked, "Have you considered that when they look at us, we're the ones who seem different? We can't do much about how we look, only the way we think. I, for one, don't want to waste my energy hating people because they aren't like me."

Allise paused, waiting for someone to challenge her. Sliding back on the chair, she glanced around at their despairing faces. "I want to believe Murks will never do such a thing again. And because I want to believe, I promise not to reveal what I know. Not even to my husband." She sensed her hold over them. "But, if anything like this is directed at our Negroes again, you will be suspect, and I'll go to the sheriff. This isn't meant to be a hateful threat. Think about it. The possible consequences could be imprisonment for destroying property. More harmful to you than what you did to the Negroes. Don't let it happen to you, Murks."

Briley bent forward, elbows on his knees, face buried in his hands. His wife and sons sneaked quick glances at him.

"You know," Allise said, "as frightening as your destruction of the church is, it's scarier to think hooded, secretive men could have done it." Feeling drained, Allise drew a long sigh. She pulled on Peter's mittens and coat, stood and walked toward the entrance.

At the door, Mrs. McPherson whispered, "Thank you, Miz DeWitt."

Allise sat in the car, clutching Peter. She shook with latent fear as he grunted to be free. *How could I speak with them in that way? Mr. McPherson has been in prison. If Quent knew …*

She stood Peter on the seat and cautioned, "Hold onto me, darling."

In the days that followed, Allise was beside herself in search of a plan to help the farmers survive the winter. She wrote another letter to the American Friends Service Committee, reminding the members of its social commitment:

**Since the 1600s in England, you've given without fuss or fanfare to less fortunate souls. You opposed slavery and unfair treatment of Indians and provided relief to civilians during World War I. Even when persecuted for religious practices, Quakers respected the religious freedom of others.**

She reminded the committee of the farmers' plight. Soon a monetary donation arrived. Elfreeda helped Allise buy food and fabric, then she, Rebekah and Mrs. McPherson organized black and white women into sewing circles and quilting bees. Through the women's efforts, and the farmers' chickens, pigs and cows, their families survived the hard winter.

If Quent knew of her involvement, he never said anything. Apparently he wasn't aware of her visit with the McPhersons, either. Allise guessed they had honored her trust and said nothing.

With the hard winter behind them, spring promised new beginnings. Trees budded, bulbs pushed shoots to the surface of flower beds along the DeWitt's driveway, and farmers turned the soil. The rhythm of sameness comforted Allise.

That evening, she lay on the chaise, her father's latest letter on her lap. Her thoughts went to that day when she had wanted to embrace Mrs. McPherson, but hadn't. *I didn't even try.* She wanted to understand her resistance. After all, she had given Brother Rigdon such a discourse on comforting others. *Anyway, it felt good to offer my trust.* She made a mental note to write her father that the farmers didn't freeze or starve because the Friends and women had helped. She would tell him that blacks and whites still clung to a stubborn existence with pride and determination.

She took up her father's letter. It mentioned the past decade of self-indulgence and prohibition. Allise surmised most Southerners emerged from the Twenties with little experience of decadent pleasure. Maybe through writers like F. Scott Fitzgerald, she thought. His giddy, brazen women and roguish men in *The Great Gatsby*. She had come to know a South that was unfamiliar with urban life.

Quent was once roguish, she thought. *What happened to change him?* She didn't like the direction her mind took and returned to the letter.

Her father asked: "Would the common fate imposed by depression make people kinder and gentler?" He told of businesses extending credit to the limit, and some forgiving unpaid debts altogether. Alarmed by problems outside the country, he wrote:

> **On the other side of the world, Japan withdrew from the League of Nations. Germans suffer the same worldwide financial collapse and have granted enormous power to Hitler. Aryans boycott Jews. You're too young, Allise, to remember the recent war when soldiers were poisoned by German gas. Our men went on to help defeat them.**

Off on another track, Allise asked herself, *How do Germans come to such stridence against Jews? Do defeated Germans feel depressed? Vengeful? Frustrated?* She wished she could discuss these things with her papa.

He had read *Lost Horizon; We, the People,* and Jung's *Modern Man in Search of a Soul.* Reviews, he warned, suggested certain current books might be risque and may indicate a trend in modern American literature. "Did you hear the court ruled to allow Joyce's *Ulysses* into the country?" She smiled. He wouldn't say not to read certain books, only to use good judgment. With such a hungry mind, Allise wondered if she would remain in this place if not for her child.

Sighing, she put the letter away, went downstairs and sat on the hooked rug beside Peter, listening to Quent and Daddy Joe pore over the market ledger. Much of their land and other southern farms were still cultivated by blacks. Under government controls, cotton acreage had dropped. The last crop brought twelve cents a pound. Quent had convinced his father to apply for a government subsidy offered for leaving acres out of cotton production.

Across the room on the sofa, Sam read *The Progressive Farmer.*

Peter moved into Allise's folded legs, and they played pitty-pat. She enjoyed the precious moment while at the same time hungering for adult discourse. At times, she feared losing her ability to hold a rational conversation. Soon, Peter settled heavily in sleep on her arm. Suddenly, she said, "Papa's ecstatic that New York won the World Series. We went to the games in Philadelphia. Seems a long time ago." She raised her voice. "If not for Papa, how would I know the Steinheim skull was discovered?"

Sam lowered the paper, and the men glanced up from the desk. "I don't know, honey," Quent said. "Why do you *need* to know?" He returned to the shuffled papers.

Allise stood, her moment of recognition was already forgotten by them, and her smug smile went unnoticed. "I'll take Peter up to bed." Returning, she stopped halfway down the stairs, listening for any disturbance from the baby's room. Continuing down with a glance into the living room, she saw Sam had lowered the paper, and his eyes followed her.

As she re-entered the living room, he shook the paper open, hid his face behind it and said, "Balloon tires are being made for tractors. Says here farmers hafta think about tractors to replace manpower. 'Em Nigras keep going North, how we gonna plow a thousand acres?"

"Hell!" Daddy Joe looked up. "Excuse me, honey. Sam knows we cain't buy a black-eyed pea for the pot, much less a tractor."

Quent laughed. "Sam gets these grandiose ideas."

"Oughta consider it, Quent. Need to plan ahead. Get caught in a bind, it's too late."

No one argued with him. Allise sat down and said, "I think Sam makes a valid point."

"Who asked you, Allie? There isn't going to be a trac—"

"Listen, Quent!" She jumped up. "I don't expect to be asked. Until I married you, I was considered a normal part of adult conversations."

Sam lowered the paper and stared in disbelief. "Now, now, kids." Daddy Joe rose from his chair. "Time for us to go, Sam."

\*    \*    \*    \*

Two weeks into spring plowing, Maizee watched the wagons lumber down the lane, taking her family and other tenants into town. She and Nate hadn't been to town since returning from Jefferson, but her animal-like instincts tuned to all movement and sound had relaxed somewhat since Mista Quent didn't frequent the farm. While Nate slept, she finished her chores and went out to the vegetable garden. She bent over a row of English peas, snapping off handsful of pods. As she dropped them into a pail, someone spoke behind her. Jerking erect, she turned slowly.

Quent stood a few feet from her at the edge of the garden.

Maizee bent slightly, pulled the knife and held it behind a fold of her dress.

"What you doing here, girl? You supposed t' be sick. Supposed t' be in Texas."

Maizee couldn't speak. Then, recalling Aunt Althea saying black men had an illness because they messed around, she eyeballed Mista Quent and said, "I been in Texas. You know, I got syphil—" She struggled with the word.

"What? *Syphilis*? You got syphilis?"

"Yassir. That's it, syphilis."

"Damn!" He turned and left in a run.

Maizee's body shook with fright. Then, she heard the car engine turn behind the wagon shed and listened as he drove toward the east entrance to the farm. Her senses returned, and she thanked God for reminding her of the scary disease. *How long it gonna take him t' get to a doctor?* She laughed. *Won't bother me anymore. Still gotta keep Nate outta sight.*

Back in the house, Maizee pulled the battered old rocker to a window. Popping the pods, she pushed peas into a bowl and looked out at the tree line near the Chalu River. Beyond it, a blue ridge rose at the far edge of the flood plain and extended down into Louisiana. She finished shelling, washed the peas and started them to simmer on the cookstove before Nate was heard to cry. Diapered and content, she took him to the rocker. Looking out on the lane approaching the tenants, suddenly she clutched her baby.

Spinning up a cloud of dust, a big black car sped up the road. Maizee rushed to the front window. It stopped before the Spinner's house. "Is that him?" Doke Spinner stepped out, stood beside the open car door, and stretched his arms abroad as if he'd been behind the wheel for a long time. Leona be expecting him? Maizee wondered.

He entered the house and returned with a cloth. Working on the dust, he revealed parts of the car already polished to the nines.

Pulling the rocker to the front window, Maizee watched. Leona hadn't said anything about him coming home from Chicago. During eight months away, he had written about working five hours as a night janitor in a shoe store and earning enough pay for food and a bed in a slum flophouse. Later, he added a daytime foundry job. Both paid enough to rent in the same south-side black district. He got little sleep between cleaning the shoe store and rising early to shovel coal for eight hours. Two money orders in small amounts had arrived for Leona and the kids. She had said she suspected he stayed liquored-up and lost most of his pay in Saturday night craps games.

Maizee wondered if he was home for good. *With two jobs, he oughta be rolling in money.* "If he ain't," she muttered to the baby, "don't seem his life done change that much. Work and sleep, jes like on this farm." Doke disappeared back in the house, and Maizee dismissed any idea of a man in her life. She returned the chair to the window with the lane view, and soon the mules' heads were seen bobbing and weaving toward home. Rushing to the porch, she waited to see reactions to the fine-looking car parked across the road.

Jonas halted the animals beside the sedan, and Doke rushed out the door. Leona jumped from the wagon with a loud whoop, and noisy greetings erupted from all but Dalt and Cass. They walked around the handsome car, wearing big grins.

Sunday morning, before services in the Hattens' tenant, Leona sat at the Col-sons' table. Everyone wanted to hear Doke's stories but she said, "He be dead tired and flat broke. Won big at craps, but the winnings burnt a hole in his pocket. Spent ever'thing t' get here. Doke came home t' get us. Take us back t' Chicago." Her eyes beamed. "His boss said he may not have a job when he got back." She revealed he had bought the car on credit and intended to ask Mista Sam to let him plow.

Maizee listened to Leona and thought her going up North would be a relief. She wearied of the woman telling her how to raise babies. I listen to Momma, she thought. When Leona walked back across the lane, Maizee told Jonas and Rebekah about Mista Quent in the garden.

"He what?" Rebekah yelled. "What he doing out heah, anyway? Ain't no reason for that man t' be out heah on a Saturday!" Her mother fumed and paced about the kitchen.

Jonas stood and stretched to his full height. "I'm gonna kill that sorry son of a white dog." His ominous words hissed like they came out of a dream.

The venom pouring from him frighted Maizee. "No, Daddy!" Grabbing his shoulders, she stood eyeball-to-eyeball with him. Jonas sagged, but she didn't let go.

"Did he see Nate? *Did he?*" Rebekah demanded.

"No, Momma! Hush!" Relaxing her grip on Jonas, Maizee's hands slipped down to her side. "I told 'im I got syphilis. You know, y' get it from messing around."

Appearing stunned, her parents sat down again. "Maizee, how you know about that?" Rebekah seemed to disguise a smile behind her hand.

"Oh-e-e! Ooh, haw-haw." Jonas bent over his guffaws, then drawing a recovering breath, said, "I bet that scared the Almighty outta him."

Later that day, Maizee and Rebekah sat in chairs on the porch. Jonas leaned against a post, and soon, all the tenants sat around the edge or stood about the yard. Dalt and Cass milled about as if not knowing what to do in the presence of one who had seen a big city. Having inspected Doke's car, they had no place to go in their Sunday best. Maizee watched them sneak glances at the sedan and move closer to its proud owner, who leaned against the porch. He jammed hands in his pockets and crossed one foot over the other as he told about the big metropolis. Pointing, he said, "That Oldsmobile out yonder, that's *mine.*"

"Man! How much you pay for it, Doke?" Cass asked.

"More'n you got, boy." Doke strutted around like a peacock fanning its royal tail feathers. "I tell ya, Cass, they got jobs up North. You can have a car jes like that."

His show-off manner amused Maizee, and Rebekah moved forward on her chair. "Doke Spinner, don't you hang round heah talking big t' git my boys way off up there."

"Now, Bekah"

"Don't you Bekah me, boy! I ain't joking," she said, and Doke grinned.

Jake Hatten leaned against the four-by-four post, facing Jonas across the top step. He appeared marginally impressed. "If I was young, I might move up there, too," he said.

"Man, you gotta take a risk sometimes," the craps player declared.

Maizee saw cautious doubt in her daddy's face. He asked, "What you do up there, Doke?" He had heard it from Leona, but Maizee guessed he wanted a man's version. She reckoned her daddy and Jake had racked up more toiling years than Doke Spinner. *Daddy backed up agin that post, dead tired. Ain't no room for hope and dreaming.*

"Cain't ever'body work two jobs like I do," Doke said. "Y' gotta be young. Take Cass and Dalt, they'd get jobs quick. Burn coal up there and dump it right on the sidewalks. Need delivery men." His voice droned on, leaving Maizee to imagine city sights. Then she heard, "I be heading North with Leona and the kids soon as DeWitt plowing's done. Get enough money, we be lo-ong gone from here."

Apparently fresh out of tales, Doke ambled off toward the Spinner tenant house.

Jonas pointed to the sun hanging low in a fiery ball over the river. It dropped below the ridge line, leaving a panorama of gray, orange and purplish pink across the horizon. "I wonder, do they have pretty skies like 'at up North?" he asked.

No one answered, but Cass gazed at the shiny car as Doke rubbed the front fender with his shirttail. Maizee stared over the edge of the porch. She wondered how rain could pour off the tin roof with enough force to make a deep rut in a rock-hard crust. Following the roof's outline in the ground below, she saw not even Doke's pacing had wiped it out.

Always been there, she thought. It was something she could count on for as long as rain would fall.

A month later, Maizee stood in the early morning light with the other tenants, watching the Spinners and Dalt load their possessions and themselves into the Oldsmobile. Doke had helped plow fields, and now his family and Dalt were ready to leave for Chicago.

Rebekah, unable to keep her oldest son from going up North, seemed to ignore Cass' disgusted looks. She refused to let him go to Chicago. Watching the car leave, he said, "I swear someday, someway, Momma."

Her daddy had waited for the car to roll down the lane, then, he ambled off toward Mista Sam in his fresh planted cornfield. They stood beside the field watching the car move down the lane and out of sight. Mista Sam walked up to the picket fence with Jonas and called to her momma, "Couldn't keep him here, huh? Be one less cotton picker this fall."

"I don't know why he wanna go off up there." Rebekah had shaken her head, and Maizee had wanted to cry. She was fond of her younger brother, and now after six months in Chicago, Dalt was coming home.

Maizee read his note again. "'I'm hopping a freight South before you start picking cotton.'" She expected him any day now.

It was mid-morning, and she listened to her mother fret about Dalt being a hobo. She peered out the window, hoping to see him walking up the lane. Then, at the front window, she looked out. "Dalt," she cried.

He slept on the porch, his head cradled on a bundle of clothing. Aroused by her cry, he came inside, and like Doke after his long ride, slept for hours.

At supper that night, he told of riding a train bound for Texas. It would turn around with a load of livestock meant for the Chicago meat packing houses. The empty cattle car with slatted sides and open top offered no protection from the elements. After a long day and sleepless night on the straw-strewn floor smelling of manure, "I felt like somebody at the high end of a jackhammer," Dalt said. As daylight peaked, the train slowed to cross the Chalu River railroad bridge. He climbed over the top of the car and down the side to hang just above the tracks. Beyond the bridge, before the engine picked up speed, he jumped. Sore and exhausted, he had walked two miles to the tenant house.

Doke's big car was repossessed, he said. His family seldom saw him. Craps games and liquor took his earnings, while Leona cleaned rooms in a downtown hotel. She made the rent for a rundown apartment where Dalt subleased a room.

I don't need a 'no-count' man messing up my life, Maizee thought.

"The city ain't clean like home, Momma," Dalt was saying. "It's noisy. People be fussing and fighting and screaming all the time. Cain't get much sleep."

"Uh-huh. Don't sound like no decent life t' me." Rebekah shook her head. "You ask about Maizee going up North. Don't you think I gwine t' let her go to Chicago. She afraid Mista Quent gonna learn about Nate, but she safer here wid him than in that nasty town."

Maizee took her plate to the dishpan then slid down on the chair again to listen.

Propped on forearms, her mind wondered into savory smells and colorful sights as Dalt talked. She giggled when he mimicked frantic street shouts and close-quartered families in tenements, then she rose and sank more plates in the hot sudsy water.

Jonas leaned over his plate, chomping an ear of Sam's corn. "Son, you heard about old Huey P. Long down in Louisiana? Old Huey P. sees things the way they is. Mista Sam, though, he telling me he talking politics making it sound like things gonna get better for po' folks. Mista Sam don't agree wid 'im. But Old Huey say he gonna build roads 'n' bridges 'n' schools in Louisiana. Maybe you better stick round here and see—"

"Ah, Daddy, that man's a clown! Most colored folk I know cain't see him helping 'um. Anyways, I cain't see no sense in staying here."

Maizee, standing over the dishpan, asked him to tell more about the city. "Well, y' got electric lights and a in-door toilet," Dalt said. "Don't hafta freeze my tail off running to the outhouse. They's got dance halls ... piccolo houses with machines y' plug a nickel in and jazz music plays. Dancing, laughing, screaming, lotsa drinking 'n' fighting going on."

Rebekah sent her son an irritated look. "Think Maizee gonna go off up there! Uh-uh!" Her indignation sounded clearly against any attempt to entice her daughter away.

"Well, Momma, it ain't much of a life, but it's better than slaving for the DeWitts. Maizee asking Daddy ever'day if Mista Quent coming to the farm. Up there, she be okay. I ain't got much, but I got money in my pocket. Even send some to you now and then. I ain't gonna be a coalman forever." He shook his head. "Nawsir. Friend done teach me t' drive and I give my name at the Chicago Transit office t' operate a streetcar."

"You want her t' live like Leona? What she gonna do with the baby?" The question hung there between her momma and brother.

Maizee leaned on the table again, waiting for Jonas and Dalt to finish their meals. Life in the city sounded too fast. She had never known days cast in a heated rush to "good times." Her reality was the bond of family love. Days flowing one into the other in a constant course of southern seasons. Too much a part of the rich river loam, of mockingbirds trilling from willow trees at the edge of Moon Lake, she was secure in her knowledge of what must be done to get through each day. *Ain't nothing I wanna change, except he ain't wanting me no more.* She smiled. Nate and my family, that's what counts, she thought. *Some things jes weigh more than worry about that old white man.*

She frowned at Rebekah's distress. "Don't fret, Momma, me 'n' Nate ain't going nowhere. I jes like t' hear about Chicago. Anyways, I told Mista Quent I got syphilis."

"You told him *what*? You joking?" Dalt looked from her to his momma and daddy. He seemed to realize his sister had lied. "Good thinking, girl."

They laughed so much, Jonas complained, "Oh my," then, catching a breath, "If I could git by with it, I'd kill that white so-and-so." Laughter reached near hysteria until dawning consequences brought them to look at each other with half-wise, half-silly grins.

Maizee didn't want Dalt's visit to end, but on the fifth night, he leaned back and patted a stomach full of roasted corn. "Gotta be on the railroad bridge before daybreak."

Early the next morning he was gone, and Maizee walked out to Mista Sam's corn field with Jonas. They went down the rows, pulling an ear here and there and shucking it when Sam drove up in the truck. "Two or three long ears to a stalk," he said. "How about that? At least it's something we can eat and feed to the livestock."

"Yessa, we sho can," Jonas said. "We need t' build a corn crib, Mista Sam."

"Yeah. When the cotton's picked, we will do just that and fill it with corn for the pigs. In late November, the fatted hogs we slaughter will hang in the smokehouse behind your house, Jonas. Then, we can be sure of food for the cold season and spend our winter days in the tool shed around a barrel fire. I can talk to you, Jonas, about my ideas. For a Nigra, you're no dummy. Have some good notions of your own."

Maizee knew Mista Sam meant to compliment her daddy, but it sounded insulting.

# CHAPTER 6

▼

Acres of DeWitt land would lie fallow if not sown in crops other than cotton. Quent had applied for a government subsidy given to leave cotton out of production. Fields, other than those to be left bare, had been plowed.

One morning, Allise and Peter had gone to the farm with Quent. He stood, thumbs hooked over back pockets, watching Jonas trudge along behind the corn seeder when Sam walked up. "That corn's all yours to cultivate and sell," he said. "Corn never has brought any money. Cotton's always been the only cash crop."

"You don't think I can make a crop, do you?" Sam had walked away with a look of disgust and shouted back over his shoulder, "I'll show you, Smart Alec!" Quent picked up a dry clod and threw it, striking his brother's back. Sam had turned as if to rush back at him; instead, he shook his fist and continued on.

Later that evening, Allise overheard her husband on the phone with Sam. "Keep your ears tuned to any Nigra talk about government money. That smart ass Nigra's been up North." He meant Dalt. "He may have heard about the allowance and told Jonas."

Although she grappled with the realities of the times, Allise felt guilty about getting money for not producing. She had heard Quent indicate to Sam that he had no intension of sharing the subsidy with the tenants and wondered if she tried hard enough to understand him.

More than six months later, Sam had raised a good corn crop. During that time, Allise was trying to convince herself that if she couldn't accept southern ways, then she would just have to love beyond understanding them.

Now, waiting for Quent to come from the market, she switched on the radio and sat down on the rug with Peter. Alphabet blocks lay strewn about the floor. Picking up the letter "C," she voiced the symbol and showed it to her son.

"C," Peter repeated. Approaching his third year, her child was strong, confident and aware of himself as a separate entity. Handing him the block, she encouraged him to place it on a teetering structure. Suddenly, the radio crackled loud static, and above the din, Allise caught Amelia Earhart's name. Clambering up from the floor, she hurried to the arch-shaped console. Walter Winchell announced:

**Yes, ladies and gentlemen, Amelia Earhart! First pilot to solo over the Pacific landed in Oakland, California some thirty minutes ago at 4:31 p.m. Pacific time. She took off from Wheeler Field in Honolulu yesterday, January 11, 1935 at 10:15 p.m. and made the historic oceanic flight in something over eighteen hours. Oh, the excitement here at the airport!**

Turning from the radio, Allise saw Peter running toward Sam who leaned in the dining room doorway. "Sam, Amelia Earhart just landed." She switched off the sound.

Sam held Peter above his head. "Some woman, huh? Stopped in t' see my boy."

"Did Quent go upstairs?" Allise asked.

Sam removed a wool cap, placed it on the floor next to the sofa and sat beside her with Peter on his lap. "Quent uh, I dropped him at Rooster's."

"So *that's* where he ... I should put his dinner away." She stared, but didn't move.

"Him and Daddy came to the farm t' see if Jonas and me were tending to chores. Said tell y' he'd just play a couple of poker games."

She sagged, and Sam reached for her. "Allie"

Drawing back, she said, "Oh, it's all right." But all the time, she knew her hus-band's waywardness wasn't right.

Sam left and Allise bathed Peter, put him to bed and closed his door. Pulling on a gown, she crept downstairs and dozed on the sofa when Quent came in. Meeting him in the foyer, she watched him hook a brown fedora on the hall tree. He stooped to kiss her cheek, but she whirled away.

Shedding his corduroy jacket, he hung it, giving no excuse for tardiness. He stood for a moment then walked past her into the living room. She followed, wanting to hear excuses so she could accuse and scold him. Testing his mood, she said, "You missed the report of Amelia Earhart's flight over the ocean."

"Amelia Earhart! Why don't you women stick t' home and babies, and leave such things as flying airplanes to the men."

Allise held a scream behind tight lips. She picked up Peter's blocks and threw them into a bag, each crack of wood against wood resonating her contempt. Tying the bag, she cast it in the toy box, making the crashing sound an expression of what she couldn't bring herself to say. Then, fighting temptation no longer, she screamed, "You enjoy making me unhappy, Quent. There are times when I hate you. Hate you!" Her moan brought a flood of tears. He took her in his arms, letting her sob until quieted, then he carried her upstairs.

Watching him undress, she felt in jeopardy of drowning in sheltered womanhood.

Quent crawled into bed and pulled her to him. "I want you, Allie." With impatient passion, he pulled up her gown. Moments later, gratified, he rolled back.

Allise lay awake, listening to him breathe. I'm not a passive person, she thought. *Why do I fear losing him more than myself? What does he want from our marriage?* She thought she knew. What did she want? *Affection, security. Did we marry for all the wrong reasons?* But I love him, she told herself.

April brought rain. Sam and Quent came from the farm and told Allise of finding Jonas, Cass and several hired hands waiting behind teams hitched to plows. "Jonas said it was too wet to put plows in the soil." Sam said he was afraid of that. "We'll be late planting this year."

Allise left them talking and went upstairs to check on Peter, who was napping. Returning, she reached the bottom landing and stopped to listen. Quent said he had sent off a letter declaring their unplanted acreage. "Heard anything from the Nigras about subsidy money?"

"You still worried about that?" Sam asked. "Anyhow, Jonas knows. He's talked about subsidy money. He knows you ain't fair, but him and Rebekah ain't going nowhere."

"Fair! Hell, that land belongs to us. That Nigra just has t' work it."

The two men sat on the couch with their backs to Allise. Sam turned to Quent. "I haven't figured it out, but something's damned odd about you, Quent."

"Huh. Well I'll be damned. Tell me about it, little brother."

"Like right now. You wearing that off-putting smile at the same time you making me feel like dirt." Sam exercised his palms. Quent's smirk vanished. "You're nice one minute and turn into a devil the next. Tell me how you can turn good days into gloom like shutting off water at the faucet? It's like you're two different people. I don't know how Allie lives with you."

Quent leaned toward Sam, and almost in a whisper, said, " 'Cause she *has* to, little brother. She has three choices, live with me, live on a teacher's salary or go back to her parents in Philadelphia. Allie isn't going to take Peter away from me. It's hard on women, Sam. Can't survive like a man. Another thing, baby brother, I love Allie. I just have needs that …." He heard Allise reenter the living room.

She knew what he said was true. She had three choices. At least he said he loves me, she thought.

Two weeks went by before the fields were dry enough for the hands to plow. Meantime, Allise saw Quent off each morning to work on store and farm ledgers in the back room of the market. She had stopped waiting up for him, but lay awake into the wee hours, then pretended to be asleep when he crawled into bed.

On this Friday evening, she felt tired from household chores. Turning on the radio, she was ready to stretch out on the couch when the doorbell sounded. "I was home by myself," Sam said. "Daddy wasn't around so I came t' listen to the radio with y'all."

"Come in, Sam. I was about to sit my worn body down." She explained about cleaning and not sleeping well.

Sam said he had stacked market shelves all day. "After the store closed, Quent asked me to drop him at Rooster's. I tried to get him to come home, but he slammed the truck door like it was an explanation point at the end of a warning 'Ask me no questions, I'll tell no lies.' Allie, I'll keep an eye on Peter if you doze off."

Sam turned the radio volume down, but she couldn't sleep. Sitting up, she heard H. B. Kaltenborn's voice:

**Senator Huey P. Long, the Kingfish, was gunned down in the corridor of the Louisiana capitol an hour ago. Carl Austin Weiss, a doctor, was wrestled to the floor and slain by Long's bodyguards.**

**Long rose to power by promising he would redistribute wealth in his state. At thirty five, he was Louisiana's governor, then elected a U. S. senator four years later. When assassinated, he intended to run for president.**

"I'll hafta tell Jonas," Sam said. "He thinks the sun rises and sets in Huey P."

"Yes, you must." Allise yawned. "I'm sorry, Sam. I must put Peter to bed, and I think I will call it a night, as well."

"Oh, yeah." He stood. "Come here, Peedy. Give Uncle Sam a hug." He picked up the child, they hugged, and when Allise reached for Peter, Sam pulled them close. Bending, he landed a kiss near her mouth. "Goodnight, Allie," he whispered and stumbled back as though in disbelief.

Peter's head rested on her shoulder, and Allise looked at him in stunned silence.

"I-I'm sorry, Allie. I'm sorry." His face flamed as he staggered toward the door.

She followed him to the door. "Goodnight, Sam. We will talk about this later." Locking up behind him, she muttered, "Didn't I see this coming?" Upstairs, she thought of how she had denied Sam's meaningful looks and done nothing to discourage them.

Soon after Long's assassination, she, Quent and Sam listened to the late news. Will Rogers, the cowboy comedian, and his pilot were killed in a plane crash in Alaska. "Daddy Joe loves Will Rogers," Allise said. "He could walk onto a stage, twirl a rope and with sophisticated humor educate an audience."

"Yep," Quent said. "Just from what he read in the newspapers. Everyone liked him. He was a real American."

Daddy Joe never came for dinner and radio entertainment on Friday evenings. "Where is he tonight?" Allise asked. If his sons knew, they didn't say, and she asked them to turn off the radio. Her husband asked why. "Because Sam and I have something to tell you. We have a problem."

"A 'problem!'" Quent exclaimed without bothering to move toward the radio. Allise switched it off, and Sam sat forward, wringing his hands.

"Quent, it's taken some time to come up with a way to say this. A few weeks ago you weren't here." She related what had taken place between her and Sam. When she told about the kiss, Sam was on his feet, pacing, his shoulders drawn up around his neck and hands rolling over each other.

Quent jumped to his feet. "I'll kill you, you sorry son-of-a-sneak!"

"No, you won't!" Allise shouted. Rushing at him, she pushed against his chest. "Sit down, both of you! Now!" She felt her husband sag. "Didn't I know you would react like a crazy man, Quent? Sit down over there. Sam, sit!" She stood between them. "Well, now you know, and I'm telling this because it will not happen again. Will it, Sam?"

She glared at him, and he shook his head. "It won't, Quent. It won't." Her husband sat on the edge of the leather chair, eyes blazing, fists knotted.

"Sam lost control for a moment," Allise said, facing her husband's anger. "He's my brother. That's how I love him, and he's going to accept that truth. Aren't you, Sam?"

"Yes, I-I promise," he said, and silence pervaded the room. Sam stood. In the foyer, he snatched a light jacket from the hall tree and left.

Allise sat down. There seemed nothing more to say.

Nothing more was said about the incident. When October brought a collage of red, purple, orange and yellow patched among the pines on Arkansas' rolling hills, and golden autumn sun highlighted the colors, Allise led Peter out into the brisk morning air. She told him the colors were the work of Jack Frost, a mysterious little elf who slipped up on a year. She said Jack Frost came quietly in the night to leave something beautiful before the trees took a winter nap. Sinking down to his level, she had put an arm about Peter and watched him take in the season.

The autumn leaves were brown and dropping when President Roosevelt captured a second term in November. Switching off the radio, Quent turned to Allise. "You rave about him benefitting poor folks and Nigras. Well, his so-called 'New Deal,' how's it helping Nigras?" He seemed waiting for her to react, and when she didn't, he said, "The South ain't gonna waste funds on black birds. Did he sign that anti-lynching law? No! Eleanor's the one talking up Nigras. A woman, for God's sake!"

Allise thought on his words, then she said, "You want such remarks to anger me, don't you?"

"Well, whatcha gonna say?"

"He's put people to work. I admit it doesn't seem to be helping Negroes."

"Damn right." Quent looked pleased.

It was apparent her husband had awakened in a foul mood. He muttered something about the subsidy check and left with his nastiness resonating in a bang of the back door. Allise felt the sound in every nerve of her body. Assuming he started for the post office, she stood in the kitchen thinking about fields producing weeds and the government paying for them. There's something unreasonable about it, she thought.

At lunchtime, Quent hadn't returned. Allise sat at the table watching Peter, who stood at the dining room window waiting for his daddy to drive in. Dark clouds sailed past the window, and thunder rumbled with sudden streaks of lightning. A loud clap caused the child to jerk back with a frightened face. Allise picked up her son and pointed to leaves clinging to the red oak's limbs as though defiant of the season. "See how the raindrops make the leaves dance like fairies."

Just then, Quent drove past the window. "Daddy!" Peter broke from her and ran to the door. Water clung to Quent's coat. He shook it off on the porch and grabbed up his son in a quick hug. In the kitchen, he laid the coat over a chair and sat at the table with Peter on his knee. He held an envelope in front of the child. "See what daddy has?" He shoved it toward Allise. "The subsidy check. Wanna see *Anna Karenina* at the movie tonight?"

Recoiling from the envelope, she was unable to remember a time when he had displayed such elated emotion. She needed the tenderness of his arms more than a movie. Would I rush into his arms or resist? she wondered. Jarred by her thoughts, she nodded agreement about the movie then asked, "Will the tenants get some of the subsidy money?"

If she had pricked an inflated balloon, her question could not have been more provocative. "Gawddamn it!" He pitched the check and other mail on the table. Standing, Quent placed Peter in the high chair then sank down in his chair again. Allise hesitated to take her place at the table, and he released an aggravated sigh. "Allie, I try so hard to make you see the way it is. We don't whip them into obedience, but a Nigra has to be kept in his place. You never pay 'im more than he needs for food and clothing. That way he'll keep working because he has to."

Something strange and scary rose from her depths. Choking back hurt, she blamed herself for changing his mood. *I should regard him above all others, but how can I and be true to myself?* She folded down on a chair. Eating in silence, Quent ripped open another envelope. "A letter from Uncle John!" His outburst made her jump.

Uncle John, Daddy Joe's younger brother, was a Mississippi farmer. He was every bit as shrewd and determined as Allise's father-in-law. The owner of two hundred acres, he had recently acquired eighty more and moved Aunt Minnie and their brood into a large house situated on the new property.

Quent looked up. "Corn, potatoes and cane for molasses brought more than his cotton." Turning back to the letter, he shouted, "My God!" causing Allise to jump again. "He opened a store near Greenville. Took all his money to stock it. Says his 'old cronies' warned he'd stack up credit and was a fool to open a business with trade slow as it is."

Quent kept glancing up at her and reading. "'I fooled all of 'um. Do a real good business with Nigras.' Uncle John says he gives credit according to the cotton Nigras expect to gin. He read from the letter: 'They buy everything from my store. Food, clothing, equipment. If they don't pay up, I strap on my six-shooter and go after 'em.'"

"Great God!" Allise clamped a hand over her mouth and glanced at Peter.

Quent chuckled. "Ah, Allie, Uncle John scares 'em. He has t' keep 'em in line."

Allise mumbled under her breath, but her frustrations went unacknowledged. Peter gulped his milk and swiped an arm across his lips. She wiped the milk line above his lip and put him to the floor. The diversion pushed back her inner conflict. She told herself Quent's good points far outweighed their differences.

He appeared past his upset with her, and she remembered how little she knew about the tenant farm system. Her questions were always met with shrugs, or "Why do you want to know about that?" This might be the moment to learn how Negroes and some poor whites were kept in a state of servitude.

Counting on his excitement about Uncle John, Allise brought up sharecropping. To her surprise, Quent seemed eager to enlighten her. He explained how each DeWitt tenant family was given ten dollars to last from March through September. "Takes 'em through planting, chopping and picking. When cotton seeds are sold, their shares go to pay debts. If seed money doesn't cover their debts ... I don't think it ever has. Anyway, when cotton's sold and books are tallied, the rest of their debt and charges for the use of livestock and equipment are deducted from their share of the cotton money."

"Did last year's cotton sell for fourteen or fifteen cents per pound?" she asked.

"Yep. A five hundred-pound bale brought seventy to seventy five dollars. We got half of that and split the other half between the Colsons and Hattens. That's less the furnishing money I gave 'em and less what they still owed. They never know what the cotton sales come to. Just split what I give 'em. That's how smart they are."

Allise thought of falling for Quent's charm half a decade ago. *Somewhere beneath that smirk is that person but is charm enough?* Careful not to disengage him, she said, "Sam says Cass plows, out-chops and out-picks everyone. All of them work fourteen-hour days. Is furnishing money the same as wages?"

Quent bellowed, "Lord no! They don't get wages! Listen, Allie, Jonas and Jake are in good shape. Most times after debts, I hand each almost a hundred dollars in cash.

He doesn't even try to sense what it's like to be a Negro, she thought. *To be under-appreciated and feel worthlessness.* Suddenly she was aware that Quent had caught her inattentive gaze. "A hundred dollars puts them in 'high cotton,'" he said. "With milk cows, hog meat and dry beans, they fare from October t' March. By then, hog meat hangs skimpy from the smokehouse rafter. Their last bucket of sorghum syrup is opened. They scrape the bottom of the barrel for the last weevily cornmeal, but they will make it. They always do."

Allise heard shady reasoning behind his comments. Guessing she would never understand the peculiar relationship between Negroes and southern whites, she was certain something was happening between her and her husband. A loss of something precious, something she had known for such a brief time. Shuddering, she recoiled from dismal thoughts and remembered

Sam saying southern men didn't burden women with their affairs. That may be how the women hang onto their sanity, she thought.

Quent's moods always slipped up on her. One day he was content, the next, on the edge of an abyss. She clung to her love for him, but his complexities ripped at the pattern of her deepest feelings and beliefs. At the fabric of her life.

✳     ✳     ✳     ✳

Shelves lining a kitchen wall in the Colson tenant house held many more empty Mason jars than filled ones. It was time to prepare a spring garden. Maizee watched her daddy reach to a shelf and pull down a jar containing seeds collected from last year's dead plants. He unwrapped pieces of paper and poured small seed piles on the table. Running a finger through them, he determined which ones he needed to buy.

Suddenly, the kitchen erupted in an uproar. "Stop!" Li'l Joke shrieked at Dessie and Nate. "Momma, make 'em stop!"

"Dessie! Nate! Stop that chasing round and git yo clothes on." Rebekah turned to Maizee, "Come on, honey. You been t' town twice in three years."

"I'm tired, Momma." Maizee saw Rebekah's black eyes snap at her and recognized her own inherited trait. Thing is, Momma's holding more years of anger, she thought.

"You ain't tired, girl, you hongry. I know that gnawing in the belly. Reckon we all tired and hongry. Cain't nobody work like we do and eat like we do and look like they alive. Naw sirree. Coloreds walk round like dead lice falling off 'em. Worked too hard and they be hongry!" She flounced about the kitchen, opened the firebox and pitched in a stick of wood. Coals flamed and a whiff of smoke bellowed out before she latched the door. Rebekah kept ranting. "Coloreds hongry all their lives. Jes tighten their belts and keep on going."

Maizee waited for a pause. "Jake and Daddy talking bout more coloreds going up North. Saying WPA paying thirty dollars a month, but it's hard for blacks t' git work."

"Do you see niggers working on public works? They ain't working on WPA up North, neither. They leave here and come dragging their tails back in a few months. They ain't got no job, they ain't got nothing." Sarcasm coated Rebekah's words like the moisture mopped from her face. Wringing the rag, she swung it over a line above the water shelf. At the kitchen door, she slung dirty water from the enameled pan as if to dump pent-up emotion. Maizee heard the water meet the resistence of a hard-pan surface and splash back.

"Come on, Maizee, you need t'git outta this house. T' see how folks hardly able t' hold their heads up. Talking about hard times and jes half listening to what somebody says. Some went up North. They didn't git no work. Didn't bring no pride back, neither. Ain't no coloreds got pride less it be Joe Lewis, and what he hafta do? Git his head bashed in."

Maizee didn't argue with her momma.

Li'l Joke leaned on the table, making a cat's cradle from a circle of string. "We's called river niggers," she said. "That what Mista Robbins say. Come outta his dry goods store and say, 'You river niggers move on. You blocking the sidewalk, laughing and smelling t' high heaven. White folk ain't coming t' my store with you hanging round.'" The string creation went limp between her hands, and her eyes gleamed questions at Rebekah. "That his zack words. He say we ain't gonna buy anything anyways. Them town coloreds looking at us like we trash, too. I wanna git away from this place. Dalt be lucky."

Nate walked in and Rebekah snatched him by the hand. "You don't hafta like the way we's treated. Don't you ever forgit it, girl." She led Nate outside to the wagon and struggled up into it.

After they pulled away, Maizee lay on the bed, listening to the stillness. Dalt is lucky, she thought. *Got a job with the bus system. Cass be leaving soon. Awways the same ... if boll weevils ain't eating up the crop, it gonna be something else.*

For a moment, old anger boiled up, but she reminded herself that Mista Quent hadn't been near her. Not since I got the syphilis. She smiled. Lying still as death, she waited for safety to sink in again, then she rolled from the bed and set to the day's work.

On the porch that evening, Maizee hummed tunes she'd heard Rebekah sing. Soon, the mules' heads bobbed like undulating waves up the dusty lane. She thought about how they stayed on course with little direction from the reins.

The animals were still moving when Nate jumped from the wagon and ran toward her. "Momma! Momma!" He belly-flopped across her lap. "Guess what? We got a soda pop! It was co-old but burnt my nose." He rubbed his wrinkled nose. "I bring you one, but Grandpa say it be warm fore we git home."

The memory of an ice cold Coca Cola tingled across Maizee's tongue. "Did Grandpa find nickels on the sidewalk for them cold pops?" Laughing, Nate said he didn't know, and she hugged him before pushing her son an arm's length away. Gazing into his strange gray-blue eyes, she said, "Chile, you don't hafta know. There'll be plenty time for yo pain. Jes like Joe Louis, we gotta stand the pain but Grandma Bekah say, we don't hafta like it."

She saw in Nate's frown a total lack of understanding.

# CHAPTER 7

▼

After Quent's explanation of the sharecropping process and before spring planting, Allise read that the Supreme Court had declared the cotton production mandate unconstitutional. Crop controls were dropped, and she was glad there would be no more subsidy checks to argue over. Undercurrents of hazings and lynchings in other parts of the country worried her, but despite deprivations, the Colsons and Hattens made it through another winter. Just as Quent predicted, she thought. Surely, Quent would be happier now that cotton could again be planted in normal acreages.

The Great Depression was in its eighth year. People still had little money for more than bare necessities, but the DeWitts were more fortunate than others in Deer Point.

Allise listened to the broadcast diatribes aired against Judge Hugo Black. It was said he was unfit to sit as a Supreme Court justice. One commentator told of Judge Black's earlier connection to the Ku Klux Klan. At the time, the newsman said, Klansmen wore badges of southern honor and "lured many young men into thinking the Klan had a noble cause." He mentioned a 1915 movie, *Birth of a Nation*, which depicted Negroes as court jesters and stirred up prejudices. The broadcaster went on to say that Klansmen made moralistic judgments through religious beliefs and vilified anyone not of the white race. Seeing only black and white, no shades of gray, they distrusted foreigners and moderate thinkers.

After hearing his comments, Allise muttered, "President Roosevelt would never appoint anyone to the court who still held Klan views." *What point of view would allow a group like the Klan to exist? Judge Black's knowledge of the Klan may be an asset to the court.* Picking up the pen, she began a letter to her father:

*Papa, I doubt there's a Klansman in Deer Point, or that the KKK has a big membership in the South. Klansmen or not, those who look different, hold opposing opinions and beliefs, or come from some other place are distrusted. Defensiveness is worn like armor and blame lies at the door of outsiders. These attitudes aren't restricted to those hanging onto old ways. It grips the young, too. I don't see much self-examination. There's a contradiction of gentleness laced with violence.*

*I've thought about the humiliation Germans must have felt after losing World War I. Are Jews an easier target for German anger than their victorious enemies? Papa, isn't it possible German anger is misplaced?*

*Can it also be Southerners hold anger for the victorious North and misdirect it toward Negroes who are also easy targets? On one hand, gracious people here—as do other respectable Southerners—proclaim distaste for the Klan. They allow the indignities of "Jim Crow" laws and clothe such attitudes in righteousness. Here, separation of the races is so complete that I seriously doubt non-sheeted Southerners are aware of their own similarities to the Klan. They hide beneath subtlety, which allows prejudice to reside under the most genteel mannerisms.*

*This bothers me. I'm baffled and intrigued by the contradictions. Quent, however, isn't in the least subtle. There are disappointments but much to admire about Southerners. They are my people now, and while they don't pretend to claim me, I feel prodded to understand them.*

Laying the pen aside, she heard Quent on the phone. "Yes, damn it! Fields that laid out four years, Sam." Slamming down the receiver, her husband walked into the room rubbing his forehead. "Government controls didn't bother Sam. He argues about planting cotton. His corn didn't bring any money, and he reads that damned *Progressive Farmer*."

Allise agreed with Sam and the farm paper about the ill-advisement of relying solely on one crop. She heard Quent complain loud and often about battles with the boll weevil. He said he didn't know if cotton prices were expected to improve, but extra bales would beat the subsidy money. He seemed in a rare good humor entering the picking season. Spending more time on farm and market accounts, he left the farm to Sam. She thought that development should make Sam happier.

Whether he was happier, or not, he did well through the crop and gathering times.

Allise was happier. She suspected another baby was on the way. Doctor Walls had confirmed it. She was eager to share the good news with Quent, but delayed when he came home that night worried about the November rainfall. It had begun in demon-like torrents and settled into a slow steady downfall, seemingly without end. Mentally and physically consumed by the threat of flooding, her husband was among other farmers watching over the rising Chalu River. He fell into bed each night around twelve o'clock, tired and distraught.

Rain continued falling, and Allise heard Quent on the phone. "In the morning, Sam, you move all of 'em outta there," he ordered his brother, then turned to her. "Sam's already moved some hogs and livestock to farms south of Deer Point. He left wagons and teams of mules so the tenants can escape." When he left the house, she called Doctor Walls to ask his advice.

"Tell your husband," he said. "Good news is what he needs now."

That night, Sam stopped by to tell Quent he was unable to remove all the hogs before dark.

He left, and Allise waited for Quent to settle in bed. Putting an arm over his chest. She cuddled into the curve of his back. He rolled over, and she caught his cheek in her hand. Heeding Dr. Wall's advice, she said, "Darling, we are going to have another baby."

Without acknowledging her statement, he left the bed to pace the floor and rant. She barely understood his words. He talked about planters deserting the unsafe river plain years earlier and moving east to build the town. "Baled cotton stood in water then," he fretted, seemingly to himself. "It's going to happen again. Dirt levees are about to blow."

Preoccupied with his dilemma, he didn't hear her choked hurt. Allise dabbed tears on the sheet.

Maizee lay in bed thinking about the levee breaking while they slept. *How would they get out if water swamped the road? Where would they go anyway?* Her questions kept coming. She listened to her mother thrashing about across the room and knew she worried about Jonas and Jake wading the fields to keep day and night watches on the river. One stayed on the levee while the other ate and rested. It had been that way for several days when her daddy left Jake on the levee and came in at midnight, wet and chilled.

Next morning, Jonas returned to relieve Jake just before the sheriff came to warn the tenants to head for higher ground. Cass ran to tell his daddy. Racing back, they jumped on the hitched wagons already loaded with those waiting. "I knew the water-logged levee was gonna break soon and was headed home when I met Cass," Jonas said.

He and Jake whipped the teams to the highway, then east toward Deer Point. The flood plain ended at Athens Hill, the highest point, four miles away. Ditches held water level with the road. Charging behind others running from the river, they arrived last on the dismal, wooded crest.

Maizee watched blacks and whites mill about ill-defined spaces marked by intangible barriers. Night fell, and her family joined others huddled and shivering in wet clothing. Some sat on tree roots, enduring drips from the leaves, or back-to-back on wagon seats, and cramped together in wagon beds. Others sat beneath their wagons.

Despair and a feeling of helplessness kept Maizee awake. Her daddy appeared exhausted and weak. Her own belly gnawed from hunger, and she thanked God when Nate stopped fretting and fell asleep in her arms.

Early next morning, the sheriff roused the restless refugees. The levee had broken during the night. Overlooking the slope down to the flat land as far as Maizee could see, water covered loam laid down by the river eons ago. Tree tops stood above the mirror-like surface, and cows lowed as they waded one behind the other in water up to their bellies.

By mid-morning, half the population of Deer Point stood on the hill beneath patches of black umbrellas, looking out on a watery scene. Soon, groups moved back to talk and wag their heads.

Maizee huddled apart from her family and beneath a moth-eaten Red Cross army blanket. Her attention riveted on the back of Mista Quent's black rain slicker. Mista Joe and Mista Sam stood with Miz Allie, crouching beneath her umbrella. She held her son's hand. Bridled in the wool blanket, four-year-old Nate squirmed. "Be still now," Maizee said. "When we get warm, you can go to Grandma Bekah." Her eyes wandered over to the the designated white area, and she spotted the McPhersons. Turning back to the DeWitts, she kept an eye trained on their movements.

$$\ast \quad \ast \quad \ast \quad \ast$$

Allise tried to estimate the number of people who would need shelter and food. She heard Sam say he reached Athens Hill at sunrise, then the sheriff stopped him. "Found the croppers right there." He pointed. "They slept under that gum tree." Before he could tell more, Maydale, his girlfriend from high school, walked up.

After greeting her, Allise spotted Jonas a few feet away. Quent was asking him about the hogs. "Had to be six left down there, mostly sows."

"Yassah, they was. We didn't know when that levee was gonna break. Sheriff come round saying we gotta leave. Cass opened the pen and shooed 'em out, Mista Quent."

Suddenly, a voice broke through a bullhorn, and volunteers went to set up tents. Allise took five-year-old Peter's hand and stepped back to a cluster of tenants standing hooded in blankets. "When did you eat last, Rebekah?"

"This morning. Gave us donuts and coffee. First thing since yesterday at noon."

"I will bring food," Allise said. She moved on through the sea of misery. With the exception of Briley, the McPhersons seemed glad to see her. Saddened by forlorn faces, she knew words wouldn't ease weariness and hunger. First, physical needs must be met. She spotted a man with a Red Cross armband and hurried to him. "Can the Red Cross meet the needs here?" she asked.

He looked surprised. "Lady, we have some clothing and a little food. Not nearly enough." Scribbling on a pad, he said, "Drinking water and toilet paper are needed. We need help on a daily basis, because they're gonna be living here in these tents for awhile."

Most of the refugees were black. Again, Allise sought help from the churches, and Sam delivered goods to the camp. One day, Rebekah complained, "Been wearing the same clothes so long they jes stand on their own, they's so dirty."

Allise took the soiled clothing home, and Elfreeda helped her launder them. Returning to the camp that day, she learned a sickness had befallen the refugees. She and Rebekah worked with Doctor Walls to ease the retching stomach cramps. That evening, Quent said he didn't want her going there anymore. "You're gonna harm yourself and the baby."

Standing at the sink, Allise relaxed the dishcloth into sudsy water and turned to stare at her husband's back. The baby wasn't mentioned after she attempted to tell him they were to be parents of a second child. Maybe he does care, she thought. She went to Doctor Walls with Quent's concern. He examined her and said she was as healthy as a horse. "Camp work will do no harm so long as you eat, sleep well, and wash your hands. Poor sanitation is causing what these people have."

Despite Quent's warning, she returned to the camp and learned Rebekah had the sickness. Overcoming her bouts of morning sickness, Allise helped Maizee attend her mother. Soon, a white woman and her child were the first to die. Doctor Walls ordered their corpses buried as soon as graves could be prepared to avoid complicating the health problem.

They were taken in a long black hearse with draped windows to the Deer Point Cemetery. Allise and Mrs. McPherson joined a small band of mourners near the grave sites as Brother Rigdon and Brother Thomas said a few comforting words.

Before noon the next day, Rebekah and two black children had died. Allise helped Maizee care for her mother, but Doctor Walls said the black woman's body just couldn't bear up to the burdens it was dealt. That afternoon, she and Elfreeda rode ahead of a short mule-drawn caravan formed behind two wagons bearing the dead. Allise reached Deer Point and turned onto the street leading to Mt. Zion Cemetery. She parked outside the cemetery fence and waited in the car.

Holding Peter's hand, Elfreeda walked through tall grass and weeds to grave sites. Soon, she brought him back to the car to pick off the beggar lice clinging to his tweed coat, cap and knickerbockers. Laughing, she said, "He sho do ask lots of questions, Miz Allie. He asked me how do they jump on 'im."

"Yes, he's curious." Turning to her friend, she said, "Elfreeda, I don't know how to put this. Some Negroes on Athens Hill are light enough to pass for white. Others are as black as ink."

Elfreeda laughed. "Uh huh, Miz Allie. We comes in all shades."

The wagons bearing the dead arrived and they followed them to the open graves, Allise and Peter were the only white mourners among the few blacks. She watched the grieving faces and wondered what Jonas and his children must be feeling. She tried to sense their loss. *Sometimes Quent seems lost to me. Not permanently, not like death.*

Maizee appeared stoic. She treated her mother with great tenderness, Allise thought. *Does she hide a wounded soul behind that masked face? Others look inconsolable, who is that small boy on Jonas' lap? Why haven't I seen him before? About Peter's age. A grandson?* Allise wondered. *Doesn't look like the others. Light-complexioned.*

Suddenly, a sweet clarion pitch broke into her thoughts. Rising above the low moan of mourners, she mistook it for her imagination. Realizing it wasn't, she heard *Rock of ages! Oh Sweet Jesus.* Eyes closed, Maizee seemed to forbid any other images than Jesus gathering the earthly one into his celestial abode. Mourners' hums wrapped around her words. Peter tugged her hand, and she loosened her tight grip and swayed with them until Maizee's song faded into the hum.

Allise's eyes teared, and she couldn't sort out the feeling that evoked them. It wasn't sadness. There was beauty in Maizee's release of her loved one. Death had never taken a precious one from her, and she was grateful for the young black girl's lesson in letting go.

After the funeral, Allise watched Maizee take responsibility for her family. She demonstrated an inner strength and was never rude, but her import defined a wall between herself and white people. Allise wanted to penetrate the wall, to know her as she had known Rebekah. Since Maizee made that next to impossible, she had questioned Jonas about their needs, careful not to show her growing curiosity about the child at the funeral.

One morning, the young black girl sat on a sawed section of tree trunk when, near collapse, Allise looked for a place to rest. "May I sit here until I feel better?" She pointed.

"I don't mind." Maizee sounded more indifferent than welcoming. Allise's nausea passed, and she rose with a few words of departure and wondering what sad secret may lurk behind the girl's veiled comeliness and dropped gazes. *What was it about the way she wore life? Like the kerchief covering her hair as if to hide it. How would she look in a hat?*

Allise left the camp with images of those whose nightmare seemed unending as they waited for flood water to ebb back toward the river. From Athens Hill, the delta spread in mud flats or stood in still pools. Washouts in the highway blocked routes back to their farms.

Trapped in the make-shift shelters, victims had run short of needs. Allise made another search of her closets. Coming up empty-handed, she reached up to a shelf and pulled down the hatbox. Removing the shallow-brimmed, straw hat interspersed with white daisies and worn long ago on the train to Arkansas, she saw it still looked fresh. Before the mirror, she pushed permed ringlets under the crown and studied herself from all angles. Turning from her image, she laid the hat back among the tissue paper and replaced the box lid. Then she remembered trying to imagine Maizee in a hat.

Hurriedly, she grabbed the hatbox and rushed back to the camp. She found people in a frenzied state. The sheriff had visited and said it was safe to return to their homes. Already packed, some were leaving and others scurried about, loading their wagons. She snatched up the hatbox and ran to Jonas where he waited on the wagon. Reaching the box to him, she explained it was for Maizee. "Jonas, if she doesn't want it, I'll offer it to someone else." Mrs. McPherson, she thought.

From a distance, Allise observed Maizee climb into the wagon and Jonas hand the box to his daughter. She turned the hat, inspecting the daisies. Her face, most often devoid of emotion, came alive. She tried it on and laughed with her sisters. Jonas flicked the reins and commanded the mules to "Git up!" Waving, she saw Maizee's face return to that of forbearance. She sat in her mother's place on the wagon seat. They're going home without Rebekah, Allise thought.

Later, Sam stopped in to tell Allise that the Colsons, on returning to their house, had found silt almost to the ceiling in every room. They shoveled it out of the kitchen where they now cooked, ate and slept. Sam said farmers were in a sad state. All had lost cotton and some would lose their land. The DeWitt farm, he said, may be the only one insured against flooding. "It covers some of our loss, but Quent says a check will not come for awhile. The land is covered in cracked mud and the cotton's gone."

He told about seeing dead animals partially consumed by predators.

Suddenly, Allise bent forward, heaving in a wave of nausea. Sam planted Peter on the floor and ran for a wet towel. He stammered apologizes and mopped her face.

Soon, she overcame the morning sickness, and now months later, she slumped in the winged chair, swollen legs elevated on the ottoman, and her body ballooned with baby. From the edge of the rug, Peter banged Lincoln Logs together or drummed them against the hardwood floor. She wanted to scream. Her husband and Daddy Joe sat at the desk. Above the din, she heard Quent say, "no furnishing money, just credit." Frowning, she thought Daddy Joe wasn't himself. *The flood levied a toll. Another grandchild will put a spark in him.* Allise was fond of her father-in-law.

She studied father and son. Daddy Joe sat sideways at the desk, propping on an elbow, chin cupped in one hand, the other on his knee. Shirt sleeves were rolled to avoid market soil, and black suspenders hitched up his dark trousers. Claiming the market's backroom for his office, Quent now dressed in a serge suit, white shirts and neckties.

Peter abandoned the logs, and Allise heard Daddy Joe say, "We caint let the Nigras know about this flood insurance money." Just then, Peter returned to the logs and sent them scattering across the floor. The unexpected noise startled her and caused Daddy Joe to turn. Lifting his hat from the chair post, he plopped it on the back of his head and pushed himself up. His trousers sagged below a protruding belly, stretching suspenders to the limit.

At the door, he tugged on the britches. "I left that kid in charge. Better get back to the store." Picking up Peter, he swung him in a circle, then mocking an engine drone, soared him overhead and swooped him near the floor. The child's giggles clearly delighted his grandfather. "Whew, I'm dizzy," he said, releasing Peter. Reeling, he staggered outside.

Peter staggered behind him. Laughing, Allise and Quent watched him wave after Daddy Joe. Calling Peter indoors, she turned to her husband. "Your father isn't well."

Back at the desk, Quent straightened papers. "Ah, Daddy just needs to get away from the market more."

Early Saturday morning, a colored man, walking along the highway toward town, came upon Daddy Joe slumped over the car's steering wheel. "Mr. Joe died of natural causes sometime last night," the county coroner had told Quent, Sam and Allise. The corpse reposed in an open, dove gray coffin resting on a bier in the great hall of the Filbert Street home. Throughout the day, people had come with food and condolences, and paused to view the body. That night, friends came to "sit" in a death-watch.

Soon, a pall settled over the house. Quent and Allise retired to an upstair's bedroom. Overhead, a fan whacked the air with more noise than relief. Peter fell asleep, and Quent took him to Sam's room. Returning, he lay beside Allise. She tried to block the monotonous fan sound and drone of voices from the hall below by thinking of the affection she and Daddy Joe had shared. He had seemed pleased about another grandchild. *Sad, he died before seeing our baby,* Allise thought, remembering then that her parents had never seen Peter. Her hand circled her bulging belly, sensing the new life she would soon deliver.

Unable to concentrate on pleasant things or bear more sleepless minutes flat on her back, Allise slipped from bed and tiptoed downstairs. Darting into the parlor, she paused to listen for signs of discovery by those in the great hall. Light from a street lamp fell across the room like a fine mist, allowing her to distinguish objects. She sank into a pillowed armchair near a window open to the front porch. Pushing back into the shadows, she unbuttoned her nightgown at the neck and listened to voices in the hall. Mildred's clicking tongue and the Widow Burns' grim inflections were clearly distinguishable.

*Where are the men who came to sit with Daddy Joe's remains?* Suddenly, she became aware of a presence on the porch. Leaning toward the window, she made out shadowy figures in the dim light. Men sat in the swing and rocking chairs. Allise hoped their show of respect for Daddy Joe was a consolation for Quent and Sam.

Words drifted through the window. "Yep, old Joe was a colorful character. Be missed, but he sure had his shady side, didn't he?" Easy, throaty laughter followed the voice recognized as Eldon Howard's. "Frank said, like always, Joe came in the liquor store for a bottle of bourbon Friday afternoon. An empty Jim Beam bottle was in his car."

*Shady side? A liquor bottle?* Their talk was taking a hurtful shape. Allise knew good things about her father-in-law. Most of these men used credit to buy at his market. He was kind to his lady customers and a loving grandfather.

"Yep," another said. "Jimmy, that part-time kid, said the bottle was in a brown paper bag on the car seat when he took boxes out back." Allise couldn't place that voice.

The men talked about Joe coming back late from lunch at Quent's. He tied on his old striped, bibbed apron and worked till six o'clock. The store was busy, but he laughed with the ladies and teased the kid about his girlfriend. One said you could keep time by Joe DeWitt on Fridays. "He'd take off the apron, roll down his sleeves and button the cuffs. I've seen him do it many times. Crease that old brown hat, put it on the back of his head and yell, 'Sweep out and lock up, Jimmy. Be sure that hot date don't keep you out late.'"

The account of Daddy Joe's last afternoon reminded Allise of Quent's stories after a Saturday night visit to the barbershop. He said it was a time when men shared sordid tales and chortled over shady capers unfit to tell their wives. His father's friends envied Daddy Joe because he didn't have a wife tying him down.

There in the armchair, Allise wondered about husbands and wives, their expectations of each other. The men on the porch probably wouldn't tell their spouses about Daddy Joe's "shady side." Southern men protected the moral well-being of women.

Heaving a long sigh and fearing her presence was detected, Allise peered out the window. Assured they hadn't heard her, she eased back into the shadows. Resting against the chair pillows, she mused over Daddy Joe's indiscretion. *Was drink his only flaw? Did he gamble at Rooster's, too? Sometimes, The Philadelphia Inquirer told of gamblers doing away with each other. Silly thought! Of course Daddy Joe died of natural causes. I saw he wasn't well.*

Voices from the porch laced the late hour and soon lulled her to sleep.

✳    ✳    ✳    ✳

The Colsons' life didn't vary in the flood's aftermath. Tenant families had little to lose. They finished a week's work, went into town on Saturday and walked next door to the Hatten house to hear Jake's sermon. They gathered from lush gardens, caught buffalo and catfish from the river, and fished in Moon Lake for perch, bass and blue-gilled bream.

Moon Lake, created in some long-ago unfolding of the Chalu, covered more acres after the flood. It clung in a mysterious way to the land it claimed, as though it were an ancient mare whose source of constant fullness remained unknown.

On a Saturday, Maizee sat on a down-turned bucket on the bank of the lake. Other blacks stood along the shallow edge or sat backed against cypress knees. When the mood to move struck, a tree trunk or a log would do to lean against. Some planted cane poles in the bank between their legs and watched for nibbles on the bait, or held their poles and watched corks bobble. If a fish was serious about a worm, it pulled the cork under and caused an upward jerk of the pole. Snared fish were whipped from the water. If one choked up the baited hook and landed back in the water, Maizee heard a disappointed shout.

Snakes slithering too close for comfort on the water's surface evoked loud screams, caused overturned buckets or poles to be dropped in the water.

The sun would soon give way to the moon far too soon. Maizee sat in the shade of a drooping willow near the water's edge. Holding her pole, she listened to baits splat the water and fish jump for flying insects. They created widening circles up and down the lake's still surface. But for those sounds and the sun moving onto the western horizon, time was as motionless as the lake itself. Content with a day well spent if she caught a meal at only the cost of time, she stared at the murky water.

If the fish don't bite today, she thought, a Sunday platter piled high with fried frog legs will be just as good. Men always came prepared with gigs. They waited for the moon to lay a light blush on the dark water, for cicadas to end their noisy cadences, and rhythmic frogs to herald the night.

Suddenly, a dragonfly swooped down and skimmed the surface. Maizee wanted the moment of dragonflies skimming and her people fishing to go on forever. She knew her river land, its fields, its people. Nate was secure in this place of wild growth.

While she waited for the "big one," a fish to make his gray-blue eyes flare, Nate looked to be daydreaming. His cork bobbed above the nibble of a small fish.

Maizee wondered if the two of them would ever be free of that long ago September evening. Would she be free to bring her son out of that place between existing and being? Would she be free to run barefoot with him in furrowed fields, to take Nate to places her people couldn't go, to say things they couldn't say, and ask questions they couldn't ask? *Would it always be this way for Nate?*

Late that evening, she fried her catch from the lake when Jonas welcomed Elfreeda and Brother Jedadiah to stay for supper. They drove down in their "new" used car. After the meal, they sat on the porch, talking and laughing when Brother James mentioned that Mista Joe DeWitt was found dead and would be buried on Sunday. The visitors were ready to leave, and Elfreeda told Maizee to fetch Nate and ride home with them. "We'll bring y' back Sunday evening."

Jonas cajoled his daughter into accepting the invitation. "We'll survive despite Li'l Joke and Dessie's cooking." Maizee bundled their Sunday clothes, grabbed the yellow straw hat, and she and Nate climbed into the sedan.

Sunday morning, Brother James delivered a blistering sermon not unlike the Almighty's powerful summer heat. After the service, the congregation stood outside the church, mopping sweat and whipping the air with cardboard fans and handkerchiefs. Maizee stood apart from the loud talk and laughter. She felt ill-fit-ted, except for the hat with daisies. A heavy-set woman pulled off her hat, crimped the brim and fanned. "I don't think I ever seen a June this hot. It's like the devil done decided t' burn us up."

Now and again, Maizee caught Mista Joe's name. *Do they know he's Nate's grandpa?* She dropped Nate's hand, wiped a hankie beneath the hat brim and wanted to scratch the rash nettling her skin beneath the concealed knife binding.

Soon Elfreeda said, "Let's go, Maizee. Dodd be at the door before we get home."

Dinner was on the table when Brother James came in. He had just offered grace when a rap was heard. Chairs scraped on the floor, tightening the circle around the table to make room for Dodd. Without uttering a word, he pulled up a chair as sliced tomatoes, green peas, mashed potatoes, gravy, and biscuits rising two inches high made a round. Nate reached for the fried chicken. Maizee grabbed his hand and put a chicken wing on his plate.

With dishes passed, speculation turned to what had caused the white man's death. Dodd reached for a chicken thigh, chewed and grunted satisfaction. "I'll tell y' zackly what happen, cause I was there."

Elfreeda looked like lightning had struck. Brother James stopped in mid-chew, and Maizee didn't understand the interest in a dead white man. Dodd held a thigh before gapped teeth, and Nate gnawed the wing, imitating the old man's grunts.

After a few chews, Dodd said he sat in front of his store when Mista Joe passed. "Like on all Fridays, he gwine t' Vickery's. Gets outta the car with a bottle of Jim Beam whiskey in a paper sack." He giggled. "Been going on ever since Miz Berniece died."

Chewing slowly, the others waited for him to go on, and Dodd said Vickery had come to the store for liver. "Makes him smothered liver jes about ever Friday.

U'Orleans style with rice." He chuckled, through a full mouth. "Anyway, what did that old white man see in that shriveled up, old, colored woman? Her cooking?" Rolling his tongue around sparse teeth and bits of chicken, he giggled again.

Elfreeda giggled, too. Brother James flipped a red polka-dotted necktie over his shoulder. His sternness appeared to struggle with an oncoming laugh. Maizee watched his dilemma swell and couldn't contain her own giggle. Covering it behind her hand, she pondered a time when Nate would have to know about his white granddaddy. Wiping his greasy cheeks on a frayed napkin, her eyes swept those around the table. *Do they know?*

She hadn't said a word, and Elfreeda began giving her the ins and outs of Dodd's story. "Chile, do you know Vickery?" Maizee shook her head, and Elfreeda explained Vickery was known as 'the bag woman.' She said Vickery walked the streets in dresses down around her ankles and wearing a dark turban on her head. She carried a short pole over her shoulder with a bag tied to one end for collecting rags and used clothing. "She lives next door t' Dodd. He lives behind his store. Don't know why she begs." Elfreeda prompted the storyteller. "We don't care bout her cooking, Dodd. Get on with it."

A red-checked curtain, matching the napkins and tablecloth, fluttered at the open window. The breeze did little to relieve the heat. Dodd wiped sweat with his napkin and said he'd been to Vickery's many times when Mista Joe was there. "You know he give her a radio? They be listening t' Amos and Andy and having shots of Jim Beam."

The preacher's eyes flashed heavenward. "Lawd! Lawd!"

Undaunted by the reverend's calling on The Above, Dodd said, "They musta been romping in bed, cause bout three-thirty in the morning, Vickery is pounding on my door. 'It's Vickery, Dodd! Come quick!' she say in a squeaky voice, fraid she wake up folks."

Maizee fingered the butterfly sleeve of her dress. *That man needs to shut up. Does Nate understand anything he's said?*

But Dodd didn't shut up. He went on to tell of still being half asleep when he got up and opened the door in his drawers. Vickery stood there in a white nightgown. "If I hadn't knowed her, I woulda thought she was a ghost." A slow easy drawl slid over his tongue like molasses dripping from a half-eaten biscuit.

Hearing the word *ghost*, Nate dropped a spoonful of potatoes. Dodd peered around the table from beneath his crumpled hat and chomped into the biscuit. He laid it on his plate and picked up a chicken wing. Maizee stopped eating altogether, and Elfreeda's meal was hardly touched. On the edge of her chair, elbows on the table and head in hands, her patience seemed exhausted. "Man, you gonna git t' what happened or ain'tcha?"

Dodd said they ran into Vickery's house, and there was Mista Joe face down on her bed. "Naked as a baby bird and deader 'n a doornail." He laughed, gasping for breath. "Vickery say, 'Hep me git 'im outta here.' 'Em itty bitty, black eyes be full a fright. A mulatto, she be white awready. We ain't saying a word, cause I'm scared, too."

He took a bite of chicken and chewed. Then, he said they pulled on his underwear, and with the body face down, worked with his pants. Vickery slipped an arm in one shirt sleeve and Dodd the other. "We latched up his s'penders in back, roll 'im over and pulled that heavy body so it hang mostly off the bed. Man! You know what happen then?"

They leaned forward on their chairs. "That dead man slid off the bed. Slump over wid his head on his chest." Nate went bug-eyed, and Elfreeda drew taut as a strung wire. The button on her red frock strained, ready to pop off. Her hand dangled a half-eaten piece of chicken. Maizee and Brother James patted Nate and waited.

Dodd seemed to sense their appetite for more. He fastened Mista Joe's front suspenders to his trousers, and Vickery buttoned his shirt. They pulled socks and shoes onto lifeless feet, and had been at the gruesome task for some time when Vickery stood back to inspect for anything left undone. Satisfied, she unfurled a patchwork quilt, letting it fall to the floor beside the lifeless man. Each lifted a leg, pulled the body even with the quilt, rolled it to the middle and folded the cover over it. Tugging it to the porch, they stopped to catch their breath before heaving the body the short distance to the ground.

Dodd grimaced. "We breathing hard. Hurt t' gulp air. We be scared and wore out. Guess we look like goblins under that moon shining on her gown and my under drawers."

Dodd's eyes loomed large and luminous in the kitchen light coming through the only window and screen door. He said they listened for any awareness of the commotion they made. "Jes some old alley cats meowing a few doors up. Vickery whisper, 'Anybody hear us, they think I going t' the privy.'"

He chuckled and said he asked what they were to do next. "Vickery said put Mista Joe in the car, drive down to the highway and push it in the ditch. Said folks think he died behind the wheel. I told her I be in trouble if white folks find out he died here instead of the car. She say, 'Shut y' mouth! You in trouble anyway if they know you hep move 'im.'" Dodd turned his head from side to side. "There didn't seem any other way. I was in deep."

He continued, saying he folded the quilt back and reached in the dead man's pocket for the keys. Opening the door, they heaved the quilted body up on the running board. The cat fight grew louder and someone cursed. "We was like statues. Couldn't hardly breathe." Vickery held the corpse upright until the night quieted. Dodd went to the driver's side, stretched across the seat and took the quilt corners held toward him. She picked up the lifeless feet, and he inched the dead weight across the front seat. Dodd held the body under the armpits while she jerked the quilt from beneath it.

Two feet hung over the passenger side, keeping the door from closing. Vickery lifted them to the open window and pushed the door shut. Telling Dodd to wait, she ran inside with the quilt and returned with the empty whiskey bottle. "She say, 'git in the car.' I say I cain't cause they ain't no room. 'You crazy!' she say and tell me to slide in and put that dead man's head on my lap. Lawd God!"

Dodd was the picture of a ghost, and Nate might as well have seen one. He pulled the napkin from his shirt, covered his face and peeked from behind it.

He said he turned the engine, and Vickery hopped onto the back seat. Backing to the street, he guided the car to the highway. No traffic came or went at that time of night, and he steered toward town before stopping near the ditch. Jumping out, Vickery urged him to hurry. Shoving and pulling, they positioned the body under the wheel. "I panted like a hound dog off the chase, but Vickery say the sun be coming up any minute."

She pushed from the rear as Dodd pushed and steered through the car's open window toward the ditch. "Lawdy God! That dead man's head fell on the wheel. Beeeeep. The horn blowing." Nate threw down his napkin and snickered. The childish and toothless old man paused to enjoy his amusement, then he said, "I tell ya, I thought I's gonna die."

Dodd's predicament had Maizee and Elfreeda laughing tears. "Ahem-m." Brother James cleared his throat, and laughter faded as awareness of sacrilege unwound around the table like a ball of yarn. For a moment, quiet prevailed under the preacher's unyielding stare. Then, Dodd continued, Vickery pulled the head off the horn, banged it down on the open window and threw the Jim Beam bottle on the floorboard.

He pushed back from the table, and rubbing his stomach, said, "Then we hightailed it back up the street."

Nate giggled, and Maizee snickered behind her hands. The old man may stretch the truth, but she would tell his story back on the river when her son wasn't around to hear.

# CHAPTER 8

▼

In the shadow of the tall DeWitt headstone in Deer Point Cemetery, Daddy Joe was laid to rest beside his late wife, Berniece. An account of his unexpected demise appeared in the *Weekly* on the following Thursday. Allise read the story and thought his death would give people something to talk about besides the weather and crops and the latest Saturday night stabbing over at Rooster's.

His death didn't remain a preoccupation for long. Daily life still banged up against harsh realities, dashing any hopes of a return to pre-depression normalcy, and the flood left farmers with added worries. Baled cotton was lost, and raging water carved more crooks and crannies in the Chalu, leaving new twists in its torrential, southeasterly sweep toward the Mississippi River. Where large, contiguous fields once unfolded, smaller parcels now stood divided by new streams and stagnant ponds, which claimed more land. Cass Colson joined the ranks of those migrating to Chicago, and seasonal workers took sawmill jobs or worked on railroad repair crews. Jonas and Jake couldn't keep up with spring plowing, so Quent ordered Sam to hire workers.

In the kitchen, Allise watched Sam pace and wring his hands. "I found a few bums under the railroad bridge. They ain't never walked behind a plow, but I hired 'em anyway. Cain't depend on hobos. Never stay in one place long before catching another freight to another place. Quent's gonna be madder 'n hell if them fields don't get planted."

She saw her husband plunge into yet another abysmal pit in the aftermath of his father's death. He seemed unable to pull himself into the present day. While making their evening meal, she tried to make sense of what ate away at him.

Whatever reasons for his despondency, one question always pushed at her logic.

*Was she the source of his despair?*

Suddenly, angry shouts came from the living room. Stepping through the dining room to the living room door, she listened to Edward R. Murrow saying: "The National Emergency Council released its findings concerning the South." Rooted there with Sam behind her, she saw her husband's face tighten and flush so that it read like a high fever registered on a thermometer.

"Where in God's name does *he* get off saying the South is the nation's number one economic problem? Bunch a damn Yankees and New Dealers thinking up lies t' tell about us! Never say anything good about the South," Quent shouted.

Disgust flooded her mind. Throwing a surreptitious look in her husband's direction, she said the meal was ready and returned to the kitchen.

Seated at the table, Sam directed himself to Quent. "I hired those hobos, but you oughta know they ain't—"

"Listen, Sam, I don't give a rat's rear end about that farm. Daddy isn't here anymore t' push me. The point is, I want no part of it. It's yours." In his forceful way, he added, "I'll keep books, handle money, pay bills but don't talk farming to me. Don't wanna hear it. If you go bankrupt well, that's your problem."

An awkward moment played between them, then Sam stood, fists clenching. "Gawd damn you, Quent!"

Her husband stood up, and Allise rushed between them. "Go outside!" In a low voice, her words were slow and deliberate. "Get out! Go beat each other until you're rid of whatever drives such hatefulness. Our son is watching all of this."

Sam sank back onto the chair. "Come here, Peedy."

Allise saw Quent grab his hat from the hall tree and slam out the door. The room was quiet as a tomb, and she wanted to hold Sam's hands and say his brother wasn't himself. I mustn't, she thought.

Sam filled the silence with a long sigh and pulled the pale-faced child between his legs, circling him in his arms. Allise was grateful for his protective gesture. "Darling," she said to Peter, "your daddy and Uncle Sam love you. Daddy just isn't himself tonight. He'll return soon." She held out her arms to her son.

Sam stood up with a long sigh. "I need t' get on home. See y' soon, Peedy. Allie."

Sitting with Peter, she wondered if Sam's sigh was one of relief. Maybe if Quent were free of the farm, he would spend less time at Rooster's. At times, his steel blue eyes, veiled and insensitive, gazed into a place that shut her out. *How could her heart feel heavy when it was empty of his love?* With ache almost consuming her, Allise thought of the life in her womb. Her innocent child wouldn't come into a world empty of love.

Hugging Peter, she prayed for patience to see her family through its trials and get her through the pregnancy.

Allise had thought she didn't have the strength to bring another baby into the world. But her time came, and Doctor Walls said, "Lay back and let it happen." A baby girl was delivered and named Clariece. *Cleesy* was the name Peter gave her, and it stuck, but under births in the DeWitt Bible, his mother wrote: *Clariece Lyle DeWitt, July 24, 1938, named for Clara Weston and Berniece Lyle DeWitt, her grandmothers.* Under deaths, she recorded: *Joseph DeWitt, 20 June 1938.*

Cleesy was colicky the first three months. Most nights, Allise walked the floor with her. Sometimes she caught naps between feedings or read. Her father had sent Huxley's *Brave New World* and Faulkner's *Light in August.* Now, laying aside Faulkner's book, she recalled her father's last letter. He wrote that Cleesy's grandmother was pleased her granddaughter carried her name. "Your mother is frail and cannot travel," he wrote. Allise was lonely. *I need my parents,* she thought, *but only Quent can fill my most desperate need.*

Elfreeda, now full-time help in the DeWitt household, came into the room. Laughing, she repeated what Peter said about his baby sister. "He say, 'She cries all the time. I don't want a baby sister.'"

"What would I do without you, Elfreeda? You give me time to read with Peter and play with Cleesy."

Allise made it through the colicky stage and teething in her daughter's first year. Quent missed Cleesy's first roll over, her first smile and first steps, among other wondrous things all babies do. She wondered how can he be so inattentive to his children's achievements; although, he surprised her sometimes when he took Peter to "shoot 'em up" movies. *I never know how to read his unpredictable moods.*

It was Saturday, and Allise let seven-year-old Peter go to the farm with Sam in his new pickup truck. Sitting on the rug while Cleesy played, she thought about the settlement of Daddy Joe's estate. Joe's Market went to Quent and the farm to Sam. Money was divided between the two, and his will stipulated the brothers were to share profits if the Filbert Street home was sold. Sam was to live there until such a time. Allise thought the farm ran smoothly under Sam's direction, and it was good of him to entrust Jonas with upkeep between busy seasons.

About mid-afternoon, Sam returned with Peter. Her son complained, "A nigger boy stared at me through the fence while I waited in the truck for Uncle Sam."

His mother begged him to call them Negroes and asked if he stared back at the boy. Peter nodded he had, and she asked how then could he complain. She tried to convince him the other child was as uncomfortable and curious as him.

Sam played with Peter and Cleesy, and shared his farm ideas with Allise. "I know so little about farming, but you make me feel needed, Sam. When are you going to bring Maydale for dinner again? If Quent works late, we will eat without him." She knew Quent wasn't working late on the evenings he didn't come home, but she made excuses for him.

He promised to bring Maydale soon.

Allise thought the girl was no great beauty. *More on the attractive side. Trim and a fashionable dresser. She comes across quite level-headed when she allows herself to be heard.* It was apparent that Maydale loved Sam, but would he propose marriage? She thought them well-suited for each other. "You need someone special in your life, Sam."

"Yeah, but I have you special people in my life." He chucked Peter under the chin. "Hey, the circus is in town for two nights. Peter will love the clowns. Let's go tonight."

The next day, Allise rested on the chaise, her papa's letter open on her lap while she revisited the circus performances. Peter had loved the clowns. Black-faced minstrels had rolled their eyes in white painted circles, waved white-gloved hands and mouthed Sambo jokes through thick, reddened lips. Peter hadn't seemed to comprehend the jokes.

"Just as well," she muttered. Picking up the letter, she read: "Hitler eats away at Europe. America's leaders voice disagreement with Japan over Manchuria, and the president threatens an oil embargo. The threat of war is far too real." He wrote about taking her sisters' families to the 1939 World's Fair in New York City.

Hearing heavy steps on the stairs, she looked up to see Sam bound into the room. "Here, read this." She pointed to a place in the letter. "Papa tells about a short movie at the fair, which forecast an agricultural revolution. It showed farmers swinging scythes to harvest wheat, and the word, 'Revolution' appeared on the screen above them." They looked up from their task to see a field bathed in sunlight with harvesting machines doing their work.

"Probably too good to come true in the South," Sam said. "Cotton prices are gonna bottom out, Allie. Did I tell you Jake took a job at the lumber yard? Moving his family t' town."

After he left, Allise considered her father's invitation to visit Philadelphia and the fair. How could she explain Quent's state of mind? Even though manufacturing for war-torn Europe had eased the economic depression, there still wasn't money for a trip. Quent struggled to keep the market afloat. She wanted to tell her papa they were happy, and he would see his grandchildren. Maybe next year, she thought.

That evening, she begged Quent to leave business accounts and listen to the broadcast of Armistice Day events. Seemingly reluctant to let his work go, he sat with her as Kate Smith sang *God Bless America*. Rubbing his eyes, he tried to sound unaffected by the song that moved him close to tears. "God has a special plan for this country, Allie. Every foreigner wants t' be here. It's worth fighting for if need be." His words sent prickles down her back.

He stood. "Come here, darling." Pulling her up, he nudged toward the stairs.

Gratified in the bedroom, he slept while she lay awake. His words about fighting for the country haunted her. The depression decade was ending, but Quent still fell into moods.

Some nights later, the hour was late when the doorbell rang. Quent wasn't home, and Allise peeked from behind a window shade and went to the door. "Sam! Anything wrong?"

He came from a date with Maydale and saw the house lights. Allise led him into the living room, and he slumped down on the sofa. "Is Quent home?"

"He'll be here soon." She swallowed her embarrassment and changed the subject. "Did you see a movie? When are you going to marry that girl, Sam?"

His neck went red. Avoiding the question, he said, "We saw *Gone With the Wind*. You'll want t' see it even if it is long and costs more." He rattled on about the expense of dating. "How long can this depression go on, Allie? It's gotta end sometime."

She reminded him the economy was improving because of European orders for arms and equipment. "For some, but it ain't getting better for farmers," he said, leaning forward with elbows on his knees and wringing his hands. "Top soil's blowing away. They say it's cause we plant in un-terraced fields. Lookey, this drought ... They're calling Oklahoma and Arkansas a dust bowl! Farmers are leaving the land. Going t' California. How can they jes leave their land?"

Allise listened to his concerns of a new season with Jonas as the lone tenant. She didn't have answers but reminded him the depression affected everyone. He agreed and ceased exercising his hands. She saw him to the door. "Sam, I'm taking the kids to the baseball game, Saturday. Are you going?"

He stepped from the porch into the darkness. "Maybe."

On Saturday, he stopped the truck in the alley and honked the horn. The kids ran out, and Allise came bringing a blanket roll. He shouted, "Come on, let's go."

South of town, they crossed the railroad and entered a grassy parking area. Deer Point was to challenge Bladon on the sandlot ballfield. Nodding greetings, Allise looked about for a grassy knoll on which to spread the blanket. Telling Peter and Cleesy to stay nearby, she and Sam settled down in the spring sunlight.

He said the fields were being plowed, but Jonas kept talking about wanting to leave the farm. "Jake's left and if Jonas leaves I gotta do something."

Allise's mind drifted. She caught enough words to respond, "Yes, you do." His concerns couldn't blot her image of Quent leaning in the kitchen doorway that morning. He rubbed his forehead and said, "We're headed for war, Allie. Poland is lost, and Denmark and Norway are being blitzkriegged. Now, the Germans are going for England and France."

She had turned from making breakfast. "There mustn't be a war. Leaders must talk to the Germans."

Her husband yelled that the president had declared neutrality. "Hell! We cain't wait for bombs t' drop over here just to satisfy folks who think we can stay out of the fracas. What if we're attacked?" He had gone on about Roosevelt gearing up the Army, poking fun at the armed forces, saying during last summer's maneuvers sticks were used for guns and military trucks for tanks. "Mounted poles on tripods to simulate artillery pieces. That's how our soldiers are trained." Quent's laugh had dripped sarcasm. "If we fight, I don't want to be in the Army."

Just then, Cleesy dropped a ball in Allise's lap. The unexpected gift made her jump. Sam touched her arm. "You okay?"

Allise smiled, said her mind was elsewhere, and told the child to return the ball.

Sam repeated his idea for enticing Jonas to stay on the farm and asked her opinion. She agreed he should set aside an acre behind the Colson house for vegetable patches so Jonas could peddle produce from the farm truck. He said he would hire extra workers so his girls can tend the patches. "All the money will go to Jonas with no charge for using the mules and truck. Whatcha think?"

She took a moment. "It's only fair to invest in Jonas. He's given years of faithful service. Have you spoken to him?"

"Nope. Wanted to hear what you thought." Sam said *The Progressive Farmer* had a story about two Memphis brothers working on a mechanical cotton picker. "Expect to get it on the market by year's end. Won't that be something? Bet it'll cost a fortune." She nodded and said it would be wonderful if such a thing worked. "Allie, I gotta invest in a John Deere tractor before this time next year. Only way I can do it is t' get a loan."

Cleesy brought the ball again, asking her mother to toss it. Rolling it to her a few times, she said, "Now, take it back, Cleesy." She caught Sam's pensive gaze. He smiled, and looking sheepish, turned away. Allise quickly diverted his attention. "Why didn't Maydale come today? Sam, have you considered marriage?" She wanted to bite her tongue.

Silence stretched between them. When he braved another glance in her direction, he appeared annoyed and squinted into the sun. "Nope! It ain't in the books. Maydale wants t' marry someone who'll take her away from here. That ain't me! We're jes friends."

Allise waited, thinking he wanted to say more, but the pitcher and batter stood ready on the field, and their attention was drawn to the game.

The ball season ended and school opened. Allise poured glasses of lemonade and waited for Peter when Sam popped in. Apologizing for prying into his and Maydale's private lives, she poured another glass. Peter banged through the door and swung his book satchel on the table. "Saw the truck. Knew you were here, Uncle Sam. Let's ride my bike."

Sam asked for Cleesy's sweater, and Peter complained about including her, but Allise settled the question, and all three raced outdoors. She watched Sam catch Cleesy's hand and follow Peter down the street. What would we do without him? she thought.

She peeled an apple at the sink when they came inside. Sam stood nearby. "I hafta go in a few minutes," he said over Peter's objections. "Need t' ask y' momma something." Allise set apple slices before the children and returned to the sink. Sam rubbed his palms together. "Allie, me and Quent, we were sorta partners till … Well, we never agreed on much, but I needed him even if he didn't need me. I hate t' make decisions. Would you be my farm partner?" His neck turned fiery. "I'm always coming to you anyway."

Taken aback with the unexpected request, she stood stone still, wanting to say "yes." To show she was flattered. She couldn't. Sam stopped hand-wringing and worked his jacket zipper. He leaned against the cabinet looking as if he expected a negative answer.

"Let's talk about it later?" She didn't need to think about it. Delay was in deference to her husband's opinion.

Sam let the zipper rest. "Okay, later."

That night, Allise put Cleesy to bed and returned to the living room. Quent worked at the desk, and she draped her arms about his neck. "Sweetheart, do you know how much Sam misses you at the farm? He loves turning the soil, seeding, and watching plants grow, but when it comes to decisions …

Well, you two didn't always agree, but Sam would rather disagree than make decisions. He depended on you."

Quent uttered a ho-hum sound. His absentmindedness galled her. "What if I told you he wants me to be his farm advisor? A partner of sorts." She rushed on. "Before you say I don't know anything about farming, and I don't, but you can teach me."

"Suit yourself," he said, without questions or even a glance at her.

Allise withdrew and stumbled back. Suddenly, old fears were overcome with anger. What was the use of having him if she lost herself? She stepped around, facing him. "Look at me, Quent! I'll learn about the farm, if not from you, from someone else. What's more, I'm going to give it a try for Sam's sake. And by the way, he wants to buy a tractor. I didn't tell him so, but I think he's right. We'll ask Dro McClure for a loan."

Her commanding tone grabbed his attention. "I assure you, Allie, any loan will be repaid without help from the market or us. I'm trading our car for a new model soon."

The mildness of his tone tamed her. She settled on the leather chair, giving thought to his remarks. *His attitude about a tractor was to be expected, and we have outgrown the roadster. I'll give him that, but if he can't take me seriously, then it's not going to matter anymore. I'll hold my own counsel.*

Allise woke the next morning from a good night's rest. Yawning and stretching, she stepped to the window and peeped between the sheer curtains. New beginnings greeted her. Birds flitted about lacy-leafed branches, singing and calling for mates. A squirrel chased another, round and up and down an oak tree. Hyacinth and jonquil bloomed purple and yellow bouquets. Nature was alive, and she felt an awakening. A challenge awaited her. Dressing quickly, she made sandwiches. After seeing Peter off to school, she put Cleesy in a day outfit, and they rode out.

The child, nearing two years old, stood on the seat and wrapped an arm behind her mother's neck. Morning sun warmed them through the back window, and Allise sang, "You are my sunshine." Cleesy picked up a word now and again, sounding along with her. Passing a farm of tall, tended pines, she pointed, and her daughter bent to see splotches of dogwood blooming at the edge of the tree line. Entering the farm, Allise drove to the equipment shed.

Sam left a hired hand to change the plow point and ambled over. "Allie, I need to say that being my partner was jes—"

"I will, Sam. I'll be your partner."

Jerking Daddy Joe's old hat off, he slapped it against his thigh. "Hot damn!" Laughing, she handed him a basket of sandwiches.

With a few parting words, Sam waved over his shoulder and turned back to the shed. Allise started the car forward and seeing the distant pecan grove, she shouted at him, "Sam, tell Jonas I want to bring the kids out to gather pecans in the fall."

"I'll tell him not to sell all of 'em before you get out here." Holding up the basket, he shouted, "Thanks."

While Allise found new meaning to her life, war news consumed her husband. She was at a loss for a way to be with him. Quent kept any thoughts about what he might do if the country went to war to himself. She lived in a state of fear. Reports from Europe were both heartening and unsettling. Near the end of May, British forces were rescued at Dunkirk. Germany, Italy, and Japan signed a mili-tary-economic pact, and Italy declared war on France. By mid-month, the Germans had entered Paris. Congress passed the Selective Service Act in August and American forces began to mobilize.

Allise tried to allay her fears in devotion to the children and learning about the farm. She had come to appreciate Elfreeda's southern treatment of vegetables. Gathering from Jonas' patches gave her an excuse to be with Maizee. Each time she saw her, the young woman made clear she wasn't ready to give any more than was asked of her. Curious about Nate's light skin and his relationship to the Col-sons, she sought a way to break the black girl's reluctance to accept her friendship.

One day when they worked side-by-side in the patch, Nate and Cleesy played hide-and-seek among the vegetable rows. Cleesy counted "one, two, ten." Both women laughed. Allise took Maizee's amusement as a hopeful sign. Observing her frailty, she thought she had Jonas' endurance and Rebekah's quick movements and snappy eyes. Allise waited for an appropriate opening, but time passed without a break in her shell.

At home, she plopped the basket of vegetables down on the kitchen floor. "Elfreeda, tell me about Nate. Is Maizee that child's mother? Since Rebekah's funeral—"

"Didn't you know Nate's her kid?" Elfreeda seemed surprised but offered nothing more, and Allise let the subject drop. Curiosity nagged her, yet she feared what she might learn about the light complexioned boy with the unusual eyes.

In November, still no headway was made with Maizee when Jonas sent word by Sam that the pecans were dropping. On Saturday, Allise drove the new Buick to the farm and parked on the tenant lane. Walking across the field toward the grove, she saw Maizee and Nate beneath the trees. She greeted them. "I thought you would be in town."

"Yes'm." Maizee held a burlap sack open for Nate to drop nuts. When he ran off to play with Cleesy, she paused often to glance in their direction.

Allise looked up. Peter engaged Nate in a stare-off. She recalled her son's gripe about a boy staring through the fence. Now, he held his ground. Soon, Nate gave up the stare and stood, hands in pockets, scuffing his shoe into leaves caught in the grass. She turned to Maizee. "Every year, I've missed gathering nuts for holiday baking." Then, she called, "Come, kids! Let's see who can fill their sacks first." Cleesy tossed a handful into her mother's pail. Nate grabbed a bulging burlap sack, and Peter said that wasn't fair.

As if to distract from the task and show his agility, Peter turned a few less-than-perfect handsprings. Nate dropped the sack, tried a handspring and flopped belly-down. Jumping up, both boys ran away laughing, and Maizee gig-gled.at their childish capers.

"Isn't that just like kids?" Allise smiled. "The boys are having fun."

"Uh-huh," she agreed.

Now seemed the time to challenge her trust. "Maizee, does Nate go to school?"

"Nome. Ain't no school. I'd sho like 'im t' go. Don't seem no way, though. I'm teaching him t' write ABCs, and he can read some from old books I learnt on."

"I miss teaching." Allise dropped pecans into the pail and looked thoughtful. "What if I came several times a week to work with Nate? For that matter, with all the farm children around here? What if we opened a school in the empty tenant house?" Her excitement swelled. "Do you think they would come?"

Her enthusiasm pulled Maizee along. "Would you do that, Miz Allie? I'll see if some of 'um can come. Can I help? Kids might feel better if I help."

Saying she could help, it occurred to Allise that Maizee may want learning for herself as well as Nate. She went straight to Sam about the vacant Spinner house. He said the tenants use it for worship, but it could be a school just like the burned church had been.

Allise was elated, and before Quent engaged the radio that evening, she told him about her plans. "I shall go to the school board for books and supplies."

"I don't like it," he said. "It'll be a waste of time. Nigras never will amount to a hill of beans no matter what you do."

"Quent, I can *teach* and they *will* learn. Blacks are wasted resources simply because they aren't educated—"

"Resources! They know nothing but farming." Lowering his voice, he said, "We need 'um to farm, Allie. Lookey, those who left farming are outta work and on relief. Farmers cain't do without their labor."

"But one day tractors will replace them. Sam read about a mechanical cotton picker. Heavens, if a machine can pick cotton, what's next?" He didn't answer, and she conceded. "You're right, Quent. They can't find work and are on relief because they aren't schooled or trained for jobs. More will be on relief when there's no work on farms."

"Why do you care, Allie?" His stare was like blue ice.

"They're human. That is sufficient reason." She hissed like air escaping a balloon. Neither spoke, then, "Quent, would you let them go hungry, or steal and rob to survive? Why not teach them to care for themselves? Educate them so they can contribute to the entire country."

With diamond-like hardness, he said, "Educate 'um and they won't farm."

He was unmovable, but Allise was adamant. "Farmers with machines won't need Negroes." She groped for an analogy. "If our children were denied an education and forced to depend on us, how would you feel? Worse, how would they feel about themselves?"

"Think what you will, but educated Nigras will be nothing but trouble. Never have been anything but trouble anyway. Like kids, can't make it without us taking care of 'um."

"I thought I said that. They're dependent because they are forced to be. Dependent people require care from some source. They own no property and have nothing to pass on to their children. Count on it, farmers will abandon them when machinery does the work." She was determined. "Remarks such as: 'Niggers have no mental capacity,' 'The more they're degraded, the more they act the buffoons they're thought to be,' or 'They're machines created for use by the white race.' Thinking or saying such is disgusting."

Quent said nothing more, but having the last word wasn't satisfying for Allise. Until such attitudes stopped passing from one generation to the next, she couldn't rest.

Their conversation reminded her of John Dewey, a twentieth century educator and philosopher who differentiated between the living and nonliving. He said the nonliving went through life without knowledge of their aliveness, and the difference between the two states of being was the experience of need and satisfaction. She had studied Dewey's ideas at Swathmore, and her father had just sent his most recent work, *Logic: The Theory of Inquiry and Experience and Education*. His wisdom made her consider her own inaptitude. *So many questions, so many angles from which to view them.* We're constantly being shaped, and I don't have answers, she thought.

Thoughts ran tracks through Allise's head. Each time she challenged Quent, he dug his heels deeper. Their game of resistance meeting resistance was tiring. She felt as though she existed on an unknown plane, a misfit in her time being pushed by some inborn trait to learn and to teach. If I can't move him, I can teach our children to be tolerant, she thought.

Days later, Allise approached the school board. Their response to her request for assistance in teaching the black children begged the question: "You know, doncha, that you won't be paid by the board to teach those kids?"

"I don't expect compensation," she said. "Just a few books and supplies. However, I do have a question. Why aren't Negro children bussed into town to the colored school? Whites are bussed from the river and all around to the Deer Point school."

"Huh! Nigra kids aren't bussed from anywhere. Just isn't done. Never has been. They don't wanna go t' school."

The rebuff forced her to write to the American Friends Service Committee. She related her plans and requested a small number of books and supplies for grades first through the third. Some weeks later, the materials arrived and classes began for Nate and nine other youngsters on two mornings each week.

Her students showed up each class day through the summer. In a letter to her father, she wrote, "The school is a start for the black children." Planning lessons and meeting farm challenges energized Allise.

One night in August, fans whipped at the heat as Sam helped Allise clean up after dinner. He suggested a movie. *Grapes of Wrath* was showing at the Rialto. She came home full of hurt for the Joads. After seeing the children off to bed, she joined Sam at the kitchen table. "Well, Steinbeck's account of the Oklahoma family in California moved me," she said.

"Yeah." Propping elbows on the table, he rubbed his hands. "Shows what folks went through when they left their land. Allie, it's time t' think of hiring cotton pickers. When cotton's sold this fall, we need to ask Dro for that loan—"

Bang! The sudden noise came from the back porch. Quent rushed past them without a word, and they heard the radio. "Come listen, y'all!" he called. Allise and Sam walked to the doorway and stood listening to the announcer say one hundred and eighty German planes were shot down. Raising a fist, Quent shouted, "Damn! Did you hear that? A hundred and eighty. Kill them bastards! Kill every one of 'um!"

"We heard." Sam turned to Allise. "I don't wanna go another season without a tractor." He walked back to the kitchen, but she stood transfixed, absorbing the news and her husband's reaction. She groped her way back to the table, and Sam grabbed her arm.

Quent walked in behind her and stood glaring at his brother. "How can you talk about a damn tractor? Doesn't the war concern y'all?"

Silence deadened the room, then Sam whispered, "I'll talk t' ya later."

# CHAPTER 9

▼

Allise listened to Quent talk about the war. He said months of Nazi losses and the downing of the German planes lifted spirits despite setting off three months of all-night bombing raids on London. She feared his patriotic enthusiasm, but she didn't complain for he was home at night to hear the latest news. Pausing, he said, "Allie, let's ask Dro for dinner."

Surprised by his request, she agreed to have him on a night when Elfreeda could stay late and make the dinner. She said her knowledge of his friend was limited to seeing him at church and occasionally at the bank. Allise laughed and said, "I won't risk my culinary skills on someone I hardly know."

On the appointed evening, she fussed with table dressing when the doorbell rang. Quent ushered Dro into the living room. He held her extended hand as she invited him to sit. Over glasses of wine, they waited for Elfreeda to announce dinner, and Quent quickly moved the conversation to the war. "Britain managed to reopen the Burma Road, but German U-Boats are sinking more merchant and military ships. Dro, why do you suppose Americans are so much against entering the war?"

"It's an isolationist view. Anyway, the conflict is far from our shores."

"Well, I don't agree with Roosevelt on much, but I do think we ought to get into this war before the Germans bomb over here."

"Yeah, the president pushes for American support of the war. Many who voted him in for a third term may be disagreeing now. You have to give it to him. His 'fireside' chats make people feel good."

Allise contributed nothing to the conversation. Intent on listening, she admired Dro's studied view of how the country fit in the world conflict, and his shock of well-groomed white hair. Suddenly, she was aware of staring at him, and he stared back.

Elfreeda appeared in the doorway to invite them to the table. Quent stood and led the way into the dining room. Allise directed Dro to her husband's left, and she sat to his right. The meal provided a respite from war talk, but not for long. Back in the living room, Quent sounded ready to join the fight.

The evening of conversation was informative, but Allise took no pleasure in Quent's preoccupation with the war in Europe. He kept her unsettled, and one evening, he came home from the market with the farm ledger. Handing it to her, he said he was finished with farm finances and record-keeping. As far as she could tell, even after turning the farm operation over to Sam, he knew no peace of mind. *What was he up to?* Shaken, she guessed at his intentions.

The next day, Sam blasted through the door, beaming over profits from the cotton sale. "War's creating a demand for cotton products, and now I can buy that tractor. Will you go to the bank with me, Allie?" Nodding, she laid the ledger on the table and related what Quent had said. Sam appeared flush with relief. "Awright!" he whispered, smiling.

At the bank, they approached the door to Dro's Loan Office, and he stood and waved them in. Allise saw a rush of flustered pleasure surge across his face as he thrust a hand toward her and motioned them to leather-bound chairs. He stood until they were seated, and she sneaked glances at his hair. It made his eyes appear darker, she thought. Twinkles in those fields of blue hinted of flirtation. Embarrassed, she turned attention to the wall hangings. Studying each framed scene, she caught only parts of the conversation.

Sam asked her to review the papers. Glancing up from them, her eyes locked in Dro's gaze. Giving him a hesitant half smile, she toyed with the forgotten pleasure of flirting. Flustered, Allise resisted the temptation to let Dro play with her emotions.

When their business was completed, Sam stood and shook his hand.

In the parking lot, he leaned over the hood of his truck. He appeared crestfallen. "Dro's a charmer, Allie. His wife died two years ago and he's lonesome."

Allise nodded. He had seen the interaction between her and Dro. *He shouldn't worry. The distinguished-looking banker will remain nothing more than Quent's friend.*

Several days passed before Sam phoned to tell Allise the tractor had arrived. "Come on over, Allie. It's a beaut!" She and Cleesy walked to Filbert Street and found him waiting on the curb. The John Deere tractor was chained to the flat bed of a delivery truck.

She was thrilled for him but wondered what the machine would mean for the Colsons. *Would he still need Jonas?* If she knew Sam, he would.

Her concern for Quent was far graver than fretting over Jonas. War in Europe had grown more ominous and spilled onto the Asian and African continents with the German invasion of Russia and North Africa. Allise heard a dire radio pronouncement. "America may not be attacked, but young Americans might be sent overseas to fight." Quent had given her reason enough to think he would enlist.

On a Sunday morning in December, Brother Rigdon was about to finish his sermon when the sanctuary door flew open. The choir dropped the invitational hymn in mid-note, and everyone turned toward the commotion. Gunther Hill stood in the center aisle, coatless despite the seasonal chill and clearly shaken. "We've been attacked, y'all!" His words were incomprehensible, and he yelled again. "I said we been attacked! Some place called Pearl Harbor. It's on the radio. Japanese bombed this morning. Bombed Hi-waii."

No one moved or made a sound. Allise heard the deathly silence lift in a wave of mumbles. Quent stepped into the aisle, and other men followed in Gunther's direction. In the surreal motion of a slowed movie reel, others left the pews, whispering among themselves.

Stunned and immobile, Allise remained in place. Looking about, she noticed Brother Rigdon still stood like a wax figure beside the pulpit. His usual dark complexion was ashen. He appeared incapable of controlling the situation and no longer fit her image of an eccentric old man couched within a body of intimidating size.

Fearing for him, she rushed up to the pulpit. "No no, I'm okay," he mumbled, and took a step or two holding onto her arm. "The news is alarming." He stopped to look about the empty church, then together they walked through the door.

Leaving him in a cluster of parishioners, Allise joined Quent and Sam on the sidewalk and heard someone say, "It's unbelievable! Must be a mistake."

"Probably not a mistake," Quent said. "Been coming for a long time."

Slowly, people drifted down the sidewalk toward their homes or cars. The DeWitts climbed into the Buick, still shiny in its newness, and rode home in tomb-like quietness.

In the garage, Quent jumped from the car and rushed past Allise. He listened to the radio while she prepared dinner in the kitchen. She could hear little of the broken and confused descriptions of the Japanese attack.

Peter must have sensed something dire had occurred. "Mother, where is Pearl Harbor anyway?"

"In the Hawaiian Islands way off in the Pacific Ocean." Allise wanted to cry.

Next day, before going to the market, she listened to President Roosevelt and the British prime minister declare war on Japan, and sensed the world was about to be changed in a drastic way. On the street, Allise halfway expected the town to be turned topsy-turvy, but she had a vague awareness of everything being upright. People went about their business as usual, from post office to courthouse, to market, and Robbins Dry Goods Store. She was greeted with astonishment that such a crazy act was perpetrated against the country, and an apparent yearning for the confusion to just go away.

Leaving the market in a headlong rush, she looked up and was nose to nose with Dro McClure. Both stopped and diddled in awkward movements from side to side as though trying to avoid contact. With "Good mornings" they settled at a comfortable distance from each other, and he asked, "How could such a thing happen, Allie? Our Navy's wiped out. Just like that!" He snapped his fingers. "Oceans on both sides, but we can't feel safe anymore. Our boys will have to fight. You know, the military draft was re-instituted months ago."

Towering above her, his words drifted down into her pool of dread, and she guessed he tried to make sense of the recent events and bring a reality to something so utterly unreal. She looked up into the square set of his jaw and read anxiety etched there. Collecting her wits, Allise searched across the pattern of his words as he fumbled with a red striped necktie, pulling at the knot and drawing it tighter around his neck.

The word "draft" stuck in her mind. In a contemplative manner, she mumbled, "At this point, I don't know how sane it is to think that some good is meant to come of this." Troubled eyes, greened by her cardigan, looked up into his. She wondered if she made sense. Somehow, questioning herself verified her sanity.

Silence between them thickened. She stared at the tall handsome man, and he gazed down at her with that mysterious glint. It intrigued her. *Did he know more about her than she wanted him to know?* Disengaging her eyes, she pushed long strands of hair from her face and dismissed him. *I don't care a whit about what Dro McClure is thinking.* However, with stillness stretching between them, she felt compelled to explain her effort to rationalize. "I was brought up to hate war, Dro. To detest man's inhumanity but we were assailed and can't just turn the other cheek." Her usual Yankee clip slowed, giving way to thought. From some corner of her mind came the shady madness of war. "Why are we pushed to the edge before we try to stop a thing from happening? What drives us to war?" She spoke as though demanding answers. When he had none, she felt so alone. A single tear trickled down her cheek. Confused and embarrassed, Allise turned to leave.

Dro's face saddened. He reached out, as if to draw her into his arms, but pulling back, he took a white handkerchief from his breast pocket. "Oh, Allie"

"Oh, Allie! Is that all anyone can say?" Sagging in defeat, he held out the hankie in a limp offer.

"I-I'm sorry, Dro." She accepted and uttered behind it, "So sorry." Ashamed that her ugly side was seen, she wiped her eyes.

"Everyone's worried," he said. "Worried about who's going away to fight. Lots of men. Why Quent and I might have to go. Apt to be drafted."

He struck the chord of her grave concern. "Quent's going to volunteer." Allise confirmed the statement he had made only the night before. "He itches to become a warrior." She glanced up at Dro's stunned look. "Yes, he said the Marine Corps. Sam said he should be the one to go, since he's younger. He said Quent could be exempt because he has a family, b-but he—" A nervous sound, closer to despair than a laugh, caught in her throat. "My husband's eager to go to war."

"Now, Allie, I don't know about the Marines. The Corps has restrictions. Quent and I, we're on the older side. Anyway, he's just talking. I wouldn't be concerned."

"I would say it's a foregone conclusion. He'll manage some way, come heck or high water." All the resentment for Quent's cavalier attitude was stored within her brassy tone. "How can he leave the children and me?" The question dogged her.

Dro attempted to console Allise, but she dismissed it with a wave of her hand. "Quent wonders how he can locate a recruiting office."

"I think the postmaster might have that information."

"Well, you tell him, Dro. I can't bring myself to be a part of his plan." For a moment, peering up at him, she felt hollow, as though some deep cavity of hurt was emptied out in anger. Remembering her husband's disregard for her opinions, she said, "Dro, if I resist Quent, I won't win. No one wins in a war, do they?"

Leaving him, she felt there was nothing to do but prepare to accept the inevitable.

Allise moved through a fog as the reality of conflict gradually sunk in and each day brought more disturbing events. Disbelief, confusion and yearning for it to go away turned to fear, then to determination. The difficulty of comprehending a future in a world so suddenly gone crazy was something she must deal with.

Upcoming was the most holy celebration of the Christian world, and it mustn't be ruined for her children, even if their father was determined to go to war.

She mustered all the normalcy possible around the holidays. The first day of the new year came and went, and two days later, a cold rain turned first to snow, then overnight to ice. Allise awoke to nature's breathtaking beauty. It was a rare Arkansas occurrence not experienced in her years in Deer Point. Sunlight blinked from tree limbs. Long, sharp prisms clung to the eaves of the house, and the lawn sparkled as a field of jagged grass blades. For a moment, she relived winters in Pennsylvania.

After lunch, she helped Cleesy into her mittens, coat, and cap. Peter grabbed a bag of breadcrumbs, and Allise held their hands as they crept out onto the icy surface. Precarious slips and slides brought squeals of laughter until they stood in front of the garage shielded from the January cold.

Blue jays, crested cardinals, and gray snow birds scurried for a share of the crumbs. Each time Peter raised his arm to throw more, the birds took flight, and Cleesy giggled.

Allise pointed to a strong, far-reaching limb halfway up the oak tree. "Look up, Peter. See the ice crystal, how it catches the light?"

"It's winking at me!" he shrieked. "Look, Cleesy! Look up there." Shading her eyes with a mittened hand, Cleesy squinted at the brightness, but the birds fascinated her. When the last crumbs were shaken out, she shoo-ed them away.

Allise crouched down to her level. "Someday you'll see Grandmom Weston's crystal chandelier. It hangs from her dining room ceiling, and when the light is on, it looks like this. When I was your age, I thought the prisms were like teardrops. The most beautiful things I had ever seen. But, you know something, this is much prettier."

"When are we going to see Grandmom and Grandpop?" Peter asked.

"Someday," she said. "Listen! Did you hear something?" Peter pushed his red knit cap above his ear. Another loud pop from the front lawn made them jump. A redbud tree, burdened by age and a coat of ice, broke at the trunk. Allise assured them the rifle-like explosion was nothing to fear. "Before that sound startled us, I was thinking of the stillness that settles over a winter scene. Do you hear the stillness? Next time it snows, we'll listen to the falling flakes. It will sound like a world at peace."

Then, a war cloud overshadowed her moments of peace. Pushing it away, she told them about ice skating on a frozen lake near Philadelphia and tobogganing downhill at Swarthmore College. Cleesy wasn't captivated by her stories. The birds flew away at the sound of the loud crack as a redbud tree gave under its ice burden. The three-year-old rubbed her eyes and tugged her mother's hand.

Peter skated on his shoe soles down the frozen driveway some distance before landing with a thud on his backside. Cleesy broke into a cackle and tried to pull away, but Allise wouldn't release her to try the same antic. She led them back indoors.

Exhilarated by the fresh air, she sat at the desk making notes and wondering if there was a lesson in the storm for her farm students. *Can they relate their experiences of the winter wonderland?* It took a few thoughtful minutes to work up a plan, then she sat back, watching the children play with their Christmas toys.

Soon, the thaw dried enough for students to walk the dirt paths to classes. Maizee had a roaring fire in the cast iron heater when Allise arrived with Cleesy. The women moved the rickety old dining table, used as a common desk, and chairs closer to the heat source. Then, while Allise collected supplies, Maizee tried to quiet ten, unruly pupils.

Once settled, their teacher handed out paper and crayons and reminded them of the storm's pristine beauty. She told of tossing crumbs to colorful birds, of the tree breaking with an explosive crack, and bright sun making Cleesy squint. "Now, I want you to draw and color a scene you remember from one of the days when everything was coated with ice. Did you see something beautiful? Maybe you heard a sound. We heard the tree crack." On a tablet, she sketched a tree and printed the word 'POW!' above it.

Holding it up for them to see, she said, "Think about smells. Did the air smell fresh? Did you touch an icicle and taste it? Do you understand what you are to do?" There were no indications otherwise. "When finished, you can show and tell what you created."

The classroom quieted. Only Cleesy's scratching across her paper with a red crayon was heard. In the light from a kerosene lamp, Allise admired her small daughter. The child swung leather-bound feet between the legs of her makeshift highchair, an open-sided box screwed to the top of a four-legged stool. In a red sweater and corduroy jumper, she was the only bright note in an otherwise drab room.

A glance at Nate revealed Peter's handed-down clothing. He was first to finish the assignment, showing a diligence that pleased her. Fearing boredom might discourage him, she whispered he should practice writing the alphabet while waiting.

When most of the other students had completed the work, she called on Nate. As she had taught them, he stood and held his paper for all to see. Gray clouds were sketched over a box-like house. Smoke curled over the roof from a stovepipe. Pointing to the house, Nate said, "I live here." Below the house, he had drawn a horizontal line with vertical ones dropping from each end. A round shape rested on the horizontal line. He said the bottom picture represented a water table and bucket in the kitchen. "I tried to wash my hands, but water in the bucket was ice. Momma heated it on the cookstove. It was too cold t' go outside. Slick, too. She said I might fall and break a leg."

His classmates laughed. Apparently their images of Nate falling were funny.

With arms resting across her bosom, Maizee stood back from the students and listened. Alllise saw unadulterated pride in her face. Nate glanced at his mother and continued. "We stayed close t' the fire t' stay warm. The ice was pretty, but it hurt my eyes, too. Oh, and I smelled bacon frying. That's all," he said, handing his paper to Allise.

Other students showed fields of vertical lines with swirls of brown at the top. They said their pictures showed dead cotton stalks. Some drew bare trees. Allise praised their efforts. "It's hard to see details when the world is all white, but we should look for beauty even when we think it's not there," she encouraged them and took up the object of her lesson. Holding up five fingers, she reminded them of their natural senses. "Nate, did you feel the cold bucket? Did you hear bacon sizzling in the skillet?"

"Yes'm. I heard the bacon frying, and the bucket sho was cold."

"Nate, when you say 'sho' what is the word you mean?" He answered, "Sure," and Allise said, "Good. Now, all of you drew something you *saw*. You used your eyes." She said Nate saw the water shelf and bucket. What else did he sense?" She waited.

"I felt that cold bucket and the warm water Momma made for my hands," he said.

"Yes, Nate used his eyes and his sense of *touch* to feel cold and warm. His nose and ears picked up the odor and sound of frying bacon. Did you taste it?"

"Yes'm. We ate it."

"All right, then. You used all five of your senses. She named them, "Taste, touch, smell, hear and see," while touching her mouth, hand, nose, ear, and eye. "We learn about things around us through our five senses. Now think a minute before answering this. If we hear nothing, are we hearing *something*? If there's silence, do we hear it?"

The students shook their heads from side to side, but Maizee spoke from the back of the room. "I guess when you don't hear something, you be hearing nothing."

"That's right, Miss Maizee!" Allise cupped her hand behind her ear. "Everyone, sit perfectly still. Listen. What do you hear?"

"Nothing" came the students' answer, but she assured them Maizee was right. "Our ears sense no sound as silence. Do you hear it?"

"Yes'um!"

She suggested they listen for silence during the next snowfall. "I love the quiet of falling snowflakes. It seems the whole world stands still, awaiting its beauty." Her voice dropped quieter and quieter. "Close your eyes, use your imaginations and see the snow drifting down, covering everything in a pure white blanket. Hear the peacefulness." The room fell quiet enough to hear a snowflake drop. Allise allowed mind pictures to run their course, then dismissing the students, she hoped she had sparked a bit of thought.

Making a mental note to give Nate extra work, she wondered how to challenge him.

Little thought was given to his challenge for anxiety dwelled just beyond the daily demands for Allise's attention. Chants of "Remember Pearl Harbor" fed American patriotism, spurring citizens to gear-up and wage battle. Deer Point had no industrial plants to retool for warfare, so families moved to the cities where jobs were plentiful and the pay was good. Allise witnessed the pride of townsfolk in offering up their boys to enlist or be drafted and sent off to train for the fight.

*If Quent leaves, what will I do?* Already, he had asked Norman Grady, a long-time butcher in the market, to oversee the operation. "You do the farm accounts and can handle market accounts without difficulty," he had told Allise. *Can I?* Allise sat at the kitchen table with Sam, trying to be attentive to his minor farm problems when Quent called from the living room. Walking to the desk, she laid a hand on his shoulder, and he covered it with his. "I want you and the kids to go with him to Little Rock on Friday." The address of the Marine Recruiting Station lay there for her to see. Her chest felt ready to explode. She had struggled with the build-up to this moment, always stopping short of imagining its actuality.

"We'll stay overnight and see the state capitol. It won't hurt for Peter to miss a day of school." He turned pleading eyes up to her.

It had been a long time since he had needed her. Allise nodded consent.

Sam yelled from the kitchen. "I'll see y'all later."

Quent stood and motioned her to the sofa. Putting an arm behind her, he rubbed a bit of her sleeve fabric between his fingers. She said they would enjoy seeing the capitol. He pulled her closer, and while welcoming the affection, Allise tried to find some meaning in what was taking place. Something not so dreadful as what she was thinking.

He smiled down at her. "You're beautiful, you know. Eyes, it's always been your eyes. This color turns 'em blue. Sometimes, that old sweater makes 'em green. Bet you think I don't notice. I love you, Allie. You've gotta know that." He sighed.

She raised his hand to her lips. Mustn't cry, she thought.

He drew in a deep breath and exhaled. "This volunteer thing, honey it's something I hafta do. Don't understand it myself. Just know I hafta go if they'll have me."

Pulling back, she gazed into his pale face. Hasn't been sun-touched in ages, she thought, feeling him sag deeper into the cushions as if releasing an imposed curse. Wiping a tear with her hand, she no longer cared if he saw crying. As unsure of her future as she was, he needed her now. Needed her to understand. Clearing the lump in her throat, she whispered, "I know. Sometimes, I think I've accepted that you may go away, b-but it's difficult."

"You're a strong person, Allie. Very strong."

Strength wasn't what she felt, but she understood Quent suffered, too, in his own way. They sat there, holding each other.

Early Friday morning, Quent backed the Buick down the driveway. Smiling out the window, he yelled to Sam, who stood at the curb beside his truck, "See you later, bud." Allise turned to watch Peter and Cleesy wave to Uncle Sam through the rear window.

Ten-year-old Peter, so much like his father it made her heart heavy, wore a bright blue shirt. It made his light, blue eyes darker. At the end of winter, his corduroy knickers were shucked for long trousers. He was the more docile of their two children. Cleesy dares the world, Allise thought. *She's cute as a porcelain doll. My hair. Grandmother DeWitt's piercing blue eyes. Have I made her too fancy in that lace-trimmed dress?*

They had traveled some distance north of Deer Point when the gravel road became a paved highway. She and the children counted cattle grazing in pastures and sang songs until Quent turned on the radio. He called their attention to a woman churning for butter on her front porch. On beyond, he pointed to the west. "The only diamond mine in the United States is near Murfreesboro. We'll go there someday."

Allise wanted their lives to hold such adventures, but she had misgivings about their future.

Before they reached the Little Rock hotel, Cleesy had fallen asleep on her lap. Peter hopped out on the sidewalk and peered up at the tall marble-faced building. Quent settled them in a large, high-ceilinged room on the fifth floor, ordered two roll-away beds and dashed off to the recruiting station. Allise laid a veiled hat, handbag and gloves on the chest of drawers and lined shoes in a closet. Curling next to Cleesy on the bed, she watched Peter stare down from the window at traffic crossing the Arkansas River bridge. This is how it's going to be, she thought. *Just us. Oh God, let him be rejected. No, he would be despondent. I must love with all my heart and let him go. I must be strong.*

Hours later in the hotel dining room, Quent ordered their meals and waited for the waiter to leave. "Well, you wanna hear what happened this afternoon?"

"Yeah, Daddy!" Peter said, and his sister mimicked him.

He smiled at Allise, as though expecting her to show the same enthusiasm. Nodding, she returned a weak smile. "I think I'll be a United States marine soon," he said.

"What's a marine, Daddy?"

"A soldier, son. Fights for his country." Grinning, he turned to Allise again. "There's this program, if completed you come out a 'ninety-day wonder.' A second lieutenant! Why, I may even be an aviator! What y' think of that?"

He looked as if begging for equal excitement, but Allise, unable to bring up the expected emotion, cut Cleesy's meat. "Yes, go on," she said.

'After Pearl Harbor, the Marine Corps lifted its age and marriage restrictions."

"Dear God." Allise muttered, hearing more enlistment reality than rejection.

Quent said the volunteers had medical examinations. "Doctors found nothing wrong with me. Said age and being married were obstacles to pilot training." Pausing for her reaction and hearing none, he said, "Someone suggested I ask our congressmen to send recommendation letters for officer's candidate school. My college degree is an advantage."

"But you're not sure of anything now. What's next? When will we know?"

He had two weeks to put affairs in order and report back. "I'm likely to go in as a non-commissioned person. A corporal. Those west of the Mississippi River usually go to California for boot camp. I'll know soon."

That night, Allise listened to his deep breathing. How would she live without him? California was so far away. Unable to sleep, she slipped from bed and sat looking out the window at North Little Rock lights across the river. How could she support him when she felt just the opposite? *Friends will want to say goodbye. That's it. A farewell party.* Pulling knees under her chin, she began a mental guest list.

Less than a week later, Quent was notified of his acceptance into the Marine Corps. Allise began preparations for a party, telling him it was to be the children's Easter picnic and egg hunt. For the first time in her life, she didn't look forward to the special, religious holiday, but party preparations helped keep his departure a distant thought.

Easter Sunday made a splendid entrance. Sunlight fell on yellow jonquils, purple hyacinths, and irises along the driveway. A lilac bush would soon droop clusters of dark lavender, and the latticework trellis of Wisteria showed pale purplish blooms. Arkansas spring floated on the air on the drive from the Easter service. Allise took in the beauty, and leaving the car, she sniffed the fragrances.

Sam and Maydale rolled in behind the Buick as Elfreeda whipped a white damask cloth over planks spanning between sawhorses under two large oaks. Inside, Allise and Maydale doffed hats, gloves, and handbags and returned with bowls of chilled punch and lemonade for each end of the makeshift table. Bringing a vase of flowers, Allise stopped to ask Elfreeda if she thought Quent was happy. "Uh-huh. He change quick though, don't he? Awways that way. Miz Bernice had a time with 'im." She shook her head.

Allise put a vase of trumpet honeysuckle on the small dessert table and admired baskets heaped with dyed eggs. Henmann's Bakery had made the white-frosted cakes topped with shredded coconut nests filled with Jelly Beans. Placing her Brownie camera on the table, she listened to sounds of a kick-ball game on the front lawn.

Maydale brought purple iris and yellow jonquil to the long table and stood with Allise, watching the guests arrive. Two couples were invited because they were new in town. She greeted each one, then directed them to punch being served by Maydale. When everyone arrived and stood about visiting, she and Elfreeda brought out platters of fried chicken, Old Tate's barbecued beef, sliced ham, deviled eggs, potato and green pea salads, coleslaw, and trays of condiments. Lastly, Elfreeda came with baskets of fresh-baked rolls and butter.

After Brother Rigdon offered grace, Allise invited everyone to the table, then she stood aside, watching them serve themselves and find a place to sit. Serving her plate, she looked about for the two new couples. She wanted them to feel welcomed.

Earlier, Quent had laughed when he saw Brother Rigdon speaking with them. "He tries to convert everyone but Nigras." Allise thought her husband wasn't too serious about his religion. She suspected his mother had insisted on him and Sam attending church.

Glancing toward the children, she thought Cleesy would get grass stain on her dress. Then her attention was drawn to Dro. He stood with plate and fork in hand as if to go for more food. Above the hum of conversations, she heard him say, "Only Quent would consider volunteering. What got into you anyway, old buddy?" Laughter rippled across the lawn.

Quent paid him a roguish smile. "I guess to get away from the likes of you."

Allise paused behind Eldon Howard. His words drifted up to her. "If you ask me, he didn't have better sense than to volunteer." His chuckle reeked of smugness, and Mildred nodded. "Always was wild," he said. "His mama and daddy had a time with 'im. Tried t' git my brother and me t' go to the Willow Fork Honky-Tonk with him and Dro. They got drunk on moonshine and came ripping back into town raising all kindsa Cain. My folks woulda killed me. Now Sam, he never was wild like that."

The Rigdons shook their heads as though Quent's youthful indiscretions doomed him to hell. Allise wanted to explain her husband's love of country, but defensiveness might spoil the party. Looking across the yard, she spotted Maydale and Sam. Seeing his gaze fixed on her, a wan smile flickered across Allise's lips, and she thought, dear Sam.

Most of the guests had finished eating and stood talking among themselves. Allise ate quickly when Elfreeda came to her. "Miz Allie, y' think ever'body's done? Can I start clearing the table? Chil'ren begging t' hunt eggs. You see to them, and I'll get the food."

Before she could answer, Mildred shoved soiled plates at Elfreeda. Without a glance at her, the black woman took them to the trash container. Mildred arched an eyebrow at Allise and scoffed in Elfreeda's direction. "They do have to earn their money, don't they?"

She recoiled, knowing Mildred's vindictiveness was meant for her. Just then, Sam took her arm. "Excuse us, Mildred, we hafta take down tables." Steering Allise away, he murmured, "Don't waste your breath on her."

"Elfreeda, can you forgive—"

"Yes'm, I can," she said, glancing up. "Been doing it all my life." Allise heard the echo of generations of giving in and saw decades of hurt in her friend's dark eyes. Unable to bear Elfreeda's scrutiny, Allise cast herself in the same pit of do-nothing humanity as those she criticized. Masking her guilt, she asked if Reverend James had come to eat. Assured he ate in the kitchen, she said they should clear the tables and get on with the hunt.

Fifteen restless children waited behind her, but Allise called for attention. Peter moaned, and the kids giggled and nudged each other with baskets. Ignoring them, she said, "Thank you for coming. Quent will be surprised to know this party is for him, too. As you know, he leaves soon to serve in the Marine Corps. Most of you hold special places in his life, share special memories with him. Today, we honor him for what he's about to do and offer an opportunity for you to bid him farewell. I wish we could have had all of Deer Point here, for only in a small town are lives so closely entwined that each citizen is ..." Close to tears, she struggled to carry on. "What I mean is, when one person goes away, the community seems to ... When you leave, Quent, our lives will be lacking."

Embarrassed by her sentiments, he avoided the eyes of those watching. Allise swiped her eyes, and parents shuffled uneasily as the children scattered over the lawn. Delighted squeals punctuated the discovery of eggs. Little Bobby Tilletson smashed one underfoot, leaving one white shoe smudged green. His sobs were loud.

Allise shaded her eyes and watched his mother appease the distraught child when Quent ambled over. He planted a kiss on her forehead and mumbled in her hair, "It's been fun, but if you had asked me, I wouldn't have wanted all this attention."

"I know, darling, but it will be a wonderful memory when you're far away." He answered with another kiss on top of her head.

Children straggled back with baskets of eggs. Allise took a group picture of them and a snapshot of Cleesy presenting a stuffed bunny to Margaret Winslow, who found the most eggs. She took pictures of guests leaving Quent with handshakes and parting words. Dro lingered to the last, and she snapped the shutter just as he shoved a hand toward her husband. "I ought to know you well enough to understand why—"

"Don't trouble yourself, Dro. Just tell Allie here how much you enjoyed her party and be off with you. I'll see you before I leave."

# CHAPTER 10

▼

Robot-like, Allise dressed Cleesy and brushed her hair, giving automated responses to the child's chatter. Dismissing her, she stood before the open closet, pulling out frocks. Holding up each one, she chose a Kelly green shirtwaist and belted it with a green and white-striped scarf. Brushing shoulder-length hair into a page boy style, she swept bangs across her forehead and gave a final glimpse in the mirror. It revealed an unhappy face, one she didn't want Quent to take away and remember. Staring at the image, she tried to smile.

At the Bensburg station, he secured a ticket minutes before the train was due to depart. Out on the station apron, Peter lagged behind. His mother waited, caught his hand, and together they walked up to Quent. He dropped his bag, scooped up Cleesy, and pressed her head to his shoulder. She threw tiny arms about his neck, then struggling, demanded that he put her down. He released the child. Allise clutched her handbag underarm and covered her face in her hands.

"It's all right, Allie." Tears streaked Peter's face, and his father said, "Come here, son." Two fingers hanging from Peter's mouth couldn't contain the aching sound escaping from him. Quent crouched and placed his hands on the child's shoulders. Looking into his eyes as though wishing to stamp out the fear seen there, he said, "Son, will you help Uncle Sam take care of your mother and sister?"

Flinching at the request, Allise sensed it was her husband's way of pushing at pain.

Peter nodded as his body jerked with uncontrollable sobs. Nose secretions ran across his mouth and dripped from his chin. Quent struggled with the sad, awkward situation. Pulling a white handkerchief from his back pocket, he wiped his son's face and placed it in Peter's hand. "Here, keep this." Taking him in his arms, he clamped his eyes shut as if to hold an image there forever.

A burst of steam shot from beneath the locomotive and dissipated in the air as the conductor called, "All aboard!" Quent pulled them into a last embrace, and Allise felt her heart would burst. "I love y'all." He released them, grabbed up his bag and without looking back, stepped up into the train. It inched away from the station, away from them.

He leaned from an open window, and Allise waved as long as he could be seen. Then, she pulled the children close, trying to laugh through tears until her voice came. "Daddy will call tonight," she said. "He is going to Little Rock where we went recently. Think about what you will tell him when he calls."

Cleesy seemed to react more to her brother's unhappiness than to her father's leave-taking, and Peter was more distraught than Allise had expected. Feeling limp as a rag, she took their hands and started back through the station. She threaded their way between benches of drab-clad young men staring through vacant eyes or sleeping on duffel bags. Some stood about the waiting room, blowing cigarette smoke.

The experience had exhausted the children, and on the way home, they slept on the back seat. The Buick clipped off the miles without Allise's awareness. Never having seen a marine, she tried to imagine Quent in a uniform, but she couldn't dispel the image waving from the train. How will I get through the night? she wondered.

Allise walked into a house that felt hollow of life. She took up neglected tasks, stopping often to check the clock, tallying two hours, then three since Quent's train departed.

Already time was her enemy, and the children's ill-tempers wore on her. She rang the neighbors, and asked if playmates could come over. Peter set up lawn croquet, located a sack of marbles and helped Cleesy round up other toys. Soon relief came in peals of laughter from carefree children.

When their friends had left that evening, Cleesy sang in the bathtub, and Peter played in the living room. Allise stared at the bedroom clock, allowing a few more minutes of play before lifting her daughter and toweling her off. The phone rang just as she gave an impatient tug on pajamas clinging to Cleesy's clammy body.

Heart pounding, she raced downstairs and jerked up the receiver. "Oh Quent!" she said. "Time seemed like an eternity, darling."

"Hi, honey." He apologized for being later than intended, saying he was among fifteen other sworn marines just back at the YMCA for the night's stay.

They had run here and there all day, and a more thorough medical exam again found him in good health. After a long pause, his near-inaudible words came: "Honey, I catch a train for Camp Pendleton, California, early in the morning."

Allise felt her breath snatched away. Quent's alarm was heard over the phone. "Allie! Are you there?" She swallowed hard and asked if Peter and Cleesy, waiting beside her, could speak with him. Brushing a hand across her eyes, she glimpsed Peter climbing upon the Hitchcock chair, a wedding gift her parents had shipped from Philadelphia. Her mind wanted to stay with that happy occasion but Quent's words interfered.

On his knees, Peter leaned into the long-necked phone. "I miss you, too, Daddy. When are you coming home?" Allise watched his expression fade from an afternoon of fun to sadness, but he responded softly to his father's voice.

Scrubbed to a shine, Cleesy wrapped around her mother's legs. "My turn! My turn!" She squinted deep blue eyes up at Allise, who shushed her with a finger to her lips.

Peter yielded the earpiece and left the chair to his sister. Cleesy listened, uttered "uh-huhs" and sometimes nodded. "Bye bye, Daddy." She gave the receiver to Allise and ran off with a bedtime story book in her hand.

"They're tired," Allise said, explaining their afternoon of play.

Quent said he was glad they had a good day, and asked that she tell them how brave he was when faced with so many needles in his arms. "I know how they hate typhoid shots. Tell 'um they will have to be brave, too." Was he dancing around their pain, she wondered, then she heard, "Hey, honey, I miss y'all. It hurts, but it will hurt more if our country is overrun and I don't do anything t' prevent it. I love you."

She heard the choke in his throat. "I know, darling. I hurt, too, and love you more than … I must be here for our children, else I wonder if I could bear it." His words were like sweet caresses, caresses she had needed on too many lonely nights. She wanted to scream at that loss, and yet if she could reach for him, touch him, listen to him forever, but metal wires and faraway stood between them.

He whispered, "I have to go now." Then, in a stronger voice, "Boys are lined up behind me waiting t' call home. I'll call from California. These fellows … Being older, I'm more like their pappy. Some have heard about boot camp. They say there isn't time for anything but training. Be patient, will you, honey?"

She grumbled, "I'll try, but California sounds like the end of the earth, Quent." Allise hung up and sat down on the stair step. With his endearments and betrayed emotions lingering in her thoughts, she tried to settle on the idea of faraway. When it had played to an end, the dull, ache of loneliness filled her being.

In the days that followed, Allise moved through time with a disconnect between mind and body. Her reason for existence, the center of her life had escaped, leaving the shell of a person she saw in the mirror. Clouded, lifeless eyes stared back at a pale, drawn face not unlike Quent's moody one. "You won't go into depression," she lectured the image. "You will not fall apart today."

Many mornings began with the ritual before the mirror, opening her days with a determination to deal with her lot. Nights brought a desperate desire to recreate her world. To make it so she wouldn't have to anticipate letters, wait for calls and feel such loss.

Quent's first call from California was a recitation of his new life. He told her of riding in a troop car for three days and two nights. Sitting upright on the wooden bench, he managed to catch forty-wink naps. The train was delayed at every little "whistle stop."

At the base depot, a big burly sergeant had awaited them. The marines loaded into a canvas-covered truck bed and made for the barracks. "Sarge ordered us off the truck with our gear and yelled, 'Fall in.' He said, 'Your souls belong to God, but from now on your asses belong to the Marine Corps. Guess what?' he said, 'I own your asses!'" Quent laughed, and his attempt to create a light moment elicited a giggle from Allise.

Marching to the barracks, they made a great effort to distinguish left foot from the right. Inside, the sarge fired off names "like spitting bullets" and pointing two fingers, he assigned bunk beds. Then, they marched to a warehouse for bedding, returning with it under their arms. "Bunks hafta be as smooth as glass, else Sarge lifts all the covers off with his swagger stick, and we make 'em again till they're right." Quent's lighthearted laugh reached out to her. It held a ring of happiness, like the person she knew long ago.

Having mastered bunk-making, he said they marched to get issued clothing. "Shoes too large, fatigues, brown socks and underwear. With helmets in our hands, we trooped back to the barracks before chow. Hup, two, three, four," he mocked the cadence. "First night, we took a three-mile march. March everywhere. Bet we learn left foot from right."

Weeks passed before Quent phoned again. He spoke first with Peter, then with Allise, talking on and on as though reluctant to say goodbye.

He said he had half an hour to shave and shower before double-timing to the mess hall for coffee, dehydrated eggs and bacon or chipped beef on burnt toast. There were more immunization shots and heads were shaved. The guys didn't know which was worse, shots or shaved heads. He laughed and said she wouldn't recognize him. He told Allise to address her letters to Platoon 402, Company F, First Squad, and said he would write when time allowed.

Later, Peter told her his daddy had said a bugle blasted him out of bed at four every morning. If he didn't get up, the sergeant rolled a trash can down the barracks' aisle. "It rattled so loud, Daddy bounced right out of bed." It was good to hear Peter laugh.

Allise established a routine around loneliness. Daily rhythms included writing to Quent, seeing Peter off to school, playing with Cleesy and preparing lessons for farm students. On certain days, she sat in the back room at Joe's Market with Mr. Grady, discussing debits and credits before posting the ledger.

Days passed while she waited for a letter or a call. Sometimes she wondered if Quent was really short of free time.

Each morning, wound tight as an alarm clock, she talked to the mirror and thought sooner or later someone would overhear and think her as daft as she thought she might be.

Her father pled for her to move to Philadelphia. Allise was tempted. It would be easy to run from misery to the safety and comfort of her parents. Peter and Cleesy would like Philadelphia's tree-lined streets, Fairmont Park and picnics near the Schuykill River. Her papa would take them through doors opened by Benjamin Franklin, George Washington and Betsy Ross. Her children needed to know their Weston kin.

He sent W. J. Cash's book, *The Mind of the South*. and she sat on the chaise reading it when Sam popped in. Weariness carried on her voice like a clock needing to be wound.

"Y' gotta pull yourself together for your sake and the kids, Allie. I hate Quent for making you unhap …" Sam's fierce blue eyes peered at her, defying rebuff.

Half-stated expressions and his anger implied more than brotherly affection. Uneasy, she asked if he thought there was such a thing as loving someone too much. "I mean the way I love Quent?"

"Maybe you do, girl, love too much." He leaned forward on his elbows and wrung his hands. He didn't know why men had to go to war, he said, but he knew she couldn't change the situation. He gazed at her, and said he had just dropped in to check on her. "If everything's okay, I'm going over to Maydale's."

Sam's well-meaning, she thought. *It's not my nature to drown in self-inflicted pain.*

At last, Quent's letter arrived. Training was more strenuous than he had imagined, and it made no difference that inoculations left men sore. They did calisthenics anyway.

**In this desert-like weather, men march and drop like flies. We run obstacle courses wearing 60-pound knapsacks and rifles slung across our chests. Climb up and down a 50-foot tower strung with cargo net to train for boarding and disembarking over the side of a ship.**

**We slosh across streams, rope hand-over-hand 30 feet above water and crawl on our bellies through reels of barbed wire with live ammo zinging over our heads. Hearing a ping is enough to make me keep my head down. Blank ammo is used for target practice. I can fire a 1903 bolt-action, single-shot Springfield rifle from all positions—sitting, hip, and prone.**

He wrote Bataan had fallen to the Japs. "It's not going well, Allie, but it has to turn around. I want to help do that." She read about the fall of Corregidor and how the battle for Midway proved American resolve. "God's on our side," Quent wrote. "I'm not the same person, Allie. I'm proud to be a 'leatherneck.' Can't explain it. Some men wonder why they joined up. It's hard, physically and mentally. Still, I find satisfaction in it."

Words seemed to jump at her. She felt threatened by an unknown. *Should she be happy for him or sad for herself?* Then, she read, "I'll be coming home on leave."

Like a prison inmate, Allise marked off another day on the calendar.

Pages of his letters frayed from folding and unfolding. She sat at the desk, pen in hand, writing flashes of people he had left behind. It's a way of keeping him close to us, she thought.

The next time he rang, Allise expected to hear, "I'm on my way home." Instead, Ethel Merman was belting out *Chattanooga Choo Choo*. The tune changed to *Praise the Lord and Pass the Ammunition*, and Quent came on the line. He sounded somber. She called Peter and Cleesy. Their father spoke to them for some time.

When she took the phone again, Quent asked about friends and other concerns, as though to prolong the connection. Edginess ate at her concentration, then he blurted, "I won't be coming home, Allie." The line went silent for what seemed eternal time. Then, "The First Marine Division moves to the docks tomorrow morning. We will load on a troop transport bound for an overseas destination. I don't know where or for how long."

Warding off the bad news, she asked if he'd heard about flight training. He hadn't, but was told he *might* be called back for flight school. "Such things move slowly up the chain of command," he said.

122 Southern Winds A' Changing

She latched onto that possibility. His throaty "I love you" was guarded and "goodbye" was abrupt. *Was he crying?* The click on his end was like the crack of a rifle.

She could cry forever. Wrapped in despondency and vaguely aware of Peter and Cleesy in the doorway, dressed for sleep, she extended her arms, and said, "Let's go up to bed."

The next morning, Allise rose early. Her farm school didn't take a summer recess. On the way there, she told Peter her students had lots of learning to do before catching up to his fourth grade level. She glanced at him. "Your father is going faraway, and Grandpop Weston wants us to move up there."

"I don't want to go to Philadelphia to live. I just want to visit."

Allise stopped at the shed where he was to work with Uncle Sam. "I know, son, and we're not moving anywhere. We will be right here when Daddy comes home." Driving on to the tenant house, Nate popped into her mind. Maizee had never spoken Quent's name, and she couldn't talk about him because he might be Nate's father. *Someday I must know the truth about that child*, she thought.

In the classroom, students' needs held her attention. After dismissing them for the day, she returned to the shed for Peter. Sam ambled over and leaned against the car. "Peedy wants to stay. Feels important out here. You know, needed."

"His self-worth is important, Sam, but he might ought to take the farm in small doses. We don't want him to come to hate it, do we?" Looking into the dark recesses of his eyes, Allise found them capable of reading her soul, and she wasn't being truthful. She gave a nervous laugh. "Sam, what would we do without you?" Somehow, she found words to tell him that Quent had called, and he wouldn't be coming home before shipping out.

He laid a sandpapery hand over her arm resting on the car door. It was brown against her light skin. "Truth is, I can't bear to be away from the children, Sam. I need … Am I selfish? I mean for using them as a crutch to help me through this?"

He stared down at his dusty shoes. Then shuffling about, Sam lifted his hands as though resigned to unspoken words. He gazed at her for a long moment. "I'll get Peter."

"Wait, Sam." Reigning in her emotions, she said, "I'm curious about Maizee's Nate." The names fell like a whisper. She wondered why at this time, she wanted to know.

For a moment, he appeared stunned. When he began turning his hands, she felt compelled to explain. "Obviously, that child's of mixed race. His fa …" The word stuck on her tongue. "Maizee never volunteers anything about him.

Her son is bright and should have the advantage of an education." Skirting around her real issue, she peered at Sam, trying to read his thoughts.

"Whatcha thinking, girl? Cain't do any more than you're doing t' educate that kid."

His remark wasn't altogether unexpected, but she was more disappointed with herself for being unable to push for the truth. "I think I can do better for Nate. It's a matter of finding a way." She watched him take off the dingy, sweat-stained hat and replace it at the same angle his father had worn it.

"You're beating a dead horse t' death, Allie. Don't worry your pretty head about such. You got enough t' worry about without that. I'll get Peedy."

He stood there for a moment while she mapped out his face, much like Daddy Joe's. She knew he meant to protect her.

Weeks later, the overhead fan flicked the sounds of a bird's wings. It cast light and dark patterns across the bedroom ceiling like a movie scene. Allise's mind danced with the disturbances. She wanted to shut them out, but the reel had a life of its own.

Leaving the bed, she went to the chaise, switched on the lamp and began a letter to her parents. She needed them as never before, but she wouldn't mention the inheritance from Daddy Joe and their savings had gone for the new Buick. She wrote the children were already traumatized by their father's absence, and she wouldn't add to it by packing them off to a strange environment. Too, the market and farm classes depended on her, so a trip to Philadelphia would have to wait.

*Do they think I am incapable of being responsible for my family? What am I thinking?* Her parents would never harbor such notions. Caught-up in their love for her and the children, they felt an obligation to see to their well-being. True, she hadn't told them things. May never reveal her unhappiness. If only someone was there to tell her she was capable when self-doubt tried to overwhelm her.

Allise pushed away the stream of thoughts and wrote that Quent's letter from Hawaii was full of excitement. Then, laying the pen and unfinished letter aside, she stared at the large hand-tinted photograph of Quent in his marine uniform. It had arrived only days before. What lay behind the blue eyes and half smile? The cap looked like an inverted loaf pan with no useful benefit for his head. He's smashing in his uniform, she thought. *Who is this father of our children? Have I ever known him? Will I ever have a chance to know him.*

Standing, she returned to bed, hoping to capture sleep.

Next morning, Allise sat at the table watching Elfreeda swing cantilevered hips about the kitchen, banging pots and pans from stove to sink.

Stopping in front of her, she said, "Miz Allie, there ain't no troubles too hard t' bear cause God gonna see to 'em." She gazed at her, waiting. "Chile,

e

you know how I know that? Momma's grandma and grandpa was slaves. When the war's over, old massa said for them t' leave. Herded 'um right off the plantation jes like animals t' fend for theirselves." Elfreeda paused, as if to let her slaves' plight sink into Allise's mind. "They didn't have nowhere t' go, didn't own no land and didn't have no money. Even if they'd had money, they wouldn't knowed how t' spend it. They be like babes in the woods. Crying like babies, too, but didn't nobody hep 'um."

Allise felt her share of the load of inhumanity. "What did they do?" she asked.

"Well, some got sick and died. They moan and cry and pray. So hongry, they boiling dirt t' eat! Momma's grandma say it tasted salty. They be begging white folks for meat bones so's they can scrape the marrow out t' boil in pokeweed and dandelion greens. Nearly starved t' death. Winter come, some the chil'ren died. Momma's grandpa said, 'We was free, but we didn't know what t' do with it.'"

She felt Elfreeda's eyes on her. "We human beings heap universal wrongs on each other. God isn't going to destroy us. We will destroy ourselves with war and other inhuman acts."

"There, Miz Allie." Shaking water from big brown hands, she dried them on her apron and pulled Allise from the chair into her strong arms. "You jes a pale slip of a girl, honey, but this thing ain't too big for you. Jes like my slaves, you gonna make it, too."

Allise's acute need for comfort melted in her friend's offered tenderness. Her body wracked in the release of pent-up pain. Elfreeda rocked her like a ship anchored in a safe harbor. When she quieted, her friend set about humming as she worked. Soon, hum turned to chant. "When the sun go down t'night, it be coming up with de morn, cause the Lawd ain't gonna let go. He knows them that bear and them that bow."

Allise surmised the lyrics were contrived for her benefit, but she knew their friendship had a shape of its own. It required no rules and was without obligation to blood bonds or property. Held together by a mutual liking, it was rare and precious on its own.

She held the few letters that Quent had written from island stopovers. The most recent one came in August from Guadalcanal. She unfolded it yet again, and read:

**We viewed the island from the ship's deck, and the captain warned us about what to expect. Yesterday morning, we descended the ship by cargo net into Higgins boats bobbing and heaving below. A misstep and we could land in the drink. Thirty-six men to a boat, many seasick on the ride to shore. Navy guns bombarded the island as we arrived.**

**Nips were here but they escaped into the jungle ahead of us. Haven't seen hide or hair of them. There wasn't a shot fired. They didn't even try to defend the airstrip they were building.**

**We're dug in on the beach, and tonight I'll sleep in a foxhole, if there is any sleep to be had. We were told the jungle is full of screaming birds and wild pigs. Little sand crabs scurry all around. Wouldn't be surprised if they dropped into my hole tonight.**

**My darling Allie, I'm far away and thinking of home. Tonight, I'll bay at the moon and dream of you. Do you feel my kiss each night? Hug the kids for me. Love you all. Must go. Our gear is being unloaded, and Sarge ordered us to relieve troops that have been moving supplies onto the beach.**

**Your loving leatherneck, Quent**

Glancing up, she caught Elfreeda watching her. Tucking the letters in her apron pocket, she knew her depth of feeling for Quent was beyond description. *He rarely demonstrated his feelings. We are so different, but I love him beyond measure.*

Elfreeda's talk about her slave ancestors had fortified Allise. Determined to push through her troubles, she stood before her mirror. Momentarily, flashes of Germans pushing across the Volga to the outskirts of Stalingrad took her mind. Then, "We're safe here. Cotton is being picked, it's the first day of school, and life is almost normal."

Each day, she saw Peter off to his classes, and left Elfreeda playing with Cleesy in her imaginary world while she went to the post office. Each day, finding her letterbox empty, she returned home with dashed hopes. Up one day, down the next, she thought. *If not for the kids, Sam and Elfreeda, I would simply fade away.*

Then, one morning, she and Elfreeda worked around routine tasks without much talk. Suddenly, Allise asked, "Who wrote 'Nothing stays the same? The moon waxes and wanes.'" Trying to remember, she mumbled, "'Mist and cloud turn to rain, Rain to mist and cloud again. Tomorrow be the day.' Why can't I remember who?"

"Yes'um, Miz Allie." Elfreeda looked concerned. She called Cleesy to the kitchen for lunch, and they sat at the table when a knock sounded from the front door. Hurrying to answer it, Elfreeda returned with a small yellow envelope. "Man from the telegraph office brought it, Miz Allie."

Examining it, Allise pondered. Was it her parents? Had something happened? Then, newsreel images of wives and mothers opening telegrams came to mind. Her heart skipped a beat. Sagging on the chair, she handed it unopened back to Elfreeda. "Read it, please?"

Tearing it open, she read, "We regret to inform you—"

Allise snatched it from her and ran upstairs. She sat on the chaise, the telegram dangling from her hand. *How? Japanese went into the jungle. He was safe.* Her tearless eyes closed, but a heartbeat proved she wasn't dead. I should have thrown it away, she thought, as if not acknowledging the telegram would change things.

Her eyes fluttered open, and Elfreeda stood in the doorway, holding Cleesy's hand. Allise swung her legs over the side of the lounge and began rapidly inhaling and exhaling.

Dropping the child's hand, Elfreeda rushed to her side. "Miz Allie, what's the matter? I'm gonna call Doctor Walls. Cleesy, stay here by yo momma, y' hear?"

Puckering as if to cry, Cleesy lay across her mother's lap. Allise couldn't stop the heavy breathing to calm her.

In minutes, Elfreeda burst back into the room. "There, Miz Allie, the doctor's coming. Cleesy, baby, you set in the rocker." She shushed at Allise until her breathing slowed, and she heard the doorbell. "Come on, Cleesy, you gotta eat your lunch."

Allise heard her let Doctor Walls in the front door and direct him up to the bedroom. He administered a remedy and waited at the bedside to see if it appeared to be working when Elfreeda returned. "Call me about four o'clock, Mrs. James," the doctor instructed. "She should come around by then. If I have no emergencies or calls, I'll check in at the end of the day. Can you stay here tonight?"

The doctor and Elfreeda talked to each other as though she wasn't present in the room. "Yassir, I sho will," she said. "Is it Mista Quent?" She handed him the telegram.

Dr. Walls went across the room to the window and read in a whisper, "Yes, killed in action on fourteenth of September." Handing the notice back to her, he said, "A cold way to announce a death. Should we call anyone other than Sam?"

"Nawsir, just her folks way up north. Town folks I don' know about them."

"I'll call Sam—No, I can't. He's picking cotton and will come home late. Allie should be fine. She will sleep. Hyperventilation brought on by shock."

As he left the room, Allise called Cleesy's name. "Sh-sh, chile. I'm gonna check on her right now. I'm gonna take care of the chil'ren. Don't you worry about nothing, honey."

The next morning, she stirred, and her eyes opened slowly. Sun beamed through sheer curtains over the east window, laying a warm autumn glow across her bed. Blinking, she sensed life much as a baby bird breaking out of its shell. Sitting up on the edge of the bed, she met a room void of any other presence, but the surroundings looked familiar. The portrait was the last thing she had seen each night before turning out the bedside lamp, and the first thing seen each morning. With a searching gaze on the man in uniform, she waited for meaning to come. Then she remembered.

A primeval scream reverberated throughout the house. She slipped to the floor, burying her face in rumpled covers pulled along with her. Beating her fists into them, her cry grew woeful.

Suddenly, strong arms lifted her, and she turned a tortured face to the blue depths of Sam's eyes. He sat on the bedside holding her like a rag doll, pressing her head to his broad chest. Sobs shattered her body, emptying it of the anguish, and he tried to wipe her face on his shirttail. She clung to him until wrenching cries became sniffles. "Sam, what am I to do? I can't bear it."

"There, girl. S-sh." Tightening his arms about her, he buried his face in the turns of her long, unkempt hair. She pushed back from him, and he swallowed hard as if resisting some rising emotion.

Allise took the gulp as a sign of his grief. "I'm sorry, Sam. You're so thoughtful of us, and I'm so grateful. You're the brother I wanted. Always here when I need you."

"Allie, I love you uh, you know, the sister I never had." Like a school boy, he looked away as she removed herself from his lap.

Arms folded across her bust, she walked to the window and looked out. On the sidewalk below, Elfreeda approached with Cleesy in tow and a grocery bag under one arm.

Sam crossed the room and stood behind her. She asked how long she had slept. He said through the night. Turning to him, she noticed his gaunt appearance. Eyes were ringed in dark circles, and he slumped. "What is today?" she said. "Did you sleep here? Who saw to the children? Did you tell them?"

"Elfreeda stayed over last night. Slept with Cleesy, and I slept there." He pointed to the chaise. "Told 'em nothing except you weren't feeling well. Didn't think we oughta."

Voices drifted upstairs, those of Elfreeda and Cleesy.

They stood peering at each other. Allise searched Sam's face for clues to help explain a father's death to his young, impressionable children. Seeing none, she said, "We must have a proper funeral. I can't bear to have him far away."

Sam turned from the window, rubbing his eyes. "I'd jes' gone downstairs to call Brother Rigdon when you woke up. I think he can contact the Red Cross."

"Quent would want to be here." Touching his arm, Allise asked if he would call the minister. "There's this awful need to do something, to have something that shows this is real. Not just a bad nightmare."

"I'll go downstairs and call now." He squeezed her hand and took a few steps toward the bedroom door.

Fighting back tears, she said, "Wait! I'll go with you." Following him, she wondered how she would tell the children. Her parents needed to know, too. Dread hovered over her. "Sam, I should call Philadelphia before you talk to the minister."

On the phone, she heard her father saying he would come right away. She told him she needed time to be alone, to sort things out. "I'll need you more, Papa, when we get his remains home. Sam and Elfreeda are taking good care of us. I love you, Papa. Give our love to Mama."

Sam spoke with the minister, and she asked Elfreeda to send the children upstairs.

They ran into her room, and Allise motioned them to the chaise. Peter nestled in her arm, and Cleesy lay her head in her mother's lap. Both paid her puzzling glances as she searched for a soft beginning. "Do you know how much I love you? I love you bushels, and I want us to have a talk."

Peter rolled his eyes. "Mother, kids are waiting outside. Can't we talk later?"

"I'm sorry, Peter, but we must talk now." Her voice dropped almost to a whisper. "Listen and think about my questions. Does a flower die when it's cut? Cotton grows until its picked, then the plants die. That's the way it is with living things."

Peter nodded and gazed toward the window through which children's banter drifted. He was distracted, but she struggled on. "We cut some plants, but most die because they've completed the time they're supposed to live. You know this, don't you?"

"Yeah, Mother! So why are you telling us this stuff?"

"Because I want you to know that just as we take the lives of some things, so does God. We have reasons, so does God. We know why we do it but don't always understand why God does." She was tempted to send them outdoors and delay another day when more thoughts came. "We can't know God's reasons, but God sees everything. We fit into God's plan like pieces in your jigsaw puzzles. If we accept death—"

"How does he see everything?" Cleesy asked.

"Well, Cleesy, you've heard God spoken of as 'he,' but I don't believe God is a 'he' or 'she.' No one has ever seen God, so each of us may feel differently about what God is. I see God as all creation, a big, pulsing, thinking everything. If this is true, then God sees and knows everything." She stroked her daughter's hair, waiting for thoughts to come. "If you think God is in heaven, it's sort of like looking down from an airplane."

"Uh huh," Peter said, and Cleesy echoed him. Now, she had their attention.

"Yes! Well, God sees like that up and down, into and out of and all around. Sees the big picture, things we don't see, and God does things that we don't understand. Things we may not like." Her voice caught. She pulled Peter close, stroked Cleesy's hair and wondered how she could go on. Somehow, she found the words. "Sometimes painful things happen, like a cut finger. The pain doesn't go away. What do you do?"

"Put a Band-Aid on it!" Cleesy sat upright and held up a bandaged finger.

Laughing, Peter said, "You have to wait for it to heal."

"We feel the hurt, put a Band-Aid on it and wait for it to heal. And we must wait to heal when God causes us to hurt." She wanted them to understand God dwelled within them, in the same place the memory of their father would be, but it was all too complicated.

As though reminding herself, Allise's voice dropped to a whisper. "God makes decisions for the good of everyone, so we accept and wait for the hurt to go away."

Moments passed before she noticed their waiting faces looking up at her. Clinging to some inner strength, she went on. "Imagine a movie in which bad guys plot to beat up a good guy and take his cattle. You want to warn him, but can't. You watch your hero being ill-treated and know he will find a way to right the wrong. When the movie ends, your hero wins. That's how it is when God tries to make a better world."

Cleesy nodded, and Peter searched his mother's face. "What you need to know is that in the big movie of the whole world, God chose a hero. Your daddy.

Picked him as we would a flower maybe to use in a way that's helpful to everyone. God chose him, and he will *never* be here with us again."

Tears ran down her cheeks, and Peter asked, "Why are you crying, Mother? Why are you saying Daddy isn't coming home?"

Allise wiped her face and regained her voice. "Because he isn't, son, not as we remember him. But if Daddy's happy where he is, and we think of him, talk to him and to each other about him, even cry if we feel like it, can we let it be all right with us?"

"I want Daddy to come home." Peter looked at her with pooled eyes.

Before Cleesy could become upset, she pulled them close. "I know, darling. I want him home, too, but we can have only what's left after his soul went to God. I believe he sees us now and is trying to tell us to remember him, that he loves us and someday we will be with him. I think your daddy is very happy where he is, don't you think so?"

"Maybe." Allise watched Peter struggle in a feeble attempt to understand his father was taken for some good purpose. "I guess so," he added.

She squeezed them and reached for the crumpled, tear-stained handkerchief on the table. "For a time, we'll be sad and feel sorry for ourselves. But you know something? In time, the sadness and sorrow will go away, and we'll have a happy memory of Daddy."

"Are you angry at God for taking Daddy away?"

"Yes, Peter, I am. And sad just as you are, because I miss him being here."

Swiping his eyes, Peter asked, "May I get something from my drawer?"

"Yes, darling. And we'll talk about him anytime you wish, I promise. Cleesy, let's find something for you." From Quent's highboy, Allise pulled out a plaid woolen muffler. "This is special," she said, kneeling to place it around her neck. "Your father wore it that cold December we were married in Pennsylvania. You can look at it and think of him."

The child clutched the scarf as if hugging her father. Peter reappeared with a limp white handkerchief. "Here, Mother, you can use it, but I want it back. It was Daddy's."

Accepting the damp hankie, she wiped the tears she couldn't suppress despite a half-smile Peter's remark evoked.

Several days later, Allise answered the door, and Brother Rigdon appeared ready to dive back down the steps. Did he fear the gossip that followed his calls on widow women, or think she would go into hysterics? Maybe he expected to be challenged. Pondering, she invited him inside. An awkward moment passed, each waiting for the other to speak. She offered coffee, but he declined. The leather chair crunched beneath his weight and groaned with his movement as he hurried through his reason for calling. A Red Cross person had promised to begin the process for shipping Quent's remains. "I wanted to tell you personally," he said.

At the door, she thanked him and turned to answer the phone. It was one more condolence call. She knew she should feel grateful, but so little thought was given to her at other times. More than superficiality, she needed genuineness. Not similitudes. Not duty-bound piety. If only the issues between her and the people of Deer Point were resolved.

Replacing the receiver, she eased down on the Hitchcock chair. I can live each day in suspension, awaiting a final ritual, a burial, or not waste another minute in limbo. I have my children, Elfreeda, Sam and Maydale to count on.

That evening, Allise told Sam he must go home. "Sleeping with Peter can't be restful," she said. "I have the rest of my life to rely on myself. Best to start now." As he quietly collected his things, she was tempted to say, "Don't go!" She needed someone to cry on.

On a Sunday morning, Allise saw a picture of morbidity approaching. Unable to deal with Mildred, she hurried inside the church. Barely seated, she felt a tap on her shoulder. Turning, she met a face struggling for sincere expression. "I'm sorry I haven't called. Time gets away, but I know what you're feeling."

She wanted to scream, "How can you know? Your husband is alive!" Instead, she swallowed hard and patted the hand on her shoulder. Sandwiched between her children and Sam, she slipped into her comfort zone and was unaware that he held her hand. Not a word of the sermon penetrated her brain, and when the closing hymn began, Sam nudged her.

Standing on the church stoop, Allise gazed past Brother Rigdon to fathers taking their families home for Sunday dinners. People clustered about her on the sidewalk. What a messy business death turns out to be, she thought. Listening and nodding, suddenly she felt a gush of anger. Anger at Quent for dying, anger at her consolers. "Do you really want to help?" Their looks of startled expectancy didn't stop her. "This community has never accepted me. I don't know if that's because I'm a 'Yankee,' a Friend, or what! You try to be kind, but you don't offer friendship not true friend ..."

Mildred Howard's gaping mouth and Ellen Crews' arched eyebrow cut her words short. She noticed Dro McClure standing nearby, and in a softer voice, said, "I shouldn't have come today. I need time." Wanting to make sense of her feelings, she threw up a gloved hand and said, "Later, when things are less confusing, I'll want to be involved so that all my thoughts won't be sad ones. I've made this place my home, and I need your friendship. I want to love you and you to ..."

She felt wounded, and through tearful eyes saw Dro's solemn face coming her way, but it was Sam and Maydale who took her arms. Together, they led Allise to the car.

Behind them, Mildred's tongue clicked. "Poor thing, too emotional for her own good."

Allise didn't need Mildred to tell her she was on an emotional roller coaster. She tried to be as strong as the day she had sent Sam home, but the initial shock, relating Quent's death to her parents and the children, and riding the wave of grief left her shipwrecked.

On Monday morning, she stood holding a letter Sam brought from the post office. A letter from Quent. It's a mistake, she thought, tearing open the coarse textured envelope. With the joy of expectation, she read the date, September 13, 1942. *The day before he* … Numbness crept over her and for a moment, she stood there, incapable of reading more. Sam waited, then he took her arm and led her to a chair.

Focusing on the page, she recognized Quent's handwriting. It must have been written in haste, words are barely readable, she thought. Almost inaudibly, she read:

**My Dearest Loved Ones,**

**We've engaged the Nips on a ridge south of the airfield. My unit's relieved for an hour and moved back from the action. I want to finish this before we move up again. I think of you all the time, darling. Everyone walks around singing, "I Walk Alone." I want you by my side, Allie.**

Pausing, she laughed lightly in Sam's direction and wiped a tear from her cheek.

She read again:

**The first night, a big naval battle forced our ships to leave with all our supplies onboard. We ate all the rice and other rations left by the Nips, who escaped to the hills. I've lost a few pounds. We hope the ships return soon with reinforcements.**

**Mosquitoes chew on us. Each morning we line up for malaria and salt tablets. My fatigues stink to high heaven. I sweat alot. Feet! That's another story. Mine are in bad shape. We're warned about jungle rot.**

**Every night Louie the Louse and Washing Machine Charlie fly over to drop green flares and a load of bombs. No one sleeps. We hear them coming, throw off our blankets and dive into foxholes.**

**I've spent most days, up until the ridge attacks, filling craters in the airstrip made by Charlie and cleaning my weapons. Oh, we pray a lot, too.**

**The Nips landed reinforcements in August. They charge our foxholes, machine gunning and screaming "banzai." We**

**fight back with our rifles and 37-millimeter canisters. Next morning, their bodies lay on the sand. War is hell, Allie.**

Breaking off abruptly, she read the rest in silence. Quent wrote he wanted to share an ocean sunset with her. Just the two of them under a coconut tree. "I remember the farewell party and all the love we have shared. I love you, darling, and the kids." Writing they were told to move back up the ridge, he signed, "Love, Quent," and added, "P.S. Written on rice paper left by the Japs."

Biting her lower lip, Allise folded the pages. She felt faint with the realization that Quent was killed after the letter was written.

Half rising, Sam banged his cup down onto the saucer. "Allie! Al—"

"What!" She jerked around to his startled look.

"Are you okay?"

"It never occurred to me a letter would come after ..."

Sam swung around the table and grabbed her up into his arms. "Let it all go, girl." His voice broke. "I'm here t' help you through this. It's gonna take time, that's all."

She surrendered to his tenderness.

Several months passed, and somehow, with Sam and Elfreeda's loving care and the passing of time, the constant ache ended. Allise stashed Quent's letters, worn from reading, in the paisley-covered box and waited. Without knowing what to expect or how the remains would arrive, she focused on the burial and found solace in her Quaker way.

Venturing out for the mail, she stopped in Joe's Market. Mr. Grady showed her the shoe box where he had stashed receipts and sales chits. She went to the back room to post them in the ledger, then, she made market deposits at the bank before returning home.

Sam came by. He urged her to resume the farm classes suspended since notification of Quent's death.

That evening, she and Elfreeda sat at the table with cups of coffee. "I'm stronger now," Allise said. "Up to doing chores and caring for Cleesy. Elfreeda, you might want to cut back to one day a week."

"As much as I love you and Cleesy, Miz Allie, I be glad to have time at home."

The doorbell interrupted. She went to answer it and returned with Brother Rigdon.

He held out another telegram and waited with a guarded look.

Allise read: "Remains of Cpl. Quentin DeWitt in U.S. Stop Advise date to arrive by train for burial Stop Advise if military ceremony is desired Stop" Sighing, she glanced at him. "Thank God, the wait is over. I don't want a military ceremony, Brother Rigdon. When is Christmas? Will we have time for the funeral before the holiday?" She had no tears, and noticed the pastor had dropped his guard.

He nodded. "We'll see."

"Will you conduct the service? Quent would want that. Sam and I will come up with a date and call you."

"I'll be glad to," he said. "Meantime, I'll wait for your call. Good day, Allie."

She thanked him and turned to her friend, standing behind her. "Oh my!"

Flashing a grin, Elfreeda pulled her into a hug. "Mista Quent be coming home, chile."

Allise made arrangements, and was told in so many words that her funeral plans strained sacred traditions. Quent was Deer Point's first dead war hero, and townspeople hummed like bees after nectar about the arrival of his body. "Taking the body straight to the cemetery for the service messes up the ritual. It oughta go to the church or his home for viewing." They complained and rumors floated. She thought it wouldn't matter what she did. *They will think I fouled it, but if Sam and I agree, that's good enough for me.*

Elfreeda's friend agreed to fashion her funeral garb, and Allise entered Rob-bin's Dry Goods Store from the side street. She went straight to the fabric counter and fingered a bolt of black crape when a saleslady walked up. A short distance away, a young clerk and another female stood staring out the large front window. Their backs were to her, but it was impossible not to overhear what they were saying. "What I'm hearing about the service is just unbelievable!" one said.

"Hey, lookey yonder!" the other said. "See that white Nigra across the street? Speaking of Quentin DeWitt, he's got two or three of 'um down on the river. Betcha that's his, too, or his old dead daddy's."

"I know," her friend said.

Allise looked out to see a light-skinned Negro youth walking past Spud's Café. The saleslady cleared her throat, catching the attention of the young clerk. Seeing Allise, she fled to the rear of the store. The other woman darted out the main entrance.

Taking a deep breath, Allise measured her control. To the saleslady, she said, "I need a pattern before you cut this yardage, and I need a sheer black fabric suitable for a veil." The woman avoided her eyes and led her to the pattern books.

Steeped in humiliation, Allise took her purchases and reaching the side street, she hurried to the car. Sitting behind the wheel, old thoughts and old images pounded in her head. She broke into sobs. Since the day she and the children gathered pecans with Maizee and Nate, she had wanted to deny Nate's resemblance to her husband. What if Peter had heard those women? The thought sobered her.

Regaining decorum, she forced her thoughts to the upcoming arrival of her father and sister. Heartache and sadness would reunite them after many years. She longed to see her disabled mother, but she would be left in the care of Allise's older sister, Margaret.

# CHAPTER 11

▼

On the way to Bensburg, Peter said Allise looked sad, and he felt sad, too. She smiled and rumpled his unruly hair. "Let's not be sad. We'll soon see Grandpop and Aunt Norine." She anticipated their warm smiles and arms embracing her, and imagined herself being equally magnanimous.

Right away in the crowded train station, she spotted a tall professorial-looking man in a dark fedora and black suit. "Father!" she called, and years of unexpressed emotions erupted as they embraced. "Norine, for a moment I thought you were Mother. You've changed hardly a whit." Her sister's arms opened, and Allise rushed into them.

Surrounded by their love, she felt safe, and their grandfather won over Peter and his sister right away. Cleesy seemed awed by him and enchanted with her aunt. Since old enough to listen, Allise had shared stories of her family with them.

That evening, she and Norine talked quietly in the living room when Peter yelled, "Cleesy, you let Grandpop steal your man!" All three stretched out from the checkerboard on the floor.

"Oh my gosh!" Cleesy said, and Peter and his grandfather laughed.

"Papa wasn't this playful with us," Allise said. She remembered her father reading to them with Norine cradled on his lap, and she and Margaret astraddle the arms of his overstuffed chair. They were spoken to as adults, and family outings were always educational events, but she never doubted her parents' love was anything less than abiding.

Now, lying there in stockinged feet, her father looked to be having the time of his life. Norine turned to her. "Do you suppose a son would have made a difference?"

"I wonder. I suppose it's different with grandchildren." Allise spoke of the difficulty of separating himself from the teacher's role. She said his intent was to mold them into mature, worthwhile citizens. "Papa's legacy to us is an appetite for books and learning. I see myself in him, mired in self-examination and the motives of others. It gets tedious, trying to fix things." She laughed. "Oh, if only I had humor and patience"

"Well, someone has to fix things," her sister said. "Who used to say that?"

Both exclaimed, "Uncle George!" and Allise said, "I turn things over in my head to the point of distraction or maybe distortion. Do you find yourself doing that?"

Norine smiled. "No, I get bogged down in 'good' works. Remember, we received a large dose of responsibility to others."

Their father stood, and leading Peter and Cleesy upstairs, he said they would read from books he brought and look at the carved chess set on which he had played. An hour or so later, he came back into the living room and took a seat. Locking his hands behind his head, he said, "By the way, Allise, did Cash's book help you to understand the Southern mind? The man took a critical look at facets of regional society." He explained to Norine that her sister wrote intriguing thoughts about Southerners, and he had sent the book.

"Papa, it made me more curious about the Southern psyche. Caused me to consider what shapes their thinking and helped me put local mores into perspective." She talked about settlers from Georgia, Alabama, and Mississippi who left post-Civil War destitution behind. Their destination was Texas, but reaching the rich loam along the Chalu River, they settled here. Looking to carve out a better place for themselves, they found unmarred landscapes, the river, and lakes. Wildlife was plentiful, too, she told them.

"Arkansas' rolling hills forested with pines and hardwoods must have looked far better than the war-torn land they left behind," she said, pausing to think. "The summer heat was no different from what they had known. Fall is beautiful here. Snow and ice are rare, but recently we had a lovely ice storm." She laughed at how she went on. "You probably wonder what holds me here. I never gave a thought to being anywhere but with Quent. This is home, a place of Southern mystique in which fierce-prided, independent people still harbor racial biases more than seventy-five years after the Civil War ended. It intrigues and disturbs me."

A hush fell over them, she absorbed in her own thoughts. Then, Allise said, "The current war makes me think the attitude toward Negroes might be misdirected revenge." She looked for her father's reaction. Seeing none, she spoke of the Germans being humiliated by World War I defeat. "Did

Hitler lead his people into war with sweeping revenge in mind? Does he go after Jews because they are easier targets than Germany's conquerors? Is the ill-feeling for Negroes miscast? After the Civil War, Southerners couldn't do much about their Northern masters, so Negroes became easy targets for their revenge. Papa, am I off base or is there a similarity?"

"Your questions make sense, Allise. I've not given much thought to the 'whys.'"

"It's apparent," she said, "that white people don't need to fear Negroes. Their greatest fear is of black men befouling white women, but it may be black women who need to be fearful. I can't see white prejudice coming from insecurity." She didn't wish to generalize but was convinced that whites still suffered from a humiliating defeat. "They may not even be aware of it. Blacks *and* whites suffer, and both pass the suffering from one generation to the next." Her tone implied inconceivability.

The room fell quiet again, then she continued. "Each suffers differently. Negroes suffer the indignities of being lesser human beings and having a next to nothing chance of achieving. Whites may not realize they're lesser humans themselves because of their treatment of the coloreds. Is it hatred? Seems beyond the mere emotion of hatred, more like institutionalized browbeating. Intimidation that's become a way of life."

Her father seemed to be giving great thought to her words. "Suppose it will ever change?" he asked.

Allise took time to think. "Yes, it has to. But it will likely be a very long and slow process. Years, even generations of sorrow and forgiveness."

Norine yawned. "I'll leave you two to solve the Southern dilemma. If you will excuse me, I'm tired and want to read for awhile."

Dismissing her with a fond look, Allise said goodnight and welcomed private time with her father. She returned to her train of thought. "I'm amazed that Negroes are so pliant, childlike, really. Probably the only way they can survive in a world of mistreatment." She said Southerners had much to hate. Northern raids, Sherman's burning and pillaging, plus ten years of Yankee reconstruction. "When Yankees returned North, what could the South do with their anger but turn it on Negroes about whom they had fought?"

Her father was quiet, and she continued. "People came here, hewed out a new life for themselves and their descendants, and they can't understand why Negroes can't accomplish what they did." Remembering Quent's disrespect for them, Allise said, "They seem unwilling to look at reasons why it would still be difficult for Negroes even after all these years. Fed, clothed and sheltered like children, they were worked to the limit."

He listened without interruption as she told of childlike dependence after the war. "Negroes were turned off plantations with nothing and no place to go. They knew farming but had no land, well later, maybe twenty-five acres. Without an education, what could they do? How could they advance themselves?" She told of farmers needing labor and taking them back on the land, enslaving them in a different way. "Poor whites were used, too, in the sharecrop-tenant system. Quent's uncle farms in Mississippi and keeps Negroes indebted."

"Hmm." Her father shifted in his chair. "I agree it will take generations to free society of racial hatred and hurt feelings, but I don't know that the South has a corner on racism. I see it in Philadelphia. As to Jews, biblical tribes always fought each other."

"True, but does it have to be that way? On the surface, harmony exists, but there's pain in Negro eyes. What's the limit of that pain? What does the future hold?" Her father had no answers, and she added, "Isn't it sad that so much energy is wasted on hating? When looking at the rate and caliber of achievement by both races, one can't help but think of wasted energy. Southern energy could have been better used to educate both its white and black citizens for industrial skills and professions." Her face held sadness for a world she dreamed could be better. "The whole of society would benefit from it," she said.

Her father looked thoughtful. "I'm proud of you, Allise. Keep reading and studying, turning thoughts over in your gifted mind. Above all, be tolerant."

She laughed. "You lavish me with such praise I'm embarrassed, Papa. I know I'm driven by impatience and intolerance and need to work on both."

"You should be close to family, daughter. Close to your Quaker roots."

"Yes, Papa, there are reasons for returning to my native home." One, she said, was a concern about bringing up her children in an atmosphere of prejudice. And, there was her weariness of being an outsider. But the loss of the children's father and their link to the community were reasons enough to remain in Deer Point. "If I can find a way to express my convictions and be more patient of other persuasions … It isn't that I don't know the more I resist their way, the more resistence I meet. I do, Papa. It may be my mission to be a thorn in their side." Looking at the time, Allise apologized for running on.

"No need for apology. Expression opens opportunities for insights and gaining knowledge. I've always taken pleasure in our conversations, Allise."

"Oh, Papa!" She walked behind him and put her arms around his neck. "I love you. Thanks for coming when I needed you. You've always understood me." Releasing him, she said, "Shall we call it a day? Tomorrow will be difficult for all of us."

The next day, Allise and Sam waited in the cavernous freight depot for the hearse to arrive. She stood resting a hand on the coffin. Her beloved husband, so removed from her. She lay her head on the field of stars, then, unable to bear more, she walked to the door where Sam waited for the vehicle.

A depot worker walked in and looked askance at the flag-draped casket. Shipment of bodies to Deer Point wasn't a common happening.

Thinking she had no more tears to cry, Allise dabbed her eyes and fled to the loading dock with the tulle veil waving behind the crown of her black felt beret. Sam followed her, and they watched the hearse back to the dock. Taking her arm, he walked her to the car and stood by for the loading.

Inside the Buick, Allise tugged at the veil, straightening until it fell over her face.

Sam slid behind the wheel and followed the somber carriage proceeding slowly toward the Newtown Church. The funeral cortege waited, and the hearse pulled to the head of a long line of cars, leaving a gap for the Buick.

Elfreeda guided Peter and Cleesy onto the back seat and climbed in beside them. They peered at the veiled woman in black, and Elfreeda crossed her lips with a finger. Their mother reached a hand to them as the cortege pulled away.

In the cemetery, a gray, November overcast kept the mid-morning sun from touching earth. Seated beneath a canopy at the grave side, Allise was vaguely aware of low murmurs around her. She escaped to that place where despair couldn't possess her. Moments passed, then a hush fell over the gathering and caught her attention.

Dro had started the eulogy. "Quentin DeWitt was a misplaced man. For as long as I knew him, a lifetime, he wanted to fly airplanes. Instead, he farmed and ran a business." Pausing, he looked out on the crowd, then continued. "He volunteered for the fight we're in. He fought to keep tyranny from our door, and though short-lived, his fight was gallant. Quent gave his life in a September battle on Guadalcanal, the first war casualty from here."

He paused again, focusing on Allise. "Quent respected the people in this community, and above all, he loved his wife and children. He was my boyhood friend a-and he was my manhood friend, too." Coming to a finish, he said, "May he be remembered." Choking on emotion, Dro collected his notes and strode back to his seat.

Allise recalled his astonishment when Quent volunteered. He knew my husband well, she thought. She listened to the choir sing *In the Garden*. It was Sam's selection.

On the last note, Brother Rigdon stepped forward, placed his Bible on the lectern and flipped to a marked reading. Mopping a handkerchief across his brow, he cleared his throat and began. "Mrs. DeWitt wants to remind us with these scriptures that we are to love and not hate, to forgive and allow ourselves to be forgiven." He gazed on the crowd. "That we should allow our souls to be joined together in our lifetimes, as they are joined with God in death." He read from First John, then Proverbs: "'Hatred stirs up strifes, but love covers all sins and a friend loves at all times.'"

As the minister read on, Allise saw Elfreeda try to control Cleesy's banging of a foot against the metal chair. Peter clamped a hand over his mouth and looked up at her.

Brother Ridgon paused at the commotion, then continuing, he took up the soul and soulfulness. "We're reminded that the soul is an immortal or spiritual part of humanity and having no physical reality." Swiping his forehead, he said, "God's the final judge of the soul." Turning to Ecclesiastes, he read: "'Then shall dust return to the earth as it was, and the spirit shall return unto God who gave it.'" He asked that they pray for his soul, then called for a moment of silence to remember Quent. Uttering "Amen," he closed his Bible.

Moving from the lectern, the minister glanced in the direction of an audible gasp rolling over the crowd. Allise didn't have to guess about it. Brother Rigdon had frowned when told the black woman would sing. Perhaps he wondered what those at the funeral would think, as well as Quent, if he were alive.

Allise had been adamant. Elfreeda would sing a spiritual to lift hearts as Quent's soul was committed to God. Waiting for the song to begin, she thought the old Quent would have disapproved, but now he saw things from God's view.

The black woman stood before them with the same steely resolve she had shown when Allise warned her of what to expect. Closing her eyes, she began to sway and hum, deep and throaty, until her voice rose as a trumpet summoning to a band of angels. *Swing low, sweet chariot, Com'n for t' carry me home.* She looked over Jordan and saw angels coming after. *And if they git there a 'fore me, then tell all my friends, sometimes I was up, sometimes I was down. They a com'n for t' carry me home.* Dropping to a more mellow tone, she beckoned in the angels. *Swing low, sweet chariot, Com'n for t' carry me home.*

Eyes closed behind the veil, Allise envisioned a drawn chariot and Quent running to meet Elfreeda's powerful voice reaching out to his transcended essence. Suddenly, there was stony silence, then a shouted "Amen!" Jarred, she opened her eyes and saw Dro smiling down at Elfreeda and clasping her hand between his.

Someone nearby muttered, "Well, it sure was an unusual service."

Allise had no time to consider the remark. Brother Rigdon was reaching for her hand. People followed him with condolences, then they clustered in groups outside the canopy where she joined her father and sister. Soon Mrs. Rigdon came around and took her hand. "So brave for so long, my dear. I don't know how you've borne up."

Pulling her hand free, Allise lifted the veil. Let it all show, she thought. Pain and anger, the sadness and loneliness. "Thank you, Mrs. Rigdon." She struggled for a respectful response. "I've felt a range of emotions, none of which I thought were handled with bravery. It took time to realize I wasn't grieving for Quent. His spirit is happy. I grieved for myself and the children, and for Sam. Our loss."

Realizing she wasn't sounding respectful, she said, "Have you met Papa and Norine? Papa, this is our pastor's wife, Mrs. Rigdon. My father, Mr. Weston, and sister, Mrs. Mason, of Philadelphia."

"Nice to meet you. If only under different circumstances. I just told this dear child how brave she is. She bears up remarkably well. Most would be devastated."

"Mrs. Rigdon." Her father bent over the gloved hand. Straightening, he glanced at Allise and said, "Well, yes, in Western civilizations, I suppose grief is a private matter. I've read of ethnic groups whose grieving women wail."

"Hm-m." The woman withdrew her hand and walked away. Turning back to him, she stared a silent, accusatory "Yankee!"

Puzzled, he asked, "Did I offend the dear lady?"

"I'm afraid so, Papa," Allise whispered. "She isn't accustomed to having her sweetness challenged. That you shared something you've learned was undoubtedly missed. Now, come help me invite these people to the wake."

The next day, Allise drove her father and sister to Bensburg. Although an unhappy occasion brought them south, their visit had strengthened her. At the train station, they said goodbyes.

Back in Deer Point, she dropped Peter at school before going home to the empty house. Taking Cleesy's hand, they walked into the kitchen. To Allise's surprise, Elfreeda greeted them. "If y' don't mind, Miz Allie, I'll stay with y' till evening. Ain't good for the house t' be so quiet today. Besides I got something t' tell ya." Whipping a dishcloth over her shoulder, she flopped down at the table.

"Oh, Elfreeda, I dreaded the emptiness. It's so good of you to be here." Allise took a chair. "Tell me what?"

"Well, my husband, y' know he cuts timber, doncha? A tree fell across his leg."

Allise drew in a deep breath and asked, "Has he seen a doctor?"

"Yes'm, but he might never walk agin, probably be in a wheelchair. I didn't wanna upset you. Dodd's with 'im now, but I cain't leave 'im there ever'day." She paused, and looking at Allise, reached for her hand. "I wish … Miz Allie, I gotta be home with Jedadiah. He's gonna be down a long time, but I got a idea. What if Maizee and Nate could come live here?"

Allise looked doubtful. "Here?"

"You got that big room over yo garage. It'd make a fine place for 'em t' live."

"I don't know, Elfreeda. That's something I would have to think about."

"You say Nate's past the books you teaching from. He needn't be held back cause of them other farm kids. Move 'um here, and Maizee can see after the house and Cleesy."

Allise wanted to teach English again at Deer Point High School. She could do it if Maizee kept Cleesy. "Do you really think she would leave her family to live here?"

"She wants that boy educated. And you don't know till y' ask, does ya?" Cleesy climbed onto Elfreeda's lap. She cuddled the five-year-old against her bosom, hummed in her ear and watched Miz Allie work through her doubt.

Allise thought of what she heard in Robbin's Store. Townsfolk had protected her children from Quent's secret, but would having a black family here put them at risk?

Elfreeda said Cleesy was heavy with sleep. She trudged upstairs, complaining the child would have to eat lunch when she woke. When she returned, Allise said she would speak with Sam about the idea. Watching her friend move about the kitchen, the near certainty of Nate's father nagged. Her heart raced, but she knew it was time to ask someone she trusted. "Elfreeda, is Nate Quent's child?"

"Miz Allie! You don't wanna—"

"Oh yes I do!" She was determined to hear the truth. "I need to know." She told Elfreeda what she had overheard in the store. "I've suspected for a long time. If it eases your discomfort, I've forgiven Quent and have no animosity for Maizee and Nate. I'm sure it wasn't her fault, and I want only the best for them. So, are you going to tell me?"

Elfreeda sank onto the chair again. "I believes you, Miz Allie. Maizee's innocent." The black woman's face contorted with worry. "If you jes gotta know, Nate's his kid. He's looking so much like 'im."

"Yes." Allise's body felt wooden. As long as she merely suspected, she was able to hold onto delusions. Had she really forgiven? She tried to tame her thoughts. "Well, I know, and that's enough for now."

"I think you's right, chile. Jes let it be."

"I'll miss you, Elfreeda. If Maizee agrees, maybe life will become normal again."

The knife bound to Maizee's leg was a constant reminder of Mista Quent. He and the McPhersons had caused her only fears. Now, the McPhersons lived in Bensburg, and one lay in a cemetery. Behind the bedroom curtain, she lifted her dress, unpinned the binding, and her long-kept secret dropped to the floor. She stood gazing down at the knife and loose length of torn, bed sheet. Untied. Free! She grinned.

# CHAPTER 12

▼

The first holidays without her husband, came and went. They weren't the joyous occasions of the past, and Allise put them behind her. She must consider how to entice Maizee and Nate to live in Deer Point. Her former position was open for the 1943-44 school term, and she wanted to apply.

Sam was devoted to her and the children, but in recent weeks, she noticed he wasn't himself. He seemed preoccupied. That night, he helped clean up after supper and didn't mention the farm once. A sure sign of something amiss. When the children went to bed, Allise caught him gazing into space. "What are you thinking, Sam?"

"Oh, about Quent, about the war. Guess I feel guilty. Ever'body old enough to go is over there fighting. Ever'body but me. I'm gonna give up my deferment and enlist." She couldn't believe what she heard and started to object. He held up a hand. "Nope! Don't say it, Allie. I know how you feel. You gotta understand, it's eating away at me."

She sat forward. "What about the farm and cotton you provide for the war? What of us? I can't bear another ..." She buried her face in her arm on the back of the sofa.

He moved next to her. Their heads close, he reached for her hand. "One thing will keep me here, Allie. I love you. Always have. Wanna marry—"

"Great heavenly host!" Allise jerked away and stood, sending glances back at him.

"Oh, n-not now!" he said, then almost whispering, "When enough time's passed."

Blushing, he stuttered, "I-I know you don't ... but it's true, Allie." He stood, pacing and rubbing his hands. Turning to her, he said, "I never intended, t' tell ya, but I've wondered how you could've missed it. Since the first time I saw you, it's like a disease eating at me. I know you don't feel the same, so I want t' do what's best for us."

Her face softened. She returned to the couch, and he said, "I never intended just slipped out." Throwing his hands up in resignation, he gave a sad little laugh.

"I love you, too, Sam. Just not that way."

"I know, and I cain't make you feel the way I do so, I think I oughta go away."

"There's no need to throw yourself on a sacrificial altar, for heaven's sake! Sell the house, move to Bensburg or near the farm. Marry Maydale and make a home"

"You're spouting nonsense now. Be still and listen t' me." On the edge of the sofa facing her, he worked his hands. "I've thought of all that. None of it's right. I ain't marrying no girl just to make a home. Put both me and Maydale on the sacrificial altar."

Allise heard some of Quent's pluck coming from him. "You're right. I'm grasping at straws because I don't want to give you up to war. You're one of the most decent people I know, Sam DeWitt. Any girl who gets you for a husband will be fortunate indeed. You honor me with an honest expression of your deepest feelings, and I almost wish—"

"Please, Allie! Nothing you say can make it easier. I-I feel strong about doing my part in the war, filling Quent's shoes, so t' speak. Maybe when I come back, my head will be screwed on straight, and we can grow some different crops." Sam stood again, took a few steps and turned back. "I've been thinking about Jonas. He has lotsa years left in him, and he knows the farm backward and forward. If you support him with extra help at critical times, well, Jonas can handle the farm. Whatcha think?" He sat down, waiting.

Allise let the question hang, thinking all this talk was an attempt to lift the weighty issues looming over them. She was tempted to reach for him but dared not. His gaze turned pensive, and he hid his face in big hands. He's serious about entering the war, she thought. "I'll support you, Sam, as difficult as it will be. And Jonas, he'll do a fine job."

Sam sagged as if he'd reached the rewind point of a spring-loaded toy. "Yep, he will. I wouldn't want the farm to be a burden for you, Allie."

"It won't be. Sam, I've given some thought to a suggestion Elfreeda made, and I need your opinion. Peter probably won't like it." She rushed on, telling him that her old position at school was open. "There's a huge void in my world, and if you're leaving, I want to return to full-time teaching. Cleesy, well, I had thought Elfreeda could care—"

"It'll be good for you, girl. Do"

"Let me finish." She touched his arm. "Elfreeda can't keep Cleesy." She told him about Jedadiah's accident and the plan. "Elfreeda and I think the garage space would make a home for Maizee and Nate. Nate can go to school, and Maizee can tend to Cleesy." She hurried on. "What do you think?"

When she had thought to speak with Sam about Maizee and Nate, her imagined scenario of how it might go had been reason enough to delay. Now, he leaned back frowning and began anew with nervous hands. "I don't know about having the Colsons—"

"Sam, I know about Nate." Allise stood and pushed up gray cardigan sleeves as though ready to spar. Taking a few steps, she turned. "I know he's Quent's son."

Appearing stunned, Sam jumped up and paced, rubbing his palms over each other.

"It doesn't make any difference, or maybe it makes all the difference in the world. Maybe I want to see after Nate because he is Quent's child."

"Who told you this?"

She took a place back on the sofa and related the women's conversation in the store. "After overhearing that, I asked Elfreeda."

He stopped pacing and sat facing her. "You have something special, girl. Not many women would see things the way you do." Their eyes met for a moment, then slouching back, he said, "I suppose the kid deserves it. His mother, too." They sat without speaking. Then grinning, Sam said, "You realize you'll dig a deeper hole for yourself in this town? And I won't be here to walk you away from it."

Her eyes were full of hurt and pleading. "Sam, don't go."

"I have to, Allie. It's like your reason for bringing the Colsons here. Do you see that?" Standing, he squeezed her hand, released it and walked to the hall tree for his coat.

Yes. She understood the comparison. They may not agree, but they would support each other. Turning off the downstairs lights, Allise wondered how she could convince Maizee to move.

As time passed, any doubts she had about bringing the Colsons to town were goaded by her convictions, and she was ready to persuade Maizee.

Peter walked across the school yard with friends, and she called to him. Grinning, he ran and hopped in the car beside his mother. "Where we going?" As they drove away, she told him about the plans for Maizee and Nate. "I don't want niggers living here!" His face turned ugly, and his words mimicked those of his late father.

Allise's chest tightened, crushing any point of reason. "Stop it!" she yelled, glaring at him. "Never refer to colored people that way again!" His hurtful look erased her anger. "Peter, that word is derogatory and demeaning. It makes Negroes feel less than human."

Glancing his way, she found him unappeased, and moments passed as she thought about how to explain. "Imagine you're a Negro. Can't have white friends. Can't sit in King's Drugstore and eat ice cream. You've done no wrong, but you have black skin. God made you that way, and you can't change it. Do you feel good about yourself?"

He pouted, and though not looking exactly contrite, he nodded with downcast eyes. Driving up the Colson's lane, she wondered if he was capable of empathy. The thought distressed her for she had wondered the same about Quent. Perhaps Peter would change once Nate lived close enough for them to become friends.

Inside the Colson house, he gazed at the black boy as if tallying a score card. As though fun shared beneath the pecan trees was a lost memory. He paid her glances no heed.

Allise laid out her plans and wasn't surprised when Maizee hedged. At planting time, she couldn't leave Jonas and her sisters to cook, plant a garden and do housework, too. Smiling shyly at her daddy, she said, "Besides, he ain't gonna like being away from Nate. They buddies. Nate's a big help with the farm."

Just then, Cleesy chased a small brown mutt about the room, coming dangerously close to the potbellied stove that warmed against the March chill. Li'l Joke grabbed the puppy and held it for her to stroke.

Allise dismissed Maizee's excuses. Nate would have summers and weekends on the farm, and she could visit her family often. "Jonas can hire help," she said. "Maizee, don't deny your son an opportunity for better schooling."

Jonas dropped his straight chair to the floor. "Sho, I'll miss y'all, but we'll be awright. Don't worry about us. Li'l Joke and Dessie can do anything you can, Maizee."

His approval must have been enough for his eldest daughter. She grinned and said, "I sho do want Nate t' be somebody."

"Well now," Allise said, waving her hand, "it's settled." Warnings flashed across her mind, and doubt in her own wisdom loomed anew, but she pushed them aside. Walking across the room to the wall bench, she took both of Maizee's hands and smiled at the young black woman. "It will be good for all of us."

Maizee astonished her with a radiant smile.

Nate leaned forward on his elbows and peeked through fingers at Peter. Allise watched him hide pleasure behind cupped hands. He looked at his mother, and his grin spread. He stood and went over to Jonas. Throwing an arm across his shoulders, he said, "We'll come see y', Grandpa."

Peter's face twitched. Was he touched by Nate's affection? Allise wondered. Her son and Nate were of an age where their opinions were important and would have to be dealt with. "Maizee," she said, "we'll get the place ready for you and Nate."

Jonas and Nate followed them to the porch. "Look!" Nate pointed. "Heading north."

Allise looked up. "Honk, honk, honk." A v-shaped flock of Canada geese winged across the sky, and she thought they were off to a new beginning. So was she.

With Maizee's move to town settled, Allise wanted to turn to other things, but she couldn't escape the news looming over their evening meals. She was as war weary as the next, but she turned up the radio volume and listened from the dining room.

America's war moved into another year. More young men trained at military bases. Nearly everyone had a relative in the thick of battle. The home front was in high gear because a national patriotism united people in a resolve to win. War plants had been built, and factories, which recently produced for civilian consumption, had retooled. Ships, planes, tanks, and military vehicles rolled off assembly lines with speed and precision.

New cars made for civilians became things of the past. Gasoline, tires, and certain foods fell under a ration system. Food substitutions were accepted, and if in the beginning, Americans had wanted to reject a war far from their shores, it was now a winning cause.

An Allied victory in North Africa brought President Roosevelt and England's Churchill together at Casablanca. Newspapers, movie reels, and the radio reported speculation of an upcoming invasion.

Peter griped about having to listen to the news, but Allise said, "It's a fact of our lives, son. Some of it is good, but I want you to know the ugly side of war, too."

"Oh heck, Mother! Why can't we just learn about it in school?"

"Because, Peter, you will be through college before this history is written." He was belligerent, but she ignored him and hoped for victories now that Sam was a soldier.

Despite the war distractions, Allise tried to plan the apartment space above the garage, but she needed help. She needed Sam. Suddenly, snatching up her crude drawings, she went to the phone and rang Dro McClure. After asking him if he could assist her, she surprised herself by inviting him to dinner.

The impulsive act tugged at her conscience and anxiety built to the appointed time. Dro's admiring gazes and the way gossip spread in town were worrisome things. Now she knew how Brother Rigdon felt when he called on widow ladies.

That evening, Allise answered the door with misgivings, but Dro's conversations engaged her and kept them at the table long after the meal ended. He was an astute student of past wars as well as the present one, and she listened with greater interest than she wanted to admit.

Peter drifted back into the room. Dro spoke of American correspondents reporting from China well before Pearl Harbor that the Japanese wanted to dominate Asia. "Where's Pearl Harbor?" Apparently, her answer that December Sunday left Peter unsure.

"On one of the Hawaiian islands in the Pacific Ocean," Dro said. "Come over to my house, and we'll have a look at my world atlas."

For one who had no children of his own, Allise thought Dro answered Peter's questions with patience. Her son's admiration for him was obvious. Without a father and Sam away, he needed a hero. *Am I trying to find favor for this man?* Biting her lip, she returned to his earlier comment. "I suppose Hitler's advances were more worrisome than Japanese incursions."

"Could be," Dro said. "Most Americans know little about the Japanese culture."

"The place seems far removed. We know them through Five and Dimes stores." Allise laughed. "Cheap novelties with 'Made in Japan' stamped on the bottom. We don't think them capable of original creations."

Dro smiled. "But they destroyed our navy at Pearl Harbor. That got our attention."

Allise suggested they move to the living room. Stretching long legs from the leather chair, Dro crossed one foot over the other and clasped his hands behind his head. He reminded her of her father. She saw Peter was mesmerized by Dro's details of the fall of France, the Japanese hits on islands, and German and Italian unity.

"Malta was bombed," he said. "We'll find those places in the atlas, Peter. Did you see the newsreel showing the bombing, Allise?" She nodded, and he told about the Germans opening a supply route into North Africa. "Good news was the Russian's keeping them out of Moscow. Hitler goofed when he sent men to fight on Russian soil in winter."

Sitting on the couch beside Peter, Allise pulled him close and kissed the top of his head. "Before your father left, he said he couldn't live with himself if his family was threatened and he didn't fight to protect it." She glanced at Dro and lowered her eyes.

Peter squirmed as if to avoid his feelings, and Dro watched Cleesy play, betraying nothing of what he was thinking. If he caught her subterfuge in trying to rid guilt by bringing up Quent, it wasn't evident.

Picking up from his last remarks, he said it took time to recover from Pearl Harbor and oppose the Japanese. "Within months after Midway, the navy stopped them in the Pacific. Now, the new Sherman tank is proving itself by stopping the German advance to the Suez."

"Our victories bring hope," Allise offered, "but war is never a good thing, Peter. When people will not reason, war becomes a necessary evil and catches everyone up in its violence. Your dad and Uncle Sam volunteered, but many young men were drafted."

Dro agreed. "There aren't many around anymore. Just old folks and young ones like you." Looking at Peter, he laughed.

"I see young Negroes on the streets, Dro. Why aren't they in the military?"

He guessed they didn't have the skills to fight or work for the country's defense. "Some fill lesser jobs left open by whites," he said. Shaking her head, Allise said it was shameful they were denied knowledge and training, and the country didn't have the benefit of their help when it was at war.

"It doesn't make sense," he said, but his true notion was indiscernible to her.

Peter yawned, and Allise urged him and Cleesy upstairs. Dro threw his leg over the chair arm and looked too comfortable to be thinking of leaving. A recent widow, she felt uneasy and clumsy being alone with him. Faking a cough behind her hand, she said, "Quent didn't live to see the Japanese leave Guadalcanal, but I think he knows."

"I suppose." Dro smiled as though he knew her game.

"Did you hear Mildred tongue-lashing the Doss twins because they enlisted in the WACs?" Allise grinned. "She said they aren't fit to be called women, then set in on those working on defense lines. 'No telling what's going on, husbands off at war. Nobody to keep them straight. Working on Sundays. Don't go to church, dis-s-graceful!'"

Dro chuckled at her mimic of Mildred. "She would die if not allowed to judge."

"Cleesy says Mrs. Howard is a mean old lady. Children tramp in her yard, and she tells them to stay out of her flower beds." Allise laughed and said her own yard was a war zone. "The neighborhood kids pull Peter's old Red Flyer wagon around town to collect scrap metal. They pick up every foil gum wrapper they find."

Smiling, Dro looked at his wristwatch and yawned. "Gosh! It's this late?" At the door, he took her hand and held it for a long moment. "It's been a pleasant evening."

Alone, guilt eroded the pleasure she'd found in his company. Quent's funeral, her children's holidays without a father, it was all still too fresh. She thought of how time stands still with pain and races through pleasure to get back to pain as if attracted to it. What had transpired between her and Dro? Did she betray her feelings? Show how much she enjoyed him? *Will I ever feel happy again?*

Allise turned out the lights and walked slowly up the stairs.

Sometime later, in a letter to Sam, she wrote that Maizee had agreed to move and Dro had sketched a plan for the garage space. She was careful not to mention that Dro, too, had reservations about moving the Colsons to Deer Point. She dropped the letter at the post office and found one from Sam. Along with vivid descriptions of army life, he wrote, "I will work on the apartment when I come home on leave in a few weeks. After leave time, I go to Camp Hood, Texas."

At the end of the month, Allise waited at the train station. She met a leaner Sam with a spring in his step. He approached her with arms outstretched, and she ran toward him, shouting that he looked great. Dropping his duffel bag, he pulled her into a muscle-hardened hug. Then, holding her at arm's-length, he said, "It's good to be home, girl. You are as pretty as ever."

A blush warmed her face, and she thought he appeared more confident. "We must hurry home before time to pick up Peter from school and Cleesy from a birthday party. They can't wait to see you."

Back in Deer Point, the kids jumped in the car and romped all over Sam in the back seat. "Gee whiz, I could have gotten basic training right here at home."

When Allise sent them to bed that night, he said, "We need to get an early start on the garage in the morning." Gathering up his gear, he left to walk the few blocks to the Filbert Street house Allise had made ready for him.

Next morning, Sam took measurements, then he set off for the lumber yard. Returning about mid-morning, he said, "Folks asked why I was buying lumber. When I told them, they got in a snit about Nigras moving in here. No one remembers a time when a colored person lived in white town."

Allise felt uneasy. Her own doubts resurfaced, but she said nothing. They were going over the plans, when Peter rushed in from school. His clothing was soiled and knees and elbows scraped.

"What happened?" She examined him.

"This kid pushed me to the ground during recess."

"What kid?" Sam asked.

"Jimmy Aberson. He's in my class. Someone told him about niggers coming here. I just walked out the school door, and he yelled 'nigger lover.' Then he shoved me. I got up and socked him right in the face. Made his nose bleed."

"Peter!"

"Now Allie, hold on. You had a right to sock—"

"Sam!" She gave her brother-in-law a stern look.

"Son, let's go over this situation. He made a degrading remark and knocked you down. Was he wrong?"

"Yeah! He was."

"Is it wrong to love Negroes?"

"Jimmy thinks so."

"Do *you* think it is?"

"I don't know."

Sam paced and wrung his hands. "Allie, the kid's gonna have trouble if you—"

"Sam, hush! I will not have my children … Peter, is it wrong to hate Negroes?" He uttered a feeble "yes," and she felt guilt and anger about what had happened to him. She stormed, "Sam, will you stop pacing and that outrageous thing with the hands!"

He slipped his hands in pockets and stood still. "I'm sorry, I …" Peter looked as if he would cry, and Allise felt like crying, too. "It's awright," Sam said. "My sergeant said the same thing. I been trying t' stop the habit."

"I am sorry, Sam." Pushing hair from her forehead, Allise pulled Peter to her side. "Sit here, son." She took his hand and explained that Jimmy Aberson implied it was wrong to think well of a whole race of people. "It's like saying every single Negro is guilty of something that should cause all of them to be hated. Jimmy was wrong to shove you, and he is wrong about the colored race."

"He was wrong to push me, alright," Peter agreed.

"I suppose you couldn't have reacted differently in this instance." She said the boy tried to intimidate him in the same way some white people keep black people cowed. "Think about that, Peter. Now, go wash your wounds and bring the Band-Aids." Turning to Sam, she asked, "What do you think of all this, Peter's run-in and the town's upset over the Colsons?" She wondered if there would be more such trouble after he left.

"I don't know folks talk. They're not much for action, but I cain't remember having anything like this to act on. It's not gonna be easy for the kids. I'm thinking they'll have a rough go of it." After a moment, he added, "Allie, I never saw the situation the way you put it. Makes sense, though."

She sighed. "Yes, well the question is will my children see it my way? When Peter was a baby, I vowed they would not hold biases. But can I keep them from it?" She felt sad. "Sam, I appreciate your help, but please don't interfere when I want them to understand how we should be with other people."

"I gotcha," he said with a salute.

The next morning issued in a cool, blustery, March day. Allise and Sam began work on the apartment. They noticed people standing at the end of the alley and staring up at the garage. Sam said they were curious and laughed it off. One day during the week, they saw three cars, one behind the other, idling on the side street. Neither had recognized the cars or drivers. "Just looking. I told ya they're all talk." Sam had tried to assuage her, but she hadn't missed his concerned gaze out the window. She recalled Rebekah's warning about Elfreeda riding in the car with her. What might happen after Sam leaves for Fort Hood, she had wondered.

Now, on his last morning, he arranged for hired workers to finish the remaining work on Maizee's quarters then rushed off to the farm. Finding it set for spring planting, he returned and told Allise that Jonas was doing a good job. His satisfaction with the farm operation pleased her.

That afternoon, she saw him off on a train to Texas, and without his comforting mantle, braced herself to carry on as the children's lone protector.

Weeks passed and nothing untoward had happened. Allise dismissed idle talk, gawking neighbors, and strange cars. She thought Peter's confrontation was likely due to a young boy's urge to fight.

The apartment was finished, it was Saturday, and she waited to receive the Colsons.

Listening to Frank Sinatra ballads, she whispered along with him, "I'll be seeing you in all the old familiar places." Nights were lonely, and sometimes it was impossible to anticipate the future without Quent. Allise argued with herself about inviting Dro to dinner again. Would it be inappropriate so soon after her husband's demise?

Her thoughts were interrupted by the sound of the farm truck in the alley. Running out to help unload the sparse furnishings, she noticed neighbors walking up the lane toward them. Seeing Maizee's nervous glances, Allise waved and called, "Hi! Nice day, isn't it?" Returning feeble waves, the curious passed on by, and she hoped Maizee would think their stroll was a common occurrence.

No sooner were they gone than she overheard Cleesy tell her friends that she went to school with Nate. Good heavens, Allise thought. *Only Sam, Elfreeda and the children know. Not even the school board knows about the farm classes.*

*What might happen when those children tell their parents?* She decided to face that problem if and when it occurred.

A more immediate concern was how to handle the boys. Peter sat on the back steps. His eyes spoke volumes when Nate glanced his way. *What was he thinking? Sam said it wouldn't be easy.*

Over the time it took for the Colsons to settle in, Allise observed Nate's happy disposition turn sad. Peter and his playmates didn't call for Nate to join them. He played with Cleesy. Allise thought when school ended, the boys would get to know each other.

One morning, she looked out the kitchen window to see Nate leaning against the uprooted stump removed from the site of the Colsons' kitchenette. Turning from the window, Allise suddenly jerked back. Peering out again, she muttered, "What is that? A sign!" To Maizee, she said, "I'll call Nate for breakfast."

With him seated at the table, she slipped back outdoors and ran to the Farley Street sidewalk. A crude cardboard sign leaned lop-sided two feet above ground. Red paint bled from the words, "Nigger Lovers." Heart racing, she pulled up the sign, rushed into the garage, pitched it onto the back floorboard of the car and paced.

Slipping back through the front door, Allise picked up the receiver and dialed. The sheriff answered, and barely above a whisper, she identified herself. "Sheriff Banes, I have a problem in need of your attention. I'll be in your office right away." She hung up, went for her car keys, and without explanation asked Maizee to see to the children.

Marching down the courthouse hall with the sign underarm, she passed open-door offices. In his office, the lawman wrote at his desk. He didn't look up, and she waited."

Standing, he placed the small pad and pen in his shirt pocket. "How are ya, Miz DeWitt. Look upset, how can I help ya?"

"Oh, I'm upset." She held the sign for him to read. "This was on my lawn."

"Well, you sorta brought this on y'self. You should've expected—"

"No, Sheriff! I expect people to be decent. Tell me what law has been violated by moving a Negro family onto my property?"

"Now Miz DeWitt, I don't know of a law, but it's jes understood down here that niggers live in Colored Town, and we live in—"

"Ah, no law has been broken. You should take note, Sheriff, that I came to you, the law enforcer in this county, with evidence of an implied threat to my family. I don't know who did this, but you've seen the evidence and been apprized of the problem." She pointed a finger at him. "If harm comes to any of us well, I intend to write a letter to the *Weekly* about this incident and mention that this evidence was brought before *you.*"

The beam faded from Sheriff Banes' eyes.

Allise told him Maizee and Nate came from hardworking blacks who farmed for her late husband's family. "It's unbelievable that law-abiding people are thought of in this derogatory manner." Again, she held the sign for the sheriff to see. "I doubt there's a thing about Maizee and Nate that should worry anyone. If they cause trouble, I'll be the first to admit I made a mistake in bringing them here." Turning, she looked back at him. "It's not my intention to be a trou-ble-maker. Can I count on your help, Sheriff?"

"W-well sure." With a fifteen-year span of catching crooks, he hitched up the belt slung low on his hips and rested a hand on the holstered pistol. "I understand, Miz DeWitt, but like you said in so many words, you know you may have put y'self in danger."

"Yes, that I admit. But we're beyond that to the reality of this." She raised the sign. "This shines a new light on our responsibilities, wouldn't you agree?"

Looking confounded, he stared at her. "I suppose."

"Good." Remembering Cleesy's blab about the farm school, she added, "I intend to be alert for the sake of my family and the Colsons." Smiling as graciously as anger would allow, she thanked him and tucked the sign under her arm. "Sheriff Banes, I'm depending on you to be responsible under the oath of your office."

Back home in the garage, Allise looked around for a place to hide the sign. There was no such place. Just as she thought to slip inside and turn it to the wall in her bedroom closet, Maizee popped around the corner. "The kids are asking where you went, Miz Allie." Her young black friend stared at the red-lettered sign, trying to read it.

Allise gave a nervous little laugh. "Oh, I uh, I just ran downtown."

"You acting strange, Miz Allie. I'm worried. What's wrong?" Allise's arm covered only the letter 'N' on the sign. Craning her neck, Maizee read, "igger lovers. Nigger lovers! I'm scared, Miz Allie."

"Sh, now. We mustn't scare the children. Help me sneak this upstairs. I want the sign as evidence. I went to the sheriff and told him if anything happened to anyone of us he would be responsible." Seeing Maizee's eyes were full of fright, she said, "We must be strong. I told him I was writing a letter to the newspaper
about this so that others will know—"

"Miz Allie, that ain't gonna do no good if we done dead."

"It isn't going to happen, Maizee." Allise wanted to be as confident as she tried to sound. "Now, you must help me get this past the kids."

"Whatcha gonna tell 'em about where you been?"

"That I ran to the courthouse on business. Now, let's get this inside."

While Maizee distracted the kids, she slipped upstairs then returned for breakfast. Apparently their curiosity about her whereabouts had been satisfied.

Allise didn't waste any time before writing her letter to the *Weekly*. Her words to the sheriff had belied her courage. She was frightened and full of doubts. And despite disclaiming the role of trouble-maker, she knew she pricked everyone like a thorn. Even as she deposited the letter in the post office, the sheriff's warning resonated in her ears. She had chosen a head-on course. It would be lonely and full of pitfalls.

A few days had passed when Peter ran onto the porch looking fearful for his life. Nate and Cleesy worked a puzzle, and he jumped up. "What happened, Pete?"

"Shut up!" Peter yelled. "Get out of here!" Nate's face crumpled with hurt.

Allise rose from a porch chair and motioned for Nate and Cleesy to continue. She followed Peter inside. His face contorted in a mixture of anger and fright. "Peter, come with me." On the living room couch, she waited for him to speak.

Slumped over his knees, he huffed and puffed, and rubbed his eyes. Groping for words, he appeared ready to cry. Finally, he managed to say two high school boys waited for him behind shrubs. "They chased me home. Called me a 'nigger lover.'" His stare asked what she intended to do about it.

"Come here, Peter." Allise pulled him into her arms, and they clung to each other. "My darling child, you can't compete with older boys. So, what can we do?"

He pulled back. "Well, you caused it! If you hadn't brought the—"

"Yes, Peter, I brought them here, but for the life of me, I can't see the wrong in that. Tell me what they've done that should keep them from being here."

"Those boys did me wrong because *they* are here."

"Excuse me. Did I hear you say the boys were wrong?"

He squirmed under her gaze, and wouldn't repeat what he had said. She saw his mind grappling with the point. "We shouldn't be intimidated, and we mustn't intimidate others. We should speak out about what is happening to us. Will you help me do that?"

Peter wouldn't commit himself, and Allise said, "There will be many times, son, when we have difficult things to do. This is one of those times."

His gaze left her uncertain of her mother-role. In another minute, she would cry.

On the evening of the parent-teachers' meeting, Allise's mind was set on her son's problem at school. Taking him and Cleesy along to the school auditorium, she told them she meant to raise what had happened to him. "I'm not a tattler," Peter said. "Don't even like colored people." There wasn't time for a rebuke. Their mother herded them to a seat.

At a proper time in the proceedings, she stood and asked to speak. Her children slid down in their seats as she told about Peter being chased from school by older boys. "My child suffers because a colored family lives on our property. The sheriff says I have broken no law. The Colsons have violated no law, harmed no one—"

"Yeah, but you teach them Nigras on the river. Let your kid sit with 'em." The loud voice came from behind her. Turning, she saw Charlie Wise standing in the back row. "Miz DeWitt, you're an offense to the way we do things. What you say about that?"

An awkward moment passed while Allise thought of how to address his question. "Before he left for the war, my late husband and I spoke about the Negroes' plight. Quent wasn't in favor of schooling them. He said they would never amount 'to a hill of beans.' I disagree. If educated, they can earn their way and contribute to society—"

"Malarkey!" The man, still standing, was joined by the mutterings of others.

Allise, determined to be heard, said, "Mr. Wise, I'll ask you the question I asked Quent. If your children were denied an education because they're white, because Negroes thought them incapable of learning and wouldn't give them an opportunity to show whether or not they could learn, how would you feel?"

The man sat down, but loud mumbling continued. Peter looked frightened, and she raised her voice. "It feels different when we walk in their shoes." The undertones quieted, and Allise captured the moment in a more complaisant manner. "Please consider the energy that's wasted in hating the Negro race. Energy that can be used to prepare them to be independent. Everyone would benefit from such an effort."

All was quiet. No one stood to leave until the chairman dismissed them.

Back home, Allise read on the chaise when Peter came in and asked what difference such talks would make. She said a difference wouldn't be seen right away. "We're taking a chance on parents and community leaders rethinking old ways. That they, over time, will redirect their children's thinking. I must fight back, Peter. Do what I can to see that anger doesn't continue to be misdirected against innocent people. You, for instance." She waited for his reaction. He looked confused, and she continued. "I would like for white people to look at their anger, to ask what it is really about. To notice hurt in colored eyes."

"What are white people angry about?" he asked.

Allise was pleased with the opening. "That's the question, isn't it? Not for harm inflicted by the Colsons or us, would you say?" He nodded agreement. "No, it isn't us, and it isn't Maizee and Nate. Were it any other colored family in our apartment, the reaction would be the same. Those, who try to frighten us, act out of long-held feelings about all Negroes. I think they're angry at a different set of people. Yankees who defeated them in the Civil War. Whites vent anger on a race weakened by the way they are treated."

Peter was quiet, and she couldn't tell from his expression if he was spurred to think of the angles she presented. If only Quent were here, she thought. *No, the burden is mine.*

∗    ∗    ∗    ∗

That night, things his mother had said rattled around in Peter's head. Her words, those of his father, and friends buzzed incessantly, keeping him awake. He remembered a picture card from Sunday School. Jesus sitting with white, black and slant-eyed kids. On the back was: "Suffer the little children to come unto me."

Lying there in the dark, he tried to sort it all out. His daddy didn't like Nigras, and kids made fun of them. His father's words popped into his head. "Take care of your mother and Cleesy." *What am I supposed to do?*

The question lingered in his mind without an answer, and the eleven-year-old's eyes grew heavy with sleep.

∗    ∗    ∗    ∗

Allise's attention was drawn to the children playing in her yard. She intended to write to Sam, but laying pen and paper on the porch table, she watched Nate make a bold attempt to be included. Peter and his friends warned him away. Nate's persistence is admirable, she thought. *Peter plays with him when other boys aren't around. His peers have a greater influence than I.* She had given them teamwork projects, but a thaw in their relationship was yet to come. *What can I do?*

Watching their childish maneuvers, she thought of her relationship with the people of Deer Point. *No inroads there either.* Provincialism wins, she told herself. *Expression of my views and standing by my convictions lead to a lonely existence.*

Maizee brought out a pitcher of lemonade and poured two glasses. Taking a seat, she waved a heart-shaped fan that read in bold, black letters, "Carvell's Funeral Home." Allise used one from Rabern's Hardware. "I hope this heat breaks soon," she said, taking a sip of the cool drink. "Maizee, have you overheard talk about you and Nate?"

The black woman nodded. Allise shook her head in denial. "It couldn't be farther from the truth, Maizee. I don't consider you a 'live-in' servant even though others say you are. But, it might be wise to let their conclusion stand rather than dispute it." Reaching out, Allise covered her hand. "We serve each other, but most of all, we share friendship."

With a shy smile, the young woman said, "We sho do, Miz Allie."

"Nevertheless, Maizee," Allise emphasized, "what they think is important. It will affect our children. Our boys are trapped between two diverse viewpoints, ours and that of the townsfolk. I've watched the boys. Sometimes Peter's intolerable, but I think a stronger relationship will result if we don't push them. Let them find their own way."

Maizee nodded again, and glanced in the direction of the large stump near the alley. Grotesque roots served as cockpit seats and pilot controls for white boys' imaginations. Staccato gunfire and battle cries came from pretend-warriors running from behind trees. Peeking out, they poked stick rifles out of bushes. Some crawled on their bellies and ran across the lawn until falling wounded or pretending to be dead.

Sad-faced, Nate sat on the apartment stoop watching the players act out what they had seen on movie screens. Allise watched him pull a blade of grass into strips. *Did he imagine black boys flying airplanes and soldiering?*

Suddenly, battle sounds changed to a cacophony of shrill yells. Snapping his head in the direction of bodies rolling on the ground, Nate stood, hesitating. Then, hearing a call for help, he ran toward the tumbling pile. Peter lay at the bottom of the heap, and Nate dived into the mound of flailing fists.

Their mothers rushed out, and Maizee moved to grab her son, but Allise caught her arm. "Wait! Let them settle it." Fists shot in all directions, each blow making her cringe as though in doubt of her restraint.

When it appeared they weren't winning, Peter's pals ran away, calling threats back at him and Nate. The two boys watched them vanish from the yard, dusted themselves off and went inside for lemonade. A short time later, Allise and Maizee saw them perched on the upturned stump, machine-gunning enemy planes. "A-ak, a-ak!" Sounds of automatic fire lead the aviators into downward plunges of doomed planes and va-rooming up again in victorious climbs. "I got that Jap! Did you see that?"

"No, you didn't, Nate. I got that one!"

Smiling, Allise said, "To think I intended to have that stump removed!" Laughing, she took up the pen and began a letter to Sam:

**Peter finds Nate a desirable playmate when he's alone. I'm not always sure of my methods in handling their relationship. Perhaps in time they will accept each other.**

**Sam, everyone in town is in a state of grief. The Iverson family has a son missing in action, and the Buckley's son is being shipped home for burial.**

She wrote the most war-like spot in Deer Point was in her yard, and that Maizee still called the radio a voice box. Finishing the letter, Allise thought if the war didn't end soon, Sam would be bound for overseas duty.

"Lookey." Maizee grinned, pointing to the largest oak tree. "They be daring each other t' jump off that limb. Playing Superman with towels around their shoulders."

Allise smiled. "Better pray no one gets a broken bone. Peter will miss Nate next week when he goes to the farm." Even as she spoke, she wasn't at all sure of her son's feelings, but she liked the contented grin on Maizee's face.

Nate was excited about his week on the farm, Allise sent him and Peter outside to wait while everyone else made ready to leave. Heading for the car, she saw Peter's impatience in every kick at clumps of grass.

Letting him off at the farm shed where Jonas tied a line on a fishing pole, she called, "Jonas, keep an eye on him."

"I sho will, Miz Allie. I'll be in the field next to that boy while he be fishing."

As the car moved away, Nate watched his grandpa and Peter troop off toward the creek. In the rear view mirror, Allise thought he would rather be fishing than sitting in the classroom. "You have a whole week on the farm, Nate."

It was noontime when they returned to pick up Peter and let Nate off. As he clambered out of the car, Peter ran up to Allise. "Jonas wants to take Nate and me fishing on Moon Lake. Ple-ease let me stay here tonight. He says the fish bite early, and we will have to get up at daylight."

She looked at Maizee for approval and said, "Okay."

Summer was close to an end when Peter wrote to Uncle Sam about fishing on Moon Lake. He asked his mother to read his letter. She read aloud: "Nate and I slept on a quilt on the porch. We sweated all night and didn't sleep much because of bullfrogs going "garrumph, garrumph." He wrote that Jonas woke them early to go to the lake. "We caught bluegills, and Jonas helped clean and cook them on a wood spit over a fire we built."

Allise added a postscript. "The Moon Lake experience was good for Peter. Maybe it will turn out right between the boys, yet." Then, handing the letter back to him, she said, "Your letter will make Uncle Sam very happy."

She picked up his latest letter from Ft. Hood. He wrote:

**Soil is so dry here, the ground cracks. I fear I'm going to bake under this scorching heat. At the end of the day, I'm coated in Texas dirt. We inhale, eat, and wear dust stirred up by the tanks. All our time is spent in the field on training maneuvers. Living in a tent isn't for me, Allie. I'll be glad to have it behind me.**

Sam, unlike Quent, isn't meant for the military life, Allise thought. She put the letter away and stashed old lesson plans with fresh marginal notations in a desk basket.

# CHAPTER 13

▼

Allise went to the Colored School about enrolling Nate and placement in a higher grade. She found the black woman setting up the only two classrooms for opening day. Pulling lift-top desks with bench seats into alignment, she grumbled about missing screws that attached them to the floor. Flipping a hand in the air, she said her effort was a useless exercise. Allise compared the desks with makeshift furniture at the farm school.

Inviting her to a seat, the woman said, "I'm Lula Hart, teacher and principal, jest trying to be in charge of ever'thing."

"Miss Hart, I'm Allise DeWitt." Extolling Nate's abilities, she explained how she worked with him. "He's bright, and I recommend him for the fifth grade." Miss Lula said she wasn't about to allow Nate to advance to the fifth grade before he proved himself.

Back home, Allise tried to encourage Maizee. "If Nate shows he can do the lessons, and we continue to work with him, Miss Hart will relent and place him in a higher class. Let's drive over early Friday to make a good impression."

"I need to do things on my own, Miz Allie. I'll go with Nate to enroll."

"Oh, I didn't mean … of course you will, but the heat, Maizee." Allise didn't press when she insisted the heat and walking weren't problems.

\*     \*     \*     \*

Friday morning, Maizee was careful not to let Miz Allie see the fear that gripped her. She had not been alone with her son on Deer Point's streets. Leaving for the Colored School, as the distance narrowed between them

163

and their destination, she grew more anxious. Nate bounced along without apparent worry about anything.

Within a stone's throw of the building, his mother pulled off her sweat-stained kerchief, swiped it across Nate's face and plunged it inside his shirt. Then, wiping her face and arms, she tossed it into the weed-choked ditch.

The school sat at the southwest edge of Colored Town and back from the Bensburg highway which paralleled the train tracks. Windows sagged in whitewashed walls, giving the structure a droopy face. Dead weeds and grass wove the grounds more like a ragged, faded rug than a green carpet. From both sides of the rickety steps, trench-like paths trailed around each corner of the front.

They climbed the steps to an open hallway dividing two large rooms. At the other end, a woman sat behind a small, rough-crafted desk. Sitting there as though welded to the seat, she showed an authoritative demeanor. Without rising to greet them, she moved a cardboard fan to catch any breath of air that mercifully passed her way.

Lagging behind Nate, Maizee kept a distance from the woman. She gotta be Miz Lula Hart, she thought, taking in the stern face. Feeling nervous, she gazed beyond the head of cropped, kinky hair out onto the back schoolyard. The trench-like trails from the front intersected a single, well-worn path leading to a bare spot beneath a lone basketball goal. Minus a net, the hoop clung in a precarious way to a rusty iron pole.

Nate took the only available chair and riveted his attention on the woman behind the desk. Yet to speak, she looked up for the first time and with command accustomed to obedience, said, "Young man, let yo momma sit! You are his momma, aren't you?"

Maizee saw Nate nearly jump out of his skin. She nodded and edged onto the seat. She wondered why no one else was there. Sitting rigidly straight, she waited to be recognized again. Laying aside her fan, the older woman lifted papers as though in search of something. Then looking up, she asked, "You here to put this boy in school?"

"Yes'um."

What's his name?"

"Nathaniel Colson. We calls him Nate." Maizee stiffened as the woman gave her child a quick glance through eyes that didn't appear to really see him.

"Uh huh, he be the one Miz DeWitt wants in fifth grade. Where was he born?"

Sarcasm in her gruntled, half-mocking laugh brought even more rigidness to Maizee's back. Through pursed lips, she answered he was born in Jefferson, Texas.

"H-mmm. When?" Maizee said 1933. The disinterested woman's exasperation was evident. "What *month*! Month, day, year."

"June 20, 1933." Why she being so grouchy? Maizee wondered, as the teacher asked for their address.

Told they lived behind Miz DeWitt, she said, "Uh huh. I been hearing about you."

Behind Maizee, Nate fastened his hands on her arms and peeked over her shoulder. "We live on Grayson Street," he said.

"Uh-huh, moved here from the river. You have a phone number?" Never looking up, the woman recorded and twitched the pencil as if mother and son existed only in the task at hand.

Maizee felt her anger building, but she was determined to enlist Nate. "What's your name?" She pointed the pencil at Maizee. Her name was barely uttered before the next question came. "Your husband's name?" She prodded, filling in needed information with less and less apparent interest in the light-complexioned child, who crouched beside his mother now, gazing up at the teacher through his unusual, blue-gray eyes. "I ain't got no husband." Maizee reached out to stroke her son's short wavy hair.

For the first time, the teacher held her pencil poised in mid-air and placed a fixed stare on Nate. "Lawdy, lawdy." Then almost inaudibly, "River niggers."

Maizee bristled and stood up. "Miz'm, don't you go calling us river niggers!" Nostrils flaring and eyes flashing, she felt the anger of that evening in the cotton shed.

For a moment, the teacher was speechless, then, "You need to be rid of that sass, girl, messing round like you do." Glancing at Nate and back to Maizee, she said, "The Lawd lets you sink to a bottomless pit, but he can lift you up." Ending her sing-song preachment, she dismissed them with a hand stroke.

Maizee's fear of the overbearing woman passed. "I already knows the Lawd. Don't you go saying such when you don't know nothing about us." Wide-eyed, Nate tugged on his mother's hand, and through her anger, she saw fright on his face. Encircling him in her arm, she gazed at the woman assumed to be his teacher. "Miz'm, Nate bees a smart boy. Ain't nothing gonna stop us from getting him more learning."

Staring at them, the teacher straightened the collar of her print dress. "All right then." She paused, as if searching for words. "Nobody wants to teach our kids more 'n me. Some things git my goat, like kids without da ..." She glanced at Nate. "This old building, handed-down books, no money for anything. Kids come t' school when they feel like it. I jest do the best I can." She sighed.

Knowing a similar frustration, Maizee mellowed. "Miz—"

"Ever'body calls me Miz Lula."

"Miz Lula, you gonna be a fine teacher for Nate, and he gonna be here ever' day." Their moments of frustration passed into soft laughter, and soon they waved goodbye.

Wading back through the grounds, Nate glanced around at the building with apprehension. "Son, she gonna be a fine teacher cause she cares," his mother said.

They met the wicked overhead sun and plodded homeward. Maizee swiped a trickle of sweat from Nate's temple. He slowed their pace, and she urged him along. She seldom thought about Mista Quent anymore, but now she wondered how Miz Allie could miss Nate's resemblance to her late husband. Guessing at what she might know, Maizee knew her white woman was different. Baffled by her kindness, she was coming to think of her as a beloved sister.

Suddenly, she was aware of being back on the tree-lined sidewalks of Deer Point.

✳     ✳     ✳     ✳

With Nate situated to start classes at the Colored School, Allise anticipated her return to a high school classroom after a twelve-year lapse. Did she still have a passion for teaching? *It will be a challenge. New ideas, new ways.* How could she make the learning process interesting?

It had been a while since she thought about John Dewey's motivational values.

Shortly before graduating Swarthmore College, an instructor had elaborated on them. The Twentieth Century philosopher's theories, referred to as "Instrumentalism," maintained that educators should use values to motivate conduct and come up with programs to improve social relations. Through such a process, ways should evolve to eliminate confusion around primary issues and social beliefs, and suggest actions to meet current problems.

Are his theories still relevant today, Allise wondered. She took the paisley-cov-ered box from a bureau drawer, returned to the lounge and removed a yellowed envelope postmarked May 6, 1929. Her father had scribbled a note on it:

***Good luck, daughter. Teach to make a difference for good in future generations. Your loving Papa, W. P. Weston***

Below, he summarized Dewey's principles for educating students:

1.  Include the study of culture,

2.  Prepare students for the future,

3.  Stimulate individual growth with consideration for individual differences,

4.  Be accessible to everyone.

Allise remembered arriving in the South with the scribbled envelope in her handbag. *A newly trained teacher, awed by Dewey's ideas, I knew little about the regional differences I would encounter. Set in on my southern students with idealism and confidence.* Well, his idea of learning by doing still appeals to me, she thought. *His methods can still be a test of social practices touching on all segments of the social fiber. Science, intelligence, democracy, especially education. How can I use his methods of directed activity, experimentation, and investigation, and keep the students' attention?*

Allise sat in the quiet of her bedroom, contemplating differences between North and South. What about the black segment of society? She believed war drew a curtain over concerns for social progress. It drained energy away from improving lives, caring for the unhealthy and unloved lot. Suddenly, she realized she floundered in the same old quagmire. No matter how her thoughts began, they came back to the least cared-for souls.

Returning to responsibilities in a classroom, she made a mental note to be open to changes and careful in the application of methods. Her father had said, "discussion, compromise and patience solves most problems." Dewey's philosophy was weighty, but her papa's influence was greater. Allise tucked the envelope back into the box and sought in her Quaker way, the direction for making a difference as Papa had charged her.

Standing, she returned the box to the bureau. Despite timidity about taking charge of a classroom again, she was determined to begin anew the work she felt born to do.

School had been in session a couple of weeks, and the mid-September heat registered in the high nineties. After classes, Allise and Cleesy escaped swirling fans at home for a short drive in the country. Returning, they stopped at the post office and found Sam's letter waiting. Her worst fears surfaced. To no one in particular, she said, "He's in Europe!" She wondered if he was in the battles raging across Sicily.

Allise drove to the bank, and with Cleesy in tow, she raced in just ahead of a teller ready to lock the door. Dro glanced up and signaled her inside. Beaming what appeared to be surprised pleasure at Cleesy, he motioned Allise to a leather chair.

She held up the letter. "Sam's in Europe!"

Dro stood behind the tabletop desk, hands in his pockets. "Now, Allie, you know we expected this." Removing one hand, he shuffled a single piece of paper in what seemed an idle gesture. "Let's focus on the day this mess ends, and Sam and all our boys come home safe and sound," he said.

Leaving somewhat assuaged, she thought Dro seemed to understand her fear of another telegram. He held out neither false hope nor doting comfort. Only sensible optimism, something she could appreciate.

She needed optimism when Sicily fell into Allied hands and the forces moved on toward Italy, bringing down the fascist regime and deposing Mussolini to make an armistice with the Italians. The fight for Salerno had been bitter, and no word had arrived from Sam. Dreading to know his situation, Allise feared he was in the thick of it.

At war with conflicts of her conscience, she had reassessed old beliefs, beliefs of a lifetime, absolutes that never before came into question. Her growing hatred of Germans and the Japanese was against principles taught her from childhood. Now, uncomfortable with the angles her mind forced her to consider, she stood in the post office pondering acronyms in the return address on a small piece of mail. She didn't hear Dro approach from behind her. "Hi! Is it from Sam?"

Smiling, she held it toward him. "Yes. First one like this." Slipping a finger under the seal, she unfolded the V-Mail dated September 23, 1943.

Dro read over her shoulder. "He's in Italy. Going on two months now?" They continued to read:

**Two weeks of hard rain. We dug tanks out of knee-deep mud. It's like oatmeal, sticky like Mama made us eat.**

**Air force and navy bombers saved us from xxxxxxx. We fought four days for xxxxx. Won xxxxxxxxx ridge after 6 days. My combat jacket's in shreds. Smells like rotten potatoes. So far, no frostbite or trench foot, but many do have it. Can't shave. No razors, shaving cream, mirrors or hot water. No time if we had them. I look 110 with this beard.**

**Hope you've had no more Colson trouble. Write news of the kids.**

**Love, Sam**

"Censored. Bet he's with the Fifth Army, General Clark's command." Dro had read an account of the battle for Salerno in the *Arkansas Gazette*. "He must be miserable. What kind of Christmas will he have?"

"A bleak one, I suppose." Dro frowned and asked, "What kind of Colson trouble?"

"None since the sign." Gazing into his eyes, Allise felt his concern was real. "Thanks for asking." She had such a need to fall into strong, protective arms, but the thought frightened her. Flustered, she made an excuse about time. "See you at dinner," she said, and hurried away.

In her classroom, Allise sorted papers and books in piles on the floor around her desk. Other materials would replace them after the Christmas break. She thought of Sam, glad his holiday package was on the way. Maizee had helped her pack gloves, socks, knit caps, a sweater and cookies to send to him. Dro had reminded her that Naples had fallen to the Allies, but the Army was tied down in winter weather.

To relieve her fear for Sam, she turned to thoughts of her students. Had she kindled an enthusiasm for the English language? Had she caused them to think provocatively on world literature? *My flare for teaching still burns. I've made a remarkable connection with them*, she thought. *Couldn't have done it without Maizee.*

She felt good about the time she and her friend shared. The black girl's reservations had slipped away over the months, and their relationship seemed more like sisterhood. The love between Cleesy and Maizee was quite evident. *My five-year-old is well-cared for. Peter and Nate still victims of color.* Must keep at that, Allise thought. *Nate and Miz Lula share a warm bond. Life is good but Peter and I head off to school in one direction and Nate in another. We may act like a family, but there are things we can't do together.*

She finished sorting, packed a box, and stored some things to use after the holidays.

That evening, Allise and Dro sat at the dining table while Maizee cleaned in the kitchen. He spent more and more time with her. She told herself he filled the voids left by Quent and Sam, and Maizee liked to cook for him. Dro pulled his chair close to hers and whispered, "Allise, don't be too open about Maizee and Nate eating in here. Invites disapproval. Makes no difference to me, but others—"

"We're a family, Dro. People think Maizee is a domestic, living in separate quarters with a half-white son who's nevertheless a 'nigger.'" She promised discretion.

Maizee brought cookies and poured coffee. Dro reached for one and said she was the best cookie maker in the country. "I know, Mista Dro. You jes wriggling yo way t' more dinners." They laughed. "I got some Christmas stuff yesterday. Ribbon and Nate's gift. You coming for Christmas dinner with us, Mista Dro?"

He gave Allise a questioning look, and she smiled.

\*   \*   \*   \*

Maizee waved to Miz Allie and the children. They were off on a shopping spree in Bensburg, and she was free to bake more Christmas cookies for gifts.

In the kitchen, she made the dough and took a star-shaped cutter from the drawer. Working fast to finish before they returned, she thought about the changes in her life since moving to Deer Point. *Me and Nate have our own place. No more drawing water from a well. Like Dalt said, don't have to freeze our tails off in a outhouse.* She smiled with fondness for her brothers and wondered what they thought of her and Nate living with Mista Quent's family. *I figure me and Nate be better off than the two of them.*

Maizee tied the last cellophane-wrapped bag of cookies with ribbon when she heard the car roll in. Hiding the packets and Nate's wrapped gift in her closet, she straightened her dress and ran out to meet the returning shoppers. The children scooted past her with purchases of Christmas surprises clutched to their chests. "There's tea cakes on the kitchen table." She shouted after them, hoping the smell of spice would cover the aroma of her gumdrop cookies made for gifts. Laughing at their guarded packages, she walked over to the car.

"Let's get these things inside," Miz Allie whispered, pointing into the trunk. "The children are already too curious about what's in the bags."

They sprinted upstairs with "Santa's" surprises. Miz Allie showed her a doll for Cleesy, sweaters, shirts, and socks for the boys. Books, games, puzzles, and marbles, too. "The war leaves little variety." Her white friend pushed the bag back on a high closet shelf. "It's a copy of Ernie Pyle's *Brave Men* for Dro," she said.

Not finding Miz Allie very convincing, Maizee looked skeptical. "Uh huh, I know what you gone and done." Her cookies wouldn't come close to the hidden gift, but Miz Allie would like them anyway. Earlier, she had sat on her bedside counting coins emptied from a small pouch. Left over from Nate's gift and ribbon, she still had enough money for remnants to make dresses and bonnets for Cleesy's doll and marble bags for the boys.

Maizee had never been so excited about Christmas.

\*   \*   \*   \*

Allise rushed Peter and Cleesy into the church hall for the children's Christmas party at Newtown Church. They were late, and the last refreshments disappeared as they ran inside the room. "Oh, man, they ate all the cookies," Peter complained.

In a corner of the room, a tree stood trimmed in biblical cut-outs and paper chains. With a "Ho, Ho, Ho!" Brother Rigdon sat nearby, dressed in Santa Claus garb fashioned by his wife and handing each child a small Bible as they filed past him.

Watching, Allise thought the scene never changed. Year after year, same cookies, same punch and gift. Same unfeeling "Ho, Ho, Ho." *Where's the spirit of Christmas?*

Christmas Eve morning, she woke thinking of the lack of joy at the party. The day arrived with a cold, damp overcast that kept everyone indoors, and she locked her bedroom door to keep intruders out while she wrapped packages. Tying the ribbons, she thought of how much Sam would miss Peter and Cleesy's happy faces on Christmas morning. Suddenly a loud commotion interrupted her. Descending the stairs, she saw Jonas trying to maneuver a six-foot cedar tree on a stand through the front door.

"See the pretty red ribbon, Miz Allie?" Maizee grinned. She explained that Brother Jedadiah had asked a timber hand to cut the tree. "Daddy brought it on the truck. It's a gift to us, Miz Allie, from Elfreeda, Brother Jedadiah and Daddy. It ain't been easy keeping their secret. Elfreeda threatened me within an inch of my life, if you went out and got another tree."

"It's a beauty," Allise exclaimed. "Let's get the decorations from beneath the staircase." As Jonas positioned the tree, she invited him to help trim it. He draped red and green roping round and round it. She and Maizee hung tinsel, and the kids hooked globe-shaped, red and gold ornaments from a decade of DeWitt Christmases. When all was in place, everyone stood back admiring their creation and watching Peter stretch from a stepladder to hook the gold star on top. Allise felt a glow of pride as he took on the role his father held in previous years.

Maizee looked awestruck. She placed a hand on Nate's shoulder. "Look at that!"

Peter backed down the ladder and yelled, "Let's get our gifts." Jonas left, and everyone scurried for presents.

Peter sat on the floor, shoving packages beneath the tree when Maizee and Nate came in with their gifts. He glanced up with a surprised expression. "You aren't putting gifts under our tree. Go get your own tree. Mother," he yelled as Allise walked into the living room with arms full of wrapped gifts, "why are Maizee and Nate putting gifts under our tree?"

Maizee and her son stood, clutching packages to their bodies. "Grandpa brought this tree for all of us, Pete." Allise heard the belligerence of Nate's mood and watched him walk over and put his gifts beneath the tree.

Peter grabbed his arm, and Maizee pulled Cleesy back. Allise laid down her gifts and watched the boys roll about the floor. They struck the library table and stood up. Suddenly, a fist shot out and blood spurted from Peter's nose. Nate staggered backwards.

"Oh, my lawd!" Maizee shouted. She picked up Cleesy and plopped her down on the leather chair then started toward Peter.

Choking back tears, he clutched his nose.

Stunned momentarily, Allise grabbed Peter and Nate by their arms and led them to the couch. "Please, a cold, wet towel for Peter, Maizee. How did this start, Nate?"

"Miz Allie, Pete said we couldn't put our gifts under the tree."

Maizee returned with a wet towel and held it out to Peter. Snatching it from her hand, he lay back on the couch, pressing it under his nose. Maizee stood in front of her son. "You two oughta be ashamed of yo'selves. Nate, you listen to Miz Allie. She tell you right." Taking Cleesy's hand, she led her out toward the kitchen.

"What Peter said to you and Maizee was wrong, Nate." Allise said the whole scene was wrong. "We were happy. Did you think Nate wouldn't fight back, Peter?"

"Yes! Niggers aren't suppose to sass whites and fight them." Peter removed the bloody towel and sat up. His face held a familiar message for his mother.

"Tonight, you boys are going to see what Christmas is really about." Allise looked at all the packages piled about the room. "Meantime, we're going to put all of our gifts under the tree." She asked Nate to find Maizee and Cleesy.

At dinner that evening, Allise said they were going on a search for Christmas joy. She asked the children to help her load gifts in the car while Maizee cleaned the kitchen.

Rolling up in front of the James house, Allise announced their arrival with a beep of the car horn.

At the open door, Elfreeda beamed like a cherub behind Jedadiah's wheelchair. "Merry Christmas!" Allise offered a basket tied with a large green bow. Lined with dried magnolia leaves, it held fruits, nuts and pine cones. "Our tree is beautiful. I wouldn't have known where to look for one since my husband always brought it. Thanks for a thoughtful gift." She hugged Elfreeda and squeezed Jedadiah's hand.

Nodding agreement, Maizee handed Elfreeda a bag of gumdrop cookies.

"Well, we've set out to make this a memorable Christmas," Allise said. "Elfreeda, it will really put us in the Christmas spirit if you sing *Silent Night*. Will you?"

Twittering over their gifts, she said, "I sho will. Y'all gotta help now." Humming, she caught the tune and eased into the lyrics about a wondrous and holy night. Maizee closed her eyes and hummed along. Three sets of youthful eyes twinkled like stars in the dimly-lit room, and the precious moment brought Allise close to tears.

When the carol ended, Brother James shouted, "Hallelujah! Amen."

With echos of "Merry Christmas," the merrymakers left to pay Jonas a visit.

At the Colson house, they were welcomed into the front room crowded with Li'l Joke and Dessie's double bed, a pot-bellied stove, two cane-bottomed chairs and a low bench along one wall. Colored paper chains and popcorn roping circled a small pine tree in one corner, and a *Sears, Roebuck Catalog* and scissors lay on the floor between Li'l Joke and Dessie.

Nate motioned to the catalog. "What if Pete and me cut out pictures of toys? Momma, you and Miz Allie can thread 'em, and Li'l Joke, Dessie and Cleesy can hang 'em on the tree."

Leaning his chair against the wall, Jonas laughed. "That's good. I git t' watch."

Allise noticed Peter sitting cross-legged on the floor, sneering at Nate. "You find the pictures, Nate, and Peter will help cut."

When the last one was hung, Maizee laid a bag of cookies beneath the tree. "No peeking before morning." She wagged a finger at her sisters. "Goes for you, too, Daddy. You the worst one, jes like a little kid."

Allise placed a fruit basket beneath the tree. "Let's sing *The First Noel.*"

Maizee began, and as they sang of the reason for celebration, Allise watched their faces sober. On the last note, Peter piped up. "How about let's sing *Jingle Bells?*"

"Yeah, *Jingle Bells,*" Nate and Cleesy chimed in. Jonas dropped his chair and directed the chorus. His fast rendition broke everyone into laughter, and Allise knew she was experiencing an evening of Christmas joy.

The next morning, she was shaken awake by Peter and Cleesy. They dashed down the stairs, urging her, "Come on! It's Christmas." Yawning, Allise plodded downstairs.

Maizee and Nate waited in the living room, and she and Maizee sat, watching the young ones discover the bounty left by Santa. Cleesy snatched up a package, and in openmouthed surprise, tore wrapping from a doll box. The boys opened bright packages bearing their names. Sitting in the midst of torn paper and flying ribbons, Allise waited for the pandemonium to settle. Then, beaming at Maizee, she signaled her to "ooh" and "aah" over their gifts of candy canes, Juicy Fruit gum and pretty handkerchiefs from the kids.

When it was obvious the children knew they were pleased, she handed Maizee a red package tied with a large green bow. Her friend unwrapped a deep red, shirtwaist dress and held it up to her shoulders. Tears pooling in her eyes, Maizee said, "Oh my, Miz Allie. I ain't ever had a new store-bought dress."

Allise offered the lace-trimmed hankie Nate had watched his mother unwrap moments before. "Look, children! She's going to be pretty in this dress."

Peter didn't look up from his Hardy Boys book, but Nate pushed the shape of Nebraska into a jigsaw puzzle of the United States, gazed at his mother and said, "You sure are gonna be pretty, Momma."

Maizee handed a bag of gumdrop cookies to Allise. She pulled the red ribbon. "Cookies! Maizee, when did you manage these?" Maizee didn't answer, but her grin revealed the meaning of a magical Christmas.

Peter reached for a cookie. If only Sam were here, Allise thought.

After Christmas, her letter to Sam told about their holiday. She wrote that Dro proclaimed Maizee's ambrosia 'fit for a king,' and Maydale had declined her invitation for Christmas dinner to be with her parents. "Only your absence marred our good times." She asked about his celebration and if he knew about General MacArthur's gains in the Pacific.

In late January, Sam's answer came.

*Christmas Eve, we sang carols and decorated a tree outside our tents with Christmas cards from home. The chaplain came round for a service. I wish I could have been with you all. I'm lonesome. Course I am anyway.*

*On Christmas Day, I hunkered down in a blanket. Cold wind seeped through the tent wall. For dinner we had cans of Spam and C-rations. We've fought some xxxx battles. Xxxx have us xxxxxxxxx in this wicked wind and driving snow. At daylight, we slosh in mud. At night, the mud freezes over. Xxxxx almost had us at xxxxx when we made a xxxxxx a week ago. The good old air and navy boys saved us again.*

*I dream of home. Maybe soon. Give the kids a hug. Sam.*

The blotted words irritated Allise, and Sam's miserable Christmas saddened her. Did Maydale write to him? After Sam left, his high school sweetheart took a secretarial job in Bensburg and moved. She had confided in Allise that she never loved anyone but him.

She folded the letter and called Maydale. Over the phone, she detected a definite lilt in her friend's voice. *Did Sam propose marriage? They're meant for each other. What brought on her cheery attitude?*

Maydale wasn't inclined to tell, and Allise hung up, wishing she had pried.

By mid-year, war reports had become more optimistic. Flying Fortresses bombed Berlin, and an Allied invasion of Europe was hinted. Rumors surfaced of a fierce new weapon under development, one that would hasten an end to the war. Allise's father had sent an article by Lewis Mumford on "the condition of man." She sat in her classroom pondering the progress of civilization since God put a finger to stone and handed Moses the tablets. War goes on and on, she thought.

The school year was ending, and she packed up items from her desk. Some of her students milled about the room, complaining of needing a summer break after all of her grammar drills. She thought they moaned with tongue-in-cheek. She heard about the difficulty of understanding *Julius Caesar* and all the required reading. *As a student, I complained, too, but four books and poetry by Yeats and Wordsworth wasn't too much to expect over a semester.* Allise knew her demands had sparked lively discussions and insightful essays. She suspected most of her charges held a grudging respect for her, despite their complaints.

At home that evening, Allise tried to tell Maizee about her students, but her friend talked about Nate. "Miz Allie, Nate's learning so much." Brimming with pride, his mother said he read all the time. "Can hardly git 'im t' turn out the light and go t' bed. He wishes his school had books like the white school library."

"One of these days, Maizee, it *will* be different. You'll see. He will always have books, for until things change, I'll see they are available." She sighed, wishing Peter was more interested in reading. He takes after … Well, he just isn't," she thought.

After dinner, she wrote to Sam that Maizee made her life run smoothly, Nate did well in school, and her school year was a success. She told him that despite rationing of food and other items, they suffered no great hardships. "Joe's Market still does a brisk business. Mr. Grady secures meats, poultry, and fish from local farmers and fishermen. This year's cotton is already planted." She ended with Jonas' regards.

Sam's letter, dated May 29, 1944, came in June from a field hospital. Allise's heart dropped like an elevator when she read he had caught shrapnel in his leg. He was comfortable, and she was not to worry. "I'll be healed in no time and probably right back in the fray. When released, I might be transferred to a different group." Sam didn't elaborate. His reassuring words didn't alleviate her concerns, and she called Maydale.

Maydale said she was miserable. "No one understands. My parents worry I will be an old maid."

Allise knew all about plummeting spirits. She had latched onto any glimmer of good news from Quent and clung to it, only to plunge with the unexpected. She didn't mention Sam's injury and wondered if Maydale knew. "May I come over, Maydale?"

By the time she arrived at the Bensburg apartment, Sam's letter had come. In a state of anxiety, Maydale told of an earlier letter that had made her "so happy." Her emotions erupted. "I hoped and n-now this."

As Sam and Elfreeda had anchored her, Allise comforted her friend.

In late June, Allise and Dro viewed the newsreel at the Rialto. Rome was in Allied hands and forces had made D-Day landings on French beaches. Young men wore stark stares as they leaped from landing boats and waded onto the wet sand. Some fell in the water, others on the beach to lie still as death. Soldiers stumbled or leapt over the dead bodies to face German gunfire raining from above. The able-bodied scaled the steep cliffs ahead of them.

The sickening carnage brought tears to Allise's eyes. She wondered how men could run into the jaws of death. Dro slipped her a handkerchief.

Soon the terrible scenes faded into a sad, tender saga of *Casablanca*.

Now, back home, Maizee put Cleesy to bed and went to her apartment, leaving Allise, Dro and Peter in the living room. Dro told Peter some story about his dad and they doubled over in laughter. Catching his breath, he said, "We hightailed it out of there in your dad's little roadster." He flashed even white teeth at Allise. She was tempted to ask questions, but she didn't. Peter's growing attachment to Dro was obvious. When he went off to bed, she asked, "Dro, do you know how highly my son regards you?"

"I know. Believe me, I'm aware of the responsibility such a venerable position requires." They fell silent, but he kept glancing at her as if ready to spill some weighty issue. "Allie, I worry about the Colsons being here. Some day, some smart-mouth will say something."

His tone carried concern for what he thought was her poor judgment. Never had she detected a biased notion in Dro's head. Only worry for trouble she could cause herself. "Dro, I may face prejudice, but one day all of us will be involved in a real calamity over this problem." She studied his look. "Do you understand how I feel about Negores? Not just Negroes, for human beings? Color's not the thing. We're capable of loving—"

"*You're* capable, Allie. Not everyone is. And yes, I think I do understand."

Their eyes locked across the distance. Suddenly, she wanted nothing more than to be held in his arms, to know the joy and peace of loving again in a special way. Lowering her eyes, she said, "This changes the subject, but as much as I hate for him to suffer, I'm thankful Sam's laid up in a hospital." The awkward moment passed. "Can you imagine what goes on in a soldier's mind when he faces almost certain death? Those pictures tonight they crowd my mind. Some men looked terrified, some stoic. What thoughts went through their minds in those boats? No choice but to run onto that beach."

"Mercy, Allie! One minute we're talking Negroes, next ..." He looked puzzled.

"I'm curious, Dro. From what source does that kind of courage come? Was it courage that spurred them up those cliffs?"

He took up the course she had set. "Probably fear, resignation, and yes, a lot of courage." He latched hands behind his head. "Soldiers believe they have something to fight for. Themselves, loved ones, revered principles they're willing to die for. They had no choice. A roll of the dice, live or die. They were scared, you can bet on it, but they were courageous, too." He looked thoughtful. "Courage is usually seen as the absence of fear. Maybe, but more often than not, I would bet fear and pain summon courage."

"Hm-m. I think I agree." They peered at each other through another long gaze. "I object to being called 'Allie,' you know."

"Quent called—"

"Yes, he did, and at first, I didn't mind. Thought it was his special name for me. Then, everyone said Allie. It wasn't special anymore. Please, call me Allise."

Unfolding from the chair, he stood and stretched. "Allise. Okey-dokey, Allise."

At the door, he pulled her into his embrace and held her with a passionate kiss. She hadn't expected it, but yielding left her weak-kneed. Lifting her face, he peered into it. "I love you, Allise. For so long, I've loved you. And, you know something? You love me, too, but you won't allow yourself to feel it. Why do you turn away from it? Just let it flow in." Still holding her, he said, "I've been patient, but things need to be set straight." He released her and stared into her eyes. "But not tonight. Think it over," he said walking out.

Though caught off-guard, his declaration both pleased and scared her. She remembered Sam saying Dro was a charmer. *What did that kiss tell about this man?* She started upstairs knowing she couldn't deny that she prized his company and didn't want to lose it. *What if I love him? Can I trust my emotions?* I long for love, she thought.

In the bedroom, Allise thought about how well things were going. She didn't want uncertainty to complicate her life again? She had children's characters to mold and Sam's safe return to be concerned about. She didn't need more complications. As she undressed, her mind reeled. Maizee ran the household well. They laughed and cried together. Shared the intricacies of each other's days. The boys still squabbled, but the two families had melded into a dependency on each other. She loved teaching, and if Sam returned safely from the war, her worries would be relieved.

Nevertheless, Allise climbed into bed with a sense of something waiting in the wings to throw her life out of kilter. She steeled herself for whatever the future might hold.

More than a month had passed since the night Dro's embrace and kiss left her giddy. His behavior bewildered her. When they had happened upon each other, it was as though two ghosts passed through a void. His parting words nagged her. What did he mean, "things need to be set straight?" She dreaded meeting him, yet, her desire to be with him was more than she wanted to admit. Quent had long been out of her life. *Why do I use guilt as an excuse for not accepting Dro's love?*

Allise sat on the lounge, trying to sort things out. A Quaker from Philadelphia, she came in 1929 to teach English. After a six-month courtship, she married Quent and taught until her pregnancy became evident. The evening she gave birth to her first child, her husband raped Maizee. Nine months later, she gave birth to Nate. Quent was killed, and she moved the Colsons into town so that Nate could get an education and she could teach.

People in Deer Point disapproved of a black family living in the white part of town. Peter showed the same prejudicial attitude especially toward Nate that his father had held for colored people. *Maizee and I persevere.* We're a family, she thought. *I don't need Dro McClure.*

Allise thought about Sam and the Third Army's drive through France. In late July, he wrote he was fully recovered from his wounds and reassigned to the Fourth Armored Division under General Patton. The general had been called on the red carpet for slapping a soldier who sought medical help for "battle fatigue." Columnist Drew Pearson had written he would never hold another responsible war assignment, and Walter Winchell had predicted his demise by the hand of one of his own men. Both were mistaken, she thought.

There was Sam to be concerned for. She couldn't think about Dro McClure.

On a Saturday, Dro surprised her. He came with a large world atlas under his arm and a broad smile for Allise, but he asked for Peter. On the dining table, they scanned the book for places where Sam had fought.

Clearly confused, she wanted to cry when Dro left without engaging her at all. He had said he loved her, and she had waited for him to make another move, even if it was only to show a sign of impatience with her. Meantime, she had grown impatient enough for the two of them. Things needed to be said to bring an end to their situation. It might break her heart, but the air had to be cleared. Not knowing what to expect from him or herself, she felt directionless.

Allise took the family on outings, but neither day trips nor farm and market duties alleviated the yearning that came from Dro's inattentiveness. Summer was coming to an end, and she sat at the desk. It was an effort to keep her mind on reviewing and updating last year's lesson plans. *How can I want and not want him at the same time. He's always right on the edge of my mind.*

She struggled with her dilemma when the phone rang. Hanging the receiver, she returned with a smile for Maizee. "Dro called."

Maizee gave her a smug grin. "Uh-huh, I knew he'd come round." Then, she changed the subject. "Miz Allie, I'm gonna miss Cleesy when she goes off t' school."

"Yes. First days are hard for first graders."

That evening, she talked to Cleesy about the child's expectations of starting school while waiting for Dro to arrive. When the doorbell rang, Allise kissed her goodnight, and she and Dro left for the Rialto to see *The Lost Weekend.*

The newsreel opened with Parisians celebrating their liberation. Allise searched the faces of American soldiers sitting atop armored vehicles rumbling down a wide boulevard. Excited crowds lined the street, shouting and throwing flowers to them. Some boys slid from their moving perches to kiss French girls running alongside the tanks. Would I recognize Sam's face if I saw it? she wondered. *What will war do to his gentle soul?*

After the movie, she waited at the door for Dro to say goodnight, but he asked to come in. At the kitchen table, they had juice, and he broached the subject that had plagued her. "I'm ready for our relationship to change, Allise. You act as if we should go on just as we are."

She didn't want to admit how frightened she was of loving again. Bracing herself, Allise searched for excuses. "I hope you understand, Dro. When Sam comes home ... Everything seems ... It's like our lives have to be put on hold—"

Bang! His glass hit the table. "That's a damn feeble thing to say. How long am I supposed to hang around, Allie? A-Allise!" He stormed to the door, and pausing to glare at her, left without another word.

Stunned, she watched him disappear in the dark. Stumbling back to the kitchen, she sat down. Minutes ticked by as Allise held her head and muttered, "My God, what have I done?" She sobbed. Then, unaware of the time, she dried her eyes and climbed the stairs. *No more Quents.* No more heartaches, she thought.

Days stretched into a week and despite her resolve, Allise pined for Dro. He didn't call or make any effort to see her. At church, not even a glance her way. Maizee said, "Miz Allie, I'm not gonna spend no week down on that farm with you feeling so poorly."

Allise said she must because she promised Jonas. "I guess I hafta go keep house and cook cause Li'l Joke has t' pick cotton, and Dessie Mae ain't no help."

Assuring her all would be fine, Allise felt nowhere near all right. She knew she didn't fool her friend, either. Her heart ached, but cotton was ready to be picked, and school would open in a week.

She had astonished Peter when she insisted he was to pick cotton. Jonas had hired him and Nate, and now, driving them to the farm, Allise smiled in the rearview mirror at her son's pouted face. "Come on, Peter. Think of the money you will earn."

"Huh. I'm thinking hot sun."

Nate, an old hand at cotton picking, snickered. "Pete gonna be getting up before daylight and breaking his back for fourteen hours? I gotta see this." Peter made a fist and threw it into Nate's shoulder. "Ouch!" Nate looked ready to hit back, but Allise saw Maizee's backward glare. It clearly warned him not to.

Waiting for Maizee to get out at the tenant house, Allise said,"Boys, don't bruise your hands fighting if you want to make money." She drove to the shed where Jonas waited. She had taught him to post weigh-ins and tally bales. "Jonas, you're doing a good job. Our system is working well. Sam will be pleased when he comes home." He smiled. "I'll see you late this evening and pick up your tallies," she said and drove away.

In mid-week, she and Cleesy waited in the car for Peter's sack to be weighed and for Jonas to bring his list. Soon, her son walked toward the car with hands held away from his body like a garden scarecrow. "It hurts to touch these cotton hull cuts against my pants," he said. On the way home, Peter asked, "Why hasn't Dro been around?"

Allise ignored his reference to Dro. "I know your hands are painful, son, but this is good work experience. I want you to know and appreciate honest labor. Appreciate the pay that rewards it." She glanced his way and thought someday he would come to feel empathy for anyone who labored long hours over back-break-ing work.

Peter looked thoughtful. "Guess Dro knows I'm tired. Glad we've got Nig Negroes. One thing's for sure, I'm not going to be a farmer."

Praying he wouldn't think of Negroes as machines meant solely for white man's use, she asked, "If you don't want to farm, do you have another plan in mind, Peter?"

"No. Haven't thought about it. Mother, do Nate and me get the same wages?"

She bit her bottom lip and gazed straight ahead. "Yes." How could she handle his question with the gravity it deserved? It was too much like battling windmills. Peter fell quiet and thoughts of Dro churned in Allise's head.

# CHAPTER 14

▼

Cotton harvest would continue into the month, but Peter and Nate hung up their sacks to start school.

Allise went straight home from her first day of classes, and found Maizee and Nate full of excitement, and waiting at the door. Both tried speaking at once, leaving little to be understood. "Hush, Nate," his mother said. "Miz Lula done moved Nate t' the fifth grade, Miz Allie. I used our sugar to make cookies. They're baking now. Hope you don't mind."

Allise watched a grin spread across the black child's face. "Of course not, Maizee. We're so proud of you, Nate." She sniffed the spicy aroma coming from the kitchen and shouted, "Come, kids! Let's go for ice cream to help celebrate this occasion." Peter yelled he wanted to finish a letter to Uncle Sam.

Leaving him to write and Maizee to her cookies, Allise breezed into the drugstore with Nate and Cleesy. She ordered a quart of Nutty Vanilla from the rawboned man behind the soda fountain. A tall white hat added another six inches to his height. Allise had not seen him in town before now.

He stared around her at Nate and Cleesy. She turned to see the problem, then back to his curled lip. "You know that boy's not suppose t' come in that front door, don't ya?" He pointed at the entrance, then bent over the ice cream barrel behind the high, glass-fronted counter. Coming erect with a slap of the carton lid, he said, "Darkies suppose t' use that door back yonder." Nodding the direction, his gaze held a clear purpose.

"Oh." Allise glanced at Nate and back to the man. "I wasn't … It's hard for me to think that way."

"Well, I wouldn't bring 'im through that door agin, or I'll hafta tell Mr. King." He met her eyes boring into his and turned away.

She pointed to the street. "Nate, you and Cleesy wait in the car. I'll be out shortly." The door banged behind them, and Allise walked to the cash register. "I don't know you, young man, but I just learned a lot about you." She snatched the bills held out to her. "You don't even know that child. He was boosted a grade in school today. Your caustic remarks undermine his sense of accomplishment. Does that make you feel better?"

He grunted sounds of stifled, sneering laughter. "He's jest a nigger." He held the carton of ice cream across the counter.

"He may be a Negro but he's ten times more mature than you." Fighting for control, she saw his face change from a jeer to anger. Frightened, she said, "Perhaps we need to cool off and talk about this another time when—"

"I don't have more to say to you, lady." He washed soiled glasses at the sink.

Feeling the man wouldn't forget, she dashed out the door, slamming it behind her.

Back in the car, Allise took deep breaths and gripped the steering wheel with white knuckled hands. Aware of Nate's eyes on her back, she looked over her shoulder. "You must *never* allow anyone to cause you to think less of yourself, Nate. There are simple-minded people whose thinking will forever keep them from broadening their possibilities. But you, you will be different."

Cleesy sat quietly beside her mother. Allise felt ashamed of her outburst, but she reminded herself never to let up. She had promised her children would never be prejudiced against others.

Back home, Allise helped Maizee put dinner on the table. She asked Peter if he finished his letter, hoping to avoid the scene at the drugstore. "I told Uncle Sam I picked cotton and began Junior High," he said.

Cleesy piped up. "Did you tell him I'm in the first grade?"

"Yes, Peter, add a postscript about Cleesy and Nate." Realizing the honoree wasn't in the spotlight, Allise said, "Tell us what Miss Lula said, Nate."

His mouth spread into a shy grin, and he quoted his teacher. Everyone applauded but Peter. Nate's smile faded. He glanced at his mother. "The man at the drugstore was nasty."

"He's a mean old man," Cleesy declared.

"Who's mean and nasty?" Suddenly Peter was interested.

Allise confirmed Nate's remark with a nod at Maizee. "Okay, boys, you've had treats, and it's time for homework. Cleesy, get a bath. We'll talk about the man later." Peter objected but his mother held firm. Then, helping Maizee in the kitchen, she told her what had transpired in the drugstore.

Hurt gazed back at her, then anger. "I could kill 'im. I'm afraid for Nate, Miz Allie."

Allise caught her arm. "You're right to be fearful, but hate and anger … I lost my temper in front of that young man. Maizee, we mustn't frighten our children or encourage them to be excessively daring. Dear God, how *do we* teach them to handle circumstances of that sort when we don't act civilized ourselves?"

"All we can do is try, Miz Allie, but Momma said we don't hafta like that kind of treatment."

Allise gave a lot of thought to what Maizee said about their treatment. On Saturday, she dropped the boys at the farm shed and they rode to the tenant house where their students awaited. Some of the pupils had moved beyond the old materials. New books had arrived from the American Friends Service Committee. Maizee passed out books and supplies, then, pausing beside Miz Allie, she said, "Momma sho would be proud of what Li'l Joke and Dessie be learning. Anyway, Daddy sho is."

"Rebekah is proud. She and Quent are with …" Immediately realizing her slip of the tongue, Allise avoided Maizee's eyes. Neither uttered a word to the other until classes ended and they reached for their sweaters. "What I meant was, my husband …"

Maizee's dark eyes snapped, holding her white friend's attention. "I don't need t' hear about him." Their first cross situation left Allise glad that Nate and his mother were spending Sunday on the farm.

Cleesy waved, and Maizee waved back as she drove away. Allise felt sure they could smooth over the upset when Maizee came home.

Peter rode beside his mother. He laughed. "Jonas tells the funniest stories about his grandparents who were slaves in Louisiana." Saying he wanted to share them with Dro, he asked if he could invite him to Sunday dinner. Allise felt apprehensive, but her son would need an explanation if she said he couldn't invite Dro. Anyway, she felt she had lost something very special. It had been months since he slammed out of her house.

Straight away, Peter phoned. Sitting down for lunch, he said Dro was coming on Sunday.

All week, Allise sailed along on Cloud Nine, but not without wondering how she and Dro would handle their raw feelings.

If he was anything, Dro was prompt. At least, he was never late for Sunday dinner.

She met him at the door. "Dro, it's been so long." She felt utterly stupid. He dropped his hat, picked it up and dropped it again before managing to hang it on the hall tree.

"How've you been, Allise?" His face looked flushed.

"Good, thanks. You're well, I see."

"Yeah. Nothing to complain about."

Leading him inside with uncharacteristic timidity, she felt his greeting wasn't exactly a warm beginning. Later, at the dinner table, their glances met and held in prolonged gazes. He chatted as though to fill lost time. She lowered her eyes with a shy grin, and excusing herself, went to the kitchen for the cake Maizee baked before leaving for the farm. When she returned, Peter was telling about Jonas' grandparents. Some of the stories left them sad, others were funny. It was good to laugh with Dro again.

Peter grew quiet, and Dro said, "You're a lot like your dad. He told a good story."

Her son grinned. "Mother, you never told what happened at the drugstore. Nate said the man was mad when he used the front door. I told him he's supposed to go in the back."

The turn in conversation disappointed Allise. She wanted the occasion to be free of controversy. Relating the incident, she asked, "Why shouldn't Nate use the front, Peter?"

"Because that's just the way it is."

A breath caught in her throat, for at that moment, he was Quent reincarnated. Quickly, Allise regained decorum. "Son, the difference between Nate and us is skin color. That man has a problem." How could she tell him it was an attitude?

"Why do you keep on us about blacks, Mother?"

"Well, if you don't remember anything else I've tried to instill in you, Peter, do remember it's wrong to think Negroes are inferior. That they're meant only for enslavement. For the life of me, I can't believe they were—"

"That kid's the relative of a prominent family," Dro broke in.

Allise suggested they move to the living room. Peter sat on the couch beside Dro, who continued about the man. "He moved here recently. That family owns most of the buildings downtown. Bunch of know-it-alls. Allise, I wish you hadn't tangled with him."

"Deer Point thinks I'm a know-it-all, too." She laughed from the wing chair. "Both of us thought we were right, but I should have been more reasonable."

"Well, it's not unusual for anger to overcome reason," Dro said.

"Yeah, Mother, kids aren't reasonable. They poke fun and fight."

"Peter, kids must *learn* better, but grownups should *know* better." There was a lull, and Allise watched Cleesy play nearby. Was she teaching them to know better? *They needed a father. Dro was kind and thoughtful. She missed their conversations.* I've missed him, she thought, blushing.

The afternoon drew to a close. Leaving, Dro said, "God knows where Sam is or where he'll be tomorrow." Accepting his hat, he left without a parting peck on her cheek.

She closed the door behind him and sank into confusion.

Months went by, and Allise yearned for Dro's company. Then, it was February. She sat on the chaise, fearing to open Sam's letter. So much had happened since Paris was freed. In November, President Roosevelt won a fourth-term, but the war had taken a toll on him. After his inaugural address, commentators said he looked worn and ill. There were misgivings about Vice President Harry S. Truman's ability to conduct war in case of the president's demise.

Allied Forces attempted to cross the border into Germany. In a backward swing at France, the Germans pushed into Belgium through a swell in the border known as "the Bulge." The U. S. Third Army moved around Bastogne, and by mid-December, the forces had slowed the Germans.

On Christmas Day, a news correspondent had reported that General Patton visited his front-line commands. He found them battle-worn but every soldier, front and rear, had been served a turkey dinner. That day, vicious counter-attacks were carried out against Sam's division. Tanks were lost and troops were forced to retreat. In January, one unit was cut off from its main command for eight days in sleet and snow conditions.

Allise thought it would be a miracle if the president lived to the end of his term. *Even more of a miracle if Sam came home alive.* She tore open the letter and read:

**Our tanks bogged down in mud. We were pushing them out when old Blood & Guts showed up. General Patton stood on a little hill motioning each one out until we were free.**

**I don't know if I will ever feel warm again, Allie. I'm resting now in the rear. Maybe this mess will end soon. I have something to tell you. It's a big surprise.**

What Sam needs is a warm Arkansas sun to his back, Allise thought.

April promised warmth, but chilling news of the president's death sent the nation into mourning. Allise and Maizee wore faces of grief and malaise. Then, fighting on the European continent ended. Harry S. Truman had been president for eighteen days when Hitler committed suicide and Germany surrendered.

Fighting continued against the Japanese, but the war was over for Sam, and he was on his way home. He had written one last letter in which he broke the news of his bride, a French nurse. She had tended his wounds and would arrive stateside soon. "Allie, I wanted to know I was going home before I told you about Simone. Maybe with your concern about me marrying, this will cheer you up," he wrote.

Sam's revelation crushed Allise's hope for him and Maydale. Several days later, she opened the door to her teary-eyed friend. "How could he? I waited so long."

Allise pulled the distraught woman inside and held her until she quieted. Recalling the self-pity and anger that had vied for her emotions, Allise left off consoling words, knowing they beat on a dead drum. "It isn't much comfort, dear," she said, "but we can't know what Sam's been through. War must have changed him."

Maydale seemed calmer when she left, but Allise imagined the heartache she carried back to her empty apartment. Her self-pity and anger would turn to grief, and Sam's former, best girl would need friendship.

Then, Sam was on his way home. Allise stood on the crowded, train platform, searching faces of those stepping down from the cars. Suddenly, he was there, scanning the crowd. She waved and called, "Sam!"

Seeing her weaving toward him, he picked up a bag in each hand and rushed toward her. As in slow motion, she felt the space close between them. They stopped short of each other, and Allise looked into the strained set of his face. Sam dropped his bags and hesitated as if confused about what to do. Other times, he would grab her in a rough hug and say "Girl, you look good!"

Unsure herself, Allise waited. Suddenly, he reached out and pulled her into his arms. "Welcome home, Sam. Let me see." She pushed against his embrace and smiled up at him. "Sam, I …" Tears welled through her attempt to laugh. "I'm happy you're home."

He swiped a coarse sleeve, bearing the chevrons of a sergeant, across his eyes.

"You're a sight to see, Allie, and I think I'm the happiest man on the planet to be home." Glancing around, his eyes lingered on a soldier without arms and another in a wheelchair with the stump of a leg jutting out. His strained mask faded to sadness.

Allise caught his hand. "Get your bags. Uncle Sam must be home by the time school's out." In the car on the drive to Deer Point, long silences hung between her attempts to draw him out. He perked up when speaking of his wife, Simone.

As they entered the driveway, Peter and Cleesy rushed out, greeting him in a rough and tumble fashion. "Great jumping Jehoshaphat! I might as well have kept fighting the war." Sam laughed. Inside, for a while he seemed to absorb their youthful exuberance. Then an edginess set in. He paced, rubbing his hands in the familiar way Allise remembered. He needs time and will settle down when Simone comes, she thought.

Weeks passed and Sam's bride didn't arrive. His swings between happiness and what seemed a loss of purpose alarmed Allise. At times, he appeared stricken, looking as if to pull something from the pit, then search for a place to put it. Or, he drifted at sea without an anchor, as though he had seen too much, been too long at the direction of others. She nudged him toward the rich Chula River loam and the crop springing to life. There, he could find space to become himself again. There he wouldn't face disarming questions.

When he wasn't at the farm, he helped her clean and repair the long-vacant Filbert Street house. It must be spotless for his wife. Though disappointed, Allise was determined to make Simone's arrival pleasant. His bride must make the difference.

The house was in order, and they waited. But, entangled in government red tape, Simone faced further delay in August when the atomic bomb dropped on Hiroshima.

Allise and Sam sat in the Rialto watching the mushroom-like cloud balloon above the Japanese city. Three days later, the radio announced another bomb sent on Nagasaki. In mid-August Japan surrendered, ending the world war on all fronts.

Awed by the bombings, Allise didn't know whether to feel guilty for the slaughter of Japanese people, or to be joyful for the victory which followed. As conflicted as she felt, the means used to gain peace soon faded into uneasy relief.

Then, the day came when Simone stepped from the train in Deer Point. It was the middle of cotton picking season. She hired Old Tate's taxi to drive her to Sam's address. He was totally surprised when he arrived home from the fields, and all of Deer Point was in a twitter over the foreigner in their presence.

Allise compared the snapshot Sam carried in his wallet to the short, stocky woman she met. Raven hair fell in a shoulder-length sweep to frame strikingly blue eyes in a broad face of flawless skin. Nearer Allise's age than Sam's, Simone looked older than her thirty five years, and she was downright masculine in the way she carried herself.

With her arrival, the veil of lifelessness lifted from Sam. He rushed about as if to live all of life in one day. Seemingly unmindful of Simone's lack of beauty and aloof disposition, he appeared head-over-heels in love with the woman who nurtured him through a difficult time. Before the war, Allise knew him as one who took life in stride, who felt comfortable with himself. Now, as if fearful of tomorrow, he towed Simone about from one introduction to another, apparently impervious to his reluctant bride's feelings.

Unapproachable as Simone seemed, Allise was undaunted. She offered a tour of the farm. Pulling in front of the Filbert Street house, she beeped the horn.

Underway, she entertained the idea that war had left both Sam and his wife scarred. Attempting to draw out the former nurse's experiences, she was met with an icy glare and a retort in broken English. "You people ask too much questions. Your past is of no intre-est to me. Why you have intre-est in mine?"

"Simone, it isn't curiosity. I worry that you don't like us. It helps if—"

"You not worry and not think! Why I go to this farm? Don't know farm, I was born in cit-ty." Steely gazes threw up a wall between her and any offered friendship.

"Well, we have that in common." Allise made a quick round of the farm, and they rode home in stony silence. The woman, giving nothing of self, clung to her secrets.

If she could have a talk with Sam, show she understood it took time to pick up where he left off long ago, she would warn him of the difficulty Simone might have settling into a small town. If only she could encourage him to let his wife come to know people in her own way. Waiting for that opportunity, she braved another try with his wife.

On the way to Bensburg to shop, Allise said she had learned to make Deer Point her home. "Simone, I know you're from a large, old city that offers many cultural advantages, and this is a small, rural place with little to offer. It takes a bit of bending to live here. I still don't fit, may never, but—"

"What's problem with you peeple?" She pinned Allise with a cold stare. "I not want to bend and fit! Anyway, Sam have you. 'Al-ese' this, 'Al-ese' that. All talk about Al-ese."

*Is she jealous or using me as an excuse to leave?* With another cold rejection, Allise's impulse was to pull to the shoulder and slap the caustic woman. Instead, she clutched the wheel and drove in stunned silence. The trip was short, and again, little was said on the way home. Too much ugliness can be expressed, she thought.

Each day, Simone appeared more disenchanted with marriage and rural America. Allise had observed the widening distance between the newlyweds. More and more, they sat quietly removed from each other. Then, one morning, some months after her arrival, Sam burst into Allise's kitchen. He looked as if the worst calamity of his life had occurred.

"She's packing! Going back to France cause ain't no need t' think we have a marriage. Hates me." Wringing his hands, he paced.

Allise lured him to the table and a cup of coffee. They sat facing each other, and she watched his face twist with pain. She wanted to hold him, but her intentions might be misconstrued. "Sam, I think I've learned a thing or two about the human soul." She reached for his busy hands. "Yours is bruised, and you're struggling to hang onto what you think will restore it. That's a natural reaction, but maybe it's not best for the tender, innermost part of your being." Collecting thoughts, she rushed on. "Sam, perhaps time wasn't on the side of this marriage."

He looked like he might implode, but Allise went on. "You and Simone came away from chaotic experiences that may take time to leave behind. Remember how it was for me after Quent was killed?" She searched for words. "You two may have entered marriage with a tremendous need to have your pains eased. Simone as a nurse, what horrendous things she must have seen. Her country occupied, living under fascist rule. More than a union, perhaps you needed comfort from each other." She looked into his face hoping to find his emotion. "You lived the horrors each day, not knowing if you would have another day of life. Sam, neither of you is to blame for what's happening to your marriage."

His face contorted and pained eyes brimmed tears. Leaning forward, his head fell to her shoulder. Allise held him, thinking conventionalism and impropriety be damned.

He straightened and looked as though his world was ended. She took his big rough hands in hers again. "Sam, she doesn't hate you. Simone isn't herself. She says things she doesn't mean. If you can find strength to release her now, allow her time to regain the person she is and give yourself time, then maybe at some future date you'll know if you're meant to be together."

Sam pulled his hands free, propped on the table and held his head.

She patted him. He needed to sob, but he wouldn't. Remembering the outpourings of people, slithering and coiling like a sterile balm over her bruises, bringing wounds to the fore, she warned of what he might face if Simone left. "It will be embarrassing. People will be sympathetic, perhaps more like pity. When Quent was killed, it took a while for me to see they offered sympathy in order to feel they were helpful." More to herself than to him, she said, "I didn't see that angle then. Ashamed of the way I handled it." She patted his arm and stood, hoping he knew she meant well.

His face revealed he wasn't relating her words to what he was feeling. "I love you like a brother, Sam, and I know you're a good husband. I'll be here when you want to talk." He swiped a hand across his eyes and gazed at her as if not knowing what to think. Propping an arm on the back of the chair, he rested his head on it.

Allise sighed. If the marriage never works out, perhaps it will be for the best. Concerned for what Sam might do, she was uncertain about her words when his feelings were so raw. Eyes that once pierced her facade, now held dull recognition, and Sam hadn't spoken since announcing Simone was leaving. The untouched coffee was cold. Suddenly, he said, "I've made a mess of things, ain't I, girl?" and tried to laugh into a handkerchief.

"Nothing that can't be mended, Sam. If it turns out to be a mistake, that's what it is. I can't believe God wants you two to live with a mistake for the rest of your lives. I think the quietness of your heart holds answers. Listen for them."

Allise thought of feelings Dro provoked in her. Of the muddled mess she'd made of his declared love. Who was she to speak to Sam when she was afraid of challenges in her own life? Afraid of loving again.

Sam stood, pulled her up and clamped her shoulders in strong hands. "I sure didn't come home with my head screwed on, did I?" He peered at her, waiting.

To keep from revealing her uncertainty, she avoided his eyes, painting over the gaze with words. "It will work out. I'm here if you want to talk. The kids worship you, and you're a hero in the community, Sam. And the farm always needs you."

"Yep, the farm." He loosened his grip and ambled out.

The next morning, Sam drove Simone to the Bensburg train station.

Ironically, Dro chose this time to call again. In the dining room over after-dinner coffees, Allise told him she worried that Sam couldn't find peace. They talked about the after-war wind down, and how people were becoming aware of what they had achieved. The forging of a massive support system for an ill-prepared military that whipped itself into a mighty fighting force and won victories on the battlefields. Fighting side-by-side with other nations, they had kept the continent free of ravages suffered by others.

Dro said new technologies were emerging from the war efforts. Maizee's kitchen clatter punctuated his prediction of big changes for the future. Her noise and his words made vague imprints in Allise's head. Half listening, suddenly she said, "Dro, do you sense the intoxication that comes with being the victor? I mean the victor in a war."

Seeing his dismayed look, she realized her question must have fallen totally out of context with what he had been saying. From across the table, a flicker of chagrin crossed his face. Clearly her inattentiveness left him dashed. "I'm sorry, Dro. My mind was off in another direction." He frowned, but she insisted on his answer to her question. "We Americans feel invincible. I'm fascinated by the way victorious people act out triumph over others. What it leads the loser in a war to do."

Standing, he strode around the table and pressed his lips into her neck. Allise stood and staggered back. Uncertainty about their relationship plagued her, yet, she felt an odd tingle, as if every nerve in her body reacted to the touch of his lips.

The realization brought a warm flush to her face. "Wouldn't a Sunday drive be nice?" she asked, without knowing why. Looking pleased, he agreed, and Allise called into the kitchen, "We're going out, Maizee. Back in a while."

Dro held open the door of his pre-war Packard, and Allise climbed onto the front seat. Her heart raced, and she wondered if she was doing the right thing. She was sure of one thing. She couldn't lose Dro's companionship again.

Crossing the train tracks, he smiled and headed south out of town. Allise saw no vestige of the affront she thought she had caused earlier. Sending another smile her way, he said, "I've been waiting you out, you know. When we're together, I watch you do battle with my love. Tell me, am I right?"

He knew her so well it was frightening. His bold admission of toying with her feelings pleased Allise. He reached for her hand. "Well, isn't it so? Are we ready to talk?"

She nodded. "Your declaration that evening and disregard for my feelings caused me a great deal of anguish."

"Anguish? About what?"

"About loving and being loved." They fell silent. Streaking along the unpaved highway, she thought about this man, strong and self-assured. So was Quent when she fell in love with him, but he had bottled up his feelings. Dro will share his soul, she thought.

He grinned at her as if he knew the thoughts spinning in her head. "I'm excited about this time alone, but disappointed, too. How long have we loved each other? You've yet to say, 'I love you, Dro.' I may have to declare my love again." Allise stared at utility poles flicking past the window. When she didn't answer, he slowed the car to a crawl. "I love you, Allise. You must have seen it when you and Sam came for the loan. But then you belonged to my old friend, who went off to war and got himself killed. Quent and I weren't that close after we both married, but the only decent thing to do was to let you get through his death." He gave her a quick glance. "Can you say you're over the grief now?"

She turned to him. "Yes, I'm past that. It doesn't hurt anymore, but—"

"I've known hurt, too, you know. Lost my wife. Now, I'm hurting another way. Allise, I've been patient. Tried anyway. Wanting you, wanting to hold the woman I love. I've suffered from being close but unable to touch. I want to share my life with you, but you throw up this wall between us. It's sheer hell, and I don't like this game."

Before she could respond, Dro pulled into a service station tucked into a grove of tall pines and stepped from the car. She watched him walk beneath the canopy, pull small green bottles from an iced-down Coca-Cola box, uncap them and go inside to pay the attendant. Back at the car, he handed one through the passenger window. Standing there, he removed his hat and took a long swig from his bottle. Returning to the driver's seat, he said, "That wall, Allise?"

She rubbed the bottom of the cold, wet bottle on her palm, searching for a way to answer. How could she hold onto him without making a commitment? He had come to mean something to her, but from her experience with Quent, she wasn't convinced marriage held happiness for her.

"Uh oh! There it is again, that shield." Leaning toward her, he flipped his hat on the back seat and straightened. "Saying 'I love you' doesn't penetrate it. Right now, in front of that gasoline pump and the whole world, I want to hold you and kiss you until you faint in my arms."

He was serious, but she couldn't kill the smile his expression pulled from her.

"Heck, forget it!" A moment passed under his intense gaze. "Let's get on with our lives." He sipped from the bottle, slipped it onto the floorboard and stared straight ahead.

Allise had been singed with guilt. Now, the whole charade struck her as funny. She made gruntled sounds behind her hand. Here they were, she in her late thirties and Dro in his forties, acting more like teenagers than adults. He glared at her stifled giggle, a look which indicated the last straw was reached. She held her empty bottle across the seat to him. He retrieved his from the floorboard and went to deposit them in a half-filled carton beside the red cooler. Returning, he started the car without even a blink in her direction.

She touched his hand. "I'm sorry, Dro. You're right, it's a silly game. I'm tired of it, too, but suddenly, our 'game' struck me as funny." She squeezed his hand. "I've thought only of myself. Didn't know a man could express feelings as you do, so I didn't give much thought to how you might feel." There, she had said it. Allise felt relieved.

He looked thoughtful. "I went on and on, didn't I?" Both laughed, and holding hands across the seat, he guided the car back onto the empty highway.

Allise moved closer and put his hand, a hand that knew no toil, to her lips. "All right, it's my turn to speak now, Dro. I want to know that marriage … not that you've said anything about marriage!" A flush shrouded her face, but she stammered on. "I'm not sure marriage will bring happiness, but isn't it supposed to?"

He smiled without looking at her. "Are you making fun of me?" she asked.

"No! Never." He squeezed her hand. "I'm loving every word. Go on."

"Well, your admiring looks were never lost on me, but I loved Quent. It never occurred to me to think of another man. Did you... did you love your wife that intensely? Never mind, I shouldn't ask that, but the way you always looked at me I-I was embarrassed." Hesitantly, she said, "I must admit, sometimes I liked it."

Her remarks were strung-together, awkward. "Am I making myself clear?" Dro said he understood, and she explained her need for friendship and love. For someone to talk with and share joy. Someone to take an interest in her children. "Dro, I think they love you almost as much as their Uncle Sam."

The remark brought them again to soft laughter.

Dro didn't seem inclined to fill the lull in conversation. Allise folded her legs on the seat and straightened her skirt. "It isn't easy in Deer Point," she said. "I'm held at a distance, and much of it is my fault. I can't, or won't, sacrifice my convictions for acceptance. Having you take an interest after Quent well, it made living here easier."

She paused, questioning the wisdom of laying bare her thoughts. "Were you aware Quent suffered periods of melancholy?" Seeing no surprise in his face, she searched for words of explanation. "Sometimes he was there, but he wasn't really. Couldn't reach him at those times. I felt so alone. Yet, I loved him. Heaven knows I had doubts, but mostly I loved him. It was painful." Gazing out, she drew on memories. "Quent and I were ... I've come to think we had the blind love of youth. At least we confused infatuation with love."

"Love is blind, Allise, and sometimes it's painful."

"Yes, but in order to last, shouldn't it grow? What I'm trying to say is—"

"Two people should be understanding and forgiving, as well as loving."

"Yes, but Quent and I fell head over heels in love with what we thought we saw in each other. We never talked about what we expected or respected. I never looked beyond his charm. Maybe that's the way it is with first love. We were strangers, learning about each other." Dro said nothing, and she went on. "Well, after a while we saw things, little things in each other that we couldn't admire, and they began to consume our love. Quent and I ... we wanted to change each other. He wanted me to think like a Southerner, and I wanted him *not* to think like one."

A long sigh escaped her. "Dro, the wall, it's fear of trusting love again. Fear of the pain. I'm in possession of my identity again, Allise Weston DeWitt. For a time, that person was lost." She heard selfishness in her words but felt driven. She would not fall into another trap. For marriage, a woman sacrificed her name, and sometimes her opinions and well-being in deference to her husband. Hindsight left her thinking the only oneness in a union were the children created. Oneness of mind had been impossible for her and Quent.

Doubting Dro would understand, she said, "All of this wasn't sorted out before Quent … Let's just say that he and I fell into marriage all too quickly. Real love came a few weeks before he left."

Allise had carried on the one-sided conversation for some time. It made her uneasy, but she must have him understand. "With time, I've come to a simple conclusion," she said. "Married people should love each other, respect each other's individuality and at the same time pull together for the sake of making a family. Dro, I vowed to never again feel a lesser person to anyone, not even to a husband. I'm equal, no more, no less."

She glanced his way, expecting him to say something. He drove in silence, and she wondered if she'd made too much of her independence. Headlights flashed on the garage. Stopping in the driveway, he turned off the engine. Neither made a move to leave the car.

Still facing him, legs folded on the seat, Allise longed to reach some point of satisfaction before they parted. Lifting his hand, she held it in both of hers. "I won't lose myself in another marriage, Dro." She tried to think of a way to qualify her declaration. "Thought you should know. I want us to know each other's feelings and expectations."

Sitting in a self-imposed silence, she feared his thoughts. The pause seemed an eternity. At last, she told him they needed time to think about what had been said. Releasing his hand, she reached for the door handle, then turned back. "Dro McClure, I've been confused, b-but I think I have feelings for you."

He jumped out the car, went around and pulled her out into his arms. His lips found hers, and she felt herself melting into senselessness. Holding her long after their lips parted, he whispered into her hair, "All I know is I love you. My God! How I love you." Walking arm-in-arm to the door, he declared that time would never change that.

Allise felt light-headed. Happy.

# CHAPTER 15

▼

*What! What is that noise?* Allise raised up in bed and looked at the clock. It was 2:00 A.M. Realizing the sound was the phone ringing, she went downstairs. From the other end of the line, she heard, "Mrs. DeWitt, I've got Sam down here." It was the sheriff. "Thought you might want t' know."

"I'll be right there." She dressed and walked out to Maizee's apartment. Knocking softly, she called, "Maizee." Pulled out of sleep, her friend appeared in her nightgown, her eyes as big as moons. "Ss-h," Allise said. "The sheriff has Sam in jail. I'm going to get him."

"Oh, Miz Allie. What's that man done?"

"I don't know. Just wanted you to know I'm not in the house." She stepped off the stoop. "I'll return as soon as possible."

"Don't you worry. I be right here," Maizee whispered.

Driving along, Allise thought about how happiness seemed to elude Sam. Almost a year-and-a-half since Simone left, and civilian life is still his private battlefield. Efforts to win back the cold-hearted woman had failed. At times, it seemed his tries were more out of a commitment to marriage than love of Simone.

When wooing her didn't work, and the divorce was finalized, Allise noticed he spruced up to go into Bensburg. One Saturday evening after the children left the dinner table, she asked if he had seen Maydale since he came home." Sam jumped to his feet and shouted at her. The commotion caused Maizee to drop a cup in the sink. He paced the kitchen, wringing his hands. Allise walked out, and he followed her into the living room, eyes blazing.

She knew him well enough to see his behavior was erratic and asked if he had been drinking. He said she wasn't going to run his life. Grabbing his old hat off the hall tree, he had stormed out.

Allise only recently learned of his weekend binges with Gunther Hill, the town drunk. On a Sunday morning, Mrs. Blake had whispered about Sam's absence from church and said he was going to self-destruct. After the service, Allise asked what she meant about Sam. Telling her that he was a drunk, Mrs. Blake went on to say he and Gunther wind up at Rooster's to gamble and drink until dawn. Then, they slept it off on the floor.

Now, I'm going to get him out of jail, Allise thought, walking up to the courthouse door where the sheriff waited for her. "Come on in, and we'll go to my office."

"What kind of trouble is Sam in, Sheriff Banes?"

"Well, he and Gunther were drunk. They got in a fight at Rooster's with some white boys from Perle. Gunther beat one of 'um pretty good, sent 'im to the hospital." Standing, he motioned for her to sit, then he sat behind his desk. "From what I got out of 'em down there, Sam gave as good as he got. Not enough damage to charge him with assault. I charged drunkenness. There is a hundred-dollar fine. Pay it, and he can go home."

"That's kind of you, Sheriff. I'll pay the fine, but what about Gunther?"

"He'll be in jail till his trial's set. The boy has no one to care about him, but Sam needs to stay away from him."

Allise handed a check across the desk. "It's a shame. I'll talk to Sam, Sheriff."

"I'll go get 'im." He reached for keys in a drawer behind him. Don't be shocked when ya see 'im. He needs some cleaning up."

In a few minutes, he returned, leading a bedraggled, bruise-faced Sam by the arm.

Sam's legs sagged when he saw Allise, and the sheriff helped him to a chair. He wouldn't look at her but sat in the corner, head drooping like a scolded dog's tail. His appearance softened her anger. But only for a moment. Handing over a check, she stood and started for the door. "Thanks, Sheriff." Waving, she left Sam to make his way.

She found Maizee fully dressed when she met them at the garage and helped get Sam inside to a kitchen chair. "Mista Sam, what you gone and done?"

"Maizee, let's start cleaning him up." Allise whispered, "He smells awful."

They tiptoed about the house collecting a washbasin, cloth, towel and soap. Allise found a shirt and pants Quent had worn to the fields. "Mista Sam's a good man, Miz Allie. Why's he getting in trouble? That cranky old woman he married?" Allise didn't try to answer. Downstairs, Maizee placed soap and towel on the kitchen table and ran warm water into the basin.

Setting it on the table, she stood back. "Mista Sam, you gotta take off that shirt if we gonna git you clean."

"I can wash myself, Maizee." He looked up at her. "I ain't been bathed by a black woman since I was a baby. Mama said Elfreeda did it."

"Now Mista Sam, I won't do it if you don't want me to, but you don't need t' be rubbing 'em cuts. Let me wash y' face and neck anyway." He didn't object, and she lathered soap in the warm water. Squeezing the cloth, she dabbed his wounds, then cleaned his neck before running the wet cloth over his hair and patting him dry with the towel.

"You're a gentle woman, Maizee." Taking the towel, he said, "Thanks, I'll finish."

She and Allise went to the living room and waited. "His eyes be so sad, Miz Allie. Mista Sam's a good man. Maybe I find somebody like him, I might wanna …" From the kitchen, they heard, "I'm decent." Walking back into the room, the women laughed at Quent's pants covering Sam's feet. He stooped and cuffed them up.

"There is still time to catch sleep, Maizee. Why don't you go back to bed?"

Waiting for her to leave, Allise thought Sam had expended so much energy trying to lure Simone back, he had little time for the farm he loved. She turned to a sheepish-looking man. "Sit down, Sam. That is, if you're the Sam I've always known. If you're that other person I saw in the Sheriff's office, I don't have much interest in knowing you, and you should go home." She waited for him to react.

He stood, holding to the back of a chair. Moments passed, then he slid down onto it. "I'm sorry, Allie." For the first time, he looked into her face, eyes pleading.

Her anger spilled out. Anger at him, at Quent, and herself. "You're acting stupid, Sam. Punishing only yourself. I know the real Sam, and you can stop this nonsense." If she had her way, he would not be lost to an idealized woman. She reached for his hands. "Sam, rejection robs us of the person we think we are. When Simone left, you must have felt something was wrong with you."

He shook his head in denial. For a moment, she wondered about the wisdom of continuing her line of thought. They had never talked much about Quent. Maybe it was time. "Well, I know the feeling of diminished self-worth. All the times I couldn't reach Quent … He lived in his own world. All the nights he didn't come home, and I thought something was wrong with me. All the times he was unhappy because he couldn't tell Daddy Joe he didn't want to farm. That he dreamed of a more exciting life. I didn't know then what was going on with him. Who knows what was going on with your Simone?"

"I knew she wasn't coming back." Sam pulled his hand free and rubbed his eyes.

"Of course you did." Allise touched his arm. "But you've made a fool of yourself because you thought you were worthless. You're a fine man, Sam. Deserve better than what you've put yourself through, and I suspect you will find what you need." Allise stood. "I paid your fine this time, but if this nonsense happens again, you will remain in jail."

"I know you mean it, Allie. I don't know how to say 'I'm sorry' or 'thank you.'"

"Go home, Sam. Get some sleep."

Soon after their talk, Sam came to tell Allise he had given Simone a decent mourning. He showed he could reform by helping Jonas cleanup and store the farm equipment, and leaving Gunther to his drunken capers.

All through the months after Simone came into their lives, Maydale had waited in the wings. Even after Sam's wife returned to France, he made no move toward her. One day, she admitted to Allise, "While Sam was overseas, I poured out my heart in letters to him, but he rarely reflected similar feelings. How could I have been so stupid?"

Allise, letting the question hang, had tried to comfort her friend from her own experience of unreturned love. Now, she wanted Sam's trips to Bensburg and Maydale's unanswered phone calls to be reasons for hope. Again, she allowed herself to believe Sam had found the person he needed all along.

She stashed addressed Christmas cards in a desk cubbyhole and turned to see him rush into the room. Pulling up a chair, he grinned. "Guess what, girl!" Hands wringing, he said, "Me and Maydale, we gonna take the plunge. She said, 'yes.' We're getting married!"

Surprise swept her face. While she suspected they were seeing each other, Allise wasn't prepared for a wedding announcement. Springing from the chair, she grabbed his arms, and they danced around the room.

Maizee grinned from the doorway. She had told Allise that Mista Sam made her believe there might be some good men and maybe Thatch Gains was one of them.

Sam led Allise to the couch and pulled her down on it. Leaning forward, he peered into her smile as though trying to ascertain it didn't mean, "I told you so." With lowered eyes, he said, "You were right, Allie. I loved Maydale all along. Sorta lost my way for a time and didn't know love when I saw it." He stopped the nervous hands. "It's hard to believe a woman can love me the way she does. She waited so long I don't deserve her, but we got something to hinge a marriage on something Simone and me never had."

He looked up expectantly, and Allise took his hands in hers. "I'm happy for you, Sam. You two are among the most beloved people in my life. Things work out, don't they?" Gazing off, she thought of how she tried to force her wishes on him and how she tried to push Dro away. "Things do work out, despite my attempts to control them."

Looking pleased, Sam stood. "All I know is, we need people like you, Allie, and those who wait, like Maydale. What would us fence sitters do without ya?"

Allise stood and kissed him on the cheek.

Weeks later, she lay on the chaise, a copy of *Brideshead Revisited* face-down on her lap. Allise was spent. Sam and Maydale were married in a civil ceremony the week before Christmas, and she had arranged their reception dinner just ahead of the holidays. The newlyweds were expected to return from a honeymoon in Hot Springs today and settle in the DeWitt house on Filbert Street. That Sam and Maydale were finally teammates made her happy. She would no longer have to play the partnership role.

The porch door banged, and footsteps ran up the stairs. "Allie," Sam called, and the two of them burst into the room.

Allise put the book on the side table while Sam seated his wife in the armchair and pulled the rocker up close. He didn't give her time to ask about their stay in the spa city. "We got an idea wanna hear whatcha think. See, I was telling May-dale about this GI. He was a rice farmer from over round Stuttgart. We got to know each other at Ft. Hood. I never saw him after that. Don't know what happened to 'im." Sam paused, as though seeing what could have happened. He slipped forward on the rocker. "Anyway, my buddy thought our farm might be good for growing rice."

He leaned forward, scanning her face. Then, motioning to Maydale, he said, "We been talking. Could go on planting cotton, but all the farm labor is leaving. I'm afraid synthetic stuff is going to push the demand for cotton down. Whatcha think?"

Long ago, Sam had spoken of varying traditional farming practices, but Quent had not listened. He has Daddy Joe's savvy, Allise thought. Rising, she walked to the window and stood, gazing out. What could she say that wouldn't dampen their enthusiasm? She swung around to face them, hands on her hips. "Growing rice might be a real risk, Sam." His face fell, and she quickly added, "But this might be the time to be daring. To follow your hunch. Seize an opportunity."

Sam and his bride beamed at her. Wanting that picture to last, she said, "Such a change might call for small steps, and you will need to learn if the soil is suitable for rice."

"Heck," Sam said, "around World War I, Maydale's grandpa raised good rice crops in Arkansas not thirty miles from here."

Maydale nodded. Her grandfather drilled deep wells for irrigation and did well until the Depression when he had to mortgage the land. Sam's soldier friend had said rice required clayey loam, high temperatures, and lots of water channeled into irrigation ditches on flat fields. "Our land's mostly flat," he said. "The biggest cost would be drilling wells."

"Sam really wants to try this." Maydale smiled at her husband.

Allise nodded, reserving doubts about the endeavor. All agreed two months wasn't enough time to prepare for a crop this year. She said they should use the time to learn about growing rice and alluded to agricultural reports read in Cash's little book. Seemingly staggered by the learning she thought necessary, Sam said, "That will take months!"

"Well, Sam, time might be an advantage. You should talk to a rice farmer."

"Allie is right, Sam. We can start with a small rice acreage and gradually increase it," Maydale said. "That way, we rely on cotton while feeling our way into the new crop."

With Allise's sanctions, they left smiling. She was happy for them and would trust their judgment in the farming venture.

Now that Sam and Maydale were yoke mates, she felt less encumbered. As Sam's partner, and while working with Jonas, she learned about farming. Now she could watch from a distance as they prepared for next year's cultivation and turn to other matters.

Peter was sixteen and learning to drive the Buick. Allise wanted to teach Maizee and Nate, as well. So much time passed while she was caught up in her and Dro's dilemma, Sam and Simone's problems, and the wedding. Keeping up with school duties and abreast of business at Joe's Market, too. She reminded herself that market proceeds supplemented her beggared teacher's salary. *Must write my family and suggest a summer visit to Philadelphia.*

Some time later, she and Dro returned from an evening in Bensburg when Allise mentioned her planned trip. "Mother hasn't been able to visit us. Peter and Cleesy have never seen her and my sister, Margaret. We need to go before Peter goes off to college."

"What if I tag along? I want to meet your family," Dro said.

Taken aback, she stammered. "We'll let's think about it." Changing the subject, she said, "Dro, there's so much dissension between Peter and Nate."

"Sweetheart—"

"O-oh, I go all mushy when you use those endearing words." She smiled a tease.

He smiled back. "I'm onto your attempts to divert my attention, Allise. You know as well as I do the climate here isn't ready for your situation with Maizee and Nate. With the boys getting older, it's more ripe for trouble now than ever before."

"Yes, I know. Maizee and I try, but—"

"Well, you can think about the boys any time." He reached for her hand. "I want you to think about marriage. I'm giving you time to think, not that you deserve it." She giggled at the way he proposed, and thought she surely needed his help.

The next morning before leaving for school, Allise told Maizee about Dro's proposal. Grabbing hands, they danced around the room.

Returning from classes, she found Maizee at the kitchen sink, staring out the window. Suddenly, she went into a nervous tizzy. Looking out, Allise saw Nate and several black boys, all leaning against the tree stump. They laughed and punched at each other.

"Musta brought 'em from school," Maizee muttered. "Peter be here any minute. Miz Allie, what we gonna do?" Just then Peter and his buddies walked up. "Oh, my lawd! Gonna be trouble!"

Maizee and Allise ran outside to see the white boys advancing on Nate and his friends. His mother heard Peter say, "See that bunch of crows? You believe they're hanging around here?" He and Nate squared off, pounding each other about the head and face, while the others wrestled on the ground.

"My lawd, what I gonna do?" Maizee ran into the garage and returned with a baseball bat. Raising it, she walked into the fray. "Nate, get yo'self in that apartment. Peter, go inside." She pointed the bat. "If you don't move right now, I'm gonna pop both of ya." They did as she indicated. "The rest of ya, go on home. Ain't gonna be no more fighting."

Allise was astonished at her action and relieved that she didn't have to get involved.

Several days elapsed, and it became obvious Peter wasn't going to let Nate off the hook. Allise watched the boys and Cleesy scramble around the dinner table when Peter whispered, "You may be half white, but you're still a nigger to me."

Nate whispered, "I don't brag about being white. It's no big cheese t' me, honky!"

Hearing the word, Allise asked, "What is a honky?" Nate, looked surprised and said he didn't know, but a kid came back from up North and called white people honkies. Peter curled his lip and laughed across at Nate. They scuffled beneath the table, and ten-year-old Cleesy yelled for her mother to stop them. Allise saw Maizee deliver Nate a stern look.

The boys' dislike for each other was on her mind that morning as Allise sat in the school library completing an order form for books. Out of the corner of her eye, she saw a student aide standing in the doorway. "Miz DeWitt, you have a call in the office."

Over the phone came, "Miz Allie?" The familiar voice prompted a frown. Maizee had called her only twice before, when Cleesy had whooping cough, and later the measles.

"Is there a problem, Maizee?"

"Yes'm. The sheriff arrested me. I'm in jail, Miz Allie."

Without asking the reason, Allise gripped the steering wheel and sped over the empty streets. Racing across the parking lot into the jail, her heart pounded. She peered through the cell bars and waited for the jailer to come with the key. Maizee folded like an accordion on a bench along the wall, hiding her face in hugged knees. She shivered in a full-length coat, and Allise wondered if it was from cold or fright.

The jailer approached, swinging a key in a circle at the end of a cord. She called, "Maizee."

At the sound of her name, she lifted her head, dropped her feet to the floor and sat forward. Pulling on the tan coat, she encapsulated herself. Shame lay across her face.

The jailer fumbled with the lock and pulled the door open. Allise stepped inside and sat down next to her. Freeing one of Maizee's hands from the clutched coat, she held it and waited.

Maizee rocked back and forth. Late sun filtered through small side-by-side windows into the dormitory-like room, casting a long, slanted shadow of lined bunks on the opposite wall. Finally, she explained about going to Elfreeda's that morning. "Coming home this man ... Miz Allie, he made ugly looks at me. Followed me, and grabbed me from behind. He put his hand where it ain't suppose t' be."

Allise patted her hand. "That's contemptible, but why were *you* arrested?"

Maizee hesitated, running a thumb and forefinger along a fold in her coat. Then, she stopped tracing the fold and a peck of trouble peered from her almond-shaped eyes. "I stabbed him, Miz Allie." Her attention returned to the coat crease.

For a moment Allise was stunned. The jailer had offered no information, saying she would have to talk to the sheriff. Now, caught totally unaware by Maizee's incredible admission, she demanded, "How did you stab him? Is he dead?"

Maizee thought she stuck him in the thigh. "Wherever I could. He run back toward Dodd's store screaming." She told about buying the knife and wearing it on the streets for protection. "Don't want *no man* touching me!" Again, she creased the fold.

Allise's mind reeled. Hearing someone approach, both looked up.

The sheriff had sent his deputy to "fetch Mrs. DeWitt." Seated in his office, she heard that Maizee would probably stand trial for assault with intent to do bodily harm and for carrying a concealed weapon. He set bail and released Maizee in Allise's custody.

On the way home, she told her the unpleasant facts. Maizee became concerned about possibly going to prison and asked what would happen to Nate. Pulling into the garage, Allise said, "We will deal with it, Maizee. We always have." It's sure to unravel any plans to visit Pennsylvania, she thought. *Oh dear, what if our secret is revealed?*

All three kids ran to meet them. Maizee hurried to her apartment, and Nate shot past them, following behind her.

Inside the house, Peter blurted, "Kids taunted me at school."

Cleesy said two boys chanted a silly rhyme to Nate at school. She repeated: "Jailbird! Jailbird! Sitting in a jail cell, wishing and a wishing for someone to make bail."

Allise pushed dark red hair from her daughter's face. "That's cruel."

Peter glared at his mother. "Why was Maizee messing around with a no-good black man anyway? Fighting, shooting, cutting! Just like every Saturday night at Rooster's."

"How can you, Peter?" Allise asked. "Maizee cares for you as lovingly as any mother." How could she compete with the influence of his peers? Even eleven-year-old Cleesy acted distant toward the Colsons at times. Struggling with her dilemma, she explained what had happened.

Indignant, Peter paced the room. Cleesy stomped away in a pout. She turned at the door and declared, "Maizee wouldn't stick that man unless he did something to her."

With Cleesy out of hearing range, Allise told Peter the man made sexual advances.

Her son cocked his head as if to say, "So what?" Expectation in his mother's face didn't sway him. "Kids will say things to Cleesy and me. Embarrass us."

"Son, don't you feel anything for Maizee? She may face a trial and prison sentence. The man grabbed her from behind. He's the guilty one!" She couldn't mention why she thought Maizee carried the knife. Peter looked at her like a child who didn't want to hear another of her sermons. He asked why she thought Maizee was telling the truth about what had happened. "I trust her." Allise used her only defense. "I thought I could teach you and Cleesy to think and act in a kinder manner, to be different."

"Be different! For gosh sakes, that's the problem! We *are* different! Every day, I'm reminded of it. *You* don't go through what we do." His belligerent gaze held hers.

Allise was determined Peter would not out-stare her. "I'm hurt, Peter. I've always hoped we would be strong enough to bear up. Perhaps I was wrong to think the three of us, and Maizee and Nate, could stand alone against the judgment of others." She felt sad.

His eyes said she was wrong to inflict them with such a burden, and Allise wondered if she was.

The next morning, Maizee told her how Nate had followed her into her room and sat on her bedside. She said he fell to his knees and reached his arms around her. "We jes set there, holding each other, then he stand up and ask me what happened. I told him and he jes pacing, that forefinger across his lips. I'm so full of fear, watching him and wondering what gonna happen to my chile."

She said Nate stopped pacing and said she, and him, and Miz Allie would think of something. "He say, he'll get a job and hire a lawyer. Mr. James Beard be the best, he said. I tell him t' hush cause he be going t' school. Not t' talk that nonsense cause we sho gonna think of something." Maizee told how Nate stood there scheming. "He said he had worked on the farm for a pittance and when school ended, he was gonna ask Mr. Sam for a man's job."

Nate's plan brought smiles to their faces, but his mother's day in court lay ahead.

The day of the trial arrived cold and damp, chilling to the bones and drawing muscles taut. Upstairs, Negroes filled one side of the high-ceilinged courtroom.

As defense witnesses, Allise, Dro and Sam sat left of the aisle and behind Maizee at the defense table. Along with court officials and lawyers, they were the only white people in the room.

Opening with the prosecutor, Bud Lackey, took an inordinate amount of time to question witnesses for the complainant. He finished, and Maizee's lawyer, Mr. Beard, pried deeper and deeper into the stabbed man's personal life when Elfreeda caught Miz Allie's eye and waved from across the aisle.

Never having witnessed a trial, Allise marveled at Maizee's posture. Straight back and head held high. She whispered to Sam, "I'm nervous. What is Bud Lackey going to ask?"

Sam had no idea. Maizee's accuser was known for drunken fights at Rooster's. Nearly everyone but the out-of-town judge knew of his past scrapes with the law. His witnesses, dregs of Colored Town, looked more presentable than Sam had ever seen them.

Dro leaned over to whisper that the prosecutor had requested they look more presentable.

Just then, Mr. Beard called the first defense witness, the Reverend Jedadiah James. As his wheelchair rolled to a stop near the witness stand, Allise felt her tension relax. He told the court that Maizee and Nate had near perfect attendance at Mt. Zion. "Times they miss," Brother James said, "is when they's sick, and that ain't often."

On the stand, Elfreeda verified Maizee was at her house the day of the stabbing and gave an approximate time when she left.

Sam testified that Maizee came from a fine, hardworking family on the DeWitt farm. "Lived and worked there from the time Jonas and the late Rebekah Col-son married. Why, Rebekah's family worked on that land before it was Daddy's. Never has a member of the Colson family been in any kind of trouble with the law," he said.

Allise found it hard to breathe as she took the stand. Mr. Beard led her through Maizee's coming to live behind her home and work for her. She drew an easy breath when she was released by the prosecution without a hint at the shameful past.

Dro followed her on the stand. "Maizee, in the years I've known her in the DeWitt home, has never presented herself in any manner other than proper and lady-like. She's quiet and unobtrusive. I've never seen her act out of order. She's raising a fine son."

With that, Bud Lackey rose to cross-examine. "Speaking of her son, Dro Excuse me, we've known each other a long time, but for the court's sake we mustn't be too familiar. Mr. McClure, isn't it true that Maizee Colson's son is illegitimate?"

Every drop of Dro's blood looked to be rushing to his face, and a bomb couldn't have left a more piercing impact and dropped a more deadly silence over the courtroom.

Sam bent over, rubbing his hands. Allise jerked forward. She wanted to go to Maizee, but she eased back. Appearing stoic, Maizee held herself as if every muscle had tightened.

Like beginning thunder, a wave of discontent rolled across the blacks, who filled up the opposite side of the courtroom. Bolting back in his seat, Sam and other defense witnesses turned in that direction. The judge pounded the gavel. "Order! There will be order. Now!"

As the room settled, Allise wondered how Dro would answer. Her children had been protected from the truth. *How can I explain to Peter and Cleesy? Does Nate know about his birth?* Since Maizee's arrest, she had prayed explanation would not be necessary.

"What about her son, Mr. McClure?" Bud Lackey repeated.

"Well, I …" Dismayed, Dro looked down from the witness chair at Allise.

The prosecutor goaded. "We've known each other since childhood, Mr. McClure. Had the same influences, same experiences. Is he or isn't he illegitimate?"

"I-I've heard that rumor. Don't know the truth of it."

"Objection!" Mr. Beard sounded for the defense. "Your Honor, the prosecution cannot rest the case on rumor. May we approach, Your Honor?" At the bench, the judge whispered to the prosecutor, who whispered back. Mr. Beard threw up his hands as if frustrated and smoothed gray hair at his nape as they continued to whisper back and forth.

The judge dismissed the lawyers with a flick of his hand. "Your objection is overruled, Mr. Beard. Continue, Mr. Lackey."

Turning back to Dro, Bud Lackey showed a wicked grin. "I apologize, Your Honor, for having to put my friend in this position, but the truth must be brought out. Now, isn't it true, Mr. McClure, that the boy born to that woman is half-white?" He pointed to Maizee. "Isn't that a fact?" Extending over the witness rail, he was almost nose to nose with Dro, who appeared ready to punch him. Allise went ashen, and Sam dug elbows into his thighs.

"Your Honor, I object. What does something that happened so long ago have to do with this assault case?" Mr. Beard asked.

"Mr. Lackey, what does it have to do with this case?" the judge asked.

"It has everything to do with it, Your Honor. Proves this woman," he pointed, "has a loose character, and the man she stabbed had reason to think he could approach her."

Maizee turned to Allise with a look of stark pleading in her eyes. Mr. Beard saw her sag as she turned forward again. He grabbed and braced her on the chair. The judge allowed Bud to proceed, and he repeated the question of mixed race.

"Yes. I'd have to say that's pretty evident, but—"

"No qualifications were asked for, sir. The witness needs to answer with a 'yes' or 'no.'" The judge's patience seemed to be waning, and turning, the prosecutor must have seen it was. "Your Honor, a few more questions for this witness?" With the judge's begrudged approval, he asked, "Mr. McClure, who are the men in Maizee's life? Isn't it true, she goes down to Colored Town to meet men?" Again, gasps came from the colored side of the room.

"Why I've never known her to, but you're asking the wrong person. I've no way of knowing. Bud, I think I know why you're doing this, and I don't like it one bit!"

"Your Honor, Your ..." Mr. Beard tried to interrupt, but Dro would not be hushed.

"You think because I'm a white Southerner, I'll say what you want me to say about a Negro, whether true or not." Bud pled with the judge to instruct the witness on conduct.

"Mr. McClure, no conjecture needed. Answer the questions. Proceed, Mr.—"

"I don't know that she goes to Colored Town to meet men. I've never seen her there," Dro said. "Neither have I ever heard such a thing." The prosecutor dismissed him.

Dro gazed at Mr. Beard, but the defense didn't wish to question him. The judge dismissed him, and Maizee's lawyer asked for a thirty-minute recess. Both attorneys approached the bench. After whispers between them, the judge announced the recess.

Mr. Beard went to Allise and Maizee. He wished to speak with them privately. Pointing to an entrance off the courtroom, he led them to the anteroom, held the door open and asked the deputy sheriff sitting there to wait outside.

Inside the closed room, Allise stood behind Maizee, who sat wringing her hands.

"Miss Colson, you're going to be questioned about your son. Bud Lackey has proof your boy was born to an unwed Maizee Colson in Jefferson, Texas, in June 1933. He can produce the midwife's affidavit. She swore she delivered your son, and that you were not married at the time. Are you ready for this?"

Maizee shook with soundless sobs, and Allise knelt, embracing her. While they clung to each other, Mr. Beard gazed out the window. After some minutes, the seasoned old lawyer said, "Ladies, people are filing back inside from out there." Looking down, he said, "It's a hard decision, but time's running out."

Allise stood again behind Maizee. "I think ..." She squeezed her shoulder. "I think we both knew we would face this someday. It's come before either of us was ready. As for me, I support telling the truth." Squeezing again, she added, "Maizee, I know the truth about Nate. I've known for some time." Her black friend glanced up in teary disbelief.

"Are you willing to take the stand, Miss Colson? Remember the circumstances," James Beard warned, as though wanting a sure thing.

Allise pressed encouragement into her shoulder, and Maizee nodded.

"Well," the attorney said, drawing in a long breath, "let's get back in there and do it. I have one other witness to call before I call you, Miss Colson."

During the recess, the courtroom had filled with people. Where Dro, Sam, and Allise had been the only whites, now every bench behind them was filled, and people stood at the edges of the room. Mr. Beard consulted with the bailiff, then to Allise he whispered, "Someone spread the word that Nate's legitimacy was before the court."

Proceedings resumed, and the prosecutor had no other witnesses. The defense called Dodd Turner. Shuffling up front, he stuttered "I will" to the oath and clambered onto the stand. Questioned about the complainant being in his store prior to the incident, he said, "Yeah, he," Dodd pointed, "had a strawberry pop, and Maizee stop in for eggs, but I don't have any." He smiled a snaggle-toothed grin.

"Now, Mr. Turner, did Miss Colson give that man … Did you see her give him any kind of special look or say anything to that man over there?"

"Nawsir! She jes walk in, ask for eggs. I tells her I ain't got none. She turns round and walks out. She didn't even look—"

"Does Miss Colson come into Colored Town looking for men, and have you ever seen her, you know, flirting around?" Sniffles could be heard coming from Maizee.

"I ain't ever seen Maizee in Colored Town 'cepting for Sunday church and when she visit Elfreeda there." Dodd pointed. "I ain't ever seen her wid no man. She be doing that, I'd sho know bout it, cause I knows ever'thing goes on down there."

Laughter and shuffling was heard behind Allise. She imagined jabbing elbows. The judge beat his gavel, and Bud Lackey rose to challenge the witness. "Now, Dodd, isn't it just possible that Maizee was meeting men and you didn't know about it?"

"I knows ever'thing goes on. If I don't see it, I sho hears bout it." Again, there was laughter, and apparently Bud saw the uselessness of the witness. He had no more questions.

The defense attorney called Maizee, and she moved quickly to the witness stand. Mr. Beard led her into the rape. "Yessa, Mista Beard, I was raped."

Gentle in his questioning, he asked, "And when did this happen? At what age?"

Maizee wiped a tear from her cheek. "Sixteen."

"Where did it take place?"

The room fell quiet as a cemetery, and Maizee's head snapped up. She looked Mr. Beard straight in the eye. "In a cotton shed on the DeWitt farm."

"Who raped you, Miss Maizee?" Sam propped on his knees and rubbed his hands.

"I ain't saying. I ain't gonna say," she declared, turning to look at Allise and Sam.

Not even her lawyer could budge her, and the prosecutor rose. "Isn't it a fact, girl, that you teased that white man into the cotton shed? You took a shine to him and—"

"Objection, Your Honor. Badgering the witness without one shred of proof?"

"Sustained."

"Well, isn't it true, Maizee, you shimmed into Turner's Store, whipping your dress tail around just like the victim claimed up here on this stand? Didn't you lure him out of that store, and that's why he followed you? Isn't that right?" Snickering broke out in the white section of the courtroom and set the judge to pounding his gavel.

Tears streamed down Maizee cheeks. Wiping them, she looked across the room at Thatch Gains. "Answer me, Maizee." Bud's words jarred her back into reality.

Eyes aiming darts at her inquisitor, she said "No sir!" The strength of her voice seemed to surprise him, but he waited, watching her anger swell and push away shame.

"Your Honor, please." Mr. Beard tried to interfere with the questioning.

Without a quaver, Maizee shouted. "He lied!" She pointed with a lifetime of anger turned on the man who accused her of such carrying on. The prosecutor smiled, seemingly pleased at having brought out that state of emotion before dismissing her.

She fled the stand and sat rigidly straight against the back of her chair.

Called upon again, Allise took the stand. She looked down to see Maizee's eyes, so full of anger moments before, now blank and staring straight ahead. Mr. Beard walked from the defense table toward her. "Mrs. DeWitt, do you know the father of Nate Colson?" The room could be heard inhaling.

A suppressed scream waited to escape her lips, but she would not satisfy the silent expectancy. Her eyes steeled, unwavering, on the crowd. "Yes, I do." Maizee stiffened, her veiled gaze seemingly unmindful of Allise's sad smile. Sam slumped over his knees, covering his face in big hands. She may be under public scrutiny, but Allise saw Dro mouth "I love you." She pulled strength from it. Her words, barely above a whisper, cut through the courtroom. "My late husband." A gasp ran the gamut of the crowd.

"And what was your husband's name?"

"Quent Q-Quentin DeWitt." Anger ushered from some deep source. Anger held too long, and like Maizee she could no longer hold it. "Everyone in this town knows the truth," she shouted. "The sound of disbelief just heard, it wasn't for some newly revealed secret. It was because a white woman dared admit such publicly." She paused, thinking. "And more unbelievably, that I would do it to save a black woman from punishment for something forced on her by sexual misconduct. Maizee defended herself against that man there precisely because of that long-ago experience."

A rumble spread through the crowd. The judge pounded, and Allise leaned over the witness rail, focused on spectators. She spoke above the gavel sounds. "It's inconceivable to you that a white woman can befriend a *black* woman, much less one with whom her husband sired a child. Well, *I* can." She paused. "Nate is the result of rape! Maizee did nothing wrong then, or in this case. She gives all men a wide berth."

Appearing baffled, the judge had allowed her to finish, and sitting back, Allise stared out on the now-quieted crowd. "You're dismissed, Mrs. DeWitt." Once she was seated, he cleared his throat. "From testimony in this case, the defen-dant's only wrong doing is stabbing the complainant in self-defense. She's fined one hundred dollars to be paid for the plaintiff's doctor bill." He pounded the gavel and said, "Court dismissed."

# CHAPTER 16

▼

As difficult as it had been, the trial left Allise with a certain satisfaction. "Think of it this way, Maizee, we no longer have to live with a secret. We fooled them and mastered the situation." They climbed into the car and headed home.

Maizee still looked shaken. "Yes'm, but what about our kids?"

"That's been my greatest fear." Allise wanted to bolster her friend's fragile hold on courage. "Our children will need us more than ever now. There will always be another test for us, but Maizee, you and I will always weather the storms." She didn't add that after today, she felt she could depend on Dro to help ease her problems.

As they rolled into the garage, all three kids came running out to met them. Maizee ran for her apartment, but Allise called after her. "Please don't run from this, Maizee. You and Nate, come with us. We're going to confront this together."

Inside, Maizee pared fruit and took meat from the refrigerator for sandwiches. All three children sat at the kitchen table while Allise explained to Peter and Cleesy that their daddy was also Nate's daddy. Peter gazed across at Nate. "You're *not* my brother. My daddy didn't like Negroes. Daddy wouldn't …" He paused, looking at his young sister. "He wouldn't do that with a Negro. Why did you hafta say he did, Maizee?"

Cleesy jumped in before Maizee could reply. "Our daddy wouldn't make a baby with a Negro." Tears ran down her cheeks. "My best friend, Marianna Lackey, called and said, 'You're just a nigger lover, and my mother says I can't play with you anymore.'"

Nate waited for Miz Allie to calm Cleesy, then, "Pete, I'm not claiming the same daddy with the likes of you. Don't have a daddy, ain't never had one, don't need one!"

Held in the circle of her mother's arm, Cleesy hid her face on her mother's shoulder. Maizee sat down, and Allise said, "It isn't going to be easy, but we, all of us must face the truth. It wasn't easy for Maizee and me in court today. She and I have held this secret for years, even though she didn't know I knew. It's no secret anymore, and we're going to have to accept it." No one spoke, and she continued. "Everyone in town already knew, Peter. They protected you and Cleesy." She told about the conversation in Robbin's Store while selecting her funeral attire.

"You didn't hafta say anything. How can we live here?" Peter raged at Maizee.

"Peter, stop it! Cleesy, you can tell Marianna's father that he didn't have to bring it up. He badgered all of us about something totally irrelevant to the case." Allise paused, studying her son. How could she make him understand that Bud Lackey would have kept after them until he gained the answer he wanted? "I think the judge was wrong for allowing him to proceed with that line of questioning after Mr. Beard's objection," she added.

"She," Peter said, meaning Maizee, "just couldn't take his questioning, huh?" He sounded as if he hadn't been listening. His sarcasm was as thick as mud.

"In the first place, the truth is Maizee was raped, but she refused to say who did it."

"Who told then?" Peter screamed at his mother.

"Me. It was I."

"You! How could you?" Peter slapped a half-eaten sandwich on his plate. "If she didn't tell, why did you have to?"

Cleesy wanted to leave the room, but her mother said, "Honey, we're all in this together. Everyone needs to hear the truth." Allise turned to Peter again. "We were in a court room where the judge rules. Bud argued Maizee's conduct caused the man to think she invited his advances. He had evidence to prove Nate was born out of wedlock. To offset the defamation of Maizee's character, we had to reveal she was raped."

"You think her character's worth more than daddy's reputation?" Anger reddened his face, and his mother waited for more abuse, but the room fell into stony silence.

The apples Maizee had cut turned brown before she spoke for the first time. "I ain't ever meant to hurt nobody. Not you, Miz Allie, or Peter and Cleesy." Tears filled her eyes.

Nate put an arm across her shoulders. "You haven't ever hurt anyone, Momma. None of this is your fault."

"I don't know how I'm going to live in this town." Peter looked miserable.

"We do what we must, Peter." Even as her own strength wavered, Allise wanted to clothe him in armor. Was she wrong to sacrifice her children for the sake of convictions?

It was too late. What was she to do? How could she bridge the gaps between the town and her family? Between Peter and the Colsons? *Perhaps Dro ...*

Days were passing, and Allise was more convinced she needed Dro's help. Peter came from school to repeat the scorn heaped on him by his classmates. "Their parents say, 'The DeWitts ought to move to Africa and take them niggers with them.' One said, we should move to Colored Town. How you like that, Mother? They say, 'We don't want ya here.'"

She was accustomed to ostracism and his kind of pain. Reasoning away the intangible wall between themselves and townsfolk didn't sound plausible, even to her. Peter had become a recluse, shutting away in his room. Cleesy holed up, too.

On Sunday morning, Dro came to pick up the DeWitts for church. Peter refused to go, and while Allise and Dro waited for Cleesy, she said, "I'm at my wit's end. What am I to do, Dro? The children are my greatest responsibility, and I can't get it right."

He embraced her. "Now, darling, Peter's a DeWitt, one of our own. He's handsome like Quent and far too popular to lose permanent standing in Deer Point. Give it time, the town will come around. Cleesy is resilient. Her young friends will return."

Hearing Cleesy on the stairs, they released each other, and the three left for church.

Alone in the house, Peter lay across his bed. Staring at the ceiling, he thought life was never going to be the same. Might as well end it now, he thought.

He had lain there for some time when suddenly he sat up, resting his head in his hands. Moments passed, then he leaped from the bedside, flung open his door and ran along the landing to the bathroom. Returning with a razor blade, he slammed his door and ripped the sheet from his bed. With the blade, he cut two places through the hem and tore off two lengths. Tying them together, he made one long piece about six inches wide.

Unaware that Maizee and Nate had returned from church and were at that moment in the kitchen, he held the strip and stared at the nine-foot ceiling. Then, glancing around, he opened the closet door and tied one end to the inside knob. Throwing the other end over the door, he closed it and made a noose. Peter shoved a straight chair to the closet, and standing on the chair, slipped the noose over his head. For a moment, he stood there. His mind felt still, and he stepped off. The chair fell over. His body jerked, and he struggled, overturning the chair. His feet banged against the closet door.

Nate threw open the bedroom door and whispered, "Pete! Oh, lawd, what'd you do?" Straightening the chair, he lifted Peter to stand on it, then helped him to the floor.

"Nate, what is it?" Maizee called from the bottom of the stairs.

"Nothing, Momma. Just Pete messing around. He knocked over a chair."

Peter stood there, gasping for air. When his breath came easier, he pulled the noose over his head and sat on the bed rubbing his blood-red face.

"What the heck you doing, Pete?" Nate sat beside him. "You do something stupid, and it'll be the end of Miz Allie."

In a raspy voice, Peter said, "You won't tell her, will you? I mean it, Nate. Don't tell anyone, you hear?"

"I'm not gonna tell unless you try something stupid like this again."

Before Peter could promise, Maizee called a second time. "I better go back downstairs, or Momma will be coming up here."

"Shut the door," Peter said, lying back on his bed.

Without knowing that Peter had tried to commit suicide, Allise blamed herself for his despondency. She had perceived too late the possible causes of his father's moods. She asked herself, if to do over, would she protect Maizee? She sat at the table, peeling potatoes while Maizee busied herself at the sink. "I'm worried about Peter. He shuts himself away in his room."

"Miz Allie, I know how to end this whole mess. Me and Nate will move back to the farm with Daddy."

"You will do no such thing, Maizee Colson!" Allise pounded the table. "That would solve nothing. Some people will always call us 'nigger lovers.' Nate is Quent's child, and we're going to see that he goes to school."

Maizee nodded. "Miz Allie, you ain't ever gonna know how me and Nate feel about you. There ain't no way we can ever pay our debt." Her eyes turned misty.

Allise reached for her, and they clung to each other. "Listen," she said, pushing Maizee back to look into her face, "I know real devotion when I see it. There's plenty of that between us. We're strong, but we can use some help."

"Thatch Gains ..." Maizee began with a timorous whisper and demure downcast of her eyes. "Miz Allie, he wanting t' call on me."

"Maizee! Oh, Maizee, there's no reason why you shouldn't have a good man in your life." She smiled at her friend.

Looking pleased, Maizee said, "It's downright sad t' watch Mista Dro. I know how scared you are, Miz Allie, but I cain't help being sorry for him. He's a good man, too. Make a fine daddy for Peter and Cleesy."

"You're right, Maizee. He would be a good father, and Dro's in tune with my soul." She wanted him in her life.

Months after the trial, Allise reviewed their lives following the gut-wrenching experience. Everyone seemed to be moving on, even Maizee, who saw Thatch on a regular basis. Peter worked the summer in Joe's Market and avoided Nate. Jill, his steady girlfriend, had stood by him during the harsh months after the trial. Sam and Maydale did well. It had taken three growing seasons for them and Jonas to establish a Chula River rice producing farm. The couple built a home on the site of the burned church, and as usual, on leaving the farm school, Allise stopped to visit.

She told Maydale her black students had dwindled to two, and their parents would take them north as soon as the fields were planted. "My school is going to end," she said.

They discussed other farmers who had tried rice cultivation and ended up with failed crops. Maydale said farmers were funny. "They see a successful crop and everyone tries it."

"It's sad to see them fail," Allise said, and her friend nodded. She told about Peter finding a used car he wanted to buy. "Dro went with him to look it over. He says it's a bargain, but Peter may not have enough savings. I'll make up the difference. You know, seeing him and Jill riding about will be reminiscent of Quent and me in his roadster."

"Allie, you can't live in the past."

Standing to leave, she said, "I know, Maydale. The Thirties and Forties were decades of hardships. Let's hope this one turns out to be kinder."

Late one night, she and Dro sat on the couch when he laughed and said a lesser women would fall under his spell, but she, strong-willed as ever, ran like a fox from a hound. At forty-seven, he said he was settled in his ways and felt foolish trying to win her over. "But, I'm determined to change you from a DeWitt to a McClure."

After he left, she sat on the bedside hugging the quivers rushing through her body. New sensations, never felt with Quent, had her reflecting. Dro's eyes could strip her bare. Her late husband's eyes never left her naked. Lying back, she turned out the lamp, pulled up the covers and thought about their relationship. Convinced she had loved Quent, she asked herself, why otherwise, would she have been so miserable when he showed no interest? *We were so young. Attracted to each other. He wasn't the free spirit I thought him to be. He felt trapped, obligated to Daddy Joe. Love-making was for him. For me, it was more a duty. He could show affection and did at times, but Quent wasn't the caressing kind. So unlike Dro, who is soft, loving, sharing, passionate. If we hadn't kissed ...* She trembled and muttered, "I love you, Dro."

Just thinking of him hardened her breasts and nipples.

She wondered if a forty-one-year-old woman should be having such stirrings. It was as if her body signaled her to tell him, "I'm yours. Take me." *Dro will share his love, not just draw from me. He will share his feelings and thoughts. We will talk about everything imaginable and cherish being with each other.*

Allise was finished with giving the trite excuses Dro accused her of. She wanted to be with him in all the ways a man and woman should be.

In the spring after Peter graduated, they went to Pennsylvania where Allise and Dro were married in the Weston's living room, the same room in which she and Quent were wed.

Leaving Peter and Cleesy with her parents, they drove to Niagra Falls. A bellhop unlocked the door to a hotel room nine floors up and overlooking the Canadian Falls. Dro grabbed Allise up in his arms, and she clung, giggling as he carried her to the window.

Gazing out, they forgot the bellhop. He alerted them with a cough, and Dro handed him a tip. Closing the door, he picked her up and took her to the bed. Lying beside her, their heads touching, he said, "Allise McClure. I practiced saying that." Smiling, he pulled her into his arms. "I'm so happy you are my wife."

She put his hand to her lips. "Me, too. Thought I would never give my heart again. What have I done?" A nervous laugh followed her tease. "Can I tell you something?" Allise raised on one elbow. "Well, I have these these strange feelings. Oh, I've read of such in novels, just never experienced them. Wasn't sure they were possible, maybe figments of writers' imaginations. When I think about you, well, there they are."

He laughed at her innocence, pulling her down for his kiss. She raised again. "I'm supposed to, aren't I? I mean, supposed to have them?"

"Yes, love." Swinging off the bed, Dro walked around and pulled her upright. His eyes burned with desire. Turning her, he pulled the zipper and pushed the dress from her shoulders, letting it drop around her ankles. Nimbly, he loosened and removed undergarments until she stood naked. Turning her around, his eyes swept the curves of her shoulders, her breasts and hips. Then, lifting her to the bed, he quickly undressed.

Allise moved into his embrace and let his caresses fire a passion she had never known. Drawing him inside her, they melded into one hungered body.

Back in Deer Point, Maizee and Nate laughed and embraced the newlyweds. Maizee said their wedding news would turn the town upside-down.

Dro told her he had worn his feelings on his sleeve for years. "If the town is surprised, it isn't my fault. You can blame Allise for keeping them wondering." With that, they had gone upstairs.

She eased into the curve of Dro's arm and lay still and thoughtful. Then, out of the quietness, she said, "Darling—"

"You've never called me that before. It's music to my ears, love."

"I know." She smiled up at him. "Dro, are we going to trust our love?"

"Is this gonna be heavy stuff we're talking?" he asked, turning to face her.

"You're funny, and it's one of the things I love about you, but can we be serious for the moment? I need to trust your love and for you to trust mine. I want it to be like a warm blanket, safe and comforting. The two of us, loving and knowing the joy of being together. I love you, not for your good looks or charm. Oh, Dro!" She came up on her elbow, peering into his face. "You are handsome and charming. You are!"

"Yeah, yeah. I'm listening."

His amusement left her undaunted. "Dro, I think I see the depth of your soul." She cupped his cheek. "You are willing to reveal weakness and hurt. You have the capacity to laugh at yourself." He lifted his arm and sawed an imaginary violin with musical sounds. "Laugh at me if you will, I don't mean to put a damper on our happiness. It's just that we need to discuss our responsibilities."

She paused, gaging him. "My children are an intricate part of our relationship. Rearing them is the scariest challenge I've had. Peter and Cleesy are at an age to give us real problems."

Dro seemed content to listen. "Peter," she began with difficulty. "You know young Americans may be sent to Korea. If Peter isn't drafted, he'll go to college. Cleesy has five more years of school. She's coming into young adulthood." Allise pushed up and propped on her elbow, looking down at him. "Dro, are you comfortable taking us on?" She thought she knew his answer, but thinking of Quent's negligence, she needed to hear it.

He looked as though asking if he had heard right, but she rushed on. "Before you answer, hear me out. You know how I feel about war. I'm afraid for Peter and Nate."

"Allise, if there's war, I'll be right here. We will deal with whatever confronts us."

"That's what I wanted to hear, darling." She looked thoughtful. "There's another thing. We mustn't pull in different directions in front of the children. I mean, Peter shows no respect for the Negro race. Nate is obstinate, too. I can't give up and want your support in trying to reach them. Division between the races drives me—"

"I know," he said.

Moments passed. "The thing is, we own each other's responsibilities. You never had children; it will be a new and not so easy experience."

"Maybe I'm better than you think. Of course, we'll tackle the kids together."

Allise brought up her estrangement from the community. "People like the Bud Lackeys. When you married me ..."

Pulling her to him, he said, "I'm hurt and surprised you don't know me bett—"

"Oh, no!" She jerked upright. "I really do! Just need to hear we're in agreement. I don't want any unhappy surprises between us, Dro."

"With you beside me, I'll face all the Buds there are likely to be." Sounding reliable, he added, "You know how it is here. Deer Point will forget ..."

His thought trailed as she snuggled into his arm. "You handled Bud well at the trial, but they will not forget that I besmirched my husband's name in public."

"Bud knows where I stand." He took a moment. Then, "Besmirched, I don't know if that was the case. People will remember Maizee's trial, but our slate's gonna be so full of problems foreseen by you, there'll be no time to fret over them."

Allise warned him not to take their problems too lightly. She said they may be painful, and their love had to be strong enough to endure whatever marriage held for them.

"I don't take them lightly." A serious gaze confirmed Dro's sincerity. "I understand our leashes will be strained. There will be problems we don't anticipate."

"You think I make too much of this, don't you?" She moved away.

Dro sat up, fluffed his pillow against the headboard and said he was listening. She moved up beside him, unsure of how to convey what she wanted him to understand. "It isn't easy to explain, but you deserve to know why all this talk." She thought of how to say it. "Quent and I were happy until we learned of our differences." She looked at him. "I don't mean to blame him entirely. We just didn't seem to fit. He was self-obsessed even neglected us at times. I loved him zealously. Almost drowned in that love."

Dro pulled her onto his shoulder. "It'll never be that way with me, darling."

Out of the lulled moment, she said, "I don't know what would have become of us had it not ended as it did. Anyway, fear of a growing divide between us I think more than drowning in love, I was drowning in rejection. Quent was a long time realizing he was his own person." Allise flicked her hand, indicating the passing of that reality. "Then he enlisted, and I think we were closer to heart-felt caring just before he left."

Dro circled her in his arms. "Allise, you …"

"Please," she begged. "There are limits. After Quent was killed, it took time for this to make sense. Maybe women who revere their husbands above all else sometimes find it detrimental to themselves. My father was revered by my mother." Recalling, she said, "It works for my parents because Papa is kind and reasonable. Mother relies on his opinions. The twist is, he taught me to think and value myself. I will respect you, and I can't thrive without respect for myself." She looked into Dro's face. "Am I making sense?"

They gazed at each other. "Yes, I understand, and you should know I love you."

Suddenly, Allise felt exhausted, but there was one more thing to say. "I'm not questioning your love, darling. I feared losing Quent and never want to fear losing you. Our marriage must be a partnership. I cannot be delegated to a lesser role, one which reduces me to self-doubt. If we understand each other …" She reached her hand to his cheek. "I'm trying to explain what I feel for you is different, Dro. It's not less, just different. Deeper and better because it's based on maturity."

He kissed her forehead. They slid down in bed, and he curled around her back.

Next morning, the lamp light wakened Allise. Dro sat up in bed and motioned her up beside him. "It's like this, honey," he said. "I suspect had Ellen lived and had we been married longer, there would've been an edge to our togetherness. Most of the time I was content, and supposed she was happy, too. Who knows what the years would've brought? Ours weren't always rosy, and I would guess most marriages are like that."

He explained he had years to think about another marriage. "Hindsight and my feelings for you helped me understand the shallowness of some commitments. Anyway, those phases of our lives are behind us. They taught both of us lessons. Now we can move on with our time together."

Starting to say more, he stopped and held up a finger. "I want to share every thought with you, *except* those reserved to myself. I want to share every moment with you, *except*," he raised the finger again, "those reserved for myself. Everyone has a right to private thoughts and time alone. Otherwise, I will share my soul, my hurts and weaknesses without reservation, because I *want* to share with you."

After a long search for peace of mind, Allise felt secure. She kissed his cheek.

# CHAPTER 17

▼

Fear of war became a reality when American troops were sent to Korea. Maizee and Allise discussed what it would mean for their sons. Peter completed his second year at university, worked the summer in Joe's market and wasn't apt to be drafted. Nate graduated and worked at Willmott's Garage, but as the Asian war heated up, he kept Maizee and Allise upset with talk of enlisting.

In her kitchenette, his mother fretted aloud about him going off to fight. The heat was almost unbearable, but she kept Nate's dinner warming in the oven. The clock showed 8:00 PM when he stepped in the door. As he ate, she poured a glass of iced tea and sat down across from him. "Nate, I don't want you going off to the army. Go off over yonder, get y'self killed. Like Miz Allie says, war ain't gonna make anything right. We want you t' go to college. Thatch saying you crazy t' join up."

"Momma, anybody who wants to join the army is crazy, but you know as well as I do, I don't have any future in Deer Point." Nate pounded the table. "I ain't gonna be no grease monkey all my life. I just ain't." She recalled what Dalt said about hauling coal.

Her son's dejected look left her heavyhearted. "Seems I cain't say nothing about the way things are. Get you all stirred up and cause some white man's bullet t' find ya." She felt helpless. "What about college? Miz Allie—"

"Momma, I don't want t' hear any more about Miz Allie and Mista Dro paying my way. If I don't get drafted first, I'm gonna enlist. May learn something besides how to change oil and grease cars. I just wanna make a little money for you before I go."

He sighed, and Maizee patted his arm. "Get a bath, go t' bed, son. I'll be up in awhile." Alone, she wondered if things would ever be different for Nate. There was a time when she would have been content to run through plowed furrows with him. "Them days be gone," she mumbled. "He's grown now. Ain't free, but they can send 'im off t' the army." She cleaned up the kitchen, thinking of how little good it did to sit and brood. Finished with her tasks, she trudged up the narrow stairs.

Time approached for Peter to return to the university. Dro and Allise sat on the screened porch with him and his friend, James. "Little happens in Deer Point in the summertime," Peter said. They talked about high school graduates who left Deer Point to find jobs in a city. "I'll be glad to go back to school in a few days. Jill and I go to the movies, and if we didn't play 'chicken' with some of the guys, there wouldn't be any excitement at all. Mother thinks I'm going to be killed in one of our wild car races, James." He glanced at Allise.

James said he was ready to go back to college in Conway.

Looking out, they saw Nate, home from the garage, about to step inside the kitchenette. Peter yelled, "Hey, there's our wanna-be soldier boy."

Nate stood on the stoop, holding the door open. "Hi, Pete. James."

Peter got up and ambled across the porch. "It's *Mister* Pete and *Mister* James, *boy*."

Nate let the door fall shut and stepped off the stoop to meet the boys headed his way. "When did it become mister and boy, Pete? I ain't wanting no fight, man. I'm tired."

Maizee ran past them and met Mista Dro and Miz Allie running out.

The brothers stood eyeball to eyeball. "I don't like it anymore than you do that we have the same daddy," Nate said. "Even less when you're 'mister' and I'm 'boy.'"

Peter drew back his fist, but Nate caught his arm, pinning it behind him. He was ready to throw him to the ground when Dro pulled his stepson away and shoved him toward the porch. "Go inside, Peter. James, go on home and be sure to get the story straight when you tell what happened. This sort of thing isn't allowed here."

Nate and Maizee turned back to the apartment. James walked toward the street, and Peter shuffled into the house with his mother and Dro following close behind him.

Later, Allise heard Dro knock on Peter's door. When he returned downstairs, he told her about their talk. "I told him I had never said it before, but I loved him like my own son. I wanted him to hear it from me so he would know it was true. We talked about other things. Finally, I told him I didn't understand why he went out of his way to make you miserable. I said you loved him in spite of it."

Dro said he thought Peter knew she loved him. "Like a lot of folks, when he suffers, he wants others to suffer with him. He'll get over it, Allise."

She wanted to think her son would change. Less worry might take her persistent aches away.

Despite the discomfort she felt, Allise began the school term. One morning, she and Cleesy walked into the building just ahead of the opening bell. At mid-morning, classes were about to change when Allise sank onto the chair behind her desk. Propping on elbows, she clasped her head and asked the pupils to give her a few moments.

Students mumbled among themselves when she didn't move. One girl came forward and asked if they could do anything. "We're worried, Mrs. McClure." Allise said it was a sore throat and sent the student to the office to get someone to drive her home. They shouted get-well wishes after the moving car as it pulled away.

The young driver helped Maizee get her upstairs, then he walked back to school. She returned to the bedroom and felt Miz Allie's forehead. "You're feverish."

"I went dizzy and faint all of a sudden, Maizee. My head feels like a bowling ball." She supported it in her hands. "I've had a sore throat for several days."

Maizee helped her in bed and ran downstairs to dial the doctor. She returned, saying she wished Doctor Walls was alive. "I don't know bout the new doctor. We ain't ever had t' use 'im." She told Miz Allie the nurse listened as she repeated her symptoms. "She went t' tell the doctor and when she came back, she said he would be here soon."

She sat on the bed holding Allise's hand. "Can I call Mista Dro's office so's he'll be here when the doctor comes? Oughta call the school, too, and leave a message for Cleesy. She hafta walk home."

Allise nodded. A throbbing headache dulled her senses and left her languid. Within minutes, Dro rushed in ahead of the doctor. He and Maizee waited while he examined her. "Have you been exposed to illness, bitten by—"

"Doctah, not long ago, some of Daddy's kin from Louisiana brought a little girl t' the farm. Miz Allie was at Mista Sam's when Daddy come up there with that child. She had a bad runny nose," Maizee said. "Remember, Miz Allie? You told me."

"It's possible she was exposed to something." Stowing the stethoscope in his bag, Doctor Chance wrote prescriptions and said he would consult with the Bensburg Hospital, and she should be prepared to go there in the morning. "Meantime, she needs round-the-clock attendance. Keep all children away."

Dro's face went ashen. Maizee said they would take turns tending her. "I'll see him to the door," she said, following the doctor out.

When Maizee returned, she and Dro talked, apparently thinking Allise was asleep. They debated calling Peter. "Miz Allie be upset if we call him less she say so." She added, "Course, if the doctor say …"

Allise fought drowsiness to listen. "She is seriously ill, Maizee, and I can't imagine what's wrong. Never been sick a day since I've known her. Just when we … Why?" Dro said the doctor was evasive.

"I don't know, Mista Dro. Things jes happen. She ain't been sick but done had a heap a sadness. Awways thinking bout others and wouldn't like that worried look on your face. Wanna see a smile when she's better. You go back to the bank now. I'll care for her."

He told Maizee to phone if any change occurred.

Maizee pulled the rocker near the bed. Humming softly, suddenly she whispered, "Thank ya, Jesus. She gonna be awright." That was Allise's last conscious moment.

Next morning, the doctor had come and gone when Maizee came into the room and said she had seen Cleesy off to school.

Dro helped Allise get dressed. "The doctor thinks Allise has bulbar poliomyelitis, Maizee. He says it affects the lungs, and if bad enough requires an iron lung to assist breathing. All her symptoms indicate that. He said Louisiana had outbreaks of it, and she could have been exposed by that child."

"Mista Dro, Miz Allie's gonna be all right." Allise needed Maizee to be reassuring.

Downstairs, she was put in the waiting ambulance, knowing that Dro would be following it in the car.

In the long months Allise lay encapsulated in the iron lung, Dro visited her often. On one visit, he said so far she was the only person in Deer Point to fall victim to polio. "All the talk is about 'that awful iron lung' and the hometown boys being shipped to Korea." Most times, Cleesy came with him. She paced up and down the corridors or leaned in the doorway, sighing until time to leave. Dro had invited Maizee to visit, but she had told him the hospital wouldn't allow her in. "I asked the staff," he said, "and sure enough, I was told coloreds couldn't visit white patients."

Peter skipped classes and drove to Bensburg once a month. When time for him to leave, his mother whispered, "I love you." He appeared on the verge of wanting to make some physical response, but that being impossible, he waved goodbye.

During one visit, Cleesy wasn't with Dro. Allise sensed he wasn't sharing things with her. Asking about her daughter, she insisted he tell everything. He said Maizee had mentioned a problem with Cleesy. "She called Maizee a bitch, saying she wasn't her mother. Don't you worry, honey, I can corral our fif-teen-year-old." When she asked about Nate, Dro was evasive.

She had not read a newspaper or a book in months. *I've been seven months in this cylinder-like cage, dark, unknowing period.* Allise tried to visualize a future for Peter, Cleesy and Nate. *What will they become?* Thoughts of Dro brought her the most happiness. He brought well-wishes from her students. Smiling, she wondered how much longer she would be held captive to so much thinking.

She wearied of thinking one morning when the doctor came to the ward and said she was well enough to leave the lung. "But, you must remain for observation and therapy."

Months later, Dro came to the hospital to take her home. He rolled her wheel-chair into the living room where the family waited to welcome her. *Cleesy, Sam and Maydale, Maizee,* "Where is Peter?"she asked.

"He's taking exams," Dro said. "I told him to finish them and call tonight."

"Of course," she said, as Cleesy stroked her hair. "What is the date?"

"It's May twenty-third, Mother."

She patted Cleesy's hand and asked, "Where is Nate?" No one answered, but she watched Maizee walk to the foyer and motion, then noticed Dro crossing his lips with a finger as if to warn the others to stay quiet.

"We have a surprise, dear," he said.

Allise took in the familiar faces and surroundings when suddenly she saw Nate come through the doorway. "Nate!" Feeble arms reached out. "Dear God, I'm so happy to see everyone."

He knelt beside her wheelchair. "He got home from Korea a week ago, Miz Allie," Maizee said.

Through a stream of tears, she scanned his face. "Oh God, you're safe. Why didn't you tell me?" She looked accusingly at Dro. Before he could answer, Allise said, "I'm sorry, darling. He's safe and I'm glad you didn't." Nate was no longer the nineteen-year-old she remembered, and she thought he looked more like Quent than ever. He stood and assumed a pose she knew well, arm over his chest, finger crossing his lips. Holding Cleesy's hand, she reached for Maizee's. "We must choose a college for Nate."

Everyone laughed. "Things are back to normal, She's already planning," Dro said.

Several days later, before leaving for the market, Maizee did the morning therapy on Allise's atrophied muscles, helped her with the leg braces, brought a book and pushed her wheelchair near the window.

Just then Nate walked into the living room. She put the book aside and pointed to the wing chair. "Sit here with me, Nate. Your mother let me read some of your letters from Korea, but you didn't write anything about your war experiences."

"No. I didn't want Momma t' worry."

Remembering how long it took for Sam to put his life back together, Allise wondered how Nate would fare. "You were halfway around the world. What did you learn about that country so different from ours?"

"It's a beautiful country, Miz Allie, but the war was brutal. After one battle, wounded men lay all over, some dying, some already dead, their faces and limbs badly burned or blown away." He said their moans and cries haunted him. Stretchers of wounded soldiers lined the ground waiting to be medivac-ed on helicopters to MASH units for treatment. "Body bags were put on planes going to the States. Sometimes we joked about being in the next plane load," he added.

Alone with Allise, Nate poured out battle stories. He said his last engagement was April eighteenth, little more than a month before coming home. "My company was on Pork Chop Hill, an outpost just below Old Baldy, which had changed hands many times." The Chinese began pelting it with artillery in the fall of 1952, he said. "It fell to the Chinese, then the allies won it back, then the Chinese again, on and on."

Allise listened, watching his movements. *How would the experiences mold him?*

"That evening," Nate continued, "the lieutenant radioed he heard singing. The Chinese were moving into tunnels to be ready to attack. They had a real advantage. Watched our position from a ridge not more than six hundred yards up, and they always attacked at night. We were about to engage in one more bloody battle for Old Baldy."

She reached over and patted his hand. "Were you afraid, Nate?"

"Yes'm. Everyone was." A distant look clouded his eyes. "It was quiet eery like. About ten-thirty, a yellow tide poured out of the tunnels. They rushed the patrol and our listening posts. A few of our men straggled back."

Leaning toward him, Allise exclaimed, "Oh, my! So many dead and wounded."

Nate stood and walked to the window. A finger crossed his lips, when he glanced back. "A few of us walked away. A signed armistice and here I am. Not a scratch."

Allise tried to make sense of the incredible things she had heard and wondered if the horror of war would affect his future. *Will he be as unsettled as Sam was?*

Days later, Nate came into the room where Allise read in her wheelchair and Maizee looked at a magazine. From the edge of the couch, he bent forward and said, "I start work on Monday."

"Where did you find work, son?" his mother asked.

"I'll be patching inner tubes, repairing flats and changing tires. A general flunky down at Swen's Service Station. When's Pete gonna be home, Miz Allie?"

"He sold his car. Dro will pick him up at the Greyhound station tomorrow night. Do you want to ride down with him?"

"No. No, I'll see 'im later." His look indicated he didn't anticipate much of a welcoming home from Peter. He stood and walked out. Allise sighed and asked Maizee to bring the college information for her to review.

"After you look at these, we'll do some therapy, Miz Allie." Maizee laid the brochures and applications on her lap.

Allise scanned them and culled out Washington's Howard University and Atlanta's Morehouse College. Nate will not be a life-long service station flunky, she thought.

He had worked only a couple of months when Maizee came with the mail, and Allise asked if a letter of acceptance had come from one of the colleges. Suddenly, they heard the porch door bang, and Nate walked in. Sweat poured down his face onto the t-shirt already soiled from handling tires.

He paced back and forth, exhaling through pursed lips. Stopping, he threw up his hands and collapsed on the leather chair. Bending forward, he held his head. "I just quit. Cain't take any more."

His mother placed a hand on his shoulder. "Nate, what happened?"

"Well, Momma, I just heard it one time too many. 'Take it around back. That nigger boy will fix it for ya.' Today, a white kid with a bicycle tube was sent to me for a patch. I didn't mind making the patch, but that kid called me 'boy.' I'm a man, Momma. Mista Swen and everyone else has been calling me nigger or boy. 'Call that boy t' do it.' 'Get that nigger to come here and unload these tires,' they say. Makes me feel lower than an animal."

Maizee patted his back, but trying to soothe him was futile. "You know what? I'm the only person at that station who served in Korea. Calling me boy! And nigger! Just cain't take it. You know what? I slept beside 'em and ate at the same mess table with white soldiers. I went places with 'em. We fought side-by-side. I thought it would be different when I got home. It ain't. Just like it always was." He shook his head.

Maizee wiped her eyes on her apron. "I'd be angry, too." Allise spoke into the awkward silence. "Nate, hate eats at a person. Consumes you, then you're no different from those who hate you." She paused. "People are on different levels of understanding. Some get past hating. Once we realize life is a process of reaching, a step at a time—"

"I don't know, Miz Allie"

"If there is one thing I've learned, Nate, it is that progress happens. It has its own momentum; nothing can stop it. Look at history. Civilization moves even though at a snail's pace and through many obstacles. So much can be done and *is* done, to slow it down. That's what hatemongers do. They slow the progress of civilization."

Nate slumped back on the chair. "I just expected things to be different. Oh, I had doubts. Before my troop ship landed at San Francisco, black guys were segregated in one bunk area. Officers looked the other way when whites mouthed off to us."

"Try to keep hate from growing in you, Nate." Allise didn't tell him, but she wondered if humanity had really progressed all that far from the Stone Age.

"Miz Allie, I'm madder about this race thing than I was at the enemy in Korea. I wasn't angry at those people. Was just trying to stay alive and help keep my buddies safe." He paused as though thinking for a minute. "I'm mad as hell about the treatment black people get in this country. When my own half-brother doesn't accept me because of my skin—"

"Nate, maybe that isn't … Maybe Peter can't accept what his father did."

"I don't care what his reason is. I'm gonna fight it every way I can."

Allise felt the weight of their dilemma. One white, one black tainted with white.

That evening, Dro finished Allise's therapy session, and she walked to the couch using crutches. Peter sat across the room. "The doctor says your mother is doing well and can possibly stop wearing the braces in a few months."

"Nate left the service station job today," Allise said.

Peter shrugged, stood and headed for the door. "Who cares? I have a date with Jill."

"Pe–," she called behind him. Turning to Dro, she asked, "Why can't I reach him? He's so close-minded. Do I expect too much?"

Dro turned on the television and returned to sit beside her. "Now, honey, he has many influences. You said yourself, they have to find their own way."

"I don't like feeling disappointed in him. I want him and Cleesy to be good citizens. Peter's aspirations are no greater than being a market manager. He will probably marry Jill." She noticed Dro wasn't listening. On the end table was a stack of books, *The Catcher in the Rye*, *The Rose Tatoo* and *Requiem for a Nun*. Allise picked one, then placing it back on the table, she asked, "Dro, did Cleesy and her friend leave for the movie? They wanted to see *The African Queen*." He said they had, and she mentioned the used car he had helped Peter select. "I've been thinking, if Nate is accepted at one of the colleges, he could drive the Buick, and Maizee, Cleesy and I can tag along. Maizee could drive us back home."

"Allise, do you think you're up to riding that far? It's a two-day trip to either place. I don't know, hon—"

"Oh, I'm up to it. What's the difference, sitting here or in the car? You wouldn't be upset about us being away, would you? Dro, I'm ready to start living. Ready to teach again."

"Let's take things a day at a time. When Nate's accepted, we'll go from there." He turned back to *Amos and Andy* on the black-and-white TV screen.

Two days before Peter was to leave for the university, Nate received acceptance from Morehouse College. In a state of excitement, he said he was going to share the news with Rita, a friend from high school.

# CHAPTER 18

▼

Bathed and dressed, Nate stepped out into the still, hot evening. Leaving the back alley, he turned up the street and saw four figures looming in the dusk. Closing on them, he recognized Peter, James, and two other men. He knew one of the two as the man who had objected to him using the front door at King's Drugstore. "Hey, y'all," he called, and feeling uneasy, he walked on down the street.

"Hey, boy!" Peter yelled. "Come back here!" Nate stopped and looked back at the four who walked toward him. "Let me introduce us, boy," his brother said. "Meet the Pure Pride. There's more of us." He flourished a hand at the others. "Like a pack of lions, we're going to send you smart aleck niggers back where you belong."

Nate saw clinched fists and braced himself. Peter advanced toward him, and a black fist to the head reeled him backward. "Go inside, Pete. Tell Miz Allie why my signature's on your face." Nate didn't stand a chance. Pounded and kicked, he lay in the street, bloody and bruised. Walking the short distance back to their car, they leaned out the windows laughing as Peter drove perilously close to where he lay.

Dragging himself to the edge of the street, Nate knew if Mista Dro saw him, he would call the sheriff. His Momma would have a fit, but if he went to Rita's place, he could clean up. *Momma will be in bed when I get home.* Struggling, he got to his feet and walked the eight blocks into Colored Town.

Next morning, his mother fumed. "Yep, you gonna tell Miz Allie and Mista Dro. Go on over there. I'm going with ya, and if you don't tell 'em, I am."

Allise and Dro ate breakfast when they walked in. She gasped, and Dro asked, "What happened, Nate?"

"I ran into the Pure Pride last night."

"The what—"

"Go ahead. Tell 'um, Nate," his mother prodded.

He told of being beaten by four men. "One said they're going t' send niggers back to where they belong."

"Who were they?" Dro asked.

Maizee paid her son a commanding look. "Tell 'um, Nate."

"One was Pete, Mista Dro."

"Oh, heavens! Get him down here," Allise shouted, and Dro went upstairs.

"James was with 'em," Nate muttered. "Other two work in a garage down town. One of the mechanics is that man who told you not to bring me in the front door of the drugstore a long time ago, Miz Allie. This isn't gonna keep me from going to Atlanta."

Bare chested and barefoot, Peter walked into the kitchen rubbing his eyes. Dro followed, and Allise ordered Peter to sit down.

Looking sullen, he went to the sink, ran a glass of water and stood drinking it.

"Peter, what happened last night?" Dro asked.

"You mean he hasn't told you already?" Peter nodded at Nate.

"He did. Now let's hear what you have to say."

"Whatever he said, that's what we did." Peter glared at Nate.

"Who's we?" Dro insisted.

"The Pure Pride. We're going to rid this town of niggers. They belong over

there in Colored Town."

Nate bristled. "It'll take the whole damn Pride t' be rid of us niggers."

Standing behind Allise, Maizee laid a hand on her shoulder. Both cried with out a sound. "I'll tell you what we're going t' do, Peter." Dro's voice held authority. "Nate, you and your mother get your clothes ready for the trip to Atlanta. Maizee, we will help Allise later. This situation is going to be handled, and Peter is going to help me do that." To Peter, he said, "Get dressed, son."

✶ ✶ ✶ ✶

Peter sat in the car beside Dro. "I'm glad it's you at the wheel and not Mother."

Dro glanced at him. "Son, I don't want you to think of this as punishment, but we're going to Sheriff Banes. You're going to tell him who's in this Pure Pride, then you're getting out of it before it's too late. Do you know anything about the Klan?"

"I know they wore hoods and white sheets and scared niggers."

"The Ku Klux Klan did more than scare. Not so much here, but other places. It tortured and murdered Negroes. White men murdering blacks! That's not something to take pride in. Peter, you can't associate with anything like the Pure Pride and be my son."

"It's just that James is about the only friend I have." Peter struggled to conceal his emotions from Dro. He wanted to tell his stepfather how miserable he was. How he hated everyone. He wanted to talk with someone. Tell how he felt.

"I don't think it's true that James is your only friend, Peter. But if he is, you need to cultivate new friends. James may be a good kid, but those two older men they'll get you and him in trouble. You need to talk some sense to James. Nate's a good kid, too, Peter."

"Why do things have to be … Why did Daddy have to mess up, Dro?" He sniffled.

"I don't know the answer to that, son, but you've got to forgive your daddy. You do that, and you'll be surprised how light your burden is." In the courthouse parking lot, Dro turned to him. "Are you ready to go in there and name names?"

Hesitantly, he said he was. Those guys will be on me like a June bug, he thought.

"Thata boy." Dro ruffled his hair. "When we finish here, we're going down to the garage. Have a talk with those two. Did you notice those men couldn't whip Nate without you and James? It looks to me like they were setting you up. They're cowards, but when we tell them the sheriff knows their names, they'll sneak back in their holes like cowards."

"What's the sheriff going to do?" Peter knew he sympathized with Pure Pride.

"I haven't lived here all my life for nothing, Peter. I know things. Leave the sheriff to me."

Leaving an humbled looking sheriff, they drove to the garage. Dro greeted the men by name. One bent over an engine beneath a raised hood. The other rolled from underneath a car. Both were greasy and gripped tools. Seeing Peter, they looked at each other and walked into the light where he and Dro stood. "George, you and Mack need to see that Peter's name is removed from the Pure Pride membership roll. He's no longer a member, and by the way, the sheriff knows your names—"

"Ha!" George laughed and looked at Mack. "He's a member hisself."

Peter held onto his cool demeanor as Dro continued. "I sorta thought he might be, but thanks for tattling. I just might have to report the whole damn bunch of you to the attorney general. You mess around with this boy," he pointed to Peter, "or anyone around my house, and your asses will go to prison."

The two men didn't look at their adversary.

Returning to the car, Peter said, "I don't know, Dro. They're pretty mean dudes."

"They want you to think that. Let's go home, son, get you ready to go to school."

Not knowing what to believe, Peter was glad he had Dro.

＊　　＊　　＊　　＊

The morning after the brawl, Allise took the front seat with Nate. Driving along, he said his facial wounds would heal and while his body was sore, he didn't suffer. Traveling at a good speed, they met little traffic in the southeast Arkansas bayou country. By noon, the Mississippi River was behind them. Allise thought about Quent's Uncle John. *He ought to meet Cleesy, but I wouldn't dare stop with Maizee and Nate in the car.*

Soon, they saw patches of parasitic kudzu attached to trees and bushes along the road. The car's air conditioner was hard to speak over, but all had agreed silence was better than hot air blowing through open windows. They had made only two stops. One for Allise and Cleesy to use a service station restroom, another for Nate and Maizee to use the woods.

Arriving in a small eastern Mississippi town, they stopped to fill the gas tank. The attendant checked the oil and when he cleaned the windshield, Allise asked if there was a place nearby to get carryout food.

The man leaned down, grinning into the car. "Y' might git something at Oscar's on down the road there." He nodded in the direction.

Driving away from the station, Nate glanced back at his mother. Parking well back from the eatery, even though they were the only customers around Oscar's, he told his mother to hunker down.

Cleesy went inside to give their orders and wait for food to go. She paid the tab and returned to the car. "He's real cute," she said of the young man behind the counter, "but he stared out at the car the whole time. Why did you park way over here, Nate?" He didn't answer, and she chomped on a French fry, seemingly oblivious to dangers the others sensed. As soon as they had eaten, Nate sped away across the Alabama state line.

Allise consulted the map. "Let's stay the night some place near here."

"Miz Allie, there isn't gonna be no place for Momma and me t' sleep. We'll find you a place, and we'll sleep in the car."

"Are you sure there's no place, Nate? Tuscaloosa looks—"

"I'm sure. Don't fret about us. That's just the way it is."

Allise heard the ring of familiar words.

Nate looked rumpled the next morning as they traveled on. Vistas stretching before them weren't much different from the day before. Staring straight ahead through the rural villages, he felt wound as tight as a top. Birmingham's giant steel mills belched steam and black smoke. They held no fascination for him. *Just let us get to Atlanta without being stopped,* he thought, fearing something was bound to happen.

An hour or so later, a siren sounded behind them. A single dome atop the Alabama patrol car flashed red, signaling Nate to pull over. He stopped on the side of the highway, cut the engine and rolled down the window. "I wasn't speeding. What's he …"

Allise touched his arm. "Let me do the talking."

The man in a gray-green uniform and knee-high boots sauntered up to the open window. A hand rested on his sidearm. Leaning down, he peered at the front and back passengers from beneath a World War I campaign-style hat. "Where y' headed?"

Nate's grip tightened on the wheel, and Allise smiled. "Atlanta. Nate, here, is going to Morehouse College."

"Huh!" he snorted. "Going t' school are ya, boy?"

Nate felt the tic in his jaw. *If I look at 'im, I'll want t' kill 'im,* he thought.

"Officer, this is my daughter and housekeeper." Allise pointed. "Nate's her son. We're from Arkansas and want to make Atlanta before dark. Do you think we can?"

The trooper removed his hand from the holster. "I'll tell you right now, Ma'am, you're traveling dangerous cause niggers and white folks ain't suppose t' be riding on the same seat. If I's you, I'd put that white girl up here, and you drive on to Atlanta. Better for them t' set back there. Yep, y' oughta make there before dark."

"I had polio," Allise said, "and can't drive. If you will help, I'll move to the back."

The patrolman stared across Nate at her. Then on the passenger side, he opened the door, took her arm and helped seat her beside Cleesy. Tipping his hat, he said, "Ma'am."

"Mista Po-leeceman, will it be awright if Momma and me use the woods while we stopped heah?" Sounding the expected intimidation, Nate choked back anger and wondered why he had risked saying anything.

Cleesy grumbled, "When I get my license, we won't have this problem."

With everyone back in the car, they stopped a few miles down the road to fill the gas tank. A young attendant washed the windshield when Cleesy returned from the restroom. He eyed her, paying no attention to the other passengers. With him preoccupied, Maizee helped Allise to the restroom and stood outside waiting for her.

Back on the road and some time later, they entered Atlanta. Nate crept along the streets with directions from Miz Allie, who consulted the Morehouse letter. All at once they were on the campus. He and Maizee unloaded their bags at the hall where they were to stay and asked about a nearby hotel. Once Maizee was settled, Nate drove Miz Allie and Cleesy there.

✳   ✳   ✳   ✳

Next day, Maizee pushed Allise's wheelchair behind Nate and the student assisting him. Cleesy dragged along with one complaint or another. By early evening, Nate was properly oriented and ready for school. Allise was satisfied but exhausted. She was rested the following morning when Maizee drove out of Atlanta with her and Cleesy in the back seat.

They reached a roadside motel in Mississippi before nightfall. Allise told her friend to stop the car beyond the canopy and lie across the seat while Cleesy helped her register in the lobby.

When they returned, Maisee pulled in front of their room. Before they could leave the car, the attendant appeared at the window. "Thought you was gonna sneak her in, did ya? Well, I saw her when you drove in. I'll call the cops. She cain't sleep here."

"I've had polio, and Maizee is my nurse." Allise smiled with as much charm as she could bring to bear.

The woman looked befuddled. "I'll go ask my husband." In minutes, she returned. "He's bringing a roll-away. She cain't take a bath or use the towels," she said, glaring at Maizee. The man rolled in a bed without linens of any sort.

Behind the locked door, Maizee said, "Miz Allie, you sho think fast." She laughed. "I may be the first black to sleep in a motel."

Allise had Cleesy remove the top sheet from the double bed and take an extra cover from a drawer. "We almost pulled it off. In the morning, we will wake early, replace the sheet so it will look as if only white women slept under it, and return the blanket to the drawer. Thank goodness, we will be home tomorrow."

The remainder of the trip passed without incident, and they arrived back in Deer Point before dinner time. While Maizee made sandwiches and fruit, Dro sat in the kitchen, listening to Allise relate the highlights of their travel. "You can't imagine how glad I am to have you back home," he said.

"I'm glad to be here, darling. Did Peter get off to the university without any delays?" Dro said he did, and after dinner Allise got on the phone to him, "We're back from Atlanta. Did you get all the classes you wanted? Good. I'm proud of you, son. You can be successful at anything you choose to do. You know you don't have to manage the market. Yes, 'that black boy' made out well at Morehouse." After telling him about the trip, she hung up the receiver with a long sigh.

In the living room with Dro, Allise said that Peter's "black boy" comment surprised her. "I thought he was remorseful after the Pure Pride episode. I think I know how people ought to relate to each other, but I didn't convey it right in my own family." She was about to cry.

Dro pulled her into his arms. "Now, honey, I'll have another talk with him when he comes home."

"You're good with him, Dro. I love you." She felt fortunate to have a good man at her side. Without admitting the trip had left her exhausted, she said, "I'm going up to bed. Guess I better get plenty of rest like the doctor advised so I can resume teaching."

In a few days school opened, and Allise walked into the classroom on crutches. Whistles and cheers greeted her. Beaming, she lost no time before announcing semester requirements. Students would read Ernest Hemingway, John Steinbeck, Edna Ferber, or some other well-known American author of their choosing.

"She's back," the students said, poking each other and laughing.

"When you're finished reading, you will write an essay, comparing the writer's style with another author of your choosing, as long as it's one you studied last year. Now, the most recent books by the assigned authors are *The Old Man and the Sea*, *East of Eden* and *Giant*. Choice of an author is yours, but as you read, pay close attention to the writing style. Take the full semester for this. The two-page, double-spaced essay will be part of your mid-term exam. I expect no less than an interesting and thoughtful paper."

Leaving the classroom, her students grumbled about having to write essays. She waved them out. "Ah, but someday you will appreciate your hard-driving teacher."

Sinking onto her chair, she questioned if she was up to preparing them. She needed to catch up to all that had happened while she was in the hospital and recuperating.

The school semester passed quickly into holiday time, and Peter arrived home for the two-week break. True to his word, Dro had the promised talk with him. Now, in their bedroom, he told Allise how it had gone.

"I asked him about the Pure Pride. He said they were cowards and he hadn't seen or heard of them since we went to the sheriff. I told him he seemed hell-bent on keeping you upset, and he went into his spiel about how you had hurt him and Cleesy. I said no one knew that better than you." Allise snuggled close to him, and Dro continued, saying they talked about the terrible position, through no fault of their own, they had to endure. How she, his mother, lived in dread that he and Cleesy would learn the truth about their father.

"I told him life throws us curves. We can catch them, deal with them and move on while waiting for the next one, because sure as we lived, there would be more, or we can let the curves ruin our lives. It's our choice."

Dro pulled back, looking down at Allise. "Honey, I doubt anyone can change Peter's mind about Negroes. Heaven knows, you have tried since the kids were old enough to have an attitude." He said he told Peter to think about his reasons for punishing her. "That you loved him and Cleesy and just wanted them to be good citizens. If you didn't, you wouldn't be so hard on them."

He said Peter's eyes misted. "He said he would scream at his daddy if he could. Allise, I told him he should have a heart-felt talk with you."

She had listened without interrupting him. Now she said, "I should have married you years before I did, darling."

At dinner the next evening, Allise searched for interest in Peter's face as Maizee told about Nate taking a janitor's job. "He needs the money. Won't be home for Christmas or anytime soon." She sighed. "He said he done joined some 'political action groups.' Gonna take summer classes, too."

"His letters are full of enthusiasm," Allise said. "He's astonished at the information and complex ideas being presented to him. Things he never dreamed of."

"Has Nate mentioned a girlfriend, Maizee?" Dro asked.

"He writes about doing things with Leila. You know Nate don't say much about girls." She giggled.

After Peter left the table, Allise said she feared her son and Jill were going to marry. She laid her napkin beside her plate. "They should wait until Jill completes the university."

"There you go, Mother." Cleesy stood and slammed her napkin down on the table. "Always interfering." She stomped out of the room.

"You can't stop them from marrying because Peter will reach legal age soon," Dro said.

She didn't respond.

Later, waiting for Dro to get in bed, she said, "Cleesy will be sixteen in June, and we're losing control of her."

Dro switched off the light. "We'll talk with her. Let's get some sleep now."

"I'm scared, Dro. How did a sweet child become precocious in such a short time? We don't know where she went when she left the table, or with whom." Allise said they should chaperon at the Oak Street Teen House, where high school kids danced to jukebox tunes every Friday and Saturday night. "Do you think we should snoop into Cleesy's behavior?"

"No. If we do, and she finds out … believe me, she will, and we will never be trusted again. Let's talk with her. See how that works."

"For someone who doesn't have much experience, darling, you are so wise about children." Allise put her arm across his chest.

"I can be more objective than you can. Now, can we go to sleep, dear?"

Allise couldn't sleep. It was after midnight, and Cleesy still wasn't home. At one o'clock, a car pulled into the driveway. She woke Dro, and they waited downstairs.

The door opened, and Allise started for it, but he caught her arm. "Cleesy, you're way late, and we've been worried," he said. "Go on up to bed, but in the morning before I leave for the office, you *will be* down here. The three of us are going to talk about this. If you don't come down—"

"Yeah, what are you going to do, Dro? Beat me?"

"No. But I will come up to your room and get you."

"Huh!" Cleesy sounded daring, and she stomped up the stairs.

Next morning, when he should have been leaving for work, Dro knocked on Cleesy's door. Sitting at the table, Allise heard him call, "Maizee, come here, please." From the top of the stairs came, "Go in, see if she's decent."

Maizee called out, "She still in her pajamas, Mista Dro."

Listening to the back and forth, Allise wondered what she would do without them.

"Get her robed, then I'm coming in." In minutes, Allise heard them tromping down the stairs.

Looking like a bad night's tumble, hair in disarray and disposition sullen, Cleesy flopped down at the breakfast table. Dro took his seat. "Cleesy, we're not going to quiz you about last night"

"Well, thank God for that!"

Dro sat quietly as though giving her time to consider her smartness, then, "You're coming into young lady-hood, Cleesy. We're proud of you, but last night, we worried about an accident. If you were a parent, would you be worried about a child who came home late?" He looked to be waiting for his words to sink in before going on. "We want you to enjoy this time in your life but also to respect your own well-being and us. That's all I have to say, but from here on, you will be home at the prescribed time you and your mother agree upon. I have to leave now, so work it out."

He stood and kissed Cleesy on the forehead. "You're a good girl." Kissing Allise, he called from the door, "I love you."

Allise and her daughter went round and round before reaching the conditions of Cleesy's dating behavior. She would not see a college sophomore from a nearby school again. "He's much too old for you. Boys nearer your age want to date my pretty daughter." Allise patted her head.

"How can you say that, Mother? Their parents are sick of you."

"Cleesy, I'm the one the town ostracizes. This place could have turned against you and Peter long ago. Instead, they protected you because you are your father's children. You must not imagine something that isn't the case. Boys your age see you going out with this older boy and think they don't have a chance. Stop seeing him and they will ask you out."

Cleesy looked defiant, but said nothing, and her mother dismissed her.

Allise worried about her children, but otherwise, times were good. On the way to Peter's graduation, she and Dro talked about the changes since the world war ended. Americans had helped rebuild Germany and establish a new form of government in Japan, making friends of former enemies. The Korean War had ended, and people had jobs and money to spend. War veterans made families and built new homes. New cars put people on the move. Her father had written that President Eisenhower's road system, planned to span the nation north and south, east and west, may knock out regionalism and bring people together.

Whether it will or not, all kinds of new products are available, she thought. Television was a national mirror. Reflecting the best and worst in society, it brought the world into living rooms. Time passes so quickly, Allise thought.

From the back seat, Cleesy said, "I don't intend to make Arkansas University my destination after I graduate next year. There's nothing exciting about Arkansas. I want to study drama in California."

"One down, one to go," Dro said.

After his graduation, Peter settled in as manager of Joe's Market.

One morning, Allise walked into the store as sure as Nate that the South was on the cusp of change. The Supreme Court had ruled in *Brown v. Board of Education*, that a Kansas school board could not discriminate against black students, because it would violate the Fourteenth Amendment. Dro had said as much as he hated to be a fly in the ointment, he thought there would be trouble. "President Truman integrated the Army, and Senator Thurmond said

'Federal laws and Army bayonets couldn't force Negroes into white homes, white schools and white churches'"

"Yes, but things change." Allise had repeated what Langston Hughes wrote: "'If we can't let go of it'—racism—we're 'like the bird that can't fly because it has a broken wing.'"

Now, at the meat counter, she waited with Charlie Wise, the man who had confronted her at the PTA meeting. The gaunt, ruddy-faced lumberyard worker wore faded overalls with one suspender hanging loose down his back. Squinting, he tipped his straw hat to her. "Morning."

Feeling uncomfortable in his presence, she returned his greeting. He shuffled about as though he were ill-at-ease, too. Then, resuming an ongoing conversation, he said, "I tell you, Pete, my kids ain't gonna sit in school or anywhere else with niggers. I'll take 'em outta school first."

Peter stood behind the counter, his back to them. "I know what you mean, Mr. Wise. It has everyone in an uproar. This mess has to stop."

Allise sighed. "Mr. Wise, at risk of causing yet another upset, what do you think would happen if your children sat in a classroom with Negroes?" She waited, expectantly.

Peter walked to the end of the meat cooler and stood scowling at his mother.

"Uh, uh, I … Why, them nigger boys would be touching my girls. Next thing, be raping 'em, then dating and marrying our white daughters. Have little ninnies running all over the place. Folks are saying cain't nothing good come of this mess." His hesitant stuttering surprised her.

"Do you want meat, Mother? I'll get it, and you stay out of Mr. Wise's business."

Stung to her soles, Allise fought tears as he turned back to packaging meat. "Mr. Wise, do you really think Negro boys would risk their lives by touching white girls? Black men won't look at me when I speak to them." She turned and rushed out of the market.

That night, Allise laid her book aside and snuggled down next to Dro. "I did another stupid thing today. Don't know why I do it; it never makes any difference. Maizee said I shouldn't apologize. She said white folks down here just had to hate Negroes. They are going 'to be down on anybody that stands up for black folk,' she said, and someone has to 'sling arrows at haters.' She said I was the only person that would do it."

Dro pulled her into his arm and asked what she had done. Allise told of meeting Charlie Wise and repeated what was said. "I don't know if I did right by challenging him. He's still just as adamant. Peter's right, I need to tend to my own business."

Dro stroked her hair. "Allise, you have strong feelings and the courage to try to change wrong thinking. Unfortunately, the Charlie Wises have strong feelings, too. You're bound to butt heads. Strong-willed or not, I love ya." He tightened his embrace.

Allise thought she would be safe forever if she could just crawl inside him. Dro switched off the light, and she lay waiting for sleep. Then out of the dark came, "What are we going to do about Peter? I try too hard, don't I? I drove him into the opposite camp."

Dro reached again for the lamp and adjusted his eyes to the light. "Now, honey, you did all you could to influence Peter's character, but everyone helps to mold him. We have to accept him the way he is and love him, no matter what." He said she shouldn't let anything Charlie said stop her from expressing her views. "Allise, you *do* make a difference. Look at me. I might as well tell you, now don't be mad. I already knew about you and Charlie." Dro propped his pillow on the headboard, sat up and opened his arms.

Her mouth dropped open. "How?" One thin strap of her gown slipped from her shoulder, partially exposing her breast. Moving fingers down his bare chest, she kissed it.

Drawing back, she saw he was full of passion.

Dro breathed his fervor and nuzzled her hair. "He came in the bank right after you left the market."

"What did he say? Was he angry at you because I—"

"No." He laughed. "Said, 'Some wife you got there, Dro.'" He pulled her closer. "I sure can agree with that." She looked demure. "Charlie said he groped to answer your question. I'm groping here, Allise," he said, rubbing across her nipple.

"Wait, wait, what else did he say?"

"Said, he could only think of what his daddy and momma told him. That Peter interfered before he could say anything." Dro rested against his pillow. "There's some redeeming grace in the man, Allise. He can be persuaded. Just needs to hear other arguments. I told him that."

She kissed him on the cheek, and Dro pulled her across his body. Struggling down into the bed, both tugged and pulled the gown over her head. They surrendered to each other, and moving apart in the soft lamp light, made sated sighs. "Making love with you is like … it's like giving birth to the universe," Allise whispered.

"I can't know about giving birth, but it's sure as heck like the Big Bang."

They giggled. "S-s-sh. Cleesy will hear" Dro's arms encircled her, and his bare skin next to hers sent ecstatic shivers through her body. Soon, with sleep about to overtake them, he switched off the light

# CHAPTER 19

▼

Allise arranged for the rehearsal dinner to be held at the Braxton Country Club the night before Peter and Jill's wedding. It got off to a bad start. Mrs. Dixon, Jill's mother, introduced her to the attendants then left Allise standing alone. She and the woman were never friends, even when the Dixons lived in Deer Point. Her rudeness left Allise with less than admiration and wondering how her relationship would be with Jill.

The next day in the hotel room, Allise thought about her parents as she dressed for the ceremony. If only they had lived to be with her at Peter's wedding.

It had been a sad year. Her mother died, and after the McClures returned from the funeral, Allise's sister wrote that a part of their Papa died, too. His life ended in May, just after Cleesy's graduation. Back in Pennsylvania, Allise ended the eulogy. "I grieve for our parents; yet, as we release their beautiful souls to the unknown, their legacy of morals and education will remain with us for the rest of our lives."

Returning from the sad occasion less than a month before the planned wedding day, Allise rushed the groom's guest list to Mrs. Dixon. Of the two hundred expected at the event, fifty were from Deer Point, including Sam and Maydale.

Now, dressed in a dove gray, crape gown cascading down her willowy figure, she walked into the suite sitting room where Dro waited. He gaped. "You're stunning! Here let me pin Peter's corsage." He struggled at her shoulder with the bunch of pink rosebuds and baby's breath when Cleesy, one of four bride's maids, entered in peach satin. "Who's that gorgeous girl?" he said.

"You make us feel pretty, darling," Allise beamed.

At the church. the ceremony went off without a hitch, but Dro whispered it was all a bit too pretentious for him. They waited with Sam and Maydale to get underway to the reception. Turning to Sam, he said, "I can't wait for this show to end so I can get out of this penguin suit."

"Well, darling, I think you're handsome in a tux." Allise straightened his bow tie.

Sam laughed and slapped his thigh. "Yeah, Dro, you're the picture of a penguin."

They laughed and piled into the car. Following behind others, they came to an old, two-story, ivy-covered hotel. It had been renovated and reopened to private parties. Dro looked around and whispered to Allise, "Do you think we can afford for Cleesy to get married?"

She gave him a gentle pinch, and now, having stood in the reception line to receive guests, they sat at their assigned table. Allise watched her seventeen-year-old daughter flirt with a group of teenaged boys at the edge of the dance floor. She led them onto the floor where they gyrated to *Rock Around the Clock*. Those who had been dancing to *Three Coins in the Fountain* and *Young at Heart* moved toward their tables.

She was unprepared for Cleesy's erotic behavior. Mildred had complained about Elvis Presley "rolling his hips on the TV and corrupting all the young folk." Peter sauntered over to his parents' table with Jill on his arm. "How you like 'em apples, Mother?" His snide, spurious smile and glance at the dance floor left little doubt about his meaning. He leaned to whisper in her ear, "Don't upbraid Cleesy here and ruin our wedding party."

"No, I wouldn't, Peter." Allise was hurt, but remembering the Willow Fork Honky Tonk, she wondered what her papa would have said to her.

Back in Deer Point several days later, she recorded in the DeWitt Bible: *Peter Weston DeWitt and Jill Dixon, June 9, 1955, Baptist Church, Braxton, Arkansas.*

The wedding was now six months behind them. Peter was settled, but Allise was concerned about Cleesy. She told Dro that she didn't know how to talk to her. "I just want healthy, happy, educated kids who will be citizens worthy of respect."

"All we can do is love them, Allise. Cleesy is a pretty girl, and she knows it. She's just feeling her way into womanhood."

"I know, darling, but we have a wild ride ahead with her." She glanced around at the Christmas decoration boxes cluttering the living room when Maizee brought food on trays. The three of them settled down to watch TV.

Soon, August showed it could be hotter than any other month. Ignoring the heat, Allise offered to help Peter and Jill move into their new tract home. Jill declined her offer, and asked Cleesy to assist them. That night, after a full day of hauling and unpacking, Cleesy continued packing her bags to leave for Los Angeles. Allise, watching her collect clothing, said, "I've arranged for an upperclassman to meet you at the airport, take you to the dorm and around the campus. Look for the person holding a sign with your name on it."

Several mornings later at the Bensburg airport, Allise felt she could cry forever, but they parted in a dry-eyed embrace. She suffered the distance that had grown between her and Cleesy. Her daughter's choice to study drama wasn't what she wished for her, but she said, "Dro and I will do all we can, sweetie, to help you become the most successful actress you can be."

Cleesy promised to call upon arrival, and she kept her word, but it was some time before a letter came. Time crept up to another Christmas recess, and Allise tried to remember if she had missed Peter as much as she missed her daughter.

Maizee had removed the empty plates and returned when Dro rested the newspaper on his lap to listen to Edward R. Murrow's distinguished voice. "This evening Rosa Parks, a black woman in Montgomery, Alabama, was arrested for refusal to give up her seat on a city bus to a white man."

Astonishment flooded their faces. "That woman will be lucky if she gets out of this trouble without harm to herself," Dro said.

Maizee clasped her hands over her mouth and gazed at the TV screen. Allise sat forward and said, "Just wait, changes are coming. Despite obstacles, civilization happens."

The phone rang. It was Nate calling from his dorm. Allise listened to him tell about Negro leaders meeting in Montgomery's Dexter Avenue Baptist Church with Martin Luther King Jr., the minister and a Morehouse alumnus. The leaders, he said, thought Mrs. Parks was the spark needed to fire up coloreds to fight against Jim Crow.

Their conversation ended and back in the living room, she told Dro how he went on and on about the preacher making people want to change the world. "Nate said this King talked about protesting in a non-violent way, like India's Ghandi did." He told Allise an over-capacity crowd showed up at the church, and those who couldn't get inside spread out over three city blocks.

Nate's friend had called from Montgomery and quoted from Doctor King's talk. Nate repeated it to Miz Allie. "I think I remember it correctly," she told Dro. "King said if you protest courageously, but with dignity and Christian love, future historians will say a great people, black people, injected new meaning and dignity into the veins of civilization. Nate went on to say, his friend told him the preacher had thrown out that challenge as their overwhelming responsibility."

Allise found King's words inspiring. She understood why Nate had joined organized black groups with an intention to change things, the issues the two of them had talked about. She stopped relating to Dro and listened to Maizee speaking on the phone with Nate.

"I know you, Nate," his mother said. "You gonna be right in the thick of whatever happens. Don't you go and get y'self killed." Despite her warnings, each phone call from him was full of happenings around Morehouse.

She and Maizee took a goody basket to Jonas, the sole tenant left on the farm. Li'l Joke and Dessie were married, and he lived alone. In the front room, he had decked a small cedar tree in red and white paper chains, foil-wrapped gum balls and store-bought icicles. The three of them sat around the pot-bellied stove and drank cocoa.

Ready to leave, Maizee said, "Daddy, Nate's coming home on an airplane.

Jonas said he would be scared to get on an airplane, but he sure would be glad to see Nate. Allise told him Cleesy was flying in, too.

They left the aged man shaking his head.

After the college students arrived for the holidays, Allise sat in the kitchen listening to Maizee and Nate talk about Sugar Ray Robinson and his middle weight boxing title when Cleesy walked in. She stood listening, then said, "Getting himself beat up for money is probably all he can do." Her comment splashed on their conversation like cold water.

"Maybe so, but he won't have to be beat up many times with the money he makes." Nate slid his chair around to face her. "Cleesy, you want us blacks to be non-persons. Well, it *ain't* gonna be that way much longer." Flicking long, bur-nished-red hair over her shoulder, Cleesy flounced out. Nate turned back to his mother and Miz Allie. "Cleesy isn't interested in the civil rights movement. She talks about students stuffing themselves into a telephone booth. Yak-ing about USC football."

"Jest let that civil rights stuff be, son. You gonna get killed."

"Momma, you making old folk's talk now. It isn't ever gonna 'just be' anymore." Nate stood. "I'm going t' see Grandpa, now."

"Jonas expects you, but will you be back tonight?" Allise mentioned Cleesy's whirlwind round of parties, and said she had reminded her of their annual search for Christmas joy. "Cleesy said, my search for joy was a silly idea. That after all those years I made them go, it was still a silly idea."

That evening, Nate, Allise, Dro, and Maizee sang carols on neighborhood streets. Allise wondered what would be said about Negroes singing carols to white folk, and Dro teased. "We warmed them up tonight. Next year we will reheat them, and a year more, they will expect us because their taste for caroling will have been acquired."

The next morning, Allise and Maydale helped Maizee make Christmas dinner. Peter arrived and explained to his mother that Jill had driven to

Braxton. When he walked into the living room to join Dro and Sam, Maizee said she and Nate would eat in the apartment because Nate and Peter hadn't spoken since the night Nate was beaten.

"You will do no such thing," Allise said, then she followed Peter into the living room. "I want this to be the most beautiful Christmas ever."

Dro looked at Peter. "It will be, dear. The first person to spoil it will be leaving."

"And I will throw them out the door, myself," Sam said.

Peter laughed, and Dro cautioned, "You think I'm not serious. Think again."

Allise invited them to the table, and Dro offered grace. Allise raised her wine glass. "'Let everyone partake of the general joy.'" Glasses clicked, and when all were seated, she said, "Papa always followed Christmas grace with that Dryden quote."

Christmas day passed with tales of past ones, and laughter flowed like the wine.

With the holiday behind her, Allise again faced a roomful of seniors. Glancing up during their written grammar exercise, she noticed a raised hand. It was Charlie Wise's daughter. Trouble, she thought.

"Miz McClure, what's going to happen with those niggers raising Cain in Alabama?" Missy asked. "That preacher King's stirring them up."

Allise took a moment. "Well, Missy, I hadn't intended to have a lesson on race this morning. How many are finished with the assignment?" All hands went up. "Since it was brought up, perhaps we should talk. But let's try to refer to Negroes, not niggers. That word would be contemptible to anyone, even a white person. No one in this room would want to be called such. Neither do blacks." She stood at Missy's desk. "Now, does it frighten you that Negroes might be bolder than they've always acted? If so, why?"

"They're stupid always fighting and cutting up each other. They're dirty and stink! I don't want to sit by them on a bus or anywhere." A rash of agreement was heard.

"S-sh," Allise quieted them. "All right, one thing at a time. Let's talk about 'stink' and 'dirty' first. She told how water was drawn from a well, heated and poured into a tin tub for bathing. "There's little privacy. I'd be inclined to take fewer baths under those conditions." Giggles rippled around the room. She said fewer Negroes worked in fields now, but there was a time when she saw both white and black sweating and dirty on the DeWitt farm. "Do your mothers have black cooks and housekeepers? Do you eat from plates they clean?"

Consulting her watch, Allise asked, "Why do they fight each other? We could ask some whites that question." She said such a discussion would require more time than could be taken from class, but she didn't want to miss an opportunity to address their concerns. "Let's think about it. How many will meet me during study period?" Everyone raised a hand. "I'll let your study hall teacher know and see you in the auditorium."

Later in the large theater-like room, Allise asked her students if they had discussed Missy's question among themselves. They shook their heads in the negative. "Well, let's talk about things happening in Alabama." She mentioned Mrs. Parks was a neatly dressed woman who was arrested for refusing to relinquish her bus seat to a white man. "After her arrest, black leaders especially Doctor King ignited a fire in blacks. Galvanized them into action."

Pausing to scan their faces, Allise continued. "Alabama whites are unsettled. They see Doctor King as impudent. You hear such remarks as, 'All this nigger rousing will only lead to anarchy.' And 'Damned niggers, they need to stay in their place.' Have you heard this on TV?"

One boy spoke up. "Yes, Ma'am. I even hear it in Deer Point."

"How would you feel if it was said about you?" The student said it would never happen, and Allise said, "Think a minute. Pretend it was said to you?"

He lowered his head, then looking up, said, "I wouldn't like it."

"None of us would. Subjected to such treatment over a long time, you would lose respect for yourselves. There would come a time when your anger could no longer be contained. Can that be one reason why blacks fight and abuse each other? What would happen to a black person who tried to defend himself from a white person?" One student said he would go to prison, maybe be killed, and Allise said, "They can't fight white people, so they vent anger on each other. Does that make sense?"

Most indicated it did, and she asked them to consider how Negroes were fighting back under Doctor King's leadership. "In Montgomery and other large cities, people ride public transportation back and forth to work. Probably more blacks than whites take city buses, so after Rosa Parks was arrested, blacks boycotted the bus company." They asked what boycott meant, and she explained, "Instead of using the buses, Negroes walked or drove back and forth. Last October, the bus line was near bankruptcy for lack of passengers. The Supreme Court ruled segregation on buses was unconstitutional, and the boycott ended on December 21. That day, the Reverend King and E. D. Nixon, another black leader, boarded a city bus for the first time in over a year after Mrs. Parks arrest."

The auditorium fell quiet, and Allise wondered what they were thinking. "Not a person was injured or killed over her arrest," she said. "Dr. King encourages his followers to be non-violent." She looked at her watch. "You must go to your next class in a few minutes. May I ask what some of your thoughts are?"

A few raised hands and commented. "I don't understand why they objected to the back of a bus." "All niggers aren't clean." "I wouldn't want to be treated like them."

"We'll discuss this again, if you wish," she said, wondering how she could help them understand the back of a bus had nothing to do with black objections. It had everything to do with an attitude about their race.

Soon after the *Andrea Doria* collided with another ship off Nantucket Island, Nate and Allise spoke on the phone. She was sad about the lost lives then turned to Billy Graham, the handsome young evangelist, who drew record crowds to religious crusades.

Telling Dro and Maizee about their conversation, she said Nate told her those were concerns of the white world. That you wouldn't find blacks on a seafaring vessel and few if any in one of the reverend's audiences.

Hearing his disillusionment, they had gone on to talk about the rebellious youth and the idolization of James Dean and Elvis Presley. How parents thought they were corrupting young people with undisciplined vulgarity and didn't want their children exposed. Nate had said he doubted James Dean's movie roles made much of an impression on blacks. "He said Elvis's music was a different thing. That blacks compared him with Negro jazzmen."

Allise said Nate was more fired-up over rumors of their leaders' intent to force integration when public schools opened in 1957. "He said things were happening so fast, it was hard for him to concentrate on his studies. Before we hung up, I advised him to keep his priorities straight, first his studies, then the movement."

She stayed on Nate's case to the end of the school term, and he had arrived in Deer Point late the night before. Around noon, he strolled out on the lawn where recent Deer Point graduates lounged on the grass and enjoyed Allise's hot-dog-hamburger cookout. "Nate Colson," she said, "meet the graduating class. Nate will soon receive his degree from Morehouse College in Atlanta."

Without hesitation, he raised a hand in recognition. "How you doing? Are you glad to be graduating?"

A few students greeted him. Others looked as though they didn't know what to do, but one said, "I'm glad to finish school, but you look sorta old t' be going t' college."

"Yeah. I had to work for a time before spending a year in Korea. Miz Allie told me you were never too old to learn." He laughed, helping himself to a hotdog.

"Do you remember when we talked about the bus boycott in Montgomery?" Allise asked. "Well, when Nate could spare time from studying, he drove a friend's car to that city to transport workers back and forth to their jobs and homes."

"What do you guys know about congressional leaders from some Southern states signing a manifesto?" Nate waited. None knew about it. "The manifesto is those leaders' way of resisting the court's recent 'go-slow with all deliberate speed' ruling regarding desegregation of schools. The Supreme Court made that rule after rejecting a National Association for the Advancement of Colored People the NAACP's plea for immediate and total desegregation. Not only that, but state legislatures followed their lead by enacting pro-segregation statutes in their states. Those actions give racists their grist."

Roy sat up and cupped his knees. "I don't think it's right for races to mix in schools or anywhere else." He blew on a blade of grass and gave Nate a defiant look.

"Get used to it. Did you know the University of Arkansas admitted colored law students in 1948? It's happening slowly right here. Right in Little Rock and other places." He said blacks could sit out of sight in public libraries, and some city parks admitted them in small numbers. "Swimming pools and golf courses still can't be used. Can't enjoy amusement rides or sit at picnic tables in parks."

Allise saw Nate's anger building.

"Oh, and the zoo admits us on Thursdays," he went on. "Yeah, and a department store that denied food to blacks has opened a segregated lunch counter." Nate laughed. "Big steps! But we'll take any tokens we can get. Some stores took down 'white only' signs over water fountains, but restrooms are still segregated. A few hotels let black sports teams lodge but won't rent rooms to other blacks. Tell me, what's the difference between sportsmen and other Negroes?" he asked.

Blowing on the grass blade, Roy appeared trying to attract attention, but Nate continued. "Oh, and you really aren't gonna believe this. Little Rock's newspapers allow limited use of 'Mr.' and 'Mrs.' before black names. They've even begun to print Negro pictures. One hired a black reporter to cover the black community." He took a bite of hotdog and chewed. Then reverting back to regional vernacular, he said, "I jes caint believe all this happening when two, three years back, ever'body be calling me boy."

"I still think it's wrong," Roy said.

"Of course you do. People like you make it hard to follow non-violence."

"Roy, I believe people like Nate are going to bring about what is best for humanity." There always has to be one, Allise thought, but most of her former students clapped when Roy stood and walked away.

She was proud of them and Nate, who earned money that summer by mowing Deer Point lawns. It seemed summer passed all too quickly, and he returned to Atlanta.

Allise's fall school opening approached when he called. He said she should expect an uproar when Little Rock schools opened. Negro leaders had chosen Little Rock's Central High School to test integration because Governor Orville Faubus was thought to be a moderate politician who favored limited integration.

Shortly before Central High opened, the square-jawed governor went on the TV to declare he would call out the National Guard "to preserve peace" at Central High if the federal government tried to cram integration down the throats of Arkansans. He said telephone campaigns were underway to bring white mothers to the school *en masse*. Local stores were reporting knife sales, and he warned that segregationists would surround the school when Negroes showed up to be admitted. The governor said his actions would be necessary to prevent violence.

Frowning, Dro listened. "He's paving the road for trouble." Reminding Allise and Maizee of the political diatribe since 1954, he said, "Why, that Mississippi senator said back then that the South would not obey the court's decision. Said the Supreme Court made 'legislative' rulings, and that wasn't its function."

Maizee said it didn't make any difference what the governor did. "People gonna be killed for sure. Nate better stay outta this mess. It ain't right putting young'uns in harm's way. Let things stay like they are. Sure as they don't, black folks gonna be killed."

Allise patted her friend's hand. "Maizee, it's been almost one hundred years since the Civil War, and Negroes still suffer from a lack of education. It's way past time for change, and it will take brave souls to make it happen. Remember, Doctor King wrote that Negroes need to change the way they think of themselves?" She explained that the Supreme Court interpreted laws by way of the Constitution. "The court ruled that people of color are deprived of equal protection and rights guaranteed under the Constitution. Our justice system *will* prevail," she said with confidence.

Allise sounded braver that evening than she felt, and now, she, Dro and Maizee watched a replay of the mob scenes on television.

Reporter John Chancellor let a TV camera tell the story of eight colored students being escorted by black ministers through a white mob shouting jeers and ugly words. Spit flew at the blacks. An Arkansas National Guardsman turned them away before they reached the school door, and the mob grew more threatening. The blacks worked their way back through the meanness to the sidewalk and off the Central High premises.

The crowd lingered when a lone colored girl approached wearing a white dress and dark sunglasses. The cameraman followed her through the crowd, which had again turned to a screaming mob. "Here she comes, one of the niggers!" The camera panned on thrown rocks, on a white girl spewing venom through clinched teeth, and on white men grinning in the background as an old woman spat at the frail-looking girl.

She tried to enter the school door, but a guardsman blocked her with his rifle. She walked around him and was blocked by two other soldiers. Turning back to shouts of "Lynch her!" the girl returned to the sidewalk.

"That girl may look calm and dignified," Allise said, "but she must be terrified."

The Negro girl pressed through the mob and headed down the street toward a city transit bench, where she sat down. "Look," Allise pointed, "a white woman is helping her to safety on a bus. Thank God one person is showing mercy."

For some time, no one spoke. Allise pulled a tissue from the box and wiped her eyes. "Something's terribly out of control. A blight on society. It's so senseless. How is it, those people cannot see the consequences of such actions?"

"Those are powerful pictures," Dro said. "They are being seen all over the country. If people see racism for what it is, I think they will want to do something about it."

Allise felt useless. "What can we do, Dro?"

"You jes keep on doing what you been doing, Miz Allie." Maizee didn't appear surprised at what she had seen.

Dro switched off the TV. "I feel shame for my state. How *can* it happen in Little Rock? The city has already desegregated some places."

"Nate told me blacks only wanted better schooling for their kids," Allise said. "He said they didn't care whether colored or white schools, they just want *better* schools, teachers, and books. They want to be *equal.*" She told of hearing the hurt in his voice. "He said the only advantage in the races mixing is to learn about each other. Nate likes being in a colored college because he feels at ease with his own kind." She gazed at Dro, waiting for him to say something.

He saw her expectancy. "Learning about each other would probably make it easier to live together," he said

Maizee spoke up. "Last time we talked, he asked if we knew that Doctor King was invited to pray at Reverend Graham's crusade in New York. I told him I didn't know. Nate said he's gonna be right in the middle of the action. He say he be working hard in the movement. I won't be sleeping for worrying about him, cause I don't know what he might do." She mumbled about Dalt and Cass voting for the Chicago mayor. "Why cain't black folks vote down heah?" she asked. "I wanna vote the governor out."

Dro explained the Constitution left voting rights up to individual states. "Southern states deny blacks the ballot even though the Fifteenth Amendment forbids such. There's no law stating you can't vote, but some states require blacks to answer questions in order to register to vote." He looked as if thinking. "Not many whites could answer those questions, but whites don't have to answer them. It's idiotic."

Maizee looked puzzled, and Dro said he never thought he would see such problems in his state.

The Little Rock school opening dominated television time for days. President Eisenhower federalized the Arkansas National Guard, and troops moved into the city with half-track vehicles. Pup tents went up around Central High, and soldiers carried rifles. Near the end of September, an obstinate Governor Faubus backed down, and the nine black students returned to start classes. A handful of white students welcomed them, and the military escorted them daily to their classrooms.

Shortly thereafter, Dro came home telling about someone coming into the bank and asking if he heard about the Russians launching a space satellite called 'Sputnik.

"What is this going to mean for the future?" Allise asked.

"So much for the protection of our oceans," he said. "Always been deterrents to invaders, but now a vehicle in the sky is capable of setting off a nuclear bomb. The Cold War threats feel a lot closer to real war."

Maizee sat nearby mending an apron. She shook her head, and in disbelief, Allise thought of frightened children. "The Russians have nuclear bombs, we have nuclear. It would be utter nonsense for our countries to send bombs at each other."

"But whoever said we always use good sense," Dro asked.

"Why are human beings hell-bent on fighting each other?" Allise didn't believe war had to be an inevitable solution. "There must be other ways to solve problems."

In November, the McClure household watched the Little Rock school problem settle down. The airborne troops pulled out, leaving Central High in the hands of the federalized Arkansas guardsmen. But, every night's news brought different worries. After Sputnik, they listened to President Eisenhower warn the nation about pushing for more weapons, the danger of industrialized warfare.

Leaving the nations' concerns for a brief time, Dro and Allise drove Maizee and Thatch to Atlanta for Nate's graduation.

Maizee threw her arms around his neck and said, "My son gonna *be somebody.*" She stood back gazing through pooled tears into his blue-gray eyes. Thatch shook Nate's hand.

Allise waited her turn, then opening her arms to Quent's son, she said, "You're going to help change humanity, Nate. I'm proud of you. Torn between an education and allegiance to your race, you've reached a milestone. You will succeed and prove to naysayers that one *can* when given a chance." She went weepy. "We love you and Maizee." Wiping tears, she screwed up her face at him. "Truth is, I might love you less if you had proven me wrong."

They laughed, then Dro shook Nate's hand and asked what he planned to do now. "I'll work in the movement and go for a Master's degree at Howard University."

"It would be nice to have Nate come home, but Deer Point don't have nothing to offer him." Maizee wiped her eyes. "I'm jes glad I have Thatch."

Nate said, "Things *are* going to change. Public schools will bring us together. It's the law."

Allise didn't detect any doubt in his optimism. "Yes, Nate, we trust the supreme law of the land, but young people like you must keep prodding. Trouble with Russia must be stopped, too. We burden children with a heavy legacy."

"We must teach them early to overcome hate and war," Nate said. "I want to teach the way you do, Miz Allie. You know what an African classmate taught me to say in Swali? *El Fundi.* It means a person is given a craft to master then passes it on by teaching it to others."

"That *is* beautiful, son." Maizee's face lit up with pride.

Allise wanted Nate to do well. What fate awaits him? This young man, more like a second son than my first husband's unlawful offspring.

# CHAPTER 20

▼

Challenges in space between Russia and the United States kept everyone uneasy. Maizee worried about Nate fighting in another war. She couldn't sleep. Suddenly, she raised up in bed. "What's that?" Crackling sounds beneath her bedroom drew her to the window. Light flickered on an oak tree near the garage, and she smelled smoke. Snatching up a quilt, she threw it around her shoulders, ran downstairs and across the lawn. She pounded on the kitchen door, yelling for Mista Dro and Miz Allie.

A rumpled-looking Dro opened it. "Maizee, what in heaven's name—"

"Hurry, Mista Dro. The garage is on fire."

"Oh, my god! Allise, call the fire department." Grabbing his car keys, Dro ran out in his pajamas. Maizee splashed a bucket of water on the flames, and he shouted, "Get out of here!" Leaping into his car, he backed it to the street and returned for Allise's car.

Maizee ran upstairs and pulled clothing from her closet when Allise joined her. "Underwear and bedding in them drawers," she pointed. She heard Mista Dro downstairs, taking utensils and dishes from her kitchen cabinets.

The fire truck arrived, but it was too late. Sooty and smelly, the three sat at the McClures' kitchen table surrounded by a few piles of saved items. Maizee shivered, and Dro held his head. "How could it start in the middle of night?" Allise asked.

"We're going to find out." Dro glanced up. "We will rebuild the garage and apartment. Until then, Maizee can use Peter's room."

Next morning, Allise and Dro poked around in the ashes. He found a smoke-stained bottle on the garage floor. It smelled of gasoline. Saying nothing to Maizee, they took it to the courthouse. "Sheriff, did you hear about the fire?"

"Yeah. I'm real sorry, Dro."

He held out the bottle. "Not as sorry as you're going to be if you don't catch the sonsabitches that did it. This bottle had gasoline in it."

"Now, Dro, that bottle ain't gonna lend much evidence. Probably no prints, and *you* coulda had gasoline in it y'self."

"You better question those two mechanics." Dro reminded him of Nate's beating. "You know, the ones that call themselves Pure Pride."

Allise had said nothing, but she noticed the sheriff seemed nervous. He asked, "What y' talking about?"

Dro glared at him. "I know things, Sheriff, and you better get on the ball."

The sheriff stood up behind his desk. "You can bet I will, Dro."

From the doorway, Dro looked back. "I believe you will, Sheriff."

Maizee was on the phone when they returned. "Mista Dro says he gonna build back the garage and my apartment. I'm gonna be jes fine, son. You coming home for Christmas? I'll tell him you said to wait to build so you can help. We sho will be glad to see you, son. But what about y' part time job?" Maizee listened a few more minutes and hung up.

She turned to Miz Allie. "Nate said he been saving his money, and he may not work during his last semester. He wanted to know what we saved from the apartment and was worried about his keepsake cigar box? I told him we just grabbed up clothes, a few pieces of furniture and kitchen stuff. Miz Allie, he said the card you gave him when he graduated was in that box."

"Well, it was impossible to save everything, Maizee."

"I told him that card was jes a piece a paper. What we got in our hearts for you, and what you got in yours for us, that be lasting forever. Cain't no fire take that away. He said that was right. I sure wish we coulda saved the pictures you made of us, though."

"I do, too, Maizee, but I have some of you in my photo collection.

Allise was beside herself when she handed the pictures to Maizee. The sheriff had questioned Peter about the fire. It was all because of his involvement with the Pure Pride. The whole town was abuzz. James said he was in Houston when the fire occurred. Both boys owned up to beating Nate but claimed to have no contact with Pure Pride since then. They were released without a charge but warned they could be witnesses when the other two men came to trial for firebombing the McClure property. Now, she sat listening without interruption to Dro question Peter.

"Tell the truth," he said, "are you still connected in any way with those fellows?"

"As far as I know, there isn't any Pure Pride. Never was. Those guys at Swen's are no more than two old hell-raisers, Dro. Listen, I didn't like what I saw in Little Rock even though I still believe the races should be segregated. I would never beat up on Nate again. I guess I was mad about a lot of things, and it was easy to take it out on a black boy." Peter looked straight into his stepfather's eyes. "I haven't spoken to those men since that night."

Allise noticed he glanced away, as though something might be read in his eyes.

"Well, son, you better be sure, because they may try to drag you into their guilt at the trial. It will be safer for everyone to tell anything they know now."

"I don't know anything, Dro. I just want to help build another garage."

"Good. Nate said he would help, too." He looked thoughtful. "Peter, you ought to think about what you might say at a trial. Son, this kind of thing is the consequence of being involved with the wrong people."

"Do you really think they did it?"

"Yes, I do." He gazed at Peter. "And there is no telling what those men will claim."

When Peter left, Allise went to the phone and called Jill, "What do you mean this is what happens when the races are mixed? Who—"

"You!" She heard Jill scream. She reminded her mother-in-law that she moved the Colsons into town right under everyone's noses. "Peter wouldn't be involved if not for you."

"Jill, you try to make me dislike you, but you're not going to lay this at my door, dear." Allise listened for some time to her rant about being on Peter's back because of niggers, then, "Listen, Jill, Peter's problem stems from a white man raping a black girl. I could easily blame your attitude and irrational talk for inciting Peter. This conversation is getting us nowhere." She slammed down the receiver, but immediately regretted it.

Dro, listening from the living room, said, "That's telling her, honey."

He had held off beginning the reconstruction until just before Nate came for Christmas. By the time he arrived from Washington, D.C., the two mechanics had been proven guilty, fined ten thousand dollars for property damages, and given a year in prison.

All day, Nate and Peter worked, side-by-side, with the carpenters. Now, the night grew long, and they sat on the back stoop, talking. Suddenly, Peter apologized for beating him. Clearing his throat, he said, "What was it like over there, Nate? The Korean War, I mean."

"You mean the 'conflict?' Like hell. It was *war* all right." Nate told about the

U.S. Army band welcoming them into the country. He described the lay of the land and its people, climate, food and battles he fought. Peter asked if he was scared. "Hell yes, man! Almost dirtied my britches many times. Don't wanna fight in any war ever again. Don't wanna kill nobody and sure don't want anybody shooting at me."

They fell silent, then Nate said, "All to contain Communism in a little old country split in half after the last war. Crazy, man. Fight for the USA and come home to be treated like trash. Not taking it."

"Can't say I blame you, but if the races stay segregated a lot of this nonsense will quiet down. Gonna be more trouble over this school business, mark my words. Nate, white folks don't understand why you Negroes don't stand up for yourselves. You never have done anything about the way you're treated."

"Now, that's just not so, Pete." He cited instances going back many years. "But if you think it's so, that's all about to change." They grew quiet, then, "Pete, can you imagine buying pants or shoes that you aren't allowed to try on? Being called 'boy' and 'nigger' after offering your life for the country? Did Miz Allie tell you about Alabama? Stopped because she sat on the seat with a black boy. You know what that kind of treatment does to a person?" Darkness veiled their faces. "Less than human. I ain't gonna take it," Nate said.

The hour grew late. Peter stood and swiped a hand across the seat of his pants. "I have nothing against colored people, Nate. Just don't want Cleesy to marry one."

"Hell, man! Don't go telling me you have nothing against coloreds. That's the biggest crock of crap! All you white dudes say that. Well, I don't believe you, Pete."

Suddenly, they were shouting and pounding each other with their fists. Dro came out. "What's going on?" He shoved them apart. "Damn it, this is going to stop!"

The boys stood a few feet from each other. "Why?" Nate asked. "Why wouldn't you want Cleesy to marry ... say to marry *me*, Pete?"

"What? What the hell's this about?" Dro looked alarmed, but they ignored him.

"Because races aren't suppose to mix, man!"

"Because I'm a *half-brother*, you yo-yo. Yours, too, buddy." Nate sneered. "What we gonna do about it?"

"I'd like to—"

"You're so mad at our daddy, you'd like to kill me. Ain't that right, Pete?"

Peter sat down on the steps. Covering his eyes, he appeared to be sobbing. Dro seemed glued to the spot. Nate ambled over and stood beside Peter.

In a few seconds, Peter seemed drained of anger. "Heck, it's all too complicated for me. Mother believes one thing. Daddy believed another, and friends think like he did. In church I hear something different. Been sitting here listening to you. What's true in all of it?" Dro opened the door and walked back inside the house.

"Think for yourself, man," Nate said. "Don't listen to other folks."

Peter stood, threw up his hands and disappeared around the corner of the house.

Nate stayed on the stoop. Did he make a dent in Pete's thinking? He believed things were going to change, and a time would come when they could be friends. Maybe even brothers. The portrait on Miz Allie's wall had stared back at him that day. He and his mother had never talked about Mista Quent. *Daddy. A strange sound. Yep, I'll have that talk with her in the morning.*

He went upstairs to Cleesy's room, his for the time being.

Early next morning, he ate breakfast with Maizee. Mista Dro was heard showering upstairs. Suddenly Nate said, "Momma, how am I supposed to feel about my daddy?"

He saw shame flash across her face. "Son, how you want to feel?"

"I think I'd like to accept him." Telling his mother about the talk with Peter, he said, "I sat there thinking, then in bed I couldn't sleep. Talked to myself all night. I want Pete and Cleesy to accept me as a brother. Part of me is being denied existence."

The emotional struggle with their strange dilemma played over his mother's face.

Next morning, Nate worked with Peter when Thatch Gains showed up to help rebuild the garage and apartment.

At lunch time, Maizee called the three of them in to eat, and Nate watched Peter go for his mother's sandwiches and fruit while avoiding his and Thatch's eyes. She joined them at the table, and over the deafening silence said, "Thatch and me gonna get married when the apartment be ready. He be afraid for me t' stay out there by myself." Thatch grinned shyly.

Nate laid a half-eaten sandwich on his plate. "Wowee, Momma! I'm happy for ya." He pulled her up into a hug. "I'm getting a *new* daddy, Pete."

Peter made a sheepish face. "Good for you, Maizee. Soon, you'll be needed here more than ever. I didn't always want you here, but I'm trying to get my head together. You probably won't believe that I never liked to fight."

His confession hung there, then "I thought about things, Nate." He offered a pained look. "I've been angry for a long time."

"I'm angry, too, Pete. Mad cause Momma was raped." Maizee covered her eyes, and Nate lay an arm across her shoulders. "It's all right, Momma. You don't have to be ashamed." He pulled her close. "I can hardly remember when I wasn't mad about being this thing between black and white. Hey! You know, I bet there are enough of us to start a whole new race." Bitterness sounded in his laugh. "Just think, I'd be … we'd be the gray people. You know something? No one at More-house ever said a word about my color."

"Stop it, Nate!" Maizee ordered.

"Sorry, Momma. I don't wanna be mad anymore. I want to be black and proud of it. Pete, fact is we have the same daddy, and there isn't a damn thing we can do about it. Geez, Pete, it's a waste of time to be upset about things we can't change, man. I don't want to rage about the way blacks are treated. Time should be spent on things we can change."

Peter released a heavy sigh. "Daddy died before I knew him. Mother broadcast everything at the trial." He paused. "I don't sleep for thinking. I know nothing can be done about us being brothers, Nate. That's what I came to realize, but I don't know, man I'll have to do a lot of thinking about mixing up the races. If Mother would get off my back—"

"Pete, I hope this means we're making a start in the right direction." Nate released his mother. "Ain't nobody asking to mix up the races. Didn't I just say being between black and white ain't the most comfortable place to be? You white folks want to tell us what we want and don't listen when we say what we want."

A moment of stillness prevailed, then out of the quiet, Maizee said, "Like Miz Allie, I jes want peace. She worry about the world, she worry about you boys. I'm telling you two, peace starts here in this house. Miz Allie knows it, too." She stared at them.

\*     \*     \*     \*

Allise anticipated Cleesy's arrival for the holiday. They had spoken on the phone, and her daughter had said she planned to spend Christmas Day with Peter and Jill and would not be attending Maizee's wedding that day.

Cleesy arrived home safely, and on Christmas Eve, during dinner, Allise said, "Tomorrow is Maizee's big day. Dro, will you make a toast?"

Glasses raised, and Maizee grinned shyly. "No one deserves a good life more than Maizee," Dro said. "To Maizee and Thatch. May they have a happy life together."

On Christmas Day, following the Sunday service at Mt. Zion, Allise, Nate, L'il Joke, Dessie and their two youngest daughters stood in the back of the church. Thatch and his attendant waited on Brother James' left. The two young girls strew snippets of red crape paper and silver icicles down the aisle in front of L'il Joke, Dessie and Miz Allie as they strolled to their places. The bride, wearing a magenta-dyed, crape gown and matching veiled hat, came down the aisle on Nate's arm. He wore a broad grin and presented his mother. Instead of taking a seat, he stood beside the best man to witness their vows.

After the ceremony, Allise and Dro snapped pictures, while the church ladies spread food on two tables set up between the choir stalls behind the pulpit.

The party was ready to break up when Nate searched out Thatch. Holding out his hand, he said, "It's late to call you 'Daddy,' Thatch. To me, you're Momma's husband, and don't you ever make her regret marrying at age forty-six." Pulling the man of slight stature to his chest, he patted him on the back and hugged Maizee before they drove away.

"Where do you suppose they will stay the night?" Allise asked.

Nate's face turned sad. "Probably sleep in the car. Drive into Chicago tomorrow."

"Things will change, Nate. It's going to take time."

"I know," he said.

Shortly after Maizee and Thatch returned from Chicago and were settled in the new apartment, Elfreeda asked them to stay for an after-church dinner. Allise took the opportunity of their absence to invite Peter and Jill over. She and her daughter-in-law had not visited or spoken to each other since their angry phone exchange. Peter avoided her in the market. His mother thought their situation was ridiculous.

They accepted, and now she watched Peter stick his fork in one last morsel of roast beef and hold it suspended in front of his mouth. They had almost made it though the meal without talking about racial problems, but here it comes, she thought. "Martin Luther King is going to cause anarchy sure as shooting," he said. "It's too bad that nigger woman didn't stab deep enough to kill him in that Harlem bookstore. Would have been something, killed by his own kind."

Jill nodded with a sneer. "Ship them all back to Africa, I say."

Without a word, Allise stood, snatched up plates and rushed to the kitchen. She placed dollops of ice cream on top of apple pie servings and put the plates on a tray. Silence was thick enough to slice when she returned to the table. She wanted to stay above the fray, but her nature goaded. "Jill, why do you have Bessie clean and cook for you?" She placed a dessert in front of her. "This pie was made by a Negro. Still have a taste for it?"

"I've eaten Maizee's cooking. Just don't want her eating at the table with me."

"Shut up, Jill!" Peter ordered. "Mother, let her alone. Coming here is a disaster."

Dro's face flushed with anger. Dropping his fork, he shouted, "Not another word. This kind of acrimony isn't going on around my table. Peter, your comment led to this. When you and Jill finish dinner, it'll be time for you to go on home."

Allise slumped. Before Dro could reach her, she drew back from the blame that always tried to consume her. "Peter, ..." She watched them leave

Without reaching reconciliation with her children, Allise reconsidered her long-held belief that evil wasn't inherent. Rehashing her thoughts about it, she came around to her original conclusion.

Ironically, a week later, she stood among the church sidewalk visitors when someone remarked that human beings were born evil. Riled, she said, "How can you dismiss evil as human nature? Babies aren't born evil. Evil is learned. We can't blame God for bad deeds."

Apparently, no one wanted to argue, and the conversation turned to private schools.

"They're opening all across the South. I drove my children quite a distance every day to a church academy." The speaker's family had recently moved from Mississippi to a large Chalu River farm and become quite active in the church.

"Why?" Allise asked. "We have perfectly good schools here."

"I'll drive 'em wherever to keep 'em from being with niggers. This church oughta be planning now for its own academy. Integration will be forced on every white school in the South."

Allise was slightly taken aback. She had been impressed with the young cou-ple's devoutness. "I can't understand objections to white and black kids going to school toget—"

"They're ignorant! Niggers will drag our kids down to their level," the woman said.

Dro tugged Allise's arm, but she refused to budge. "As a teacher I feel degraded. Do you think educators aren't capable of bringing colored children to higher standards? I don't see any reason for religion to become involved in public education as long as there are Sunday Schools. Maybe Sunday Schools aren't doing a good enough job."

"If church schools don't provide a way out of this mess, what will?" a man asked, and others nodded agreement.

Allise eyed him. "Churches should encourage tolerance, not divide us."

Mildred Howard grabbed Eldon's arm. "Well, everything you've said, Allie, is debatable. The Bible is full of God's people who refused to turn over and act dead. Come on, Eldon, we don't have t' listen to an outsider." She walked away, clicking her tongue.

"Kids can deal with integration. Adults have problems with it." Dro cleared his throat. "Before Little Rock, there were already some integrated programs, and some schools opened without any trouble. Wish this sort of thing wasn't happening here. It's going to ruin our schools."

Someone grunted, and another said, "We don't need change in this state."

"It's hard to believe people in Little Rock acted that way, but I don't have to go there to see hate for Negroes," Dro said, taking Allise's arm. "Right here in Deer Point, it's subtle, it runs deep, and it's disgusting human behavior."

"Don't you say I hate niggers," someone demanded. "I jes don't want white and colored mixed. Ain't right. If God wanted us mixed, he woulda made us all one color."

Allise asked if he thought God approved of people's actions in Little Rock, and he said, "People did the only thing they could to show they didn't want 'em in the schools."

She shook her head. "In my opinion, this church should emphasize the teachings of Jesus. He didn't tell us to love everyone but minorities."

"You're not even a member of our church. A Quaker come down here telling us what we oughta believe." The woman's tongue was searing. Allise said she didn't mean to tell them how to believe, but they were heard to profess a belief in what Jesus taught.

Dro looked teed. "What do you know about Quakers?" No one answered.

He walked away with Allise, "They have no shame," she said.

The encounter was on her mind when she sat down at the desk to write yet another letter to Cleesy. Her daughter was ready to graduate, and still the many letters and phone calls Allise had made went unanswered. She wrote about her students reading Pastenak's *Dr. Zhivago*, *Exodus* by Uris and Hansberry's *A Raisin in the Sun*. The drive-in movie, she wrote, was set up just outside of town and forced the Rialto to close. She and Dro had gone to Bensburg with Uncle Sam and Maydale for dinner and a movie.

Maizee walked in as she sealed the letter. "Thatch is awready gitting calls for garden jobs."

"They want to be sure he's available," Allise said, moving to the leather chair. "We are flying to Los Angeles for Cleesy's graduation, Maizee. When

I decide on clothes for the trip, you can tell me if alterations are needed. I've broadened in the beam."

They laughed. "I bet Nate would have a conniption if he was t' see Thatch pat me on my beam and say I gotta pretty little behind." She giggled.

✳   ✳   ✳   ✳

Maizee and Thatch dropped the McClures at the airport then drove into Bensburg to shop for an apartment-size television set. Thatch didn't want to bother Mista Dro and Miz Allie in the evenings anymore. On the way home, Maizee mentioned Peter's name, and he slowed the car. "I guess I oughta tell ya I was cleaning around the Swen's shrubs, and I heard something about Peter." He glanced at her. "Didn't wanna worry ya—"

"Why you keeping things from me, Thatch?" She frowned. "What did you hear?"

"I was round the corner from Mista Swen and the sheriff when I heard them talking about them men that went t' prison. The sheriff told Mista Swen them men said Peter told 'em t' burn the garage. They be afraid t' say anything cause of what Mista Dro knowed."

Maizee gasped. "Lawd, Thatch! Miz Allie ever knows, it'll kill her."

"I know, but the sheriff say he didn't believe it."

"Well, we ain't telling Miz Allie and Mista Dro. We ain't telling nobody. You hear me, Thatch?"

"I ain't gonna tell, Maizee."

✳   ✳   ✳   ✳

Allise and Dro took a cab to a hotel near the campus. That evening, they had dinner with Cleesy and her boyfriend, Jerry. "We're moving to San Francisco tomorrow," Cleesy said. "After the graduation ceremony."

"Oh, Cleesy, stay a few days, visit and tour the city with us," Allise begged, but her daughter said their Haight-Ashbury friends expected them.

"Haight-Ashbury?" Dro looked unsure. "Isn't that a haven for—"

"Yep. Hippies. Flower children. Free love, all that." Cleesy grinned.

"If you're trying to shock us, Cleesy, you're doing a good job." Allise took a tissue from her purse and blew into it. "I don't know how you can—"

"Honey, let it go,"Dro whispered. "We're not suppose to understand kids today." Aloud, he said, "She's jerking your chain. Isn't that right, Cleesy?"

"Mother will never understand, Dro. She's in a rut."

Jerry glanced at Allise, and she thought the soft spoken kid had suffered Cleesy's acrid tongue, too. "Give it a rest, Clee," he said. "They came all this way to see you graduate. Why can't we put off going to San Francisco?"

"No, Jere! They will see us graduate, and anyway, I told friends we were coming."

After dinner, they stood beside Jerry's old car and made plans for the next day.

Allise spent a sleepless night, and the next morning while dressing for the graduation ceremony, she asked Dro to reschedule their flight home. He called the airport, and now the ceremony was over, and they waited behind the outdoor seating for Cleesy and Jerry. Soon, they ran up holding their diplomas. "We're proud of you two," Allise said. She and Dro hugged both of them.

"We have to leave the caps and gowns," Jerry said. "Meet you in half an hour."

At the appointed time, all arrived in the hotel restaurant. Lunch was ordered, and Cleesy said, "When we're settled in San Francisco, I'm heading to New York to find theater roles." Allise asked if she knew someone there. "Yeah. Guys from here. I graduated with them today." She said Jerry was staying to work on a Mas-ter's degree.

Soon it was time for goodbyes. Struggling to hold back tears, Allise held Cleesy's hands and gazed at her as though for the last time. She remembered the day Quent looked at Peter as if to capture his image forever.

Back home, Allise tried to explain to Maizee about Cleesy's decisions and their early return. "Miz Allie, all's I can say is we gotta love our kids no matter what they do."

"Yes, we do," Allise said, heading upstairs to dress for church.

That morning, an interim pastor filled the pulpit while a search was on to find a new minister. He warned the congregation, "Our kids are adrift in pot smoke and drowning in 'free' love. Too many marriages end in divorce." He stared out at them. "Not only are our children in peril, but the places where we live are infested with hate. Deer Point is one of the most racially biased communities in this state." His long pause created a deadly silence, then, "Any minister who comes here will not tell you this, but it needs to be said."

After the service, Allise and Dro surged forward to thank him. "We're grateful for your courage," Dro said. The minister smiled and said he could say it because he didn't have to live in Deer Point.

From behind them, someone said, "Now we have more than Allie telling us off."

Outside, Mildred pecked her cane on the sidewalk. "Outrageous music, cuss words in movies sending our kids t' hell in a handbasket. Disgraceful!"

Allise pulled up an image of her daughter's chain smoking habit. "Cleesy smokes." Her voice was hardly above a whisper. "She doesn't know how much she is loved."

Mildred smirked. "Uh-huh. Happens to the best of us, don't it? Your kids are just like everybody else's."

"Yes, they are." Allise stared. "Maizee says all we can do is love our children. How have your children turned out, Mildred?"

"Yeah, Mildred," someone piped up, "tell us about your kids."

For a moment, her acerbic tongue was stilled. Then, "Rock and roll music … Eldon and I really suffer when we visit them in Memphis." Hearing the laughter, Mildred grabbed her husband's arm, and they hobbled off.

Allise watched the grins of those trailing behind them. It occurred to her that others might find Mildred difficult to like.

# CHAPTER 21

▼

On a Saturday, Dro called Allise to the television. She and Maizee walked into the living room to see black and white students sitting at a lunch counter in a Tennessee eatery. The well-behaved, well-dressed youth appeared humble before jittery waitresses. Not long after in North Carolina, four black, male students refused to budge from a lunch counter. Sit-ins put in motion a testing time. Yet, many public places—parks, swimming pools and beaches, theater seating, and up-front usage of libraries—were yet untested.

While they watched, the media reported that some blacks had tried to worship in a white church, but they had been turned away. They were told, "Blackbirds and redbirds are all God's creatures, but they travel in separate flocks. God didn't mean for black and white to be together." The anchor went on to say some young demonstrators didn't understand Doctor King's reluctance to join protest marches and sit-ins.

"The man's human," Dro said. "Anything can happen. He's been arrested and could be killed."

"Nate says Doctor King don't care about his safety," Maizee said. "Says he packs the church when he talks about all races being free."

"Nate thinks King is the hope for all black people, Maizee. He may be right."

"They don't use 'black' anymore, dear," Allise prompted. "Afro-Americans. Doctor King used 'Negro,' but he received many complaints about 'black' misrepresenting their different shades. Nate says 'Afro-American' feels right." Standing, she said, "I need to call Cleesy."

Allise listened to the phone ring and a feminine voice say Jerry and Cleesy had left Haight-Ashbury for a commune ten miles away. She dialed the new number. Jerry answered. He said Cleesy had been in New York, but she didn't get any acting roles and had returned. He would have her call, but he told Allise she needed to talk to her because Cleesy was in a bad way.

Allise didn't want to think about what that might mean.

That night, Cleesy called, and her mother asked if she were ill. Allise listened to her scream about Jere saying she was sick. "I need money." Asking her mother to send it, she cut the conversation short and said goodbye.

The click of the phone shattered Allise. Distraught and sobbing, she ran to Dro, "She-e's o-on drugs. I know it." As she tried to gain control, he asked if she sounded lucid. "Yes. She needs money. Wouldn't talk." Allise wiped her eyes. "I should call Peter."

"Now, darling, you will make yourself sick. Anyway, I suspect Peter and Cleesy are in touch. Let the kids be responsible for once." Dro's patience sounded thin.

Allise made an effort to be patient over the next several months, and now Cleesy and Jerry were coming to visit over the Christmas holiday. She picked up an icicle that had fallen from the tree and replaced it. Nearby, Maizee hemmed a dress, her gift for Li'l Joke's daughter. They waited for their expected guests to arrive. "I long to hold the child she once was," Allise said. "It's like the Dead Sea separates us. How can I reclaim my children? Something vital is ripped from me."

"I know, Miz Allie." Maizee laid her task aside as Allise settled on the wing chair. "Nate's done trained t' dare white folks to beat his head in. For a college teacher, he ain't got sense enough t' let things be. I worry all the time about him."

"Yes, but Nate does worthwhile things. Cleesy is hellbent on self-destruction."

Just then, a garish-colored van passed outside the newly installed French doors. "Good heavens, Maizee! It's them." Allise ran out to meet them.

Cleesy stepped from the van in a green dress reaching to her ankles. Flowers pinned long strands of red hair behind her ear. Allise kissed her and stood back, surveying. "Darling, you're a slip of the girl I last saw, but welcome home."

An unshaven, gaunt figure at the back of the psychedelic van seemed to struggle with his unkempt appearance. He held out a hand to Allise. "Welcome, Jerry."

"Jere painted our van," Cleesy raised on tiptoes and kissed him on the mouth. "He replaced a water pump with one found in a junkyard and soon had us back on the road."

"Good for Jere." Allise watched him remove two small bags tucked beside a mattress covered in mussed bedding. She swallowed hard and invited them inside.

Without waiting for introduction, Maizee started for the kitchen when she met Dro on his way in. "Cleesy and her man just got here."

Allise offered to take their bags upstairs. "Oh," Jerry said, "we sleep in the van. Those bags hold changes of clothing." She choked back her tongue.

"It's too damn cold to sleep in the van," Dro said, offering his hand.

Jerry stood and shook it. "We do it all the time. Got plenty of covers," he said, sitting down on the couch again.

"Don't have a cow, Mother." Cleesy snuggled against him. "It's what Hippies do."

Dro shot Allise a warning glance. She picked up the bags and said she would take them to the spare room near the bath.

In time, Maizee called dinner. "Jere, you've heard of Maizee," Cleesy said.

They acknowledged each other, and Maizee placed dessert on the counter. "Miz Allie, I'm going to my quarters now."

Allise called after her. "Maizee, get Thatch. You will sit here in your places."

"I've told you about our strange household, Jere." Cleesy rolled her eyes, and an awkwardness fell over the room. After dinner, the awkward feeling followed them to the living room even as Dro tried to ease the talk around to their California experiences.

Near midnight, he and Allise excused themselves and left Cleesy and Jerry cuddling on the couch. Upstairs, before she climbed in bed, Allise peeked out at the van. "I can't see a thing out there."

"Come to bed, Allise!" Dro's gentle command pulled her from the window.

The next day, Nate came from Clark College where he had taught since earning his Master's degree. Everyone sat in the kitchen while his mother prepared his favorite dishes. He snickered over paintings on the van when Jerry and Cleesy walked in. "Jere, meet Nate, another part of the strange arrangement."

Allise shook her head as Nate accepted Jerry's hand. "Strange? Something strange going on with you, Cleesy?" A burst of laughter erupted from him, and she flopped down on a chair, glaring.

The two men talked about school. Jerry told of working toward a Master's in Russian and Slavic studies. "My grandparents came from Russia. The Cold War puzzles me. I think I want to be in the diplomatic service."

Nate scratched his head. "Hey, dude, somebody better clean up this mess. A war between us and Russia will knock both countries off the face of the earth." Allise agreed.

Maizee encouraged them to the dining table, and as food made a round, Jerry said he and Cleesy planned to work on behalf of John Kennedy's second presidential campaign. Nate talked about working in the Civil Rights Movement. "Last night we had a meeting and got those black kids all fired up."

"You gotta stop talking kids into places where they ain't wanted, Nate." His mother shook her head. "Gonna get them and yo'self killed! Nothing gonna change anyhow."

"Now, Maizee," Allise said, "Nate's involved in a good cause. I'm proud of him." Turning to Nate, she said, "You must be very careful, Nate. Use good judgment."

When the holidays ended, and Cleesy, Jerry and Nate were on their way back to California and Clark College, Maizee put the evening meal on the kitchen table. Allise said Peter and Jill's absence at the Christmas dinner should have been expected. "I was glad Sam and Maydale joined us."

For a time, they ate in silence, then Maizee said, "Lotsa bad things going on. Coloreds they the ones being killed."

Allise looked at her for a long moment. "Yes, Maizee, it's sad, but the struggle goes on, and it's a just one. It may take years, but old laws will be changed. The races will come to see each other in a better light. Wait and see. Anyway, it can't be stopped now."

"Yeah, we're moving on." Dro laid his napkin on the table and smiled at Maizee.

She said Thatch would be home and coming for her. She made a plate of food for him, pulled on her coat and closed the door behind her. Allise cleared the table, and Dro went to his living room recliner.

Soon, she eased onto his lap and nibbled his ear. "I love you, Dro McClure," she whispered, "It's good to have the house to ourselves again." She moved to the couch and swung her legs up on it. "I've been thinking about the thousands, young and old from all walks of life and professions, going to faraway countries as goodwill ambassadors. If I could leave you and my students," she said, "I would enlist in the Peace Corps."

"I'm glad you have me and your students." Dro laughed. He said he approved of the Peace Corps but his confidence in government was shaken after the Bay of Pigs invasion. "You could almost hear a collective sigh of relief when Chairman Khrushchev agreed to remove Russian missiles from Cuba." He looked thoughtful, then added, "We don't ever need to come that close to a nuclear war again. But both countries keep on building arms. That and Afro-American boldness keeps everyone constantly unnerved."

He said blacks amazed him. They were undaunted by white taunts and the demeaning signs flourishing in more and more places. Dro repeated what he had seen on the TV. "'Why don't you fight back, nigger?' 'I don't like the looks of a nigger' or 'Some niggers are eager to die.'" He paused, then remembered others. "'Niggers were born to pick cotton.' 'Go home, niggers!' 'Tickets to Africa sold here.' Demeaning," he said.

"Thank God, we haven't seen anything like that here in Deer Point." Allise yawned.

After Clark College classes recessed for summer, Nate tutored students in non-violent behavior. On the phone, he said, "Miz Allie, I'm leaving for Washington, D. C. to join a Freedom Ride. Tell Momma the action is forced on us if we expect to be free."

In the District, he boarded a chartered bus bound for the South. Riders were to challenge water fountain and restroom rules in cross-country bus stations. On the long trip, freedom songs encouraged them to face whatever lay ahead.

The bus pulled into a Mississippi bus station, and was met by a white mob with clubs and rubber hoses. A baseball bat slammed into Nate's head. Blood streamed down his face and neck, and he crawled behind a building to avoid arrest. When the scene ended, he heard voices and peered around the corner. Black people assisted the wounded lying up and down the sidewalk. Taken to one of their homes, Nate's wounds were cleaned and bandaged.

Fearing Maizee would see the event on television, he called. She yelled at him about coming to his senses and asked if he just stood there and let them beat on him. Then, she wanted to know if he was on the bus that burned. "No, I wasn't on the bus to Alabama. Now, Momma, you've got to have faith in Doctor King. If we stay non-violent, white folks will come to see we deserve our rights. Momma, tell Miz Allie I'm going to be okay."

Allise and Maizee were in constant states of concern for Cleesy and Nate, but Allise had to concentrate on preparation for the opening of school. She had tried to read Faulkner's *Mansion*, but his writing style took too much time, and she turned to Harper Lee's *To Kill a Mockingbird*.

On opening day, she made Lee's book required reading, and shelved three other new library books, Steinbeck's *Travels with Charlie*, Drury's *Advise and*

*Consent,* and John O'Hara's *Ourselves to Know* holding out *Mansion* to read at her leisure.

Later, when she called on her students to discuss *Mockingbird,* they surprised her with sympathy for Atticus Finch's Negro client, accused of raping a white girl. Allise dared to hope her students' attitudes were changing. Asking them to imagine themselves with black skins, she said, "What do you feel?"

One girl said, "I wouldn't like to live the way they do."

"I wouldn't like stepping off the sidewalk for a white person to pass, like I wasn't good enough," a young man said.

"I think you've hit on the thing black people are most upset about," Allise said. "We may lack material things, but to not be accepted as equal beings, that hurts most."

She hoped they were coming around, but there was a whole range of incidents and constant fears for her charges to deal with. Troops were being sent to Vietnam. Students practiced diving beneath their desks. And in Mississippi, James Meredith was barred from registering at the university.

One pupil asked how a governor could keep a black from going to college. "Cause he's the gov, goon," a classmate said. "States' rights, man." As they discussed the events, Allise realized her students were too young in 1957 to know what had happened in Little Rock.

The school day ended, and she sat on the chaise, wondering about children growing up in such an unnerving time. Her generation was responsible for the chaotic times which would mold the way young people came to view their world.

Maizee appeared in the doorway. "Come, Miz Allie." Leading her downstairs, they listened to the news that Eleanor Roosevelt had died at her home in New York.

The commentator was saying, "'known as the 'First Lady of the World,' she once said, and I quote: 'About the only value the story of my life may have is to show that one even without any particular gifts can overcome obstacles that seem insurmountable if one is willing to face the fact that they must be overcome.'"

Another of Allise's heroines had left this life. Time is passing too quickly, she thought.

Allise had taught for twenty-four years. She feared the education system was devolving into private, church-operated, white academies, but if that was what integration brought about, so be it. She pled with the all-male school board to integrate Deer Point High. "It's incredible the state can defy the Supreme Court." Discouraged by the brush-aside from the board members, she was unsure about continuing in her profession. She had overcome polio, and at fifty-five years of age, in a time of racial upheavals and war, her children were estranged. She agreed with Mildred Howard. *Not only young people, but the world is going to hell in a handbasket.*

That night, she told Dro about going to the school board. "Well," he said, "bad racial relations aren't just denying educations. They aren't good for the town, either." He said at the last city council meeting members agreed new businesses were needed. "Some resented me for bringing up racial attitudes, but business people worry about profits. They aren't going to waste time arguing social problems, or risk racial chaos destroying their businesses." He climbed in bed beside Allise. "Such issues distract a business from making a success. I don't know why the council can't see those consequences."

"Because they can't get past the hatred they feel for black people," Allise said. She didn't mention to her husband that symptoms similar to the long ago polio attack plagued her.

Despite the lethargic feeling, she entered yet another school term.

Several months into the school year, Dro answered Nate's phone call. He hung up and told Maizee Nate was leaving his class to see after Leila. She was clubbed at a bus station when Freedom riders sat down at a lunch counter and refused to move. Local police had pushed them outside and beat them.

Later, he told Allise about Leila. "Nate said civil rights leaders urged Doctor King to go to Birmingham. Did you hear Governor George Wallace speak from the steps of the state capitol?" She shook her head. "He said, 'No other son-of-a-bitch will ever out-nigger me again.'" He reminded Allise the governor had complained in an earlier speech that when he tried to talk about taxes, highways, and schools, people didn't listen until he talked about Negroes.

Maizee came into the room and stood listening. "I'm afraid Doctor King's gonna lead Nate to more harm. Him and Leila oughta git married before both of 'em git killed."

Dro said some Afro-Americans disliked and feared Doctor King, but others had a new sense of themselves. "Cassius Clay 'stung' his opponent 'like a bee' and won an Olympic boxing championship. He brags, 'I'm the greatest.'" Dro raised his arms in a sparring stance and grinned. "He's an arrogant son-of-a-gun in a charming way. Going to be an idol along with Jackie Robinson."

"Their pride grows," Allise said. "Nightly meetings are being held to plan massive rallies, boycotts, marches, and sit-ins in Birmingham. Movement songs keep their emotions high." She repeated the words of one she had heard: "'We hung our head and cried, Cried for those like Lee who died. Died for you and died for me, Died for the cause of equality'"

As black pride grew, racial tensions became more turbulent. Doctor King was arrested in Birmingham. He wrote from jail about those who talked goodwill but did nothing. Maizee watched the tension escalate on the television as students from Parker High, the largest black school in Birmingham, began a peaceful march that turned into bedlam.

That evening, she prepared dinner when Allise asked, "How long will we endure this turmoil before our government does something? People must have felt this way during the Civil War. Seeing the uproar day after day makes it difficult to think of anything else."

Maizee turned from the sink. "Them poor kids jest marching, and cheering, and singing, then ever'thing broke loose," she said. "Them policemen went after 'um with dogs and water hoses. That man, Bull Connor, yelled, 'Look at 'em niggers run.'" Tears ran down her cheeks. "Dogs biting 'em and water hoses sending bodies head over heels."

"It's bad," Dro said, "but now people will see America's ugly underbelly."

Allise helped Maizee put their dinner on TV trays because the president was supposed to speak during prime time.

In the living room, she and Dro listened to him announce he was sending a civil rights bill to Congress. "A great change is at hand," he said. "Our task, our obligation, is to make that revolution, that change peaceful and constructive for all."

"Do you really think it will stand a chance of passing," Dro asked.

"Y'all gonna eat?" Maizee gazed at them.

"I can't imagine that it won't," Allise said. "At last, consideration will be given to how some people live in this country." She was eager to take part in the progress.

The next morning, Dro called from the bank. Someone had walked in and said two crosses were burned in Colored Town during the night. "Did you say one was burned in front of Dodd's store and another at Mt. Zion church?" she asked. He confirmed what he said and told her, as the bank president, he intended to call an open meeting to try to convince people that cross burning didn't enhance Deer Point's image. He asked Allise to call people in Deer Point and Colored Town about the meeting to be held that night.

Elfreeda was among many others she called during the day. "I'm afraid to be seen in a meeting with Jedadiah in a wheelchair," she said. "He cain't help if somebody breaks in here, Miz Allie, but I know someone who will be there."

That night, Allise waited in the rear as the bank lobby filled to capacity. Dro opened the meeting by talking about the town's image and how growth could be affected by such things as cross burnings. "This kind of thing can't go on here," he said. "Y'all know the president of the other bank. Come on up here, Claude. We've agreed to be selective about who gets loans in this town. If you businessmen refuse credit, too, we can soon unmask these cross burners. Sooner or later, if people can't get money and credit, they will give up names."

"But Dro, just a *few* are doing it, and a *lotta* folks agree with 'em. I don't know what you expect. If we get too tough, people won't buy our goods," one businessman said.

"If they know we know who they are, we won't have this kind of thing in our town. People who do evil in the stealth of night are cowards. We're cowards if we let them do it."

Dro invited Sheriff Banes up front.

He had been elected time and again without an opponent, but he didn't appear too comfortable before the crowd. "Whoever's doing it will hafta be caught in the act. No evidence was found on the burn sites," the sheriff said, pulling up his holster belt. "It's gonna be tough catching whoever did it."

"I have something to say, if I may speak." A well-dressed black woman stood out in the crowd. Dro asked her to come forward.

Without so much as a blink, she waited for uneasy shuffling to settle. "We have formed neighborhood alerts. We're watching all over Colored Town for anything unusual. Our people are instructed to call you, Sheriff. Now, the question is, how long will it take you to arrive if and when you receive a call?" Under her long questioning gaze, he stirred, and she said, "The black community is putting the burden on your law enforcement."

"Well, I think that's a wise move," Dro said. "Better than taking the law into your own hands. Y'all agree?" He turned to the crowd. Some agreed, and others walked out.

The meeting was over, and Dro locked the bank door. He and Allise crossed the parking lot to his car. With her seated inside, he started around the car when the sheriff approached.

"Dro," he called, motioning him to move away from the car where Allise waited. They stood talking in low voices for a few minutes. When Dro got in the car, she asked what he wanted.

"Oh, nothing. Just trying to make excuses about why they may not catch the ones who burned the crosses."

She could tell Dro was being evasive, but she didn't question further.

The next day, Maizee started down the stairs when she heard Mista Dro on the phone. "The sheriff thinks the same two men who burned the garage are involved with the cross burnings and you're behind them." She stopped in her tracks and listened.

"He said you apparently don't take part in the deeds but do the planning." Dro listened for a few minutes, then, "Gawddamn it, Peter! You are going to kill your mother." He listened again, then, "Of course I'm not going to tell her, but you know how things get broadcast in this town." Dro slammed down the receiver and started up the stairs.

Maizee moved back to the bathroom. She could see Mista Dro was in a high state, and he shouldn't know she had heard.

*    *    *    *

Allise was kept in the dark about Peter. A few weeks later, she answered the phone, and Nate said Leila was released from the hospital a month earlier. They planned to be in Washington, D. C. for the big, upcoming march.

A week later, the McClures and Maizee searched the TV scene for Nate's face in the crowd of hundreds of thousands, stretching from the Lincoln Memorial to the Washington Monument. The August humidity was said to feel like a sauna. Some people waded in the reflecting pool. Others sang rousing songs and made moving speeches. Late in the day, a chant went up for Doctor King. His familiar resonance was said to lift spirits all the way to heaven as he took them along on his "dream."

That evening, one congressman commented on the news that it was a "Communist" gathering. The commentator said King's dream didn't resonate with many in the South.

"Mind you, it will. Things are going to change," Allise declared.

When she returned to her classroom in the fall, her students wanted to discuss the events happening in their time. One asked if she knew that President Kennedy had federalized the state guard after Governor Wallace attempted to bar court-ordered integration. Five blacks were admitted to the Birmingham schools, he said. Most of her charges seemed upset over the bombing of four young black girls in a Birmingham church.

"When there's so much chaos, something has to be wrong." another student said.

Allise said he was right about something being wrong, "but if everyone will do their part, we can change the way things are." She told them the Sixties Decade had burst on the scene with much hope and trust in a new president.

Now, in November, Allise and Dro watched the coverage of President Kennedy's assassination. Bullets rang out in Dallas, taking his young life.

The tragedy made her long to reconcile with her children. "Life is too short, too precious to live without their love," she told Maizee. She had no contact with Cleesy, and Peter provoked her at every chance. "My son feels about the Kennedys as Quent did about Roosevelt. What kind of hatred brings one to murder our elected leader?"

Maizee wiped her eyes. She had seen Lee Harvey Oswald gunned down on the TV. "There's too many devils around," she said, and Thatch nodded.

"Why would Jack Ruby murder the apparent assassin?" Dro asked. "It's strange."

Agreeing, Allise said, "The world is out of kilter."

Later, they listened to President Lyndon Johnson tell a joint session of Congress that no memorial could more eloquently honor President Kennedy's memory than the early passage of the civil rights bill.

Once again, Allise was hopeful, then she stood in the March chill outside the church, listening to talk about bombings and shootings. Someone remarked, "Niggers are getting just what they deserve. They gotta learn to stay in their place. God made 'em what they are"

"Don't tell me goodness has a hand in any of this!" Allise was in no mood to hear such talk. "Things happen because we … all of us allow it. We won't take blame for our vile acts, but hide our guilt for them under the guise of God's name." Disgust dripped from her words. "Unlike ancient Greece's jealous, warring gods, the only God I know loves this beautiful world and expects us to love it, too. The God I know has great pity for us."

She halfway expected to hear Mildred's tongue click or her cane tap, but her nemesis had passed away. Instead, she heard, "Oh, my lords." *Those words could have come from every generation since the Civil War.* Even if these people visualize me in hell, Allise thought, I refuse to carry the guilt they want to impose on me.

Disappointment in unyielding attitudes, and the ups and downs of civil rights battles kept her upset. Three civil rights workers were missing in Mississippi. Eight blacks, served in an Arkansas eatery, were roughed-up by a mob who waited outside for them, but Allise told Nate on the phone, that all was not negative. "My students show positive signs of attitudinal change even though much of the general public seems obstinate."

Suddenly, Allise wiped her cheek. Nate had just asked if he had ever told her what she meant to him. He struck a deep chord of emotion, and she said, "Thanks for saying I have a way, and no, you have never told me what I mean to you, but Nate, I know." She said her many flaws needed constant attention, especially intemperance and impatience. "Peter still hangs up when I call, and Cleesy is unreachable. I failed them, and that is my biggest regret."

They talked on for several minutes, and she said the McClure household soared like an elevator ascending to the top floor when the Civil Rights Bill was enacted. "Now, we will see what President Johnson can make of his 'Great Society.'"

Allise hung up and walked back into the living room. "The 'war on poverty' is apt to take a back seat to the war in Vietnam," Dro said. "Damned manifest destiny! Damned Domino theory!" He read from the president's address: "'America keeps her word we must honor our commitments. The issue is the future of southeast Asia.'"

Dro raised his eyebrows. "Did you read this? The president says there 'is a threat to all,' and that 'Our purpose is peace.' He says we have 'no military, political, or territorial ambitions,' only 'struggle for freedom.'" He laid the paper aside. "He says we aid South Vietnam and Laos so they can repel aggression, strengthen independence, and anyway the North Vietnam regime violated the 1962 Geneva Agreements." He looked up at her. "It's meddlesome to interfere in the affairs of other nations."

The eagerness to send young men off to be killed was beyond Allise's comprehension. The subject was getting to her. "Nate's back at Clark College," she said. "He went with that Mississippi committee in August to try to get its delegates seated at the national political convention. Nate said after that experience, they knew America's racist society is a long way from being democratic."

# CHAPTER 22

▼

Each day, school became more difficult for Allise to endure. She rested on the chaise when Maizee brought a letter from Cleesy. They studied a photograph of her and Jerry outside their commune. "She doesn't look happy," Allise said. "Wasting her life. How can she?"

That night, she handed the brief note and picture to her husband. "I'm catching a plane to San Francisco. Will you come with me?"

"Allise, let me fly out and try to bring her home."

"Don't just try, darling. Bring her home! I've seen those LSD users on"

"Honey, you're working yourself into a frenzy. Probably over nothing."

Several days later Dro boarded a plane to California. He returned in a few days with Cleesy's remains.

In their bedroom, he told Allise the details of how he had found their daughter. He took a cab north to Valley Ford and stopped at a service station to inquire for the commune. "The attendant said it was funny I should ask because a girl from that place was killed the night before, and the boy taken to the hospital. He said the kid drove an old painted-up van. A picture of the accident was in the paper."

Dro said he had trouble breathing, but had the presence of mind to ask for their names. "The attendant wasn't clear about the girl's, but said the boy's name was Jerry."

Allise sobbed, and Dro calmed her before going on.

He returned to his hotel in San Francisco, and after many calls, located the morgue holding Cleesy's body. After identifying it, he arranged to have her shipped home. "Before calling, I paced and rehearsed ways to tell you, Allise."

She clung to him and told how she had questioned sending him for Cleesy. "I doubted she would come, and if she did, I knew we couldn't keep her here." She said when he called, Maizee helped her upstairs. "Without her I don't know how I could have kept breathing until you were home. Dro, a part of me is dead."

"S-sh, darling." He held Allise until her sobs subsided again.

Allise said Maizee called Peter. "She told him Cleesy had been killed in a car accident, and you were br-bringing her home. Dro, he came right over. Sat in that rocking chair." Allise's body sagged with sadness, but she needed to spill the hurt. "I asked Peter if I ever told him his father had Mr. Andrews make the chair so I could rock him. He said no, that it had always been here, a part of this room." She said Peter sat there, rubbing the wood as if caressing it and seemingly gripped by something unsaid. "Then he said, 'Mother, did you love my father?'"

Allise sobbed and sobbed. Drying her tears, she said the question took her by surprise. "I told him, like all young people, we were attracted to each other and fell in love. That we married within a few months, knowing so little about each other. I told him I wanted to be with his father always and thought life couldn't go on after his death."

Looking up at Dro, she said, "I was unsure of how much I should reveal about the relationship between his father and me. Didn't say how doubtful I was that our love would endure. Just that his father and I thought what we had was love."

Dro drew her to his shoulder and nuzzled her hair. "I think you did the right thing."

"Oh, God, Dro, Peter asked, 'Do you love me and Cleesy?' It sounded accusatory." She had cried and cried, and her son had just gazed at her, waiting for an answer. "I told him my love for them was beyond description. That I didn't think they could do anything I couldn't forgive. I asked if he could forgive me for taking too seriously the responsibility of rearing them. Of trying to make them good citizens." She had admitted to not allowing any occasion of bias to pass without calling their attention to it. Peter, she said, didn't offer his forgiveness, but they had wept in each other's arms.

Allise pulled back and looked up at her husband. Her eyes held a lifetime of failures, but she said, "You know the rest. Peter and Maizee stayed right here with me."

They heard Maizee call them down to dinner. With them settled at the table, she went to the phone to tell Nate about Cleesy's death.

Allise thought other adversities should have seasoned her, made her less overcome by Cleesy's demise, but she never felt more vulnerable.

At the cemetery, she listened to Peter give the eulogy, and Elfreeda sing *Swing Low, Sweet Chariot* as the coffin was lowered in the DeWitt plot next to Quent. How could any pain ever be as hurtful as when Quent was killed? She couldn't contain her grief. An unresolved relationship with her daughter would be with her forever. Cleesy would never know how much she was loved. More than anything, Allise wanted to believe God, that unknown entity, had a reason for all tragedy. God is in each of us, she thought.

Shortly, after the funeral, Allise listened to Maizee plead with Nate. "You what? Son, you let that march in Selma, Alabama, be. You leave that march and come on home for a visit. Miz Allie sho be glad to see you after what she been through."

*    *    *    *

His mother's pleas didn't change Nate's plans. The march from Selma to Montgomery began, and he joined the two-by-two walk toward the Edmund Pettus Bridge. White men wearing hard hats and holding clubs greeted them with smirks, but the marchers passed onto the bridge without incident.

Near the end of the bridge, they stopped before a field of blue-helmeted, uniformed troopers and local lawmen. Some were mounted on horses. Then, black leaders began to step forward and others followed. Troopers donned gas masks. One man moved out front as they advanced, and over his bullhorn came, "You're unlawfully assembled. For the sake of public safety, turn back." The marchers halted again.

Down the line came a whisper, "Leaders say for us t' kneel and pray." Nate fell to his knees. Booted feet and horses' hooves pounded, closer and closer. Billy clubs, rubber hoses and tear gas forced the marchers back past a line of laughter and shouts. White people waved Confederate flags and screamed, "Get the niggers!"

Blinded by tear gas and clubbed in the head, Nate stumbled almost back to the chapel before taking another blow. Blood gushed from his temple. He sensed himself falling.

*    *    *    *

Downstairs, Maizee answered the phone. "Oh, my lawd. Is he gonna die?" Dro and Allise heard, and he rushed downstairs. She dropped the receiver and fell onto the chair. Suddenly, she stood and went into a flying dervish.

Dro heard and rushed downstairs to see her suddenly stand and go into a flying dervish. She howled and darted about without sense or purpose. Allise watched from the head of the stairs in stunned silence. "What on earth happened, Maizee?" Dro caught her arms and guided her back to the chair.

She breathed heavily, but finally made them understand Nate was in a coma in a Montgomery hospital. "They found him unconscious on the sidewalk. Somebody carried him inside the church they marched from. I gotta go to 'im, Miz Allie."

Dro called about flights to Montgomery, and Maizee went to the apartment to pack.

Thatch, located at his gardening job, was told.

"I hate t' leave you, Miz Allie, but ..."

"Maizee, if we can do anything, call us." Allise held her for a long moment, then Thatch drove her to the airport.

*Months passed and in time, Allise committed Cleesy to the creator and wrote in the DeWitt Bible:* **Clariece Lyle DeWitt died March 6, 1965. Nathaniel Colson, born June 20, 1933, to an Afro-American, Maizee Colson, and Quentin DeWitt.**

No matter how strong she wanted to appear, events were catching up to her. She thought about how she had lived her life. "Dro, I've never told you about my Quaker way. I go to this sacred inner-self to find what we call God, to find peace. This time the death of my child makes it harder to let God in. I hope I haven't worn out the way to God, for now I will be going there for Nate, too."

She had spoken with Maizee. The doctors told her they couldn't do anything more for Nate. He was being released. He hadn't spoken a word since the blow to his head. They told his mother that he may never be himself again. She was ready to bring him home.

Dro listened to her tell about Nate. He said he would fly to Montgomery and bring them home. Picking up the paper, he diverted Allise's attention, "Listen to this, people do care." He read letters to the editor about rights denied to Negroes. "People across the country are writing and calling their congressmen, asking for rights legislation. He turned the page, and read from an article. "Congress is requesting that the president submit a voting rights bill." He kept reading aloud. "The president addressed Congress and said, 'rarely did an issue lay bare the secret heart of America. Equal rights for Negroes is such an issue. We can defeat every enemy, double our wealth and conquer the stars, but if not equal to this issue, then our people and nation will have failed. We must all overcome (a) legacy of bigotry and injustice.'"

As soon as Dro could take time from the bank, he made all the arrangements and flew to Montgomery.

Nate was a constant reminder of Bloody Sunday. Allise wondered if he would ever be able to return to Clark College. *I overcame polio with muscle therapy, Nate can heal with brain therapy*, she thought. *I will not give up on him.*

She told him the Voting Rights Act of 1965 was signed less than five months after Dr. King's successful march to Montgomery and repeated things of common interest to them. Maizee and Dro talked to him, too.

At times, Nate seemed to understand and looked as if he wanted to respond. "I will not allow him to vegetate," Allise said. "He *will* come out of this. You'll see."

After what had happened to Nate, she couldn't believe her son's attitude remained unchanged. He and Jill visited one evening, and Dro discussed the escalation of violence on the Asian continent. "King's totally wrong to oppose the war," Peter said.

"Riots all over the country, costing millions in damage." Jill looked at Allise. "Peter wants to fight."

Allise caught her breath. "Peter, lives are wasted on war. Money, too."

"I don't know, son," Dro said. "You should give that some thought."

"It's a *just* war! If we don't rid the world of Communism before it spreads, who will? If Daddy were alive, he would tell me to fight for this country just like he did."

Allise's heart skipped another beat. "War never settles anything, Pe—"

"There she goes again!" he shouted. "Why do you think Cleesy lived the way she did, Mother? I bet you drove Daddy to war."

"Dear God!" Allise wailed, reaching out to him. "Peter, I love you." He stared, unmoved, holding his ground.

Dro stood and led her into the kitchen. He held her shaking body. "Allise, let Peter be and stop beating yourself over the head."

Hardly were they seated again when Peter took up the interrupted conversation. "If I had children old enough to defend this country, I would encourage them." Apparently no one wanted to travel that road again, and soon he and Jill took their leave.

"It's probably best we don't have grandchildren," Allise said.

There was a time when she wished for grandchildren, but now she fought to keep up her optimism about Nate's improvement. He stared into a void and the ugly head scar reminded them of his racist encounter. She told him he had walked side-by-side with Doctor King in a non-violent movement. That he helped shift the South and bring hope. She wanted him to understand his role. "Nate, Doctor King increasingly speaks of the causes of poverty.

Blacks are chanting, 'Black is beautiful.' Why, a Massachusetts black, Edward W. Brooke, was elected to the Senate, and Thurgood Marshall was named to the Supreme Court."

Allise read *Dr. Zhivago* to him and mentioned Leila, hoping to set off a spark.

It didn't. He turned picture book pages without recognition of what was seen. *The Sound of Music* and Beatle songs were played. Nate broke into a slight smile when he heard, "All you need is love; Love is all you need." The song seemed to be his favorite.

He watched television with Allise and Dro when Doctor King spoke to garbage workers in Memphis. Speaking of God's will, King said he was allowed to go to the mountain top, look over and see the promised land. He wasn't worried about anything and feared no one.

Later Nate's idol was shown on a Memphis motel balcony just before he was assassinated. An anchorman repeated Doctor King's chosen epitaph taken from a Negro spiritual: "Free at last, free at last, Thank God Almighty, I'm free at last!"

Summer came, and still Nate didn't realize his hero was dead. Allise sat talking with him when the doorbell rang. She opened the door to a red-haired, freckle-faced college student. "I'm Fran, a Volunteer in Service to America. You know, a VISTA worker. I was sent to Deer Point to learn about and help solve community problems. Mr. Wise gave me you name, Mrs. McClure."

Allise smiled and invited her in. Fran answered her questions and said she had talked to a few community leaders about Deer Point needs. "A few always welcome me," she said. "Most places, it's the same." Her assignment was to initiate projects and suggest improvements that would benefit everyone. "A meeting is being held tonight. Can you go?"

Allise assured her Deer Point had needs, but townsfolk were an independent bunch.

She invited Fran to dinner and agreed to go to the meeting.

At the courthouse, they met in a dimly lit room with Charlie Wise and four people from the black community. Fran explained they were there to brainstorm ideas.

"A city park with a grandstand and picnic tables is needed," Allise said. "A place where people can listen to music and speeches, and play with their children." All agreed it should be a park open to everyone, and located where passing travelers could have access to it. Other ideas were suggested and each was discussed.

After the VISTA worker returned to school, the Deer Point City Council met without taking up the suggestions.

Allise was disappointed that the park idea wasn't acted on, but she encouraged her students to contribute to society. She used the young VISTA worker as an example and talked of other ways they could become involved. "You know Missy? The daughter of Mister Charlie Wise. Missy joined the Peace Corps."

The classroom listened attentively, then she set them to diagraming sentences. Groans came with the tedious process. Then, one of the boys asked, "Can we talk about drug use or the rioting and looting going on in cities? Anti-war demonstrators are chanting about body bags coming back from Vietnam. Miz McClure, do y' like Bob Dylan's song, *Blowin' in the Wind?*"

Allise knew he tried to avoid the assigned work. "Well, Jim, his song says a lot. Do you want to lead us in a verse." Everyone laughed, but he surprised them and began to sing.

She recalled Dylan's song the night she and Dro watched presidential candidate Robert Kennedy fall to an assassin's bullet before the TV camera.

Sunday morning, standing on the church sidewalk someone was overheard saying, "another Kennedy hit the dust. Good riddance." Another said, "He was a nigger lover, even more so than his brother. Our problems started with a Kennedy. I agree, Mac. Good riddance."

Dro caught Allise's arm too late. She pulled back. "Inside those doors," she pointed, "we are told, 'Love thy neighbor as thyself.' That means all human beings. Robert Kennedy understood the needs of Afro-Americans. If he could have lived to be our president, he would have done something about their plight. You support sending missionaries to Africa, but you don't welcome blacks into this church."

"Afro-Americans," one man sneered into the laughter.

Dro tried to walk Allise away, but she resisted. "No liquor, swearing, stealing, gambling, adultery. Why not no hating and no wars. I cannot believe …"

Someone tried to butt in, but she ignored him. "You make God into a creature to be feared. God is loving and wants us to be loving, too." The crowd appeared tongue-tied.

Allise wondered when the killing would end. The decade went on for almost two more years. For a time, she had believed the Sixties offered a greater vision, one that seemed attainable. Now, she rested on the chaise, reading some wise per-son's words: "Jim Crow was shot while hiding in the law books, but the bird wasn't dead." Yes, she thought, seething hatred is alive and well.

She considered the awesome space achievements. An Apollo mission went to the dark side of the moon and sent back satellite views. Then another roared into space and landed on that distant orb. "The Eagle has landed," Edwin Aldrin had radioed back to Earth, and Neil Armstrong had stepped out on the powdery surface. "That's one small step for man, one giant leap for mankind," he had said.

Nate wasn't told about the spacecraft fire that took the lives of three astronauts. Dro made sure he knew about other space travels.

Allise remembered Nate saying the *Andrea Doria* tragedy and Billy Graham's crusades were white folks worries. *What would he say now?*

She sat there, reflecting on challenges to old ways and meeting the expectations of the times when Maizee came running into the room with a spiral notebook. She found it among Nate's Clark College materials.

Turning to the title page, written in Nate's hand, she read: "On The Way To A New South." Then began a long list of dates and events:

1. 1. May 17, 1954—Black Monday, Sam Ervin, Strom Thurmond, George Smathers and Harry Byrd signed "Southern Manifesto."

2. 2. Aug. 1955—14-yr. old Emmett Till from Chicago, while visiting in Miss., beaten to death for whistling at a white woman. (Alleged murderers acquitted.)

3. 3. 1957—Shuttlesworth and wife beaten for attempting to enroll daughter in white public school. [Earlier, their home was firebombed.]

The list went on and on, and Allise continued to read. "Feb. 27, 1960— Paul L., white Fisk U. student, kicked and clubbed (81 arrested). Look Maizee, he reminds himself to check the date." She continued, "Amzie M. sat in his home with loaded rifle. Phone rang. Told his house will blow in 5 mins., he can stay inside or vacate and be sniped." Allise said she didn't know about some of the atrocities he listed. "In 1961, Bob M., jailed in Mississippi. Local white minister said, 'You don't believe in Jesus Christ, do you, you sonofabitch?'"

Flipping though the pages of misdeeds, she said, "It appears Nate documented accounts of civil wrongs. Do you suppose he researched to write a book?" His mother said if he did, all his work was wasted. "No, Maizee," Allise said. "Nate's coming along."

On a Sunday afternoon, Allise and Dro took Nate along to visit Sam and Maydale. She told them about his spiral notebook. She complained about the slow pace of court-ordered integration across the South. "One token black admitted to Deer Point High in 1968. We're in the seventies and after thirty years of teaching and eighteen years since the Supreme Court order, I'm still waiting for it to happen. I have tried to prepare my students for the day when black students will be admitted. Try to impress on them, they must show kindness and respect."

They looked at her expectantly. "When it happens here and it will we'll be ready," she added.

"You're doing the right thing, Allise," Maydale said.

The farm couple discussed inflated food prices, costs of new cars, gasoline and postage stamps with their guests. Dro said business owners complained about raising the minimum wage to a dollar per hour, and small farmers should fear corporate buy-outs and take-overs for debt.

"Yeah," Sam said, "I know some who buy equipment they can't afford. We're doing okay. Me and Maydale don't need much, just good health so we can keep farming." He pulled her closer.

She giggled. "We don't have kids to inherit the farm. We'll leave it to Peter."

Allise said she didn't know about that. "Peter said he never wanted to farm. You should think about selling to someone who treasures the land as much as you and Sam."

"Allise is right," Dro said. "I don't think Peter would be good at farming."

Her Peter still railed about mixing the races when forced integration put blacks in Deer Point schools in 1971. He said it would soon prove to be a mistake.

Throughout the school year, Allise watched the interactions between her racially different students. They didn't mingle outside the classrooms. Social division ruled. Nate had said "equal treatment" was enough, and she thought both sides wanted it that way.

When the term ended, Dro told Allise it was time for both of them to retire. "We can travel, now," he said, when he came home from his retirement ceremony with a fancy set of cufflinks.

Allise liked the idea of traveling. She had hung on to see blacks exposed to equal education opportunity. The law finally made it the right time for her. She wrote a letter of resignation to the newly elected, younger, school board officials. An evening was held in her honor. One of the board members read from a walnut, embossed plaque:

### In recognition of
### Mrs. Allise McClure
### English teacher, 1942-1972

**Through dedicated service at Deer Point High School, her enthusiasm** engaged students and moved them to higher planes of thinking. Entrusted to teach, this educator also spoke truth.

Allise stood before the board members, guests, Dro, and Peter. "I accept this honor with gratitude and humbleness. My father would be proud. I've often been upbraided for expressing my principles and have not always been successful in reaching my goals." Pausing, she looked at Peter. "Seldom have I been accused of not speaking my truth." The audience laughed. "Teaching our youth has been my greatest privilege. Thank you."

The applause overwhelmed her.

At last, she felt an accepted member of the community, but before the year was out, Allise was bedridden. Her body was used up. "Dro, I'll bet you didn't count on this kind of retirement." She laughed. Unable to smile, his face looked ready to break.

Maizee tried to lift the sadness they felt. "Miz Allie, you and Nate gonna wear me and Mista Dro out, and we jes foolish enough about you t' let you do it."

# EPILOGUE

▼

## 1972

Maizee and Nate waited in the bedroom. She glanced across at her son. Did he worry about Miz Allie? Taking a book from the bedside table, she read when Dro came from the drugstore. He gave Allise the medication and sat on her bedside, waiting for it to make a difference.

Most of the day had passed when Allise stirred. Dro moved to the bedside and took her hand to his lips. "Did you have a good rest? You slept a long time, honey." She gave him a wan smile.

Maizee stood on the other side of the bed. Allise looked from her to Dro. Catching a quick breath, tears ran across her temple into thick white hair. Dro wiped them, and she tried to whisper between gasps. Looking close to breaking, he bent and kissed her.

Maizee smiled, wishing she could communicate her thoughts to Miz Allie. *We raised a family, but we couldn't slay the dragon between our boys. Our work's over.* She held Allise's hand, "Mista Dro, Miz Allie say, 'Mourn for them that have short lives or it be taken unjustly.' She say, 'If I live a long life, don't grieve for me.'"

Allise tried to squeeze her hand and looked about as though searching for someone. She whispered, "Nate?" Maizee went to the chair and motioned her son to the bedside.

Allise tried to reach for his hand. Tears streaked Maizee's cheeks as she held their hands together. Peter and Jill walked into the room, and she stepped back with Nate. Peter stood near the bed, shaking with uncontrollable sobs. Suddenly, Nate stumbled over and put his arms around him as others stared in astonishment.

Sam and Maydale came before Allise closed her eyes and drew her last, soft, peaceful-sounding sighs. Then everyone left Dro alone with her.

At nightfall, he came downstairs. Hearing singing, he peeked out. "They're holding candles out there," he said, and everyone moved to the front porch. Tiny lights flickered across the lawn as Allise's students sang hymns and spirituals.

Her sisters arrived from Pennsylvania, and Missy Wise, a social worker in North Carolina, called to ask if she could give the eulogy. Next day, she took the podium at the graveside service. Looking across the audience, Missy turned to the family seated with Maizee, Nate and Elfreeda. Smiling at the scene, she said, "This looks like the world Mrs. McClure would arrange. She's pleased."

Missy's father, Charlie Wise, shouted, "Amen!"

"I want you to know," she began, "I would not have joined the Peace Corps, one of two great experiences in my life, it not been for Mrs. McClure. I'm where I am today because she encouraged advanced education, and love for the unloved and disadvantaged in our world. Today, I work at that." Missy referred to her notes. "My first great experience was being her student.

"She shared a love of teaching and love for humankind with her students. Mrs. McClure inspired me to be a better person. I think I can speak for all her students. Many of whom are here today." She gazed out on the crowd.

"We didn't appreciate the grammar she pounded into our minds, and the many books she made us read." Missy laughed. "But with her reasonable answers to our questions, over time, we came to understand she tried to teach us how to live with each other in this beautiful place created for us."

She told how Allise used classical works to explain situations people set up or found themselves caught up in. How she encouraged students to put themselves in those situations and think about their actions under similar circumstances. "Mrs. McClure had the capacity to love every one of us. I've spoken with any number of students and cannot begin to tell of the love we have for her." Pausing to compose herself, she said, "At this moment, after a lifetime of concern for all kinds of wrongs, I know she's at peace."

Missy picked up her notes and whispered, "I love you, dear teacher." Leaving the podium, she touched her lips and threw a kiss.

A reverent hush hung over the crowd extending out beyond the canopy. Not a whisper sounded when Elfreeda stood. As she had for Mista Quent and Cleesy, she sang, "Swing low, sweet chariot ..."

Dro, bearing grief for the end of their love story, placed a white rose on the coffin and lingered over his goodbye. Peter, wore a look of unfinished business as he placed his rose. Sam and Maydale followed him with red roses.

As the coffin lowered in the DeWitt plot, people walked toward cars lining the cemetery lanes. Elfreeda walked away, leaving Maizee and Nate to wait for Mista Dro. Suddenly, Maizee heard, "Momma." Jolted as though by a lightning bolt, she struggled to appear normal when Nate motioned to the new grave.

"It's Miz Allie, son." She led him toward the car. Unsure about pursuing the miracle, she feared doing the wrong thing. No one would believe her if they didn't hear for themselves. Not even Mista Dro, she thought.

That evening, she put plates of leftovers on the table and sat down with Dro and Nate. They ate quietly when Nate began making forced, grunting sounds. Words came slowly. "Don't know." Dro stopped eating, looked at him, then at Maizee. Putting an arm across Nate's shoulders, he looked at her for an explanation.

Nate allowed no time for explaining. "Miz Allie gone." With seeming frustration, his eyes pled with them.

"Son, Miz Allie gonna go right on whipping devils. She done earned her angel wings. Ain't that so, Mista Dro?" Dro wiped his eyes and nodded.

With tear-filled eyes, Maizee still managed to laugh. "Miz Allie got too much left t' be done." She slapped her hands together in a prayerful hold. "Life in this old town goes on, but the South be changing even if it's dragged along with the wind. Lawd, lawd, if Miz Allie has her way, she'll be directing the wind from up there."

8221986R0

Made in the USA
Lexington, KY
16 January 2011